NCIS
NOVEL
TWO

TYNDALE HOUSE PUBLISHERS, INC. >> CAROL STREA

EVIDE

INOIS
MEL ODOM
NCE

Visit Tyndale's exciting Web site at www.tyndale.com

TYNDALE and Tyndale's quill logo are registered trademarks of Tyndale House Publishers, Inc.

Blood Evidence

Designed by Dean H. Renninger

Library of Congress Cataloging-in-Publication Data

Odom, Mel.
Blood evidence / Mel Odom.
p. cm.
ISBN-13: 978-1-4143-0307-9 (sc)
ISBN-10: 1-4143-0307-6 (sc)
1. Kidnapping—Fiction. 2. Murder—Investigation—Fiction. 3. United States. Naval Criminal Investigative Service—Fiction. 4. Women forensic pathologists—Fiction. I. Title.
PS3565.D53B66 2007
813′.54—dc22 2006037589

Printed in the United States of America

13 12 11 10 09 08 07
7 6 5 4 3 2 1

DEDICATION

A prayer of thanks: God, thank you for my wife, Sherry. I never thought I would know someone so wonderful. She came into my life at a time when I'd given up all hope. Please watch over her and continue to give her immense patience and understanding. As you know, you've given her a lot of responsibility being Mom to five kids and a husband who continues to enjoy his childhood whenever he can.

ACKNOWLEDGMENTS

Without the guiding hand and unswerving perseverance of Jeremy Taylor, this book would not be what it is. Thanks, Jeremy!

Jan Stob, as always, has been there since the beginning. The friendship is much appreciated, Jan!

Karen Watson is new to me as of this book, but we share small-town roots. Looking forward to swapping stories again, Karen!

Cheryl Kerwin works hard to keep us in the public eye. Thank you for all your work, Cheryl!

>> **SEVENTEEN YEARS AGO...**

>> ARTICLE FROM THE RALEIGH, NORTH CAROLINA, *NEWS & OBSERVER*.

SERIAL KILLER STRIKES CLOSE TO HOME

Hunters discovered the body of 16-year-old Chloe Ivers in Jacksonville two nights ago. The discovery ended a two-day search for the missing girl, who had been abducted from her home in Raleigh.

Police spokesman Craig Tyler confirmed the murdered girl's identity after her stepfather, Congressman Ben Swanson, learned of the tragic circumstances.

"That poor child was horribly murdered," Detective Tyler says. "But we believe we've got her murderer in custody."

Officers apprehended Isaac Allen Lamont early this morning. Three other police agencies want to speak to Lamont regarding murders in their cities and states.

"We've got Lamont cold on four other murders," Federal Bureau of Investigation Special Agent Ted Griffen says. "The FBI has listed him as a known serial killer for almost a year. He's just been hard to catch. It's a shame Lamont wasn't caught before this happened."

Congressman Swanson has agreed to give a statement to the press at a later date. United States Navy Lieutenant Laura Ivers Swanson, Chloe's mother, is based at Camp Lejeune and was unavailable for comment.

NCIS

NAVAL CRIMINAL INVESTIGATIVE SERVICE

1

SCENE  NCIS  CRIME SCENE

NAVAL CRIMINAL INVESTIGATIVE SERVICE

```
>> UNIVERSITY OF NORTH CAROLINA
>> CHAPEL HILL, NORTH CAROLINA
>> THE PRESENT
>> 2014 HOURS
```

"Folks, no matter how this game finishes, you'll have to admit that you've been treated to a rare night of collegiate basketball," the announcer rumbled. "Any time the Tar Heels lock horns with the Blue Devils, you can bet pride is on the line."

Will Coburn sat in one of the twenty-one thousand baby blue seats that filled the Dean E. Smith Center and watched the basketball game with avid interest. His seven-year-old daughter, Wren, sat beside him with a big bucket of popcorn in her lap. She'd never been to a basketball game before and had begged to come along when Will had asked Steven to join him.

With the tension of the divorce still hovering between Will and his fifteen-year-old son, Will had wanted a father-son night. But Wren, excitable and eager, was hard to refuse. She'd bowled Steven over before he'd had a chance.

Or maybe, Will had to admit ruefully, his son hadn't wanted to spend an evening alone with him.

Even before the divorce had finally come through a couple months ago, Will's love of the sea and his Navy career had driven a wedge between his family and him, and his marriage hadn't survived it. Even after Will had asked for and received shore duty at Camp Lejeune in his native North Carolina, the damage already done, together with whatever flaws had been in the marriage to begin with, had proven insurmountable. He'd lost his wife, but he hoped his relationship with his kids would remain solid.

Tonight was something of a test for that. School was out for spring break, and Will had gotten visitation for the next few days.

Wren had been an easy sell. Steven, on the other hand, had come only with extreme reluctance, and Will really didn't know what had turned the corner on his son's decision.

One of the Tar Heels players pulled up and shot a three-pointer that bounced harmlessly from the hoop. A Duke University player jumped and pulled the ball in, then fired it to a teammate who was already streaking down the court.

"No!" Wren shrilled, jumping up.

Will grabbed the popcorn bucket before his daughter managed to dump it all over the spectators in front of them.

The player put the ball on the ground for two quick dribbles, then went airborne, skying for the hoop. A Tar Heels player leaped after his opponent, managing to foul him on the shot but not enough to knock the shot away.

"No!" Wren shouted again. "That's five fouls, Holby! You're out! You're not going to do us any good sitting on the bench!"

The two college-age young men seated in front of Wren turned around to her, smiling broadly.

"You tell him," one of the guys said good-naturedly. He held up a hand.

Wren high-fived him without hesitation.

Will smiled. That was Wren. Open and engaging to a fault, she had never met a stranger. She was her father's daughter. She had Will's black hair and green eyes, and she was built tall and slim. From the time she was born, Wren had seemed to know that the world had a place in it for her. Her self-confidence was a marvel to behold.

The buzzer sounded as the two teams set up for the free-throw shot. The refs received notification that Holby had hit his five fouls and had to be removed. The tall, lanky player went out to a burst of applause.

"Now we're giving up too much of the paint," Wren groaned in frustration.

The audience remained on their feet, hooting and jeering as the Duke University player got ready to shoot. Four minutes were left in the half, and the Tar Heels had just dropped three points behind. The extra point made it four.

Everyone sat down again.

"How did you learn so much about basketball?" Will asked his daughter.

"TV." Wren's green eyes watched as the players inbounded the ball.

"I thought you watched *Scooby-Doo*."

"Sometimes."

"But you watch basketball."

"When baseball's not on," Wren replied, as if that explained everything.

"Oh," Will said. "I didn't know you liked sports."

"I do. They've got softball sign-ups at the rec center. I want to play, but Mom says maybe we'll be too busy."

Another Tar Heels player shot from outside and missed.

"Don't just heave it up there!" Wren groaned. "*Share* that rock! Man!"

Duke recovered and went downcourt again, but when the fast break didn't come together, the coach called a time-out.

"Maybe I can talk to your mom," Will said. "About the softball sign-ups."

"That would be cool." Wren munched popcorn, looked at the scoreboard, and heaved a despairing sigh.

Steven glanced at his father reproachfully. He looked more like his mother, with dark brown hair and blue eyes. "You know," Steven said in a cold, hostile voice, "you might want to give Mom a break. She doesn't need you rolling another responsibility over onto her."

Will curbed his immediate impulse to reprimand his son for his impudence. He took in a breath and let his anger go.

All night long—in fact, since Will had picked his son and daughter up from their mother's house earlier in the day—Steven had given him the cold shoulder. Fewer than a hundred words had been exchanged in the last four hours.

"Mom's got a lot to do," Steven went on. "She doesn't just kick back in some office somewhere and tell people what to do. She's busy taking care of us."

Anger and pain mixed inside Will. He hadn't wanted the divorce, but he hadn't been given a choice. No one seemed to realize that. Having both a family and a military career was hard, but other people managed it. Frank Billings had.

Thinking of Frank hurt. Even though most of a year had passed since Frank's murder, Will still felt that loss. He suspected that he always would. Frank had been close to him, his second-in-command on the aircraft carrier they'd served on as well as in the Naval Criminal Investigative Service unit Will commanded.

Sitting there, hurt and angry, Will wondered what Frank would have said to one of his sons if he'd been faced with this situation.

Frank wouldn't be in this boat, Will realized. Frank's relationship with his wife and kids had been solid from start to finish, and he'd even had enough time and love left over in his life to be a godfather to Steven and Wren.

Steven stared at Will, as if daring him to say something.

Insubordination wasn't something Commander Will Coburn easily tolerated. But this was family, and rank didn't have its privileges in family. And Steven's rancorous behavior was something new.

Thankfully, the Tar Heels stole the ball when it was inbounded and flipped it downcourt for a quick basket. Wren reared to her feet, and Will once more managed to save the popcorn bucket from a tumble.

Then his cell phone rang.

A quick glance at the caller ID let Will know the call was business. The number belonged to NCIS Director Michael Larkin. Larkin knew Will had cleared his schedule for this night with his kids; he wouldn't have called if it weren't important.

Will flipped the phone open and answered. Steven gave his father a look of derisive disgust, then looked away.

"Coburn," Will answered.

Larkin spoke in a clipped manner, his New York accent coming through. Before he'd taken the job as NCIS director, he'd been captain of homicide detectives in Manhattan. "Sorry to call you, Will, but something's come up."

"I'm listening."

"I know you're with your kids, but we have a situation. A fifteen-year-old girl, the daughter of a Marine captain here at the base, has been kidnapped."

The announcement sent a chill through Will. Any case that involved kids struck too close to home. "What do you need, sir?"

"You. And your team. We think we know where the girl is being held, but I want you people to take her out of there."

"Aye, sir. Driving from here to there is going to take two and a half hours. And the game is almost over. There's going to be a traffic jam."

"I've got a helicopter coming to meet you. It should be there in five minutes. Call me when you're moving."

Will folded the phone and stood up. "Come on. We've got to go."

Wren looked up at him in disbelief. "Now?"

"Yeah. Sorry."

"But there's only two minutes left."

"I know." Will took his daughter by the hand and excused himself as they made their way down the row. He glanced back at Steven, finding that his son hadn't moved. "Let's go."

Steven frowned.

"Now," Will said, his voice taking on the timbre of command. "Or it's going to be a long week without phone and Internet privileges."

Brimming with teen hostility, Steven stood and grabbed his jacket.

As Will made his way through the crowd with Wren in hand, looking back over her shoulder to watch the game, and Steven in tow at least ten feet back, he unlimbered his phone and called his team.

>> 2021 HOURS

Outside in the parking lot, the March chill slamming into him with gusto, Will returned his phone to his pocket and examined the night sky. He'd reached all his team.

Shel McHenry had been on the firing range, which was par for the course for the big Marine gunnery sergeant. Maggie Foley had been attending an art lecture in Jacksonville. Estrella Montoya had been home with her six-year-old son. And Remy Gautreau had been out with one of the young women that always seemed to flock around him.

"Is somebody in trouble?" Wren asked.

Will glanced down at his daughter. "I'm afraid so."

A troubled look tightened her face. "Is it going to be okay?"

In the past, Will would have been tempted to tell her sure, everything would be fine. But last year they'd buried Frank Billings. That had changed a lot of things. Will could no longer just pat his daughter on the head and tell her yes. She wouldn't believe him.

He squatted down, putting his eyes level with hers, and took her hands. "I hope so. I'm going to try to make it be okay."

"'Cause that's your job." Wren still looked pensive.

Will smiled reassuringly at his daughter. "That's right. It's my job."

"I just want you to stay safe."

"I'll do the best I can." Will glanced over her shoulder at Steven. He stood about ten feet away, arms wrapped around himself, not looking in their direction.

Helicopter rotors sounded overhead.

Glancing up, Will spotted the distinctive dual-rotor design of the Boeing CH-46 Sea Knight cutting through the night sky.

Will's phone rang and he answered. "Coburn."

"Commander Coburn, this is Express Zero Niner," a young male voice said. "Director Larkin sent us to pick you up, sir. You should have a visual on us from your twenty."

"Copy that, Express. Visual confirmed."

"Great. We can't put down, but we've got a basket ready."

Will took a Mini Maglite from his pocket, switched it on and waved it over his head. The bright light knifed through the darkness. The helo had already drawn the attention of some of the people loitering in the parking lot.

"I'm providing a visual, Express. Do you see me?"

"Affirmative, Commander. We have your visual. Reading you five by five."

"My kids are here. Can we get them home?"

"Roger that, sir. Director Larkin sent along a special agent to take care of that for you. We'll drop him when we pick you up."

Will folded his phone and turned to Steven. Despite his son's attitude and the pressing need to address it, Will stayed on task. *Take care of what's necessary. Deal with incidentals later.* "Steven."

Steven looked up at him.

"I don't know how long this will take," Will said. "I need you to take care of your sister."

Steven nodded.

"If you need anything—"

"We'll be fine."

"I know you will. But if you do need anything, call Chief Petty Officer McBride. She'll get you what you need."

Steven nodded again.

The Sea Knight hovered overhead. A cargo bucket appeared in the side doorway and started down. A lone figure held on.

"You feel like driving?" Will asked.

Steven looked at him. He'd gotten his driver's permit a month ago. "I haven't driven at night much."

"I'd planned on letting you drive back to base tonight. Once you're off campus, the traffic won't be as bad as it was when we came in." Will reached into his jeans pocket and took out his keys. "If you're up to it."

"Yeah."

Whatever mood gripped Steven, it would have been almost impossible for a fifteen-year-old boy with a brand-new driver's permit to pass up an opportunity to drive. Will just hoped that whomever Larkin had sent to get his kids home didn't regret it.

"Let me grab my gear." Will trotted over to his dark metallic blue Chevrolet Avalanche Z71 and keyed the electronic locks. They popped open at once. He couldn't help thinking that the 4x4 truck was a lot for Steven to handle, and Will really liked the truck. *It's your kid,* he told himself. *Let it go. You can always replace a truck.*

He reached into the back and took out the locked equipment case he carried with him wherever he went. With the NCIS posting, he was never truly off duty. He had to be ready to roll at a moment's notice. Spare gear at home and in his vehicle was a must.

He turned to Steven. "If something comes up and you need me, I'm only a phone call away."

Steven nodded but didn't look entirely convinced. Still, getting to drive appeared to have mollified him somewhat.

You're not supposed to have to bribe your kids to like you, Will told himself.

He tossed his son the keys.

Steven caught them but made no move to step toward his father.

"Hey, Dad." Wren grabbed Will around the waist and hugged him tightly.

"You have a bedtime tonight," Will said.

"Okay."

"And it's the bed. Not the couch."

Wren rolled her eyes. "*Okaaaay.*"

Will kissed her forehead, knowing the clock was ticking, thinking of the girl being held in a situation he'd never want his daughter in. Footsteps sounded behind him and he turned.

"Commander Coburn? I'm Special Agent Fulton." The young NCIS agent looked flustered. "I don't know if I'm supposed to salute or shake hands."

Most of the NCIS teams were made up from civilian sectors. Many agents didn't have prior military service. Will's team was different. Except for Maggie, who served as profiler for the unit, and Nita Tomlinson, the team's medical examiner, the rest of the team was still military.

Will took the man's hand, then quickly introduced him to Wren and Steven. "Get them home safe. They can handle it from there. Steven's driving. He just got his driver's permit. Take care of my truck."

Fulton looked uneasy. "Uh, Commander, I don't—"

"You're in the NCIS, Special Agent Fulton. You're trained for difficult situations. Riding as copilot for a beginning driver is not as hard as it gets."

Will's tone brooked no denial of responsibility.

"Yes, sir." Fulton snapped to attention. He saluted, getting it wrong but at least going to the effort. "I mean, aye, sir."

"Bye, Dad," Wren called.

Will waved one last time, then sprinted for the cargo bucket hanging from the Sea Knight's side. The rotor wash blew litter around the parking lot.

As he was pulled toward the helicopter in the bucket, Will thought about his son driving his truck and offered a brief prayer that God would see his son and daughter home safely. Then he turned his thoughts—and his prayers—to the kidnapped girl.

2

SCENE  NCIS  CRIME SCENE

NAVAL CRIMINAL INVESTIGATIVE SERVICE

>> NCIS MEDICAL LAB
>> CAMP LEJEUNE, NORTH CAROLINA
>> 2032 HOURS

Dr. Nita Tomlinson eyed the current guest in her autopsy lab.

She preferred thinking of the dead people who ended up here as guests. Death had a way of stripping away a person's individuality and uniqueness. Walking around, breathing, and talking, a person was a person. Dead, without the ability to interact any longer, a person who had passed on tended to become a commodity accessorized by a funeral home and housed in a cemetery.

But in her chosen domain, they were her guests.

She was alone in the lab. Only the sound of the equipment kept her company. She liked it that way. Five feet nine inches tall, she was slim and well built, spending enough time in the gym to keep herself in good shape despite the late nights and long hours. At thirty-two, she still turned men's heads, and she took pride in that.

Nita pulled back her long red hair and fixed it into a ponytail. Her quick gray-green eyes took in the torso of the naked man on the autopsy table.

Reaching into a box of surgical gloves, she took a pair out and pulled them on. Then she adjusted her face mask, hooking the elastic straps over her ears. Pulling the overhead microphone close to her face, she set to work.

"Open file," she ordered in a flat tone.

On one of the gleaming stainless-steel tables against the surrounding walls, her notebook computer pulsed to life, awakened by the software responding to her verbal command. The camcorder capturing the procedure also came on.

"O'Brien, Charles Edward. United States Navy senior chief petty officer assigned to Camp Lejeune as training officer," Nita said, reading the information from the chart on the table. "DOB 11-16-1953." She looked at O'Brien. "This is the body of a fifty-three-year-old male. He's at least thirty pounds over regs." *Whoever let him slide on his PT wasn't doing him any favors,* she thought.

Nita stepped forward and examined the broken purple capillaries that made maps on O'Brien's nose and cheeks. "He shows evidence of a history of heavy drinking." *The liver's going to be the proof of that.* "Otherwise, overall, he seems fit and able." She touched a scar on his left calf. "He has an old bullet wound on his lower left calf. It appears to have been treated and to have healed well."

She continued with the visual inspection of the body, going through the list by rote. Then it came time to cut.

"Chief Petty Officer O'Brien collapsed on the job at 1127 hours two days ago." Nita took up a large scalpel from the instrument tray. "The reason for the autopsy is that O'Brien didn't have a medical history and wasn't under a doctor's care for disease or a medical condition."

She pressed the tip of the scalpel against the corpse's left shoulder, leaning across the table to reach it.

For a moment, Nita hesitated. Her mouth was suddenly dry. There didn't seem to be enough oxygen in the room. She realized she was perspiring heavily.

Her hand shook. She stared at it in disbelief. What was happening to her? Her hand had never, *never* done that.

Cursing, Nita drew the blade back. *What's wrong with you?*

She sucked in a ragged breath, then pushed it out in a soft explosion. She took a firm grip on the scalpel and got set to go again. Whatever her problem was, it seemed to have passed.

>> NCIS FIELD COMMAND POST
>> NORTH OF JACKSONVILLE, NORTH CAROLINA
>> 2116 HOURS

"Maggie."

Seated at one of the computer consoles inside the command post, Maggie Foley turned to face the speaker. "Sir?"

NCIS Director Michael Larkin stood in the doorway of the mobile command center, a modified RV that had been outfitted with the latest in computer hardware. Larkin was six feet two inches tall, built rangy and fit. At fifty-four, his dark brown hair was graying at the temples now. As usual, he was impeccably dressed in a dark blue suit and smelled of good cologne.

"Will's fifteen minutes out," Larkin said.

"Yes, sir." Athletic and lean, Maggie stood only four inches over five feet. Her dark hazel eyes and shoulder-length, dark brown hair made her look slightly younger than her twenty-eight years. She wore a black battledress uniform in preparation for the night's activities. Twin Beretta M9s hung in a dual shoulder-holster rig. Extra magazines filled the combat webbing. She was fully prepared.

Although she hadn't ever served in the military, Maggie had benefited from military training. Before starting at NCIS, she'd worked as a police officer in her native Boston, Massachusetts. She'd taken several gun lessons, then further training with Shel McHenry when she joined the team. She knew about combat situations, and she'd been involved in several encounters in which her weapons training had come in handy.

"Our tech guys say they're 90 percent sure the girl is inside," said Larkin, nodding toward a monitor displaying a farmhouse. "Infrared imaging shows maybe two dozen potential hostiles and enough weaponry to outfit a small army."

"Where do you want me?" Maggie inquired.

"When Will gets here," Larkin said, "you take point on the briefing." He never used military rank even though he'd served in the Army himself for a short time before joining the New York Police Department. His people were associates, and he treated them accordingly.

"Yes, sir," Maggie replied. "How much does the commander know about what we're facing?"

"Only that there's been a kidnapping involving the fifteen-year-old daughter of a Marine captain."

Maggie nodded. "There still haven't been any demands?"

Larkin shook his head.

"That's unusual in the case of a kidnapping."

"I think so too."

Hesitating just a moment, Maggie said, "I may be stepping out of line here, sir, but may I speak freely?"

Larkin regarded her. "You're talking to me. It won't go any further than us if it doesn't need to."

Nodding, Maggie accepted that. Whatever Larkin said he stood behind. That was one of the things she liked about him. "I think Captain Whitcomb is wrong."

"What do you mean?"

"I mean I don't think his daughter was kidnapped."

Larkin didn't appear to be surprised. Maggie chose to believe that was a good sign.

"During the interview I had with Captain Whitcomb," Maggie said, "he kept insisting that Amanda, his daughter, was taken against her will. I don't think she was."

"Why?"

"She called her father from her cell phone—by his testimony and by the phone records we checked."

Larkin grinned sourly. "Doesn't stand to reason that a known criminal group would leave a kidnap victim her phone, does it?"

"No," Maggie agreed. "Especially since we were able to get a fix on her location by triangulating the cell signal. If she was kidnapped, this is the most incompetent kidnapping job I've ever seen."

"So if she isn't kidnapped, what is she?"

"It's possible Amanda is being held against her will, but I believe she was at that house by invitation," Maggie said.

"Gonna be hard to prove that."

"We don't need to prove it. We just need to get her out of there. Once she's clear, she's going to need some counseling. I just think that you might talk to the counselor and have the possibility explored that Amanda Whitcomb placed herself in harm's way tonight."

Larkin gave a tight nod. "I agree. I'll take care of it."

"Thank you, sir."

"I checked into the captain's background with the provost marshal's office," Larkin said. "I also put in a phone call to SRO Corporal White at Lejeune High School inquiring about the Whitcomb family and Amanda's school attendance."

Captain Whitcomb was newly arrived to Camp Lejeune and hadn't yet acquired civilian housing. The provost marshal's office handled security and domestic problems on base. The SRO—school resource officer—handled school problems, ensuring that the school was a safe place to learn and to teach for students and teachers and that violence wasn't an acceptable resolution in conflicts or disagreements.

"There have been a few incidents at home," Larkin went on. "Arguments between father and daughter."

Maggie nodded. Disagreements between parents and teenage children were hardly out of the ordinary.

"Amanda's had troubles at school, too. Fights and rebelliousness."

"Have drugs been involved?" Maggie asked.

"Suspected," Larkin answered, "but never proven."

"Did you get a chance to investigate Captain Whitcomb's previous posting?"

"Not yet. For the moment, I just want to get the girl safe."

Maggie nodded. That was what they all wanted, but they were going to have to enter a house full of armed men to get it done. They needed as much information as they could get.

>> NCIS MEDICAL LAB
>> CAMP LEJEUNE, NORTH CAROLINA
>> 2118 HOURS

Nita inserted the scalpel and felt it sink through the dead man's flesh. She dragged the sharp blade from O'Brien's shoulder to the lower sternum.

Slipping the knife free, Nita inscribed the same cut from the other shoulder. Then, starting at the sternum, she cut again, sliding the blade down across the trunk, slightly left of the umbilicus, and ending at the pubic bone.

Unbelievably, Nita discovered she was drenched in perspiration. Her hands quivered periodically. She forced herself to continue with her work.

Gripping the flaps of flesh with one hand, she slid the scalpel through the muscle and soft tissues connecting them to the rib cage. When she finished, the chest flap was turned back over the dead man's face, exposing the ribs and sternum.

Nita lifted the electric bone saw and sliced through the rib cage on both sides. Pulling the chest plate back revealed the heart and lungs beneath. She used a smaller scalpel to slice into the pericardium, the double-walled sac that covered the heart.

"There's no apparent sign of pericardial effusion," Nita said. The pericardial fluid was responsible for lubricating the heart and preventing friction as the body's pump contracted and relaxed. Extensive buildup of the fluid could cause the heart to stop beating or compress the heart vessels. "And no sign of cardiac tamponade."

Okay, she thought, *we're still searching for cause of death.*

She stuck a finger into the pulmonary artery where it exited the heart and felt around. There was no obstruction, no evidence of a blood clot that might have slipped from a vein in another part of the body to wreak havoc in the heart.

"We can rule out thromboembolism," she said.

She cut the abdominal muscles, pulling the flaps away from the bottom of the rib cage and the diaphragm to expose the stomach, intestines, liver, and other organs. After identifying the carotid and subclavian arteries in the neck and upper chest, she tied them off for the morticians. The funeral home would use those arteries to pump embalming fluid into the body.

Nita carefully severed the attachments holding the chest organs to the spine. Then, putting the scalpel aside, she used both hands to lift the organ block from the shell of the dead man. Turning, she placed the organs gently on the small dissecting table she'd pulled up to the man's knees.

She pulled the esophagus from the other organs with just her fingers, then picked up an eighteen-inch knife—called a bread knife in the trade—and sliced the lungs away from the heart and trachea.

As usual, the right lung was larger than the left. Since the heart lay on the left side of the body, the left lung had to compensate by leaving a space called the cardiac notch.

"The lungs are dark," Nita said, "not pink like healthy ones should be. O'Brien's medical records show that he was a smoker. But there's no sign of pneumonia or pulmonary edema." Pulmonary edema, fluid in the lungs, would lead to speculation about congestive heart failure.

She sliced the lungs like bread loaves, cutting them into one-centimeter-thick slices. Tissue samples went into jars that were labeled with O'Brien's case number.

Nita went for the heart next. Working deftly, she removed the organ and weighed it on a scale.

"Heart weighs four hundred grams. Slightly more than normal, indicating some possible stress."

She picked the heart up and crosscut the coronary arteries. "I'm detecting some signs of preliminary heart disease, but not enough to take O'Brien's life." From there she moved to the larynx and trachea, opening them up from the rear to examine. The thyroid gland likewise offered no clues.

Flipping the organ block over, Nita located the adrenal glands in the fatty tissue surrounding the kidneys. She took tissue samples from the glands, then turned her attention to the liver, finding what she'd expected. Instead of being brown and healthy, the liver looked far heavier than the normal fourteen hundred grams and was light colored with a definite orange tint.

"There are signs of advanced cirrhosis of the liver," Nita said. "Chief O'Brien, as reported by friends and family, was a chronic drinker." Even so, Nita was certain O'Brien had not died from liver failure.

She weighed the liver, took samples, and put it to one side.

Next she opened the stomach and found that the chief had eaten not long before he'd expired, leaving a liquid mass that reeked of gastric acid. Finding nothing there, she moved on to the pancreas and duodenum, then the kidneys and urinary bladder. She followed those with an exploration of the aorta, including the renal, celiac, mesenteric, and iliac arteries.

Still nothing.

Frowning, Nita stepped back from the corpse and glanced at the clock on the wall. The autopsy was taking longer than she'd expected. She was going to be late.

She didn't mind going home late. In fact, she preferred it. Being around her husband and daughter made her feel inept.

Nita hated feeling that way, but she was usually able to keep her problems at home separate from her work. Here in the autopsy room, working with the dead, she was totally in control.

So why can't you keep your hands from shaking? She pushed the thought away.

"Okay, Chief O'Brien, you can be stubborn if you want to, but I'm going to find out your secrets. Then I'm going to go have a drink to celebrate how good I am at what I do."

Nita walked to one of the cabinets and took out a Stryker saw. She placed a body block under the back of the dead man's head, elevating it. Using a scalpel, she cut from behind the left ear, over the crown of the head, and ended up behind the right ear.

Nita pulled the front flap forward, then yanked the back flap down to the nape of the chief's neck to expose the top hemisphere of the skull.

She lifted the Stryker saw and switched on the power. The whir of the blade filled the lab.

"Okay, Chief," Nita said good-naturedly as she leaned in with the saw, "let's see what was on your mind."

S CRIME SCENE  NCIS 

NAVAL CRIMINAL INVESTIGATIVE SERVICE

3

SCENE    CRIME SCEN

>> HIGHWAY 37
>> NORTH OF JACKSONVILLE, NORTH CAROLINA
>> 2131 HOURS

Will sat strapped in along the wall of the CH-46 as the helicopter dropped earthward and held its position, hovering like a dragonfly. He carried a Springfield XD-40 semiautomatic pistol under his left arm and another in a counterterrorist drop holster on his right thigh.

Given the people his team was up against, chances were good that the situation would turn ballistic. Tonight Will was willing to err on the side of being overequipped.

The loadmaster tapped Will on the shoulder. "We're clear, Commander," the young Marine shouted over the noise of the churning rotors. He yanked the cargo door open.

"Thanks." Will got up and approached the cargo door, equipment case in hand. The skids hovered three feet above the country road less than three miles from the NCIS command post near the kidnappers' house.

The loadmaster put a hand on Will's head. "Keep low, sir."

"I will." Stepping through the cargo door, Will dropped to the street they were using as a landing zone. He turned, remaining crouched as the helicopter climbed back into the dark sky. As the Sea Knight cleared the makeshift LZ, Will spotted a black Suburban parked at the side of the road.

Standing beside the Suburban, United States Marine Corps Gunnery Sergeant Shelton McHenry almost made the vehicle look small. Broad shouldered, blue-eyed, and blond haired, Shel was six feet four inches tall, every inch of it Marine. He wore combat black BDUs and carried two matte black Mark 23 Mod 0 SOCOM .45-caliber pistols in a dual shoulder-holster rig. An M4A1 assault rifle rested easily in the crook of his arm.

Max, the black Labrador retriever that was Shel's full-time partner, lay at the gunnery sergeant's feet. The dog's pink tongue looked bright in the night.

"Evening, Commander," Shel said.

Will acknowledged the greeting and trotted over to the Suburban's passenger side. "How bad is it?" He opened the door and sat.

During the flight from Chapel Hill he hadn't been able to talk to his team. The whole time he'd thought about the girl and her father and about how he'd left things with Steven.

"It's bad enough," Shel answered. "Maggie's doing the briefing when we get there."

"What are we up against?" Will snugged the seat belt into place.

Max vaulted through the open window of the rear door and lay in the backseat. As always, the dog was calm and controlled even when everyone around him was tense.

"Twenty-seven to thirty-two guns." Shel started the truck and pulled onto the road.

"All hostile?"

"All potentially hostile. Remains to be seen how many of them want to make the ante once we name the game."

"Everyone's here?"

Shel nodded. "Maggie's got the brief ready. Estrella's running surveillance. Remy's putting video and audio pickups in place at the hostile twenty."

"Remy's on-site at the house?"

"Yeah." Shel grinned as he looked at Will. "But the bad guys don't know it."

>> FARMHOUSE
>> 2133 HOURS

United States Navy Chief Petty Officer Remy Gautreau slid through the night like a shadow. Black and lean, carrying just over a hundred and eighty pounds on a six-foot-three-inch frame, he was quiet as a whisper as he closed on the house.

He was a Navy SEAL, trained for special-forces combat on sea, air, and land. Getting through the loose security maintained by the men occupying the old farmhouse had been cake.

A black watch cap blunted the moonlight that might have shone against his shaved scalp. He lay on his belly in the woods behind the house and brought a pair of light-amplifying binoculars to his eyes.

One. Two. Three. Four. Remy counted the sentries easily, marking them by the positions he'd already identified.

The men were stationary, staying within the darkness and away from the scant light that spilled from the covered farmhouse windows. A couple of them smoked, the orange coals of their cigarettes giving away their positions.

Not cigarettes, Remy thought, recognizing the sickly sweet smell of the smoke. *Reefer.*

The earpiece on the skeletal COMSET around his throat and ear chirped for attention.

Remy tapped the microphone at his throat, not wanting to speak. He replied in Morse code, sending the message quickly: HERE.

Clicks sounded in his ear and he translated effortlessly. WILL IS HERE. CONFIRM GIRL STATUS.

Meaning, was she a prisoner? Was she alive?

NEGATIVE, Remy tapped back. NEED MORE TIME.

ROGER.

Rising to his feet, staying close to a twisted oak tree, Remy circled through the forest to the blind spot he'd found in the security.

The farmhouse was easily a hundred years old. That wasn't unusual for this area outside of Jacksonville. The house was clean and looked as though it had been well kept up; it certainly didn't look like a den of evil. According to the real-estate records Estrella had accessed back in the command center, the property was owned by a man named Bryce Ketchum and had been for twenty-three years.

Over the years, additions had been made to the farmhouse. Now the structure stood spread out from a four-room core. Single rooms had been added, then wings and hallways. The second floor had been added in at least three different ventures that Remy could see.

It's gonna be a rat's nest inside, he told himself. *A logistical nightmare even for a seasoned urban-assault team.*

It would have been a lot easier if the girl hadn't been on the premises. The possibility of collateral damage made any operation more difficult.

You people feel secure in your little rat's nest, Remy thought coldly. *But that's only for now. We're going to take that away from you.*

Settling his load-bearing harness across his chest and shoulders again, Remy took up his rifle and walked toward the barn, moving quickly. He wasn't too worried about being spotted; rapid movement in the dark was a killer. He knew the guards' eyes would be struggling with the night, especially when they kept adjusting to the light in the house or the glow from their cigarettes.

The barn stank of old animal sweat and excrement, of leather tack and hay. Tonight vehicles—cars, trucks, SUVs, and motorcycles—were parked there. They added the stench of oil and gas.

No one was on guard there.

STILL WITH ME? Remy tapped on the throat mike.

YES.

Remy slung his assault rifle over his shoulder and climbed the ladder leading to the loft. Looking out over the farmhouse, he saw that he'd come out where he'd thought he would: behind the house. He'd noted a pattern in the guards' walking tours. All of them concentrated on the trail leading up to the house and not on the wooded area behind.

They were obviously expecting company, but not from the rear of the house.

Easing over the side of the hayloft, Remy hung by his fingertips for a moment, then dropped to the ground. Turning deliberately, not moving too fast, he walked to the rear of the farmhouse, caught hold of the low eave over the screened-in sunroom, and swung himself up just as he heard footsteps approach his position.

Remy flattened against the roof and didn't move. The odor of marijuana filled his nostrils. A faint whisper of country music reached his ears. The guy was listening to an iPod while he walked patrol.

Peering over the roof's edge in disbelief, Remy watched as the man headed to the front of the house, his head bopping in rhythm to the music. *Way too relaxed out here,* Remy thought. But it worked to his advantage.

Spotting the open window below, Remy reached for a battery-operated audio transceiver spike and slipped it into the window jamb. He flipped it on, then tapped a message: CONFIRM AUDIO PICKUP?

AUDIO PICKUP CONFIRMED.

Remy quickly added a small, battery-operated camera with a fish-eye lens the size of a shirt button. He placed it and turned it on.

CONFIRM VIDEO?

AFFIRMATIVE.

Remy kept working, negotiating the farmhouse's roof carefully, not entirely trusting it to hold his weight. His luck got even better when he found an attic vent big enough to admit him at the side of the house.

He used a Leatherman Multi-Tool to remove the screws holding the vent cover, then removed the grate. He climbed in and paused for a moment in a kneeling position with his pistol in his hands. Slowly his eyes acclimated.

I'M INSIDE ATTIC.

CONFIRM. GO EASY.

ROGER THAT. STAND READY. WE'RE GOING TO MOVE QUICKLY NOW.

Holstering his sidearm, Remy started wiring the rest of the house, spiking the top-floor rooms as he searched for the girl.

>> NCIS FIELD COMMAND POST
>> 2143 HOURS

"Captain Whitcomb, let me introduce Commander Will Coburn," Larkin said as Will stepped into the command vehicle.

Will took the man's hand and shook.

Whitcomb was in his late forties, fit and brown haired with gray showing at the temples. He wore civilian dress, charcoal Dockers, and a dark blue polo shirt, but someone had gotten him a navy blue Windbreaker with yellow letters proclaiming *Special Agent* across the back.

"They tell me you're good at what you do, Commander." Nervous tension tightened Whitcomb's voice.

"Aye, Captain. I am. And I've got good people. We'll get your daughter out of there safely."

Larkin gestured, and they all sat at the small foldout table near the front of the retrofitted RV, away from the tech center where Estrella Montoya worked her magic.

Maggie stood a short distance away with a small notebook computer. Will waved her forward.

Maggie sat at the table and opened the computer. She struck a series of keys, and the screen flickered to life, revealing the round face of a young girl no older than Steven. Her dark hair had scarlet highlights and was chopped in some kind of cut that left it three inches shorter on one side. Freckles covered her nose and stained her cheeks.

"This is your daughter?" Will asked.

Whitcomb nodded. He was obviously having trouble restraining himself. "It is. That's Amanda."

"Want to tell me what happened?"

"I don't know. I just got this phone call from Amanda about two—" Whitcomb checked his watch—"about two and a half hours ago. Just past nineteen hundred hours. She said she'd been kidnapped by her boyfriend."

"Who's the boyfriend?"

Whitcomb shook his head. "I don't know. Amanda and I—" he paused—"we don't talk a lot these days. I don't know why. It's just . . . it's just *hard*. Hard to talk."

Will knew what that was like and wished he didn't.

"I don't really know who any of her friends are," Whitcomb went on.

"It's all right, Captain," Maggie said, stepping into the uncomfortable silence when Will didn't. "There'll be time to figure all of that out later."

"Sure."

"Your daughter was pulled over with a young man last month," Maggie said. "Did you know that?"

"Pulled over by whom?"

"The Jacksonville PD." Maggie keyed the computer again. A new picture showed up on the screen.

The young man was in his early twenties. His hair was just stubble, showing the multicolored lines of a dragon tattoo on his scalp. A knife scar marred his right cheek. A goatee looked like algae growth on his chin. Several earrings hung from each ear.

"Do you recognize this man?" Maggie asked.

Whitcomb studied the man and cursed bitterly, then excused himself. "He's brought Amanda home a few times. I asked her to stay away from him." He cut his eyes to Maggie. "Is that who brought her out here?"

"We don't know. That's what we're trying to find out."

"Is he the only one that's holding her?"

"No." Maggie didn't try to evade the question.

"She told me she was at a farmhouse."

"Yes," Maggie said. "We've identified the location."

"Is Amanda there? Is she all right?"

"We don't know yet."

Whitcomb glanced at Larkin. "I thought you said these people were good."

"These people," Larkin said in a calm, well-modulated manner, "are the best I have."

"You've got Marines out there," Whitcomb objected. "You could send them after Amanda."

"I could," Larkin agreed. "But if it comes out later that your daughter isn't being held against her will or says that she isn't, we could become liable for any damage done at that farmhouse."

"Amanda could be hurt. She may already be hurt."

"And if she's not," Will stated, "she could get that way quickly if those men find a group of Marines parked on their doorstep."

Whitcomb held Will's gaze for a moment, then settled back in his seat. "You're right."

"We're going to try to do this as bloodlessly as possible," Will went on. "If nobody gets hurt, that means Amanda won't be hurt either."

Whitcomb nodded and took a deep breath. "All right."

"You talked to your daughter two and a half hours ago?"

"Yes."

"How did she sound?"

"Scared. Mad. She said she couldn't believe the guy was being such a jerk."

"Did she sound . . . sober?" For a moment Will felt certain that Whitcomb was going to vault out of his chair and attack. He saw it in the man's eyes.

Rage mottled Whitcomb's face. "I resent the implication in that question."

"I apologize," Will said. "But before I send my people into that situation, I want to know what I'm dealing with."

"Your daughter has a history of drugs and alcohol," Maggie said. "Even if she didn't use or drink, she was around it. She's been picked up at every base you have lived at since she was ten."

"She has trouble picking the right friends," Whitcomb replied.

"When the Jacksonville PD picked your daughter up a few weeks ago in this man's custody," Maggie said, "she'd been drinking. The police officer looked at her military ID and decided to pass on pressing charges against her. A cop drove her home after the man she was with was arrested for DUI and having an open container in the vehicle."

"If Amanda has been drinking tonight," Will said, "extracting her is going to be more difficult." He folded his hands before him on the table. "I need to know what my people are facing before I send them in there."

Whitcomb took in a deep breath and let it out. When he spoke, his voice was soft and had fear in it. "I don't know. I don't know if she's sober."

Will nodded. He stood.

"Where are you going?" Whitcomb asked.

"To see if we can't get your daughter back," Will answered.

CRIME SCENE

NCIS
NAVAL CRIMINAL INVESTIGATIVE SERVICE

4

SCENE  NCIS  CRIME SCEN

NAVAL CRIMINAL INVESTIGATIVE SERVICE

>> KETCHUM FARMHOUSE
>> NORTH OF JACKSONVILLE, NORTH CAROLINA
>> 2149 HOURS

Remy lay flat on his stomach on the boards he'd moved to span the farmhouse rafters. He was drenched in perspiration from the heat trapped in the house. The insulation was already starting to make him itch.

Using a battery-operated minidrill from his pack, Remy cut through the Sheetrock ceiling in the corner of the room. Sheetrock dust filtered down from the hole, but he was close enough to the wall that he felt comfortable no one would notice.

The whole house was shaking to Southern rock. Pungent smoke coiled in the attic, mixing with the stifling heat. The people inside the farmhouse created their own diversions.

So far Remy had wired three of the twelve rooms on the farmhouse's second floor. When the drill bit chewed through the Sheetrock, he released the trigger and drew the drill gun back.

Soft light stabbed into the attic from below, shooting through the sixteenth-of-an-inch hole.

Laying the drill gun aside, Remy reached into his pack for another of the battery-operated wireless video cameras he was hooking up. He'd already strung signal repeaters in the woods beyond the farmhouse.

The pinhole video camera needed only a sixteenth-of-an-inch aperture to film through. Its electronic iris operated automatically to provide the best picture even in low-light situations. The camera transmitted in color at 420 lines of resolution, which was better than the picture on most television sets.

Remy picked up the 2.4 GHz wireless video sender/receiver and brought the latest unit on line. He scanned the image, realizing that he'd tapped into another bedroom.

On the screen, the room's sole occupant sat on a bed with her knees drawn up to her chin. She smoked a cigarette that looked suspiciously like a joint and appeared miserably alone.

Elation coursed through Remy. He'd found Amanda Whitcomb. The girl was still alive. Working quickly, Remy cut another hole through the ceiling and added an audio pickup.

Then he tapped the throat microphone. CONFIRM GIRL'S PRESENCE.

ACKNOWLEDGED. CONFIRM GIRL.

Amanda Whitcomb was safe at the moment. That felt good. As a SEAL, Remy hadn't always arrived in time to save the people he was sent in to save. This time he could make that happen.

He moved on, working the perimeter of the attic.

>> NCIS FIELD COMMAND POST
>> NORTH OF JACKSONVILLE, NORTH CAROLINA
>> 2152 HOURS

"Remy found the girl." United States Navy Petty Officer Third Class Estrella Montoya tapped the computer monitor that showed Amanda Whitcomb alone in the bedroom.

Standing behind Estrella, Will studied the monitor. The room Amanda Whitcomb occupied was small, holding only a full-size bed and a chest of drawers that supported a small television set. Amanda was watching cartoons, which seemed incongruous to the kidnapping situation that had drawn Will and his team to the site.

"She appears unharmed," Estrella stated quietly. Full figured and five feet seven inches tall, Estrella was twenty-nine years old. Dark bronze hair framed her dark-complexioned face and her warm brown eyes. She was a whiz with anything that had to do with computers.

Will silently agreed, but he also suspected that Amanda Whitcomb was partially responsible for her "kidnapping." Whether by bad choices or a self-destructive nature, the girl had put herself in harm's way. Still, the father part of him knew that children strayed and often made mistakes. The trick was to help them survive those mistakes and learn from them. As an NCIS investigator, he knew firsthand that children didn't always get to grow up.

Investigating crimes against children was hard—too hard. But over time, Will had learned to regret the ones he'd arrived too late to help and to hold fiercely to those he'd helped save.

Tonight, he told himself, *is going to be another save.* Whether Amanda Whitcomb was responsible for her presence in the farmhouse or not, he was going to see to it that she went home.

"Tell me about the boyfriend," Will told Maggie. They'd left Captain Whitcomb with Larkin, cutting the man out of the information loop until they knew what they were going to do.

"Not much to tell," Maggie said, bringing up the guy's picture on her computer. "Dylan Moss. He's twenty-three and has a history of trouble with the law. Petty theft. Drugs. Assault. Trespassing. He's had a close relationship with juvenile services since the age of nine."

Will tried not to think about nine-year-old Dylan Moss. But it was hard not to. Someone somewhere—his parents or the system—had failed him. Maybe Dylan Moss had been the child of divorced parents. Like Steven. Maybe Dylan Moss just hadn't made it through the emotional turmoil. Seven years, maybe eight, separated Steven from the young man on the screen.

It's more than that, Will told himself. *Steven could never be someone like this.* Then he wondered if Captain Whitcomb had thought that about his daughter.

Will shifted his gaze to another monitor. This one was hooked into a satellite feed and showed the farmhouse in thermographic imagery that read the heat signatures of the people inside the structure.

The view, looking down on the farmhouse from space, was a little difficult to judge. Several yellow, orange, and red figures sat or moved inside and outside the structure. Most of them were tagged with numbers.

"How many people are on-site?" Will asked, knowing the tags were there to identify unique body masses.

Estrella opened a window on one of the screens and consulted it briefly. "Twenty-seven."

"Who are they?"

"A local gang," Maggie said. "They call themselves the Purple Royals. They're a pretty small outfit—a real grassroots operation. Only locals can get in. They run drugs and weapons."

"Weapons?"

Maggie nodded. "Pistols and rifles. Fully automatic weapons."

Drugs and weapons together were never good. Will surveyed the monitors again, spotting the guards Remy Gautreau had found. They all carried assault rifles that could have been modified for fully automatic fire.

It's going to be a combat zone going in there, Will realized. "This can't be about one girl."

"No. From the intel I've been able to gather by working with the Jacksonville PD, the Royals are currently at odds with the Almighty Latin Kings."

"They're out of Chicago," Estrella said. "They're the oldest Hispanic gang of record."

Will wasn't suprised Estrella knew that. She was from Chicago and had brothers who'd struggled with the local gangs while growing up.

"The Almighty Latin Kings have factions in several other cities," Maggie said. "Including New York. The detective I talked to told me that the Kings and the Royals are currently fighting over territory in Jacksonville."

"Why?"

"They're still investigating that. They believe it's drugs or guns."

"Who owns the farmhouse?" Will asked.

Maggie hit another key and brought up full-face and profile pictures of another man. "A man named Bryce Ketchum. He's the leader of the Royals. The farmhouse has been in his family for three generations."

Will studied the man's features. Ketchum's Native American ancestry showed in the sharp cheekbones, dark skin, and long black hair. Cold hazel eyes stared out of the mug shot. A ragged scar tracked his right profile from his ear to his chin.

"He's forty-three, lives in Jacksonville," Maggie said. "He's got a long history with the police and court systems. He's lived in Jacksonville all his life. Most of the people that are with him are locals."

"They're going to know the woods," Will acknowledged. That made things even more dangerous.

>> NCIS MEDICAL LAB
>> CAMP LEJEUNE, NORTH CAROLINA
>> 2201 HOURS

Nita handled the Stryker saw with ease, keeping just enough pressure on to allow the blade to bite through the skull. Fine bone dust sprayed over her scrubs.

She cut the skull at an angle, the way a pumpkin would be cut to create a jack-o'-lantern, beveling the sides so the section would fit back into place precisely. A straight cut would have allowed the top of the skull to slide out of place—not something anyone would want to have happen during the funeral.

When she was finished with the cut, Nita laid the saw aside. She pried off the skullcap, called the calvarium, with her gloved fingers. She listened for—and heard—the familiar wet, sucking sound that told her she'd freed the calvarium properly. Putting the skullcap on a small table, she turned her attention to Chief O'Brien's brain.

Blood spotted the brain's surface, and Nita knew instantly what had killed the chief. She sighed in sympathy, knowing that what she was going to find wouldn't have been fatal if it had been caught in time.

"Blood inside the skull indicates the possibility of an aneurysm," Nita said. "Evacuation of the brain will reveal more."

An aneurysm was a thinning of the blood-vessel walls because of age or illness or just a defect the person had been born with. Gradually, as time and stress worked on it, the aneurysm would worsen, growing thinner till it finally burst. Most aneurysms formed in the brain. But they didn't have to be fatal.

Since the dura mater, the outer layers of meninges that covered the brain, stayed with the calvarium, the brain sat fully exposed inside the skull. With a scalpel, Nita freed the brain from the spinal cord. Moving slowly, she eased her fingers down into the skull and removed the brain.

The organ was pinkish gray, so soft in its present form that it could easily be torn. She judged that it weighed around three and a half pounds, which was average size.

While a person was alive, the brain was kept more or less suspended in cerebrospinal fluid inside the skull. Without the cushioning effect of the CSF, the brain was so fragile it would collapse under its own weight.

Handling the brain carefully, Nita tied a string around it, then lowered it into a waiting jar of formalin, a 10 percent mixture of formaldehyde gas in buffered water. For the next two weeks, the brain would remain in the water, hardening and becoming rubbery like gelatin so it could be more easily handled without tearing.

Holding the jar up, Nita peered inside. After only a moment, she found the cause of O'Brien's death.

At the base of the brain, in the area called the circle of Willis, where a redundancy of blood vessels ensured continued blood flow even if one of the other vessels narrowed or became blocked from injury, she spotted a ballooned vessel that had burst.

"There is a burst aneurysm at the back of Chief O'Brien's brain,"

Nita said. "Judging from the size and shape, this was a saccular aneurysm, formed in the anterior part of the circle, a bifurcation of the internal carotid and posterior communication arteries."

The rupture was common. And if caught in time, it was treatable through surgery. Even if the chief hadn't been healthy enough for that, microcoil thrombosis could have been used. The process allowed surgeons to insert a catheter through an artery up to the brain, where tiny coils were used to block the flow of blood through the aneurysm.

Putting the brain jar on the table, Nita stripped off her gloves and threw them into a biohazard disposal bin. She picked up the chief's medical records.

"According to the paperwork," Nita said, reading through the notes, "the chief had been complaining of headaches and dizziness a few days before his death. Those are symptomatic of subarachnoid hemorrhaging. The aneurysm was the cause of death."

Nita stood and stretched, working the kinks out of tired muscles. She looked back at the hollow dead man she'd left on the table. There was still a lot of work to do before she could leave and go to the club.

Her cell phone rang.

Nita glanced at the caller ID and saw that it was her home number. She thought about not answering; she didn't want to deal with her husband or daughter right now.

But she couldn't ignore the call either. Something inside her wouldn't allow that, and she didn't know why. That was another of the feelings that made her feel so trapped in her marriage, in being a wife and a parent. She'd never planned on either of those roles.

Yet here she was, wasn't she? Doing both. And it was getting in the way of letting her be who she needed to be.

Roiling resentment coursed through her. Barely controlling the anger she felt, she picked up the phone and punched the Talk button.

"Hello." Nita knew her tone wasn't happy and didn't encourage talk.

"Nita." As always, Joe Tomlinson's voice was soft and easygoing, as if he didn't have a problem in the world. People who knew her husband usually went on at length about how laid-back and calm he was. Nothing ruffled Joe's demeanor, and Nita had never once seen her husband out of control with anger or frustration, the two emotions that seemed to plague her most.

That soft voice and easy way of speaking had drawn Nita to him initially. He had honeyed tones, a Southern accent that was pure and true, not put on or emphasized. Joe was always just . . . Joe. An inch short of six feet tall, he had broad shoulders and narrow hips, sun-kissed blond hair that hung to his shoulders, and light hazel eyes that belonged on a big cat. Their daughter, Celia, took most of her looks from her father.

Joe worked on boats at a shop he'd built himself down by the Kerr Street Marina. His father and grandfather had been carpenters, but Joe had always loved the sea and sailing. He'd worked with his father and grandfather but had added shipbuilding and motor repair to the skills they'd taught him. Now he built custom craft boats and repaired and refurbished existing ones. He had a waiting list of over two years for his new boats and never tried to hurry through to the end of a job. He did everything exactly the way it was supposed to be done.

"Catch you at a bad time?" Joe asked.

Nita wanted to say something angry, but she really couldn't. Joe wasn't the problem. She was. He just didn't know that.

"I'm just working," she said.

"I guessed that." Joe waited a beat. "Is it bad?"

"Bad enough." Joe knew the kind of work Nita did, though he'd never come down to her lab. Nita hadn't wanted him there. The lab was her space. Just as his shop was his. The difference was that she knew she was invited to his shop anytime she wanted to go.

She never wanted to.

"I just finished up an autopsy," Nita went on.

"That's good that you've finished. You sound like you could use some rest."

Nita knew that he wanted her home. He never came out and said that, but she knew it was what he wanted. Joe liked having her there. So did Celia. Again, Nita was the problem, not them. She felt like she was suffocating there and didn't know what to do about it except not be there.

"I can't leave yet," she told him. "I've still got a lot to do. I've got to put the body back together and deal with all the paperwork."

"Sure," Joe said. "I was just calling because I wanted to hear your voice."

Despite her anger and frustration, that simple declaration made Nita smile. Guys had told her that before. Those were easy words to say when two people were getting to know each other. But she never doubted that Joe meant them. He meant everything he said.

"And I wanted to let you know that I had dinner ready for you if you wanted it when you got home," Joe went on. "It's in the refrigerator. Meat loaf and a salad."

"All right."

Joe was always doing things like that. Nita seldom cooked and didn't enjoy it, but Joe was as good in the kitchen as he was in his marine shop.

"Celia wanted to make a deep-dish apple pie tonight, so we did," Joe said. "That's in the refrigerator too. It turned out really well."

As soon as Celia had developed an interest in preparing meals, Joe had worked with her, helping her make pancakes and cookies. Celia had loved it, and Nita had no doubt that her daughter knew more about preparing a meal than she did.

Nita hadn't learned to do more than open a can or nuke a TV dinner until college, when she had to make her money stretch. Only then, when she'd grown tired of eating the same thing all the time, had she started learning to cook a few simple meals.

Growing up in various trailer parks with her mother, Nita had learned to mooch meals off other kids' moms and to subsist on peanut-butter sandwiches, microwaved nachos, and canned pasta. Nita couldn't remember her mom ever preparing a meal, but there were occasional boyfriends who had charcoaled.

"Thanks," Nita said.

The awkward silence stretched between them. There were more and more of those of late.

"I should let you get back to work," Joe said. "Probably I shouldn't have called, but I just wanted to talk to you for a little while."

"Sure," Nita replied.

"Celia and I are going to church Sunday morning."

The invitation was there between the words. That was another thing that Nita couldn't understand about her husband. He went to church every Sunday morning and evening and nearly every Wednesday. People knew him at church, and he was always involved in some activity that was going on there. He and Celia did most of those things together.

"I really want to sleep in," Nita said.

"All right. Maybe next time."

It was always "maybe next time." Nita hadn't been to church with her family except on Easter and Christmas in over three years. With the way the churchwomen gossiped, she was certain her absence had been the subject of more than one conversation. Especially since everyone expected her to rise to her husband's standard.

"Well," Joe said, "take care of yourself. If you need anything, just call."

"Sure," she said again.

"Good night."

Nita gripped the phone a little tighter, wishing she could object to

Joe's calling her in the first place. She could start a fight that way, maybe even push it big enough for her to move out.

But all she said was, "Good night."

Joe broke the connection, and Nita cursed and dropped the cell phone back into her purse. She didn't need the guilt that talking to her husband brought to her. She wasn't the world's most perfect wife or mother. She already knew that. She wasn't trained to be. Neither one of those things had been on her list of aspirations.

She just wanted to be free to be herself again. To go and do whatever she wanted without someone waiting in the wings to make her feel guilty.

Get finished here, she told herself. *The bars will still be open.*

Pulling on a fresh set of surgical gloves, Nita threaded a needle and set to work putting the dead man back together.

Maybe tonight would be the night she could slip free. A chance encounter at the bar with a Marine or Navy man, or even a civilian, that could take her that one step past the point of no return. As Christian as Joe was, she felt certain he wouldn't be able to forgive infidelity. Maybe she'd have to suffer through some negative responses, but she'd have her life back. When she did, it would be small and neat and orderly. An existence that she could understand and handle, in which no one expected anything out of her that she couldn't—or didn't want to—give. That was all she truly wanted. It was all she'd ever dreamed of growing up in those trailer parks with a mother who was gone more than she was home.

Tonight could be the night. Freedom in exchange for a little guilt and a little pain. For a moment her resolve weakened; then she told herself that Joe and Celia would be better off as well. She was going to free them all.

S  CRIME SCENE  NCIS  C

NAVAL CRIMINAL INVESTIGATIVE SERVICE

5

SCENE  NCIS  CRIME SCEN

NAVAL CRIMINAL INVESTIGATIVE SERVICE

>> KETCHUM FARMHOUSE
>> NORTH OF JACKSONVILLE, NORTH CAROLINA
>> 2326 HOURS

Since Amanda Whitcomb was relatively safe for the moment, Will concentrated on the rescue effort, positioning the different units and giving them their standing orders. He stood in the darkness behind the farmhouse with Shel McHenry at his side. Three other men held positions behind them.

The big Marine wore combat black. Black camo cosmetics shaded his face. Like Will and the other members of the insertion teams, he wore impact-resistant elbow and knee pads, a Kevlar vest, and a helmet, all designed to protect him while still allowing him to move quickly.

A contingent of Marines trained in urban warfare hid in the woods behind them. All of the men were experienced in search-and-rescue efforts.

Knowing he was about to make the call to send them into action, Will felt his stomach knot up. Command came naturally to him, but it didn't come easily. No action went without a price.

Lord, please protect these men. Help us to move quietly and surely, and allow us to succeed in rescuing Amanda Whitcomb. Thank you for watching over us.

"Ready, Steadfast Leader," Maggie called over the headset.

"Acknowledged, Steadfast Four," Will replied. Shel was Three. Estrella was Five. Remy was Six. Since Frank Billings's murder, Steadfast Two had gone unused. Will studied the top of the roof, barely able to make out Remy Gautreau even though he was looking for him. "Ready, Six?"

SIX IS READY, Remy tapped back, still not wanting to use his voice around the house.

Will took a deep breath and packed away the uncertainty he was feeling. Remy was responsible for securing the girl. Will's faith in the SEAL was complete. If anyone could get Amanda Whitcomb out of the farmhouse alive, Remy could.

"You have the ball, Six," Will said. "Commence."

ACKNOWLEDGED. SIX HAS THE BALL.

Remy's shadow slithered back into the attic. He'd been in place outside to help spot for the approach and to give warning if any of the guards had noticed them.

"Time, Five?" Will said.

"Twenty-three twenty-eight, Leader," Estrella answered over the headset.

"Keep me in the loop." In the darkness, Will waited, and he said another prayer. Since Frank's death, since that whole terrorist operation had begun last year and ended in the South China Sea with nuclear weapons aimed at Chinhae Naval Base, Will had moved closer to God. The relationship and his faith had strengthened, and that gave Will the confidence to get through his divorce and to hope that his relationship with his children would survive.

He prayed quietly, but his eyes never left the farmhouse.

⊛ ⊛ ⊛

>> 2330 HOURS

The bedroom Amanda Whitcomb occupied had a closet. Remy had already marked its location and cleared the area of insulation.

When he reached it this time, he took out a keen-edged survival knife, scored the Sheetrock at the top of the closet with the regular blade, then cut through it with the saw-toothed side. The Sheetrock cut easily, and he knew the sound couldn't be heard over the cartoon shows the girl was watching.

The swirling dust clung to Remy and made it hard to breathe. He tried not to think about all the dust he was sucking into his lungs. *Gotta include surgical masks in my kit for home invasions.*

He pried up the section of Sheetrock he'd cut free and withdrew it. Below, barely visible in the light coming in around the closet door, he saw the closet. A few jackets and coats hung from a metal rod, but only a few.

He checked the video display for the room. Amanda Whitcomb's attention was still on the television as she lit another joint. The redolent stink of marijuana filled Remy's nostrils again.

STEADFAST LEADER, SIX IS READY TO MAKE ENTRANCE, Remy tapped.

"Acknowledged, Six. Make your play. Godspeed." Will Coburn sounded totally calm. Scary calm, almost.

During the last year of working with Will, Remy had learned to respect the man not only as a military officer but as a human being. Remy kept his distance from the rest of the team, but he watched. He liked the way Will Coburn carried himself, the way he led the team. He also liked the way Will acted with his kids, placing them first whenever he could. But Will had a tough job with a lot of responsibility. Keeping that balance was a difficult thing, and Remy wouldn't want to do it.

Remy dropped silently through the hole in the ceiling and into the closet, careful to avoid the few dangling hangers. He drew his sidearm. After all the years he'd carried it, the Smith & Wesson .357 felt like a part of his body. He tried the closet door and found it unlocked.

FIVE, AM I CLEAR? Remy tapped.

"You're clear, Six," Estrella whispered into his ear.

Remy pushed the door out, quickly and smoothly, and followed it into the bedroom.

On the bed, Amanda Whitcomb turned her head toward him. Then her eyes widened in shock, slowed somewhat because of the drug in her system. She opened her mouth to scream.

By then Remy was at her side. He clapped a leather glove–covered hand over her mouth and held her tightly against him. She struggled fiercely, reaching for his face with her fingernails. The joint had tumbled from her lips to the bed.

Keeping his face ducked low and against the back of her head, Remy used his forearms to block her attempts to get to him. She struggled to stand up on the bed and pull away from him, but her movements were sluggish, and he restrained her easily. Doing it without hurting her was harder.

"Amanda," he whispered in her ear. "I'm here to get you out. Your father sent me."

The girl didn't stop fighting.

"Amanda," Remy whispered more forcibly. He captured one of her arms with his free hand and brought it across her body, trapping her. He had a tranquilizer ampoule in his kit that would render her unconscious if he couldn't get her to listen. But he didn't want to use it. Knocking her out would lessen her chances of survival. "I'm not going to hurt you. Your father sent me."

Amanda stopped struggling. She looked up at Remy. The fear was still there, but he had her attention now. "My father?" Her voice was a dry whisper.

"Yes. Your father."

"I called him. They wouldn't let me go. Dylan said I couldn't go. He said they were waiting." Tears fell from her eyes, pulling black stains from the heavy mascara with them.

Remy knew the girl was well under the effects of the marijuana. He knew how easily drugs could foul up a person's hold on reality. *Keep her focused. Keep her focused and keep her alive.*

Remy whispered calmly, "Your father sent us to get you out of here."

"I didn't think he was coming." Her voice cracked, and suddenly she was shaking in Remy's arms.

"Your father called us," Remy said. "Now we're going to get you out of here." He heard Estrella telling the rest of the extraction team that he had the girl. *Having her and getting her out of here safely are two different things.*

Amanda clung to him.

Gently Remy eased her arms from around him. "We gotta move," he told her, taking her by the hand. "Look at me."

She did.

"You hearing me okay, Amanda?" Remy asked.

She nodded, but her reaction time was off, slow.

Remy pushed away the doubts and fear. They didn't have any place in his world at the moment. *You've got a plan—a* good *plan. Just stick with the plan. That's all you've gotta do.* "We move when I say move. Okay?"

"Yeah." Her voice broke.

"We can get out through the closet. It leads to the attic. We can get out that way too."

"Okay."

Before Remy could move, Estrella said, "You've got problems, Six. One of the hostiles is closing in on your twenty."

Adrenaline kicked through Remy's system. He pointed his pistol at the door as the knob turned. Still, he kept his voice calm. "Steadfast Leader, be advised that I'm about to be compromised."

>> NCIS COMMAND POST
>> NORTH OF JACKSONVILLE, NORTH CAROLINA
>> 2333 HOURS

Estrella stared at the thermographic display. She made herself breathe as she watched the yellow-and-red "ghost" image of someone walking toward the bedroom where Remy Gautreau held Amanda Whitcomb.

"Six has company," Estrella said.

On the screen, the yellow-and-red figure hesitantly opened the bedroom door and entered.

Shifting over to the video feed from the camera Remy had installed in the ceiling, Estrella watched as the man came through the door. She hated the helpless feeling that flooded through her.

Stay on task, she told herself. *You can't be there, but you can help if you'll stay on task.*

On the screen, Remy lifted his pistol and pointed it into the man's face.

"Step inside." Remy's voice sounded as cool as death, even through the tiny speakers built into the monitor.

Though Estrella had known Remy Gautreau for nearly a year, had worked with him during perilous times, those icy words reminded her that she didn't really know him at all. Remy kept to himself.

It's not just that, she told herself grimly. *You don't really know anyone in this life. Everyone can surprise you.*

Remy's words, the chill purposefulness of them, reminded Estrella of her own husband's death. She'd been pregnant with their child, with Dominic, when she'd come home and found Julian dead. Her husband had shot himself in the bathtub.

Overwhelmed by insurmountable debt, his dreams of creating a videogame company fractured, knowing he was going to be shackled to one company or another for years to make good on money he'd borrowed, Julian had given up. At the end, he'd been vulnerable.

Estrella sensed that in Remy, too. She'd seen Remy's service jacket, had gone through reports of his activities. Will and the others didn't know that, but Estrella felt she owed it to her son to know whom she could trust and whom she couldn't.

After Julian's death, Estrella doubted her own instincts. And she doubted God. God—despite her mother's insistence that he looked over his children—hadn't been there for any of them when Julian killed himself.

"Don't reach for anything," Estrella heard Remy order.

On-screen, the other man raised his hands. "It's cool, dude." The man's voice broke. "Don't hurt me."

"Close the door behind you."

The man did.

A silencer hung at the end of Remy's pistol, fat and malignant. Estrella knew the SEAL had equipped the weapon like that in case he had any violent encounters that he needed to handle quietly.

For a moment, no one moved.

He's going to kill him. The uncomfortable realization wormed through Estrella's stomach. A sour bubble burst at the back of her throat.

She'd seen men killed before. She'd even killed some herself. But it had always been in the heat of battle, during a confrontation when it was a matter of survival.

Not in cold blood.

Before she knew it, Estrella spoke. "Six, that's her boyfriend."

Remy didn't move.

Estrella could almost hear the SEAL thinking about it, figuring the odds of getting the girl safely out of the house if the young man in front of him was alive versus dead. Dead was more certain. Dead was easier.

She wanted to go on talking, to let Remy know that was a human being standing before him. But she felt certain it wouldn't matter. On a handful of occasions, Estrella had seen a colder nature in the SEAL than she'd seen in Shel McHenry. Shel killed combatants. Remy Gautreau was a killer.

"Dude." The young man's voice quavered. The video camera's definition was sharp enough to pick up the tears running down his cheeks. "Don't kill me. Please don't kill me."

Estrella cut to a private frequency with Will. "Six has been compromised by the girl's boyfriend. I think Six is going to kill him."

"Affirmative," Will responded.

Flipping back to the team frequency, Estrella heard Will say, "Six, what's the SITREP?"

"Compromised, Leader." Remy's voice was flat.

"I don't want a body count on this, Six. Not if we can get out clean."

"Understood. I'll keep it that way if I can."

Estrella watched, hypnotized by the screen.

Shifting only slightly, Remy whipped his arm forward and slammed his fist into the young man's neck. The young man stood for a moment, his mouth open as if he was about to cry out. Then he slumped to the floor.

The video reception was clean enough for Estrella to see the hypodermic jutting from the young man's neck. She knew Remy had carried a tranquilizer in with him. She sipped a breath.

"What did you do to him?" Amanda Whitcomb demanded.

"He's all right," Remy said. "Just taking a little nap."

The girl shoved her hair back from her face. Then she stepped away from Remy. "I'm not going with you."

"Amanda." Remy's voice was soothing now.

"No," she said. "*No*. You hurt him. You'll hurt me."

"I'm here to get you out of this place." Remy sounded calm, logical. He didn't make the mistake of reaching for the girl.

"No."

Remy looked at her. "You want to stay here?"

Amanda sagged against the wall. "I want my dad."

"I can take you to your dad."

"Where is he?"

"He's here."

Amanda's eyes held nothing but confusion and fear. "I want my dad."

"Six," Estrella said. "Give her the headset. I'll put her father on."

"Affirmative, Five." Remy stripped his headset and handed it to Amanda.

Pushing away from the control center, Estrella scooped up a wireless headset and walked into the RV's forward room, where Director Larkin sat with Captain Whitcomb. She felt tense. Without the headset, Remy was deaf, dumb, and blind.

Larkin looked at Estrella when she entered the forward section of the command post.

"We have a situation." Estrella shifted her attention to the Marine at once, knowing time was ticking away. "Captain Whitcomb, your daughter isn't in good shape."

The Marine captain looked scared and angry. "Has something happened to her?"

"No, sir," Estrella said. "She's frightened and confused. I think she just needs to hear your voice, sir. We don't have much time. Just tell her that you're here and that you want her to go with the man she's with. As of right now, she has that soldier's headset." She knew the captain would understand the risk Remy was taking.

Whitcomb accepted the headset Estrella pushed at him.

"Tell her," Estrella said. "Tell her *now* that you're here."

Whitcomb hesitated only a moment, then said, "Amanda. Amanda, honey, it's me. It's Daddy."

The raw emotion in the gruff Marine's eyes caused Estrella's eyes to burn. No matter what her mistakes were, that was his little girl in that house. Estrella knew how she'd feel if Nicky were in the same kind of danger. She vowed that her six-year-old would never grow up like that, never grow up without her around enough to teach him right from wrong.

But he's already growing up without a father, isn't he?

There was no denying that. And in the Hispanic community, a father counted for an awful lot.

"Daddy?" Amanda sounded surprised.

"I'm here," Whitcomb said.

Estrella closed her fist over her own mouthpiece. "Tell her to accompany that man, Captain."

Whitcomb looked at her and nodded. "Amanda, I need you to do something for me."

"What?"

"I need you to go with that man. The man that's with you."

"I don't know him."

"I do," Whitcomb said.

"She's under the influence, sir," Estrella said. "She's not tracking well."

Pain stabbed through the Marine's eyes. "Amanda, just go with him. Please. He's going to take care of you."

"We've got to hurry," Estrella said.

Whitcomb nodded. The Marine captain was more in control of himself than Estrella felt most parents would have been under similar conditions.

"Amanda, I've got to let you go," Whitcomb said.

"No," the girl pleaded. "I'm scared."

"So am I, sweetheart." Whitcomb's voice broke a little at the end. "But we can get through this thing. We *will* get through this."

Amanda started crying. "I'm sorry, Daddy. I'm *really* sorry."

"It's going to be okay," Whitcomb said.

Estrella's headset beeped for her attention. She changed frequencies and answered. "Steadfast Five here."

"Steadfast Five, this is Charlie Nine."

The Charlie groups were the outer-perimeter watchdogs that guarded the highway leading up to the Ketchum farm.

"Go, Charlie Nine. Steadfast Five reads you." Estrella beeped Will and cut him into the link. "What's the problem, Charlie Nine?" She knew Will would immediately identify the caller and know that their operation perimeters were about to be breached.

"I've got four bogeys that just turned onto the dirt road leading to your secure zone."

"Roger that." Estrella bolted for the back of the RV. As she slid into the seat, she scanned the monitors and saw the taillights of four vehicles speeding down the dirt road toward Ketchum Farm. "Was there any identification on those four vehicles, Charlie Nine?"

"I read North Carolina plates. We've got them recorded. Do you want them?"

"Negative, Charlie Nine. Hold that intel." By the time Estrella could run down the license plates, the four vehicles would already have arrived at the farm.

"Estrella?" Larkin stood behind her with the wireless headset in his hand. "Remy's back online."

Estrella nodded, shifted over to Remy's frequency, and asked, "Are you with me, Steadfast Six?"

"Steadfast Six reads you five by five." Remy sounded tense and alert.

"Get out of there, Six."

"Affirmative."

On-screen, Remy hustled Amanda Whitcomb toward the closet.

"Night Eyes, this is Steadfast Five."

Night Eyes was the designation for the helicopter that had brought Will on-site. It was FLIR equipped. The forward-looking infrared would give them a closer look at the vehicles.

"Acknowledged, Five. Night Eyes reads you."

"I need a sweep of those four bogeys."

"Night Eyes is on the way."

"Understood, Night Eyes. But I want a safe flyby only. Nothing that will spook the bogeys." Estrella tapped the keyboard in quick syncopation. Adrenaline flashed through her, reminding her of how she'd felt when she and Julian used to crack Web sites together, trashing and shredding their way through even the most secure servers. They had never found an intrusion countermeasure they hadn't been able to hack their way through.

She suddenly felt her husband's absence more than she had in a long time, and it made her wish she were with Nicky. She told herself that she'd be home soon. Amanda Whitcomb would be out of the trouble she'd gotten herself into, and Estrella would watch her son sleep for a while.

Accessing the satellite link, Estrella scanned the approaching vehicles. She tapped keys, bringing up a digital readout that showed in minutes and miles approximately how far the convoy was from the farmhouse. And there was no doubt that the vehicles were a convoy.

"Steadfast Leader, be advised that the approaching bogeys are less than two minutes out," Estrella said.

"Understood," Will replied. "If you can get me ID, that'll help."

"Working on it, Leader."

Larkin cursed.

Estrella didn't blame him. The thermographic display capabilities of the sat link revealed that a small army was inside the vans.

"Leader," Estrella said calmly, "those bogeys may be an invasion force."

"Copy," Will said.

"Have Ketchum and his people gotten crossways with anyone lately?" Larkin asked.

"I don't know, sir." Estrella moved her hands across the keyboard, focusing on all the screens in turn.

Night Eyes swept in for a closer look. Estrella brought the FLIR camera front and center, displacing the farmhouse feeds to the sides of the grid. The helicopter flew over quickly.

Even slowing the film, Estrella had trouble seeing more than blurs inside the vehicles. With the necessary magnification and loss of definition due to the speed and darkness, she had trouble making out anything.

But one thing was obvious.

"They're Asian," Larkin said.

Estrella agreed. She was already thinking of the various Asian gangs that operated in or around Jacksonville.

6

SCENE    CRIME SCEN

NCIS

NAVAL CRIMINAL INVESTIGATIVE SERVICE

```
>> EXTREME RUSH CLUB
>> JACKSONVILLE, NORTH CAROLINA
>> 2348 HOURS
```

Nita drank at the bar. She stood next to a pretty blonde in tight pants, who was talking animatedly to a trio of young Marines all competing for her attention. Sipping her rum and Coke, Nita checked the action going on in the club in the polished mirror behind the bar.

Extreme Rush catered to the military crowd as well as civilians. Tonight the two cultures mixed in fairly equal numbers, filling the club. But Nita could always tell who was military and who wasn't.

The music was loud, driving speed metal that suited Nita's mood. When she got this far down, she needed something to blow up the blues—something that would, for just a little while, allow her to forget those parts of her that were responsible for other people.

Darkness and cigarette smoke filled the club. Neon lights danced around the room.

A man shouldered in next to Nita from the crowded dance floor. His effort to escape the writhing bodies jostled her enough to cause her drink to slop over the sides.

"Hey," he said politely, "excuse me. I tripped over somebody's foot back there." He frowned. "At least, I think it was a foot. I had to step over two people on my way to the bar."

"It's all right." *Definitely military,* Nita thought as she reached for a paper napkin and wiped up the spill.

"Let me buy you another drink." He was tall and good-looking. His black hair was cropped short and he had intense blue eyes.

Nita thought about refusing but then reconsidered. So far she'd turned away three guys who had hit on her. Two of them were wearing wedding bands. She'd rejected them because of that immediately and felt like the world's biggest hypocrite for doing it.

Her own wedding ring was safely locked up in her office on base. She hadn't worn it in weeks. Joe believed her when she said she wanted to protect the ring from the chemicals she used. That was only part of the truth. Lately she hadn't been able to wear it because it felt like an anchor.

You can cheat, she told herself angrily, *but you don't want to help others do the same.* She didn't understand the impulse, but she couldn't deny it either.

"You don't have to buy me another drink," Nita said. "This one hardly spilled at all."

He smiled at her. "I want to." His cheeks dimpled, and she knew that he was younger than she'd thought. Maybe as much as a handful of years younger than she was.

She gave in, interested in him and caught up in the what-if and maybe that used to fuel her nights before she was married. "All right."

"What are you drinking?"

Nita told him.

He leaned over the bar and yelled at the bartender, which was usually the only way to get attention. He ordered two rum and Cokes.

After the drinks arrived, he extended a hand. "I'm Lieutenant David Horton, United States Navy. I'm a pilot. I fly F-18 Hornets. Those are fighter jets."

"Pleased to meet you, Lieutenant Horton." Nita took his hand; it felt hot and strong in her own. He held on to her hand just long enough to really claim her attention but not lingering long enough to make the situation uncomfortable.

Horton flashed the dimples again. "Just call me Dave."

"All right."

Horton stared into her eyes with his blue ones. "I didn't get your name."

"Nita."

"Just Nita?"

Nita smiled, mocking him. "Do you need more?"

"Not at the moment. You come here often, Nita?"

"Not often enough." Nita studied the man. He seemed arrogant and cocky, just the type to do well in the Navy's fighter-jet program.

"It's an okay place," Horton declared.

Nita nodded. The drinks were getting to her, loosening her up and allowing her to put the autopsy behind her. The fatigue and discontent lifted as well. She felt free and happy.

An unwelcome thought flashed through her mind: the man's name was David. In the Old Testament, David had been one of God's favorites and had been forgiven for a multitude of sins. As king, David had even coveted the wife of one of his soldiers, a Hittite warrior named Uriah who had served in the king's army.

Silently, Nita cursed. If it hadn't been for Joe, she'd never have heard of that story. Nita's own mother hadn't had much use for church except as a babysitting service. That had consisted of Sundays, Wednesdays, and every free Mothers' Day Out and Vacation Bible School she could find.

But Joe—back when he'd still been able to talk Nita into accompanying him to his Sunday school class—had told her the story. Nita forced the thought out of her mind. None of that had any place here.

"What do you do?" Horton asked.

"When I'm not here?" Nita countered.

"Sure." Horton nodded.

"I can't remember."

Horton's eyes dropped and he gazed at her in slight confusion. "You don't remember?"

"No," Nita replied. "I do remember that I come here to get away from whatever it is."

Frowning ruefully, Horton said, "All right. Do you remember if you dance?"

"As I remember it, I dance quite well."

Horton smiled. "Would you care to?"

"I would." Nita drained her drink, took hold of the young pilot's arm, and let him lead her onto the raucous dance floor. She danced, not thinking of her husband or daughter, giving herself over to the throbbing beat that echoed inside her. The alcohol numbed the unwanted guilt and wariness within her.

>> KETCHUM FARMHOUSE
>> NORTH OF JACKSONVILLE, NORTH CAROLINA
>> 2357 HOURS

Tension balled inside Will's stomach as he gazed in the direction of the dirt road that led to the Ketchum farmhouse.

"Ketchum and his people were expecting visitors," Shel said. "That's why there are so many people here."

Will nodded. "It remains to be seen whether they're doing business or waging war."

Shel's lips flattened into a grim, hard line.

"Six," Will called. "What's your SITREP?"

"Evacuating now, Leader."

"What's your twenty?"

"Inside the attic."

Remy's voice was hushed, but he was speaking rather than tapping his messages. Apparently, having been down inside the house itself, he felt the noise of the party was sufficient to cover his replies.

Headlights flared through the darkness, sweeping closer to the farmhouse. The perimeter guards came awake, shaking off boredom and drowsiness. Voices called out. The music coming from inside the house quieted. Several of the outside lights came on, setting the farmhouse ablaze.

Will and his team drew back more deeply into the shadows.

"Six," Will said, "hold your position."

"Acknowledged, Leader. Six is holding."

Several men emerged from the house. One of them was Bryce Ketchum. He carried an M14 assault rifle as he strode onto the long porch.

"Five," Will said, "I need intel."

The four vehicles rolled sedately into the yard, spreading out so they all had fire-free zones.

"Looks like the beginnings of the OK Corral," Shel stated softly. At his feet, Max rose to attention without a sound. Obviously the dog sensed tension.

"I can confirm several people inside two of those vehicles," Estrella said. "I believe they are Asian, but I don't know who they are."

Will radioed acknowledgment. There was nothing to do but wait and see what happened.

Ketchum went forward, swaggering slightly.

"Four," Will said, "can you get a read?"

Maggie Foley was a trained criminalist with a master's degree in psychology. Reading body language was just one of her skills.

"He's confident," Maggie replied. "Whoever those people are, he was expecting them and doesn't think he'll get any trouble from them."

Will took a compact pair of night-vision binoculars from his chest pack and scanned the vehicles. "Are we getting video on this, Five?"

"Affirmative, Leader. Five is acquiring video on all subjects."

Whatever they couldn't use tonight would be turned over to the police agencies they'd interfaced with to come this far.

One of the Asian men stepped forward to meet Ketchum. He was young, of average height, and slender. Will watched the way the wind pressed the man's black nylon Windbreaker against his body and knew the man carried a sidearm in a shoulder holster.

Two other men fell in beside the man who talked to Ketchum. They were here to make a statement.

"Do we have audio, Five?" Will asked.

"Audio is limited, but we have it. I'm patching it through."

"—merchandise is in the vans," the Asian was saying.

"Are they in good shape, Cho?" Ketchum asked. "I can't sell them if they're busted up or broken."

The Asian man took no insult from the question. "They are good."

"No ugly ones? I'll have trouble selling ugly ones, too."

A sick feeling twisted in Will's stomach as he guessed the nature of the merchandise. Beside him, Shel cursed, and Will knew the big Marine was tracking the same vibe.

"No ugly ones," Cho agreed.

"We'll see about that. Let me look at them."

Will keyed the frequency, getting everyone's attention. The parameters on the op—as well as the opposition—had just increased dramatically. "We've got noncombatants on the premises. Baker team, I want you to secure those vans when this goes down. Get as many of the bystanders out of the line of fire as you can."

"Yes, sir," the Marine heading up Baker Company quickly replied.

Ketchum crossed to the closest van.

Cho gestured at the man standing guard there.

"How many?" Ketchum asked.

"Twenty. Ten in each."

The guard at the side of the van slid the door back. The light came on, showing the mass of young women and girls huddled on the floor of the cargo van. Clad in shapeless dresses, their wrists secured by disposable plastic cuffs, all the women looked frightened.

"Party time," one of Ketchum's men said loudly. Several men laughed.

Ketchum reached into the van and pulled one of the women out. Reed thin, she barely came to Ketchum's shoulder. Her eyes were wide with fear.

The sickness inside Will swirled threateningly. He pushed it away.

During his shipboard career, he'd seen how cheap life sometimes was, especially in third world nations. Women and children were second-class citizens, the first casualties of plague or starvation because men wouldn't endanger their own well-being to provide for them.

In China, families sometimes still suffocated or drowned female children rather than take on an extra mouth to feed that would never be worth anything to the family. Or the girls were allowed to grow up, reach puberty, and be sold into sexual slavery.

Will had seen that, too. In the world that existed, women would always be commodities that could be bought, sold, or stolen. Thousands went missing every year, ending up in brothels and on the streets of foreign cities, where they had no choice except to do what they were told. When they could no longer work in the brothels, they were sold into sweatshops or simply killed.

"Do they speak English?" Ketchum asked.

"Some of them," Cho answered. "The others understand enough to know what to do."

"What about diseases?"

"They're clean."

"If any of my men come up with an STD," Ketchum said in a low, threatening voice, "I'll be wanting a discount the next time we do business."

"Our business would be more desirable if you could reciprocate in kind," Cho said.

"How?"

"A woman for a woman."

Ketchum laughed at that. "An American woman would be worth two or three of these."

Cho was silent for a moment, but the way he moved his head and shoulders told Will the man was angry at the assessment. "We could," he stated tightly, "come to some kind of terms."

"Have your boss call me sometime," Ketchum invited. "You're just the delivery boy, Cho. I want to talk to the man that pulls the strings."

One of the young Asian men started forward. Cho put his hand on the man's chest and held him in place. There was a brief, heated exchange in what Will recognized as Mandarin, though he didn't understand the words.

"No offense," Ketchum said laconically.

Slowly, Cho nodded. "I want the payment."

For a moment Ketchum didn't move. Will sensed the undercurrent of violence that moved around the men. It wouldn't take much to set it off, and at the moment, Ketchum was holding the match.

"Sniper teams, acknowledge," Will called.

The four teams checked in quickly.

"Everyone who pulls a weapon goes down," Will said. "We'll take whoever is left standing."

Ketchum gestured to one of the men inside the house. He came out with a metal aircraft carry-on. Placing it on the rear of the lead car, the man opened it and used a flashlight to reveal stacks of currency and plastic, pillow-shaped bags of white powder.

"Drugs?" Cho sneered.

"Yeah," Ketchum said.

"We agreed that the payment would be in currency only."

"I'm cash-poor at the moment. What I've got is coke. The way I see it, you can take the powder and do yourself right, maybe even increase your profit margin, or you can sell me what I can get of these girls for cash and take your chances hauling the rest around."

Will felt the increase in threatened violence. He didn't know which way it was going to go. Putting the binoculars away, he slipped the M4A1 assault rifle off his shoulder and settled it comfortably in his arms. "Night Eyes, he said, "bring it in."

"Roger that, Steadfast Leader. On our way."

"You told me you had the money," Cho said.

"Coke *is* money," Ketchum replied. "If you don't know what to do with it, that's *your* problem."

The sound of distant helicopter rotors coming in reached Will's ears. He spotted the flashing lights along the aircraft's undercarriage.

In front of the farmhouse, Ketchum and Cho stared up at the sky. Men on both sides pulled weapons even as they faded into the nearest structure or vehicle to keep from being skylined on the ground. The night was their friend.

Then the helicopter crew took away the darkness, throwing several dozen SOLAS white flares into the air three hundred yards above the farmhouse. Equipped with small parachutes, the flares drifted earthward, burning brightly at 75,000 candela. They had a burn time of thirty seconds and were often used in low-visibility search-and-rescue ops.

In a heartbeat, night turned into day.

Hoarse shouts from the men across the ground rang out. They started firing at once, spraying bullets into the air as they attempted to track the Sea Knight across the sky.

"Go!" Will ordered. "Take them down!" He surged up from the darkness, going toward the light as he led the men.

❀ ❀ ❀

>> 0009 HOURS

Amanda Whitcomb jumped when gunfire sounded outside the house.

Hunkered down inside the furnace-like attic, Remy put a hand on the girl's shoulder. "It's all right. That's just my buddies. Just TCB. Taking care of business."

"Dylan . . ." The girl's face was screwed up in fear.

"He's okay. We left him sleeping back there, remember? Nobody's going to shoot him just for sleeping. Probably saved his life. You understand?"

Amanda hesitated, then nodded.

"We need to get out of here." Remy pointed his flashlight at the back of the house. "We can get out onto the roof there. Just take it easy going across the rafters."

Amanda crawled on her hands and knees as gunfire crashed all around them. Remy identified the heavier reports of the M24 rifles used by the sniper teams. He'd used one himself on several occasions.

The girl coughed repeatedly, choking on the dust as she went forward.

Without warning, bullets tore through the Sheetrock only a few feet away, allowing finger-thick spears of light to penetrate the attic's darkness.

Amanda screamed.

Remy hoped that the sound wasn't noticed in all the other confusion going on.

"There's someone in the attic!" a man shouted from below. "They're inside the house!"

Immediately a salvo of shots tore through the ceiling. Amanda froze and screamed even louder, drawing a quick, choked breath and screaming again.

The shooter vectored in on her screams. Bullets chugged through the ceiling and threw up pink tufts of insulation.

Panicked, Amanda drew away, lost her balance, and fell onto a section of the Sheetrock. It didn't hold. Even as Remy reached for her, Amanda plummeted through the ceiling and into the room.

7

SCENE  

 CRIME SCENE

\>> EXTREME RUSH CLUB
\>> JACKSONVILLE, NORTH CAROLINA
\>> 0013 HOURS

Nita stumbled through the crowd thronging the bar. Her vision had turned bleary with all the drinking, the long hours, and the stress she'd been under while trying to work out what she was going to do to win her life back.

Horton caught her elbow and steadied her. "Easy there," the Navy flier said, smiling.

Nita tried to pull free of him, wanting him to know that she could stand on her own two feet. "I'm fine."

"You are that," Horton agreed.

Someone bumped into Nita from behind, knocking her into Horton. He wrapped his arms around her easily, as if he'd been doing it for years.

For just a moment a sense of wrongness scraped against Nita, like the stealthy probe of a scalpel. But it quickly passed. Lately it felt wrong when Joe tried to hold her too.

It can't all be wrong, she told herself. *There has to be a middle ground.*

Horton released Nita with one arm and reached back for the man who had bumped into her. The flier shoved the man away, sending him crashing against the crowded bar.

"Hey!" the man protested.

"Watch where you're going!" Horton snarled.

Nita studied the flier watching over her protectively. She tried to imagine Joe doing something like that and couldn't. She doubted her husband had ever had a physical confrontation in his life.

The man yelled a little more, but he never took a step toward Horton or Nita. In the end, with a final curse directed at Horton, he turned and walked away.

Horton turned back to Nita and shook his head. "This place is getting filled with idiots." He looked at her and smiled. "Want to go somewhere more . . . private?"

There it was. All the invitation Nita needed to reclaim her life. She couldn't believe she was hesitating or that there was even a tiny little spark of pain in her stomach as she made her decision.

"Sure," she replied. "You know a place?"

"My place," Horton said. "Quietest place in town. Interested?" Evidently confidence wasn't a problem for him.

Nita took a breath and let it out. All she had to do was go with him. Then her life would be hers again, no longer filled with household chores and expectations from her husband and daughter, no more having to plan around birthdays and other celebrations that didn't fall conveniently on weekends.

And Lieutenant David Horton was exactly the kind of guy she used to spend time with before Joe came along. Thinking of her husband caused another spark of pain in Nita's stomach. She reached past it, though, and touched the memories of the times she hadn't lived up to Joe's wants, all the looks of disappointment he'd tried to hide when she didn't get home in time to have dinner with Celia and him.

She just couldn't live with the guilt of disappointing people anymore. *No, I* won't *live with that guilt anymore.*

Horton waited for her answer, no pressure. But his eyes gleamed with confidence.

"Okay," Nita said. "That sounds fun."

"Great." Horton took her hand and led her from the bar.

As she followed, Nita felt like she'd just stepped over the edge of a very steep cliff. She'd been flirting with the idea of leaving, of getting a divorce, for over two years. But this was the first time she'd ever gone home with someone.

>> KETCHUM FARMHOUSE
>> NORTH OF JACKSONVILLE, NORTH CAROLINA
>> 0016 HOURS

Remy was up and moving even before Amanda touched the floor. He drew his Beretta, peered through the hole in the ceiling, and saw two men staring at Amanda. She lay in the middle of the floor. Broken plaster littered the floor and dust filled the air. Remy couldn't tell how badly she was hurt or if she was even still alive.

"It's the girl," one of the men said.

The other guy reached for Amanda while gunshots continued to ring out around them.

Remy knelt on the supports and freed his Mini Maglite. He flashed it over the men, drawing their attention up to the ceiling. "Put the weapons down," he ordered.

The men stood frozen for a moment; then the heavyset one pulled his shotgun up.

Remy didn't hesitate. Sliding his finger inside the trigger guard, he squeezed off two rounds, one after the other just as he'd been trained. The muzzle flashes lit up the interior of the attic. Both rounds cored into the man's center mass and knocked him backward.

The man bounced off the wall and went down. The slack way he hit told Remy he was dead.

The other man dropped his weapon and raised his hands. "Don't shoot!"

Remy gathered himself and dropped into the room beside Amanda. Holding the pistol on the man, the SEAL pressed his fingers against the girl's neck. Her pulse beat steadily. She was alive. Remy didn't know if she'd hit her head on the way down and knocked herself out or if she'd just passed out from the adrenaline overdrive. Either was possible.

"Down on your knees," Remy told the man. "Hands behind your head. I bet you know the drill."

The man did. He locked his hands behind his head and fell to his knees. He wouldn't meet Remy's gaze, keeping his eyes staring at the floor.

"Six, give me a SITREP," Estrella said.

"We're fine." Remy took smelling salts from the medical kit he carried in the front pouch of his pack. He hadn't known how drugged the girl would be when he got to her, so he'd packed accordingly.

"Copy that."

"Let the team know we're coming through the back window." The need to be up and moving raked claws through Remy's nervous system. He could hold his own in the confrontation going down around him, but the girl was a sitting duck.

He listened as Estrella passed the word.

With the smelling salts under her nose, Amanda grudgingly came around. She coughed and cursed and retched.

Remy eased her into a sitting position. Gunshots rang out all around them, punctuated by men's panicked cries.

Amanda looked at him.

"You okay?" Remy asked.

The girl nodded.

"Good." Remy smiled at her. "We're getting out of here. Can you walk?"

"I think so."

"You can," Remy told her, helping convince her with his voice. He pulled her to her feet, letting her stand for just a moment.

Then bullets ripped through the wall, striking the man who was kneeling on the floor.

Remy wrapped an arm around Amanda, covering her with his body as he hustled her to the window. "We're coming through!"

"Copy th—"

But the rest of Estrella's response was lost as Remy fired at the glass that filled the window. The panes blew to pieces and fell away. He raked a boot over the window, clearing most of the glass, then shoved Amanda through.

"Stay down!" he yelled at her as he jumped through.

Amanda huddled into a ball, tears streaming down her face.

Remy hit the ground in front of her, already tracking two shadows approaching their position. He tucked and rolled, coming up with the pistol in both hands.

Both men belonged to Ketchum. They brought shotguns up to bear, yanking them back to their shoulders.

At this range, Remy knew the double-ought buckshot would tear Amanda and him to pieces. He fired without aiming, just pointing the pistol like a finger the way he'd been trained, moving from one man to the other. Two shots, then two more.

One of the shotguns went off, the muzzle flash lighting up the man's features just as Remy's bullets chopped him down. Most of the pellets passed Remy harmlessly, but one of them clipped the side of his head, igniting an explosion of pain that left him with double vision.

Dazed, he stayed on task, firing till the magazine was empty and the slide had blown back and locked. Nausea swirled up inside him, and his head felt like it was going to burst. Warm blood trickled down the side of his face. He'd been hit, but he didn't know how bad it was.

He tripped the magazine release as he pulled a fresh clip from his belt. Snapping it into place, he pressed the slide release and seated the first round.

It took him two tries to get to his feet, and he stood on unsteady legs. Staying low, he crossed over to Amanda and took her hand. For the first time he noticed how lit up the grounds were. Then he saw the sky full of flares slowly floating down.

"C'mon," he said. "We've got to move. It isn't safe."

Amanda looked up at him. Terror filled her eyes. "You're bleeding!"

"I'll be all right." Remy pulled her to her feet. "We're both going to be all right. Move." He yanked her into motion, heading for the tree line beside the barn.

The sickness spread inside Remy's stomach. The pain inside his skull grew even fiercer. His double vision got worse till *everything* was blurry.

A shadow jumped out of the darkness to the right.

Remy had his pistol up, tracking the movement, as he pulled Amanda in closer to him to shield her body with his. Then he saw that the man was one of the Marines Will had brought in.

"I've got her," the Marine said.

Remy nodded. That proved to be a mistake. The nausea drove him to his knees as though he'd had a ten-ton truck dropped on him. He threw up, trying in vain to get control of his body. Panic surged inside him then. He smelled his own blood and heard his breath rasping in his chest.

Then it stopped.

And Remy did too.

>> 0018 HOURS

Will moved forward with Shel and Max at his side. Cradling the M4A1, Will yelled, "Naval Criminal Investigative Services! Put down your weapons! Put down your weapons *now*!"

Several other members of the force shouted the same things over and over.

Ketchum and his men, caught in the middle between the military unit and the Asian gangsters, hesitated. The Asians reached for weapons immediately.

"Put down your weapons!" Shel ordered.

But the Asians didn't even slow their efforts.

Will fired immediately. "Don't hit the women!"

The line of gangsters withered under the deadly fire. Marine snipers picked off men guarding the women.

One of the Asians seized a woman and put a gun to her head.

Will stood just long enough to acquire the target from twenty yards out, crosshairs centered over the exposed portion of the man's head, then squeezed the trigger. The man released his hostage and fell to the ground.

The girl fell too, but she started screaming in fear, and Will knew she hadn't been harmed.

Ketchum and his men broke from the skirmish area, running back toward the house.

Several Marines went forward and gathered the women, forcing them back into the vehicles they'd been in. Other Marines slid behind the steering wheels and drove the vehicles out of harm's way.

The opposition splintered then, but the Marines broke into prearranged groups and gave pursuit. Several bodies, Asian and Ketchum's men, lay on the ground. The flares continued to burn, tinting everything scarlet and burying the shadows.

For a moment, with the stink of cordite and blood in his nose and the bright, burning lights falling from the sky, Will thought that he knew what hell might be like. He'd been involved in shoot-outs before, but nothing like this one. Not one carved out of the night and the forest.

"The house," Will said to Shel as Ketchum and several of his men disappeared inside.

"I got your six," the big Marine said.

Bullets tore into the earth only a few feet away from Will as he charged the porch. He fired at targets he identified, chasing men behind parked cars and knocking some of them down.

"Reload," Will yelled as the assault rifle cycled dry. He dropped into position beside a 4x4 pickup, dumped the empty clip, and slammed a fresh one home. "Ready."

Shel knelt beside Will, his back to the truck and shoving a new magazine home himself. "Ready," he replied.

Nodding, Will stood. And drew immediate enemy fire. Bullets skipped across the front of the pickup and crashed through the windshield.

"Down!" Will ordered, dropping to cover. He glanced back at Shel. "Did you get their position?"

"They're on the porch," Shel said.

Will nodded. That was the impression he'd gotten, but he hadn't been sure.

Gunfire sounded again, and this time he realized it was a fully automatic, heavy-caliber machine gun. The pickup shuddered under the assault.

"That's a .50-cal gun," Shel said.

"Yeah. And the way they're burning through ammo, you'd think they've got an inexhaustible supply."

Several radio comments let Will know that the Marines were getting pinned down by the machine-gun fire. Not only that, but several of Ketchum's people were lining up to back the machine-gun operators.

Will kept thinking about the forest behind the house. There was no guarantee the men couldn't get there and vanish.

"I brought a couple party favors," Shel said. He held out his big hand and revealed the two grenades in his palm. "Stingers."

Also known as Hornet's Nest grenades, the stingers were made of hard rubber and packed with 20 mm hard rubber balls designed to incapacitate rather than kill or seriously injure. They were used to subdue small groups, chase emplaced opponents from hiding, and scare people that no one wanted to kill. They didn't disorient the target the way a flash-bang did, but there was no bright light that would blind the Marine unit either.

"Do it," Will said.

Shel slid forward, Max at his heels. The Marine pulled the pins, then lobbed the grenades one after the other toward the front porch.

"Stinger!" Shel yelled, hunkering down behind the pickup again. The military team knew exactly what to expect, and all of them took cover.

Someone on the porch cursed and tried to yell a warning, but his voice was lost in the detonations that followed. Yelps of pain erupted as the hard rubber balls ricocheted everywhere. Several of them hit the truck where Will and Shel took cover.

Will moved out at once, holding the assault rifle to his shoulder. He focused on the machine gun, seeing it clearly defined now. The weapon stood on a tripod, but it had been covered by a tarp.

Evidently they didn't trust the guys they were doing business with tonight, Will thought.

A half dozen men lay squirming in pain on the wooden porch. At least that many were unconscious, sprawled where they fell. The windows behind them were broken, and glass gleamed against the planks.

With no one on the porch prepared to continue the fight, Will dropped into position beside the door. He lifted the assault rifle and readied himself as Shel set up on the other side of the door.

Ducking around the doorframe, Will caught sight of movement within the house. He yanked his head back just as bullets thudded into the frame.

"Lively party," Shel observed.

"Got another surprise?" Will asked.

Shel revealed another stinger grenade. "I'm a Marine. I always come prepared." He pulled the pin, yelled a warning, and tossed the grenade in.

Rubber balls tore holes in the walls and ceiling when the grenade exploded. Glass from shattered windows arced outward, catching the light from the first of the flares as they touched the ground.

Glancing around the doorframe again, Will judged the way to be clear. He stepped inside the room and moved forward quickly.

Two men squirmed on the floor. Will and Shel quickly tied their hands behind them using disposable cuffs. Then they went on, leaving the living room area and moving toward the kitchen.

Will waved another group of men toward the other end of the house.

The rooms were small, and movement was tight. The teams moved through darkness; the exploding stinger grenades had destroyed the light fixtures.

The lights were on in the large kitchen, however.

Will led the way with Shel on his heels. Trash overflowed the can in the corner, shot through with fast-food cartons and beer cans. Pizza boxes and a sleeve of plastic plates covered the island in the center of the room. The smell of burned popcorn hung in the air.

No one was in the kitchen.

"Maybe they already evacuated this room," Will suggested.

Shel eyed the room suspiciously. "Uh-uh. No way out that we don't have covered."

Will glanced around. There were two doors in the wall on the opposite side of the room. One had a curtained window and undoubtedly led out the back of the house, but it was latched from the inside, and even if Ketchum and his men had gone through it, they would have been picked up immediately by the Marine guards outside. That left only one possibility for where the men had gone.

Walking quickly through the room, Shel said, "A place like this reminds me of my granny's house. Tight little rooms, but you knew where everything was." He looked around. "She also had a basement—what she called a root cellar—under the kitchen."

He opened the door beside the stove.

Glancing over the Marine's shoulder and spotting the narrow wooden stairs going down, Will said, "Like this one?"

"Yeah," Shel replied. "A lot like this one."

Will radioed Estrella and told her where they'd be.

Motioning to Max, Shel sent the Labrador down into the dark room. Max reached the floor without incident.

"Room's clear." Shel headed down the stairs.

8

SCENE  NCIS  CRIME SCEN

NAVAL CRIMINAL INVESTIGATIVE SERVICE

>> KETCHUM FARMHOUSE
>> NORTH OF JACKSONVILLE, NORTH CAROLINA
>> 0032 HOURS

Following Shel but leaving enough space between them to maneuver quickly if they needed to react to a threat, Will peered around the dark room. It was a cellar. The damp, thick smell of earth and closed-in spaces clung to it. In the darkness, he could barely make out the wooden shelves that occupied the center of the room.

"All right," Will said as he reached the poured-concrete floor and took up a position. "Light it up."

Footsteps sounded above. Glancing over his shoulder, Will saw that two Marines held the position there.

"We have the house," one of them said.

Will nodded. "Good."

Shel flicked on his Maglite, widening the beam so it carved a huge tunnel in the darkness. He played the beam around the room, holding his rifle in his other hand. "Seek," he told Max.

The Lab put his nose to the floor and set off through the shelves.

"Is anybody down here?" one of the Marines asked.

"That's what we're finding out," Shel replied.

"The back door is latched," the Marine said. "They didn't get out that way."

"And nobody reported anybody by the back of the house," Will said.

"We've got a satellite view of this twenty, not to mention spotters and the helicopter. Those men fled by other means."

"Found it," Shel called.

A light flared to life on the ceiling. Squinting against the sudden brightness, Will saw Shel release the pull cord connected to the naked bulb swinging from the low ceiling.

"Got a door over here," Shel added.

Will walked through the shelves containing dry goods, canned goods, and MREs. *They were prepared for a long stay.* Having that many supplies on hand also meant that Ketchum had a cash flow.

Shel stood at the narrow door in the wall. It had been designed to fit into the wall so it could not easily be seen. "Found it with the Maglite. In dim light it would be easy to miss." He knelt. "So would the trip wire."

Looking more closely, Will spotted the trip wire spanning the narrow passageway. It was connected to a block of plastic explosive set in the wall. "Can you disarm it?"

"Doesn't look overly sophisticated." Shel leaned his assault rifle against the wall, then told Max to retreat and started to work on the booby trap.

"Steadfast Five," Will called, "this is Leader."

"Go, Leader. Five reads you." Estrella's voice was calm, all business.

"We're in the basement under the kitchen."

"Negative, Leader. The blueprints we have don't show a basement."

"It's more of a root cellar, actually. And whether the blueprints show it or not, we're standing in it."

"Aye, Leader."

Shel continued working, slowly and carefully.

Sweat blurred Will's vision for just a moment and stung his eyes. He gazed around the room, orienting himself. *Which way is north?* He'd gotten turned around in the confusion. He rolled back his sleeve and looked at the compass mounted on a band on his wrist.

"The room's about twenty by twenty," Will said. "We came through on the east side. We're standing at the south wall now. There's a passageway headed due south from what I see."

"Roger that, Leader," Estrella said. "Depending on how long the tunnel is, it could extend to the barn behind the house. . . ."

"Or to the woods," Will said.

"Affirmative."

"Route fire teams in that direction. Can you get a lock on my GPS signal?"

"Roger that. I've got you on-screen now."

"Then stay with me," Will directed. "When I zig, have the teams zig. Tell them to be on the lookout for a natural construction that might allow egress from this tunnel."

"Got it."

Shel stood and took his rifle back. "We're past this one."

Will shone his Maglite down the earthen tunnel. "All right. Let's just hope there aren't any more nasty surprises along the way."

"In a situation like this," Shel said, "you have to choose between escape and being cute. They set this one, but I bet the concentration is on escape from now on."

Will nodded.

"I've got point if you want to follow them."

"I do," Will said.

Shel plunged into the narrow passageway with Will at his heels. Max loped along behind, followed by the Marines.

>> 0037 HOURS

Maggie Foley plunged through the brush south of the farmhouse with pistols in both fists. Five Marines flanked her. She wore night-vision goggles that stripped away the darkness and turned the world into green images. The human eye could determine more gradations of green than any other color in the spectrum, which was why the night-vision designers had chosen to switch everything to that color.

The broken terrain rose and fell sharply. The way was made even more difficult by the dead trees, brush, and rocks scattered over the landscape.

Estrella kept Maggie on task. "West now."

Maggie turned west.

"Not so much," Estrella said.

Maggie turned back slightly to the south.

"There," Estrella said. "That's it. You're right behind Leader now, Four."

Maggie didn't answer. It would have been a waste of breath, which she couldn't spare at the moment. She held on to the fact that she was close enough to help Will now. Learning that the tunnel he and Shel now followed was booby-trapped had unnerved her.

She hadn't profiled Bryce Ketchum, but she had profiled guys like him. Loners who felt like they were cleverer than anyone else, who figured their needs came before anyone else's and resented authority of any kind.

She couldn't shake the idea that Will and Shel could be rushing into an ambush.

"Leader," Maggie gasped. "This is Four."

"Go, Four. Leader reads you."

The radio connection popped and cracked with static. Maggie figured it was because there were several feet of dirt separating them. Will's voice sounded strained, and Maggie couldn't help imagining him and Shel plunging through the narrow escape tunnel.

"Watch for an ambush or another booby trap." Maggie charged around a large oak tree and up a steep, short incline. "Your target isn't the type to just leave his back trail clear."

"Understood, Four. We'll keep our eyes peeled."

Swinging around another tree, Maggie ducked under a low-hanging branch and kept running. The land was falling away again, going deeper into the woods.

"Hold up, Four," Estrella said. "I think I see the escape access."

Maggie threw an arm up and held her team back. Automatically they sank into the surrounding shadows.

"Where?" she asked.

>> 0039 HOURS

Estrella stroked the keyboard in front of her, bringing the thermal sat view to the center monitors. A yellow, orange, and red figure had just appeared in the woods. As she watched, several more appeared, bringing the total to eight. It was like magic. Or like eight men had just stepped out of an underground escape tunnel.

"Night Eyes," she said.

"Go," came the immediate reply.

"I need a slow roll over the tree line behind the house. Be advised that there are hostiles on the ground."

"Affirmative. We'll head there now."

Switching views again, Estrella accessed the FLIR feed from the camera mounted under the helo's belly.

In seconds the helicopter was over the position where the escapees had poured out of the ground. The thermographic view had registered the people on-site, but the capabilities were limited. She hadn't been able to see the terrain.

The FLIR ripped away the night.

Estrella was conscious of Larkin and Captain Whitcomb standing behind her, but she ignored them. She concentrated on her job because her team—her friends—depended on her.

An off-road-equipped Suburban sat back in the trees. The vehicle hadn't registered on the thermographics because it had the same ambient temperature as its surroundings, proving that it had been out there some time.

"Leader, Four," Estrella said, "the people you're pursuing have ground transport on-site."

"Affirmative," Will replied.

As Estrella watched, two of the men sprinted for the Suburban. Dulled coals ignited on the sat-feed screen as the vehicle's engine warmed.

Bright flickering lights blossomed in the hands of some of the men. Estrella knew instantly what they were.

"We're taking fire!" the helicopter pilot yelled.

"Pull out, Night Eyes," Estrella said. "I've got a fix now."

On the thermographic display, the helicopter veered away.

"I see them," Maggie said. "Four has them in sight."

>> 0041 HOURS

Maggie peered over her gunsights as the helicopter peeled away while still taking fire. "How do you want to handle this, Leader?"

The men kept firing for a time, and sparks jumped from the Sea Knight's metal hide.

"Put the vehicle down. I don't want them leaving. We're almost there."

Looking over her shoulder, Maggie said, "I need a sniper."

"Here, ma'am." A young man with his face covered by cosmetics crept forward. "Lance Corporal Wiley."

"Can you shoot out the tires on that vehicle, Lance Corporal?" That wasn't a question that had come up at the lavish parties Maggie's father had thrown in north Boston while she was growing up.

The young man grinned, showing a bright white slash of teeth. "Yes, ma'am."

"Get it done."

"Yes, ma'am." Wiley stretched out prone behind his sniper rifle.

A hundred and fifty yards away, across a bowl depression, the driver pulled the Suburban into gear and churned the wheels, throwing out dirt and rock behind it as it roared up onto a trail. The growl of the powerful engine echoed in the tree-enclosed space. The other men who had emerged from the tunnel surged toward the Suburban.

The lance corporal's sniper rifle cracked. He worked the bolt and the rifle cracked again.

At first Maggie thought the young Marine sniper had missed. Then she watched the Suburban sag to the left. Both tires on that side were flat.

"Four," Will said in Maggie's ear, "we're approaching the exit."

"Be careful," Maggie advised. "We're taking out their escape route. They're not going to be happy about it."

"Copy that."

"Do you want me to take any of them down, ma'am?" the lance corporal asked.

Like he's ordering pizza, Maggie thought. She shelved the immediate resentment she felt at the question. Although she had killed in the line of duty before, it wasn't something she was proud of. Even after all the death she'd seen, she didn't think she would ever get used to the killing.

Life was cheap. She'd learned that on the streets with the Boston PD, then again as she'd worked the homicides and manslaughter cases she'd cleared as an NCIS special agent. Those subjects weren't broached at her father's parties either.

"No," Maggie said. "We'll give them the chance to surrender."

"Yes, ma'am." The sniper remained in his prone position.

Thankfully none of Ketchum's people had identified where the sniper shots had come from. The rest of the Marines spread out, seeking fire-support positions along the ridge of the depression.

"Coming through," Will said.

Ketchum's men had spread out among the trees.

"They're entrenching, Leader. You're going to be right in their gun-sights when you come up," Maggie said.

"Night Eyes," Will called.

"Copy, Leader. Night Eyes is standing by."

"Remind those people what aerial support is all about. Then hit them with the loudhailer and tell them we're willing to take prisoners."

In the sky, the Sea Knight started another run. The aircraft was armed with two .50-caliber machine guns and a 20 mm cannon on firm points on the cargo doors. They were primarily used for defense while on a hot zone dustup.

"Somebody's going for the truck," Wiley said.

Maggie spotted the man sprinting through the woods.

"I can take him," Wiley said.

"Not yet." Maggie didn't see the need to punish desperation. She keyed the headset. "Where are you, Leader?"

"At the exit. We're waiting for Night Eyes."

The man reached the Suburban and opened the door. The interior light flashed on for just a moment; then the man reached up and broke it with a fist. Other men approached him, running straight at him.

Maggie thought they were trying to stop him, but she couldn't tell and hated to make assumptions. Then she watched as the man extended a tube, set it over his shoulder, and took aim at the escape-tunnel exit.

In that instant Maggie realized what the tube was, and a cold, leaden ball dropped into her stomach. "Take him down, Wiley!" Frantic, she keyed the headset. "Pull back, Leader! They've got a rocket launcher!"

The Marine sniper fired almost immediately, but it was too late. Fire jetted from the end of the LAW rocket launcher. The light antitank weapon was designed to take down armored vehicles.

The 94 mm HE round impacted the escape route exit. Earth and rock leaped into the sky, and the sound drowned out everything.

"Leader!" Maggie called. "Leader!"

CRIME SCENE

NCIS

NAVAL CRIMINAL INVESTIGATIVE SERVICE

9

SCENE  NCIS  CRIME SCENE

NAVAL CRIMINAL INVESTIGATIVE SERVICE

>> CAPE CALM APARTMENTS
>> JACKSONVILLE, NORTH CAROLINA
>> 0046 HOURS

Nita knew she shouldn't be driving, but she drove anyway. A tiny voice in the back of her mind said she shouldn't be going to Lieutenant David Horton's apartment either, but here she was.

She'd insisted on driving. That was one of the things her mother had taught her: Don't ever totally give control over to a man you've just met.

Not even if he was a dashing Navy flier with confidence the size of an airplane.

She pulled her dark green Mustang in behind Horton's pickup at the entrance to the underground garage. Horton had a brief discussion with the security guard then waved Nita up after him.

The security guard was young. He passed Nita a piece of paper. "Put that on your dash where it can be seen. It's for lot security."

"Sure." Nita took the paper and dropped it onto the dash.

"Another one of the lieutenant's cousins, huh?" The guard shook his head. "Man, he's got a *big* family."

That stung a little, but Nita made herself smile at the guard and drove on, following Horton. A momentary wave of indecision passed through her.

Is that all you want to be? Part of this guy's "extended family"?

Nita forced her breath out and concentrated on her driving. Horton pointed out a parking place close to the elevator then drove off in search of another. She pulled into the parking space. Then, with the engine idling, she sat there, watching the rearview mirror.

You're not here looking for a permanent relationship, she told herself. *If you wanted that, you've got it waiting for you at home. You want to be free again. You want to have fun again, to have your own life back. That's why you're here.*

She took a breath and felt the tingle of the old excitement that used to drive her through the clubs and the night. Her life was supposed to be about fun and careless abandon. It meant finding a guy in a club who was handsome and maybe a little menacing and exploring what they could do together. Any sense of permanency was supposed to vanish with the dawning of the sun.

For a moment, though, she hung balanced. She anxiously waited, looking for Horton. But part of her was inclined to start the car and leave.

She thought about Joe and Celia at home. Both of them would be asleep by now. Sometimes when she got in after a particularly bad day—like cutting open the head of someone's father and husband or trying to piece together a young sailor or Marine that had gotten mangled in an accident—she'd go home and watch them sleep.

She was going to miss that, that borrowed peacefulness she got from just watching Joe and Celia sleep.

But you're not going to miss the responsibility and the guilt, she made herself remember. She was surprised, though, to feel hot tears on her cheeks. She got mad at herself and quickly grabbed a tissue from the box between the seats.

Working quickly, Nita dabbed at her eyes and shut off the flow of unexpected tears. She turned the rearview mirror to check her makeup, hoping she hadn't ruined her mascara or left black smudges on her cheeks. Thankfully, she hadn't.

Then she saw Horton walking out from a line of cars, coming straight for her.

She drank him in, watched the tight coil of muscles, and much of the guilt and trepidation she was feeling went away. This was what she was here for: the chance to be someone's fantasy, not a wife or a mom who had to worry about cleaning out the refrigerator or fixing a healthy meal for a growing daughter.

This is what you want, she told herself fiercely.

Horton reached her door.

She rolled the window down with the touch of a finger.

"Well," Horton said.

"Well," Nita said.

"Here we are."

"I see that."

Horton appeared uncertain for a moment. "Want to come up? Or are you having second thoughts?"

"Oh," Nita replied, "I've had plenty of those. I've been thinking a lot on the way over."

"What about?" Horton smiled, all conceit and arrogance again.

He was just the kind of guy Nita realized she'd attracted so easily during her single days. Here tonight, gone tomorrow. The same kind of man her mother had brought home.

Except her mother made the mistake of trying to hang on to them and ended up messing up both their lives for years. At least, Nita's life had been a mess until she'd graduated high school and qualified for a college loan. Money had fixed a lot of her problems. Staying away from her mother had fixed others.

"About you," Nita said, knowing that was what he wanted to hear. Men like Horton were easy to read and manipulate. With a guy like Joe, however, a guy who wasn't demanding and was totally independent, it was harder to know what to say or do.

"Good," Horton said. "You're supposed to be thinking about me." He waggled an eyebrow theatrically. "Coming out? Or do I have to come in after you? I have to warn you, the parking area has cameras."

Nita laughed. Part of her reveled in the conversation. She couldn't imagine Joe talking to her like that. She pressed the electronic lock and unlocked the door.

Horton pulled the door open and offered a hand.

Nita rolled the window back up and killed the engine, then took the offered hand and allowed Horton to help her from the car. She locked the doors. The chirp sounded loud in the parking garage.

He led her to the elevator.

"The security guard said you have a lot of cousins who come visit," Nita said.

Horton looked at her as he pressed the elevator button. "Does that bother you?"

"No."

He smiled. "Good."

The elevator doors opened, and Nita stepped in with him.

⊛ ⊛ ⊛

>> KETCHUM FARMHOUSE
>> NORTH OF JACKSONVILLE, NORTH CAROLINA
>> 0050 HOURS

The explosion filled the escape tunnel with noise and force. Even though he'd turned and run at Maggie's warning, the concussive wave caught up to Will and threw him forward. He stumbled into Shel, and they both went down in a tangle of arms and legs.

For a moment Will felt as though he were submerged. The same cottony deafness he got when he was underwater filled his ears.

It's the explosion, he told himself. *You're deaf. It won't last long.*

At least, that was what he hoped. Permanent deafness *could* result from a nearby explosion.

Will forced himself up. Somehow he'd managed to hang on to the M4A1 and the Maglite. His brain felt as if it were bouncing around inside his skull. A sickening wave of dizziness that turned his stomach passed through him.

Bracing himself against the wall, Will played the Maglite's beam over Shel and the others. Max was already up, scratching at his ears. The Labrador was probably deafer than he was, Will realized, and the dog didn't know as much about his condition.

Shel got to his knees, shouldered his rifle, and ran his hands across Max, checking the dog for injuries. It was part of the buddy system a soldier had with a K-9 unit. The dog was a partner but one who couldn't communicate effectively about wounds.

Glancing over his shoulder, Shel said, *You okay?*

Will couldn't hear the words, but he could read the Marine's lips. Will nodded. He tried the headset unit, but there was no joy there. Either the headset was damaged or the hearing loss was preventing him from hearing anything. Maybe both.

"We're up and moving," Will said in case Maggie or Estrella could hear him.

He played the Maglite over the rest of his team and found that everyone was ambulatory. Turning, Will peered into the churning chaos that was the escape tunnel.

Roiling dust, illuminated by the Maglite, formed a river between the walls. Chunks of rock and earth littered the floor.

We're lucky the tunnel didn't collapse on top of us, Will thought. Turning to Shel, he signaled that they were going forward.

Shel nodded and slid his rifle from his shoulder. He picked up his own Maglite and added the beam to Will's. The Marine unit assembled behind them. All the special-ops teams knew the abbreviated sign language used for maneuvers.

Will moved through the wreckage of the tunnel. The dusty haze was so thick that he could see only two or three feet ahead. Claustrophobia had never bothered Will much, but he suddenly felt buried. He tried to estimate how much dirt might be over him; then he put those thoughts from his mind. If they couldn't go forward, they could go back.

Unless the explosion had collapsed the tunnel behind them.

There was a final swirl of dust, then he spotted the edges of the entrance. The blast had ripped the opening larger, making it two or three times its original size.

Letting his assault rifle hang for a moment, Will signaled to Shel and the rest of the team, showing them where they were.

A silhouette appeared in front of Will. He brought the M4A1 up, finger outside the trigger guard until he was ready to fire.

Maggie Foley, her face tight with worry, stood before him.

Will dropped the rifle off target, sweeping the woods behind her and seeing that the Marines were taking the rest of Bryce Ketchum's people into custody.

Maggie's lips moved.

Shaking his head, Will said, "I can't hear you."

She nodded and leaned close to his ear. "How about now?" she said loudly.

Her voice sounded like it was coming through a wall, but he could just make out the words. He nodded.

"I was afraid we'd lost you. We've got emergency services standing by," Maggie yelled.

"Good. Are all the hostiles accounted for?"

"Yes."

"What about the farmhouse?"

"We own it."

"Any casualties?"

"Two that were ours. Both of them look like they're going to make it."

Thank God. Will thought about the women prisoners. "What about the civilians?"

"We got them out safely."

More good news. Will let out a deep breath and felt fatigue settle over him. It had been a long day.

Dimly, as if the sound were a million miles away, Will heard Max barking. Turning, he looked for the Labrador and found the dog barking intently at something on the ground.

No, not on *the ground,* Will realized. In *the ground*. He shone his Maglite on it just as Shel did the same.

Revealed in the twin beams, a decomposing hand and arm lay visible.

SCENE ✪ NCIS ✪ CRIME SCEN

NAVAL CRIMINAL INVESTIGATIVE SERVICE

`>> CAPE CALM APARTMENTS`
`>> JACKSONVILLE, NORTH CAROLINA`
`>> 0101 HOURS`

"Want a beer? I don't keep wine at the apartment. I've got some vodka."

Nita sat on the couch in the small apartment. She looked at Horton, who stood in front of the open refrigerator. "Beer will be fine."

Horton reached inside and took out two bottles. He opened both and returned to the living room, handing her one of them. "Sorry," he said. "Did you want a glass?"

"Bottle's fine," Nita replied.

Horton walked over to the radio and switched it on. Soft love ballads issued from the surround sound system. Judging from the CDs in the cabinets, love songs weren't Horton's first choice. He seemed to favor a mixture of heavy metal and rap. She was willing to bet he usually had more lights on as well.

Nita smiled a little at that. Guys just didn't get that they could be so easily seen through. It was better if they were just themselves.

The apartment was neater than she'd expected.

She was used to living in a tidy environment. Joe was the neatest man she knew. When she'd married him and moved into the house he'd rebuilt with his grandfather, who had left it to him when he died, Nita had felt somewhat intimidated. Yet Joe's house—and even after six years of marriage she couldn't help thinking of it as Joe's house—wasn't neat as a pin. The home felt *lived* in. Guests could see that someone lived there, that someone had a life there. And that someone cared about that house.

Lieutenant David Horton's apartment, on the other hand, looked like a showroom. Small and carefully appointed, the only things that really looked as if they were used were the couch and entertainment system.

And the refrigerator, Nita reminded herself. She sipped the beer and found it cold and bitter.

No one *lived* at Horton's apartment. It was a den for a young animal that lived on the prowl. A lot of military guys existed like that. The apartment was nothing more than a place to keep all their stuff.

And to bring their conquests back to, Nita thought. She sipped more beer, feeling some of the buzz she'd walked away from the bar with evaporating. The club scene helped. Being here, in Horton's apartment with him, just wasn't the same. She felt nervous, like she was being weighed and measured with every breath.

Still, he was a good-looking guy. Exactly the kind of guy she was looking for.

"Want to dance?" Horton asked, offering a hand.

"Dance?" That didn't surprise Nita. Dancing in an apartment by themselves was just a prelude to what they both knew they were there for.

"Yeah." Horton smiled.

Nita put her drink on a coaster and stood. "Sure."

At first, he took her into his arms and danced slowly with her. He was surprisingly good, but then she'd seen he could move well at the club.

One song led to another. For some reason, he knew to move slowly and not talk. Nita didn't want to talk, didn't want to think. She just wanted everything to be like it had been when her life had been fun and worry-free.

She found the rhythm with him, swaying and stepping, allowing him to make the moves. He pulled her closer and leaned down to kiss her.

When his lips touched hers, that tiny voice in the back of her head started in again, telling Nita she was doing the wrong thing. But she willed the voice into silence, clinging to the alcoholic buzz that made her head feel thick and soft at the same time.

She kissed him back, and she stepped back in time to when things were simpler and what she did or didn't do really didn't matter much.

❀ ❀ ❀

>> KETCHUM FARMHOUSE
>> NORTH OF JACKSONVILLE, NORTH CAROLINA
>> 0103 HOURS

Will trained his Maglite on the decomposing hand and arm stabbing up out of the ground. The explosion had evidently dislodged an old burial site.

There was no smell of rotting flesh, which meant the body had been underground for more than six months. The flesh looked gray and leathery, and not much of it was left clinging to the bone. The skin looked like an ill-fitting glove.

He looked at Maggie. More of his hearing had returned, but it was going to be a while before he was 100 percent. "Was there a family cemetery somewhere on this farm?"

"Not that I can remember."

"I don't remember one either." The practice of having a family cemetery was an old one, not much in use anymore because it hurt the resale chances for a piece of property. But the farmhouse had been in the Ketchum family's possession for generations. "Check with Estrella."

Maggie nodded and walked away.

"Want to dig it up?" Shel asked.

Max sat calmly nearby. Once Shel had acknowledged the find, the dog had quieted at once.

Digging the body up presented a problem. This was a civilian area, and a homicide would be under the jurisdiction of the Jacksonville Police Department or the Onslow County Sheriff's Office. It had nothing to do with the military.

Will didn't want to disturb a possible crime scene. "Leave it. Notify the local PD or the sheriff's office. They can deal with it."

Shel didn't say anything. Instead he knelt and examined the arm more closely. "We've got a problem."

"What?" Will joined the big Marine.

Pointing at the inside of the decaying arm, Shel traced a tattoo that depicted an eagle, globe, and anchor. The words *Semper Fi* were written under it. They meant "always faithful." And those were words that Shel McHenry lived by.

Will recognized the symbol immediately. "That's Marine issue."

"Yeah." Shel nodded. "It's also located on the inside of the arm, where regs say you can wear one." Marines weren't permitted to have tattoos on their heads or necks or anywhere that wouldn't be covered by a service "C" uniform, which consisted of a long-sleeved shirt and a tie.

Shel looked at Will. "If this guy's a Marine, I don't want anyone else handling this."

Will nodded. "Dig him up."

Shel called for a trenching tool and a couple strong backs. They worked by flashlight. Another Marine took pictures of the process.

Working over the headset, Will kept apprised of the operation, issuing orders when necessary. Everything—everyone—was going to be processed back at Camp Lejeune. He told Estrella to have the Immigration and Naturalization Service standing by. INS would have to handle the illegals among the Asian gang members and the women.

Minutes later, Shel and the two Marines helping him donned gloves and lifted the dead man from the earth.

The body was desiccated from lying unprotected in the soil. The head had been reduced to nearly all skull. Not much in the way of features remained. The clothing, some kind of suit, had rotted away as well.

Shel played his flashlight over the dead man. Leaning over the corpse, Shel pulled at the shirt and revealed the stainless-steel chain around the neck. After a little fumbling, he produced two flat metal rectangles.

Playing the Maglite over the dog tags, Shel said, "Meet Gunnery Sergeant George Haskins." He let the dog tags drop. "He's had better days."

Will silently agreed. He took a closer look at the corpse and saw a hole in the back of the skull. "I see an exit wound. No entrance."

Shel pointed his thumb and forefinger like a pistol. He held his hand close to the dead man's mouth. "If it's suicide, there won't be one."

Will knew they couldn't make that assumption yet. He called Estrella and told her to dig up whatever information she could on USMC Gunnery Sergeant George Haskins.

"And get Nita out here," Will said. "Since this is military, we're going to have our best on it till we hand it off."

"Roger that. . . . Oh no."

"What is it?" Will asked.

"Six is down. A medic just found him. Remy's been shot . . . in the head."

>> CAPE CALM APARTMENTS
>> JACKSONVILLE, NORTH CAROLINA
>> 0112 HOURS

As Nita kissed Horton, she tried to lose herself in the sensation. There was a time, she told herself angrily, when she could do that so easily. All it had taken was being in the arms of a man, a man she'd chosen, who had caught her attention.

It wasn't working tonight. She felt stiff, wooden.

And that stupid voice in her head just wouldn't let go.

Horton backed off and looked at her. He smiled, but the effort wasn't as confident as it had been earlier. "Everything okay?"

Nita smiled back at him. "Everything's fine."

Horton just looked at her for a moment. "I hope you're right, but I'm getting this weird vibe."

"Nerves," Nita said, lying through her teeth.

Horton tried to look charming. "If you don't want to do this—"

"It's not you," Nita said. "It's me. I just had a long day."

"I hope so." Horton brushed a stray lock of hair from Nita's face. "Because I don't like being led on."

Anger stirred within Nita. She almost snapped at him. But she held her temper in check. "I'm not leading you on."

"Good," he said. "Good." He leaned in and started to kiss her neck.

Nita closed her eyes and tried to let physical desire take over. But it seemed as slow as a reluctant engine on a cold winter morning.

Horton became more aggressive.

"Hey," Nita said softly. "Maybe if you'd just slow down."

"Maybe if you'd just catch up," Horton growled impatiently.

Grabbing Horton's left elbow, Nita yanked it down and in, dragging his arm between them as she stepped back and broke his embrace. "Slow down, cowboy!"

Those were her mother's words. Nita recognized them from the countless confrontations that had taken place in the cheap apartments and trailer houses where she'd grown up.

Horton tore his arm free. Fury burned in his eyes. He cursed. "I don't know what kind of game you're pulling, but I didn't bring you up here to be disappointed."

"This was a mistake," Nita said. She backed away, heading to the couch to get her purse. She pulled her keys from her back pocket and gripped the small OC defense system.

"Not my mistake," Horton said. "I'm going to get what I was promised." He stepped toward her.

Nita didn't try to warn him any further. She didn't believe it would do any good. Bringing the OC up, she pressed the top and unleashed a torrent of pepper spray into the Navy flier's eyes.

The pungent smell of cayenne filled the room, strong enough to choke Nita as she tried to breathe. Horton screamed shrilly and dropped to the floor, rubbing at his eyes.

"Get to the bathroom," Nita said. "Stand under the shower and wash it out. You're only rubbing it in and making it worse."

Her cell phone rang.

At first she thought it was Joe, calling to check in and see where she was. Instead, caller ID showed the number belonged to Estrella Montoya's cell phone.

Horton continued to howl in pain, butting his forehead against the carpeted floor.

Maggie didn't feel sorry for the man. Horton had brought this on himself. He rolled on the carpet now.

Holding the OC container out before her, Nita stepped away from Horton and headed for the door. Before she made it, Horton leaped at her and caught her ankle. Surprised and off balance, still feeling the effects of the alcohol in her system, Nita went down.

Before she could get up, Horton was on top of her. Up close, she smelled the mixture of cologne and pepper spray. He was stronger than she was and had no problem keeping her pinned to the ground.

Fear gripped Nita. She'd never been in a situation like this before. Even before Joe, when she'd been in the bars every night, she'd never gotten herself in this much trouble.

Never let a man you don't know get between you and the door. Her mother's voice came to Nita then, but it was too late.

Horton fought to trap her wrists. "You're going to pay for that," he said, and he cursed her foully.

Nita's phone rang twice more; then the answering service kicked in. Horton trapped one of her wrists and was scrambling for the other. His weight settled uncomfortably across her stomach.

She couldn't get up.

11

>> KETCHUM FARMHOUSE
>> NORTH OF JACKSONVILLE, NORTH CAROLINA
>> 0114 HOURS

"Will," Estrella said over Will's cell phone, "I still haven't reached Nita."

"You've been calling her cell?"

"Yes."

"Call her home."

EMTs from Jacksonville had converged on the site and were in the process of ferrying away wounded personnel. The Jacksonville Police Department and Onslow Sheriff's Office had shown up to help handle traffic. The story was already breaking over the news, and there was even talk that CNN or FOX News was going to have a local work the story for them.

Things had gotten out of hand.

Estrella hesitated. "Nita doesn't like it when we call her house."

In the past, Nita had made her displeasure about those calls very well-known. No one liked his or her family brought into the work they did. Most liked to keep a separation between work and home. Some, like Estrella and Maggie, succeeded at keeping their lives compartmentalized.

Will hadn't been able to. His personal and professional lives constantly spilled over each other. The basketball game tonight—*last night,* he amended, noting the time—was a perfect example.

"I need Nita, Estrella," Will said. "I want our best people on this."

"Okay."

"What's happening with Remy?" Will asked.

"Unknown. He's alive, but I don't know how badly he's injured."

"Okay. Keep me posted. And get me what you can about George Haskins."

"I'm putting together a file now."

"Was he still active?"

"When he went missing? Yes."

"When did he go missing?" Will asked.

"Seventeen years ago."

At first Will didn't think he'd heard Estrella correctly. "Did you say *seventeen* years?"

"I did."

Seventeen years meant that somewhere in NCIS headquarters there was a box in the cold-case files that had Gunnery Sergeant George Haskins's name on it. And a trail that was seventeen years cold.

It didn't give him much hope.

"Get me the information on Haskins," Will said. "And find Nita."

"Aye, sir."

Will closed the phone and shoved it back into his BDUs, only to have his headset crackle to life.

"Steadfast Leader," a voice called.

Will pushed back his irritation. He wished he could be inside the house attending to the crime scene with Maggie. Or back with Shel, who was working Haskins's impromptu grave. Instead he was stuck dealing with all the headaches that came in the aftermath of a major operation.

Will answered the headset. "Steadfast Leader here."

"We're having trouble securing the site against reporters. So far we've caught three guys in the woods with video equipment and cameras."

"Lock them down for now. We'll question them in the morning. If they're not part of this, we'll let them go."

An EMT jogged up to Will. The med tech was young and fresh faced. He looked excited. Will figured it was probably the first war zone the guy had ever worked.

And there was no question that the farmhouse was a war zone.

"Commander Coburn," the EMT said.

"I am," Will acknowledged.

"We've got one of your men over there." The EMT jerked a thumb over his shoulder at one of the ambulances. The flashing lights strobed over Remy Gautreau, sitting there with a white bandage wrapping his head.

Relief flooded through Will. *Thank you, Lord!* Remy didn't exactly look good, but at least he wasn't dead or in a coma.

"How is he?" Will asked.

"He's refusing to go to the hospital. I thought maybe you could order him to go."

A flicker of irritation pulsed through Will. He had enough on his hands—*more* than enough—without dealing with a reluctant hospital patient. Especially one who had been shot in the head. He walked toward the ambulance.

Blood tracked the side of Remy's neck and stained his BDUs. He sat loose and easy, as if getting shot were an everyday occurrence.

"Estrella told me you'd been hit," Will said.

"Nicked by a shot pellet, that's all. I passed out, but I'm fine."

"You're refusing to go to the hospital?" Will asked.

Remy started to nod but caught himself and grimaced slightly. "It's not that bad."

Will studied the bloodstained bandage. "How bad is it?"

"Chief Petty Officer Gautreau has suffered—"

Remy cut the EMT off. "A laceration of the scalp that has been tended to, sir. A possible concussion, which I doubt because I've had concussions before and this doesn't feel like one. I'm up-to-date on my tetanus shots. All they're going to do is throw me in an ER bed for three or four hours, give me an analgesic, and tell me to take it easy for a few days."

"Is that right?" Will asked the EMT.

"He needs stitches to hold the laceration together—"

"I can do that myself," Remy said.

"—and there is a possibility of a concussion," the EMT went on.

"Commander," Remy said, "look into my eyes."

"Going to hypnotize me, Chief?"

Remy grinned then. "No, sir. I just wanted you to notice that the pupils match. There's no irregular dilation of either."

Will looked. The pupils did match. "That's not always a good indicator."

"No, sir, but given my past history with concussions and the fact that you need me here and I could use the experience working a crime scene like this, I think it'll stand."

Remy was still new to NICS. He was bright and caught on quickly, but the team hadn't worked anything like this since he'd been with them. Will knew opportunities—if something like this could be considered an opportunity—didn't come along often. *Thank God.*

"You can sew up the laceration?" Will asked.

Remy also served as the team's field medic.

"I've done it before," Remy said. "I've got a field kit. All I need is a mirror."

Will turned to the EMT. "Do you have a mirror?"

"Yes, sir, but—"

"Get this man a mirror."

The EMT swallowed and didn't look happy. "Yes, sir."

"I'll be inside the house with Maggie," Will told Remy. "As soon as you're ready."

"Aye, sir. Thank you, sir."

Will nodded and walked back toward the house. He took out his phone and called Estrella. "I just talked to Remy. He's up and around, refusing to go to the hospital. He's going to be fine."

"That's good news."

"What about Nita?"

"I talked to Joe, her husband—"

"I know who Joe is."

"Aye, sir. He doesn't know where Nita is either. She was supposed to be home by now."

A warning flag shot up in Will's mind. He knew Nita was having some kind of trouble at home, but he didn't know what it was. Any time he'd broached the subject, she'd shot him down.

"Keep trying to find her," Will growled irritably, feeling that something was wrong.

>> CAPE CALM APARTMENTS
>> JACKSONVILLE, NORTH CAROLINA
>> 0117 HOURS

Afraid and angry and stunned all at the same time, Nita felt Horton's hand encircle her free wrist. She vaguely remembered some of the self-defense classes she'd taken—not really martial arts because she'd never been interested in anything like that. They had basically taught escape maneuvers.

She rolled her wrist, twisting in viciously toward Horton's thumb and pushing her arm forward. His grip loosened; then she was free. He reached for her again.

Looking up at him, seeing his eyes filled with tears and his face red with pain, Nita knew that he was going to hurt her every way he could. But he was going to humiliate her first.

Then she remembered the brachial nerve. In her mind's eye at that moment, she could see it. The brachial plexus ran from the back of the neck throughout the body, splitting off through the arms, back, and legs. All of those areas were vulnerable to impact injuries that could cause incredible pain as well as temporary paralysis. People trained in martial arts used those areas as targets.

Nita still had her cell phone in hand. The stub of an antenna was little more than an inch long. She aimed for the soft spot below the clavicle on Horton's right side, driving the antenna into the separation of the pectoralis major over his chest and the deltoid muscle over the top of his shoulder, digging for the dorsal scapular nerve.

Horton screamed. His body arched against her.

Using that stolen moment, Nita heaved against the Navy flier and threw him from her. She rolled, got to her knees, then shoved to her feet.

Horton swore. He reached for her, one-handed, striving to get up from the floor. Nita picked up a heavy ceramic ashtray from a nearby end table and smashed it across her attacker's head. The ashtray shattered, and Horton slumped to the floor, groaning and cursing.

Nita's heart jackhammered in her chest. She grabbed her purse, fumbled with the lock on the door, and let herself out. Her legs felt rubbery and she couldn't catch her breath.

Two people, a young man in sweat pants and a young woman in an extra-long T-shirt, stood in the hallway. They looked like they'd just gotten out of bed.

"Hey," the guy said. "You okay?"

Get out of here, Nita told herself. *You don't want to be here in case someone has called the police.*

"I'm fine," she said. She forced herself to move.

Horton moaned from inside the apartment.

"Sounds like somebody's hurt," the guy in the hallway said.

I sincerely hope so, Nita thought. She kept moving. There wasn't anything she could say.

"Peter," the woman said, "call the police."

Nita walked to the elevator and pressed the button. She waited, trembling. *Adrenaline spike,* she told herself. *You're all right.*

"Miss," the young man said, "maybe you should stay here. . . ."

The elevator doors opened. Nita stepped inside. Her cell phone rang and she answered it automatically. She felt like her whole body was shaking.

She'd seen the aftermath of her mom's "dates" when they'd gotten rough. And she'd sworn something like that would never happen to her. Since she was eight years old and had figured out what was going on when her mom kept bringing men home, she'd told herself she was too smart to go through what had almost happened.

But you aren't, are you?

"Hello," Nita said into the phone.

"Nita?"

Nita recognized the voice as Estrella's. "Yes."

"Are you all right?"

"I'm fine." Staring at her reflection on the stainless-steel surface of the elevator, Nita wiped at her face. Mascara ran and left dark smudges on her cheeks. Her hands still shook and her voice cracked.

"You don't sound fine."

"It's a bad connection," Nita growled. She held on to the anger. All of her life that had been her one true emotion, the one that had never wavered and had never left her even when everything else had left her feeling dead inside. "What do you want? I'm off the clock."

"Will needs you. We've got a body that he wants you to take custody of."

"Isn't there someone else?"

"Will would like you to do it." Estrella's voice was cold and distant.

Nita knew she'd alienated the other woman. She got along with Maggie and Estrella just well enough to get through the day-to-day stuff but not enough to do the girl-chat thing. Nita didn't want to be friends, didn't want to share hopes, dreams, or secrets. She had enough responsibility taking part in a family she'd never counted on and hadn't wanted.

"Tell Will—" Nita stopped herself as the elevator doors opened. *Tell Will what? That you were almost raped while out chasing an extramarital affair?*

She took a breath and walked into the parking garage. *Or maybe you'd rather go home and explain your condition to Joe?*

Taking another breath, Nita felt panic rising within her for just a moment when she couldn't remember where she'd parked her car. Then she spotted it.

You don't want to go home. Not now. Maybe not ever again. That's what tonight was all about.

"Tell Will I'm on my way," Nita said. Doing her job was easier than going home. She couldn't remember a time when that wasn't true. She got the address and directions from Estrella and closed the phone.

Sirens sounded somewhere out on the street.

Knowing that the young couple in the apartment next to Horton's had probably called the police, Nita tossed her purse inside the car and slid behind the wheel. She started the engine and got under way.

Her phone rang again as she pulled through the security gate and onto the street. She glanced at it. The caller ID showed her home phone number. "Hello?"

"Nita, it's Joe. Are you all right?"

Nita wished everyone would quit asking her that. "I'm fine."

"Okay."

"Why did you call?"

"Estrella called looking for you. She said you weren't answering your cell."

"The battery was dead." *Then why isn't it dead now?* Nita asked herself. Lies were like the infrastructure of a skeleton, each piece dependent on the others for the whole thing to work and yet still incredibly fragile. "I'm charging it in the car now."

"Where are you?"

Nita tried to figure out if that was suspicion in her husband's voice and couldn't decide. "I went out to eat." Then she remembered that he'd left dinner waiting for her. "I had to be around people, Joe. I know you left dinner. I've been around bodies all day. I just wanted to be out where people were still alive."

"People are alive at home," Joe said softly.

"I didn't feel like talking. I just wanted to have dinner in a diner and be around people without having to talk to them."

"Sure," he said. "I understand."

Nita didn't believe that. Joe didn't understand solitude. He was at peace when he was alone and worked most of his day by himself, but he was gregarious by nature. He didn't meet strangers; it seemed no matter where they went, no matter whom they saw, Joe found something to talk about.

"I just got called out," Nita said.

"I figured that was what Estrella was calling about."

Was he trying to guilt her? "It's my job. I do have a job, you know."

"I know. Take it easy. I was just making conversation."

Nita felt even more resentment at being told to relax. She was keyed up. After what she'd been through, anybody would be. If Joe had known, he wouldn't have been so cavalier about—

But he can't know.

Some of the anger disappeared as guilt rushed in. "I know," she said. "I've got to go. The team found a body. Will wants me there."

"All right. But if you need anything, Nita—anything at all—just let me know."

"I will." Nita closed the phone, but even as she put it away she realized she had fresh tears streaming down her face. Why couldn't Joe figure out what was going on and let her go? Why did he have to be so . . . so . . . *giving* and understanding? Why didn't he understand that she hated those qualities in him?

She wiped the tears away and kept driving.

12

SCENE  **NCIS**  CRIME SCEN

NAVAL CRIMINAL INVESTIGATIVE SERVICE

>> KETCHUM FARMHOUSE
>> NORTH OF JACKSONVILLE, NORTH CAROLINA
>> 0128 HOURS

"Captain Whitcomb wants you to understand how much he appreciates you getting his daughter out of this safely."

Will surveyed the farmhouse walls riddled with bullet holes and the sheet-covered bodies being processed by the crime-scene teams. Once upon a time, the farmhouse had been a family home, not a criminal hideout.

"He would have stayed and told you himself," Director Larkin said, "but he wanted to keep his daughter and himself out of the media as much as possible."

The media, Will had learned during his time with the NCIS, were merciless. Even when they got crucial details wrong while trying to beat the clock to get a story filed, they could simply issue a retraction the next day. Of course, usually by then no one was paying attention to the story unless it was ongoing.

Will didn't blame the Marine captain for wanting to stay out of the limelight.

"We've got seventeen people dead here," he said. "Even if we keep Captain Whitcomb and his daughter out of the official story, we're going to have to tell the media something."

"We've found plenty of drugs on-site," Larkin replied.

"But no military personnel were involved till we got here. Except for Gunnery Sergeant Haskins, if that is his body we found out there. So why was NCIS here at all?"

"We were responding to a tip," Larkin said.

"A tip?"

Larkin nodded. "We were told Ketchum and his men were dealing to military personnel." He sighed. "The thing of it is, if we pursue this investigation, we'll probably find out that's true."

"All right." Will knew the cover was good and would probably hold. The media would be more interested in the body count.

"Have you found out anything about Haskins?"

"Missing seventeen years," Will said. "From the deterioration of the body, I'd say he's probably been dead that whole time. He's got what looks like a bullet hole in his skull."

"You've pulled his field-service record?"

"Estrella put in a request. But we found files on Haskins in our database."

"Interesting."

"Haskins was under investigation for racketeering and black marketeering. The agents assigned to his investigation thought he was stealing and selling military sidearms and rifles. Possibly even dealing drugs inside the camp."

"But nothing was proven?"

"No. Haskins disappeared before the agents made the case."

"Would they have made it?"

"I don't know," Will said. "I haven't reviewed the case notes. I'll get to them in the morning. I want to button this scene up first."

>> 0141 HOURS

By the time she reached the Ketchum farmhouse, Nita had calmed—and sobered—a lot. She knew she'd been taking her chances when she'd driven. If she'd been stopped and given a Breathalyzer test, she'd have been arrested on the spot.

She'd stopped at a McDonald's on the way out of Jacksonville and ordered four large coffees. Now her kidneys were protesting the combined abuse of the alcohol and coffee.

But she was—more or less—sober.

After checking in with Will, she carried the final cup of coffee with her as she trudged through the backyard where Shel McHenry was supposed to be with the body Will wanted her to look over. Judging from the work she'd seen going on around the farmhouse, there were going to be plenty of bodies to look at.

There was no way she was going to pull that load all by herself.

"Hey, Doc," Shel greeted as Nita got closer.

"You have a body," Nita said.

Shel grinned. "Thanks. So do you."

Nita frowned as she dropped her on-site kit to the ground. "Not in the mood for humor, gunney." She switched her attention to the corpse lying at Shel's feet.

Tail wagging, Max approached Nita and dropped to his haunches. Nita petted the Labrador absently.

Then the corpse consumed Nita's attention. She'd dressed in a coverall she kept in the kit in the back of her car. It was navy blue and had *Special Agent* stenciled across the back in huge yellow letters.

"This guy's been dead for a long time," Nita commented.

"He's been missing seventeen years." Shel joined her, shining his light everywhere she placed her hands, tracking her movements.

"Probably dead every minute of it." Nita pulled at the surviving material of the clothing. All of it was rotting away. "You got an ID on him?"

"I found dog tags." Shel shone the Maglite on the tags around the corpse's neck. "But we don't know if it's Haskins. He doesn't have much of a face left."

"He was buried almost immediately after being killed," Nita said. "He wasn't left out in the open. If he had been, the flies and maggots would have picked the skull completely clean. They can only get to the body when it's fresh, exposed."

Nita leaned in to take a closer look at what was left of the dead man's skin. "I don't see much evidence of flies, but there are clear indications of hide-beetle activity."

Hide beetles usually arrived in the final stages of decomposition. Unlike flies and other insects that went for soft tissues, hide beetles ate dried skin, tendons, and bone. They even had special enzymes that allowed them to devour hair. Hair had a protein called keratin in it that nothing else could eat. If hide beetles got to the body before flies, it was a sure sign of nearly instantaneous burial after death.

Nita brushed dead beetles from the corpse.

One of the Marines gagged and stumbled off.

"Newbie," Shel muttered.

"Make sure he doesn't throw up anywhere near my crime scene."

"He won't. I've already told him if he blows chunks he's gotta throw up in his shirt and carry it off."

"Awfully considerate of you."

"It's what I'm here for," Shel said. "Nursemaid the newbies."

Nita looked at him. "And you're talking too loud."

Shel lowered his voice. "Sorry. Almost caught a rocket in the ear. My hearing's off."

Nita nodded and let out a tense breath. During the drive over, her thoughts had never been far from Joe or Horton. She couldn't believe tonight had ended up so badly.

"Where did you find him?" she asked.

Shel pointed the flashlight beam toward a shallow hole. "There."

Nita abandoned the body for the moment and walked over to the hole. "You're working the crime scene?"

"Yep. We haven't found the bullet that killed him yet; I'll let you know as soon as we do."

"I'll save you the trouble: don't bother looking. You won't find it."

"Why not?"

"There's only one hole in the dead man's head."

"I thought that was the exit site."

"That's why you're a crime-scene tech and I work the bodies." Nita returned to the corpse, knelt, and lifted the dead man's head into her lap. She pointed at the back of the skull. "You thought he killed himself."

Shel mimed putting a gun in his mouth and pulling the trigger. "Boom."

"Have you ever seen a suicide bury himself?"

A frown twisted Shel's features. "I should have caught that."

"That's what I'm here for," Nita said. "Nursemaiding the would-be medical examiners."

Shel rubbed his face with a hand. "Did I mention I nearly caught a rocket round in my teeth and I was still somewhat addled when I decided on the cause of death?"

"I thought you said it was your ear."

"See how addled I am?"

Nita pointed to the edges of the hole in the skull. "Look at the fissures. They were blown inward, not out. There are still bone fragments inside the skull."

"Got it." Shel unfolded a paper bag. "Can I have his clothes? What's left of them?"

Nita took scissors from her belt pack and started cutting the clothing away. All she needed was the body, and since the man was seventeen years dead and already going to pieces, his modesty at the scene wasn't an important thing. Not that there was any modesty left.

She handed Shel the remnants of the dead man's shirt, then started removing his slacks. The polyester material had stood up well under burial. When she handed the pants to Shel, he shook them free of beetles.

A metallic object sailed from the material, winking in the flashlight beams and plopping to the ground a few feet away.

Nita started to get up, but Shel was already in motion, moving with catlike grace. The big Marine moved better than anyone Nita had ever seen.

"What is it?" Nita asked.

Shel held the object up between his thumb and forefinger. "A tiny silver shoe."

Nita held out her hand. Despite everything else that was going on in her life, she was just as curious as anyone on the team.

Shel dropped the tiny shoe into her palm. "Looks like something out of a Monopoly game."

"If the shoe in Monopoly were pointed and looked like a ballerina slipper."

"I always liked being the shoe in Monopoly. I guess I was thinking about kicking butt even back then. My brother, Don, liked being the dog. What were you?"

"The race car." She trained her Maglite on the shoe. "This isn't from a Monopoly game."

"Believe it or not," Shel said, "I got that from the ballerina reference."

"It's a charm."

"We're not talking breakfast cereal."

"No. This is a charm that would go on a girl's charm bracelet."

"A girl?"

A sick feeling twisted in Nita's stomach as she considered the implications of the find. An image of Celia ghosted through her mind.

"Yes." Nita looked back at the grave. "You might want to widen and deepen that hole. This body might not be the only one in there."

CRIME SCENE

13

SCENE  **NCIS**  CRIME SCEN

NAVAL CRIMINAL INVESTIGATIVE SERVICE

>> NCIS COMMAND POST
>> NORTH OF JACKSONVILLE, NORTH CAROLINA
>> 0237 HOURS

Maggie worked at one of the tables in the RV command post. She tried to distance herself from the tiny silver shoe she was cleaning of debris. She didn't like thinking that the girl who had owned the charm might still be in the ground somewhere awaiting discovery.

There were plenty of other explanations for why the little silver shoe had been in the dead man's clothing. But no matter how many alternative possibilities she tried to imagine, the most likely answer was that the girl had been with him when he'd been killed.

It was even possible that the girl had killed the dead man. Maybe she'd been a victim and had gotten the upper hand just long enough to save herself.

Except that Haskins's history so far hadn't mentioned anything that remotely resembled any of the scenarios Maggie had summoned up.

Stop thinking, she told herself. *Deal with the evidence. Let the facts tell the story.*

Maggie turned the shoe over and examined the bottom. What were those scratches? She squirted jewelry cleaner onto the charm, then worried the surface with a small brush.

Will had pulled her out of the farmhouse to follow up on the charm. More than anything, Maggie didn't want to hear that Shel and the Marines digging in the grave had found another body. Especially not the body of a little girl.

"Hey." Estrella stood behind her.

Maggie waited, unable to ask the question that hammered inside her mind.

"I just heard from Shel. He's certain they're not going to find another body. They've dug around everywhere and it's not there."

The knot in Maggie's stomach loosened. "That's good news."

Estrella hesitated for a moment, then said, "Something could still have happened to that girl. Just because this body was recovered here doesn't mean that another won't be recovered somewhere else."

Maggie knew that Estrella just wanted her to be prepared. "I know. But for now, no news is good news."

Walking over, Estrella looked at the tiny charm on the table. "Did you have a charm bracelet when you were a girl?"

"Yes. My mom made sure she brought back something from everywhere she and Father went."

Harrison Talbot Foley III was always Father, never *Dad.* He ruled his business empire, his political connections, and his family with an iron fist.

"Did you have one?" Maggie asked.

Estrella nodded. "Mine didn't come from Tiffany's, though." But she smiled, meaning no offense.

"Mine didn't either," Maggie admitted. "It was just commonplace keepsakes Mom picked up at bazaars and marketplaces."

"Never anything special? Never anything expensive?"

Maggie shrugged. "Every now and again. Birthday presents from my father."

"My mom made mine. Paste and zirconium and little things she found here and there. I was proud of it."

"Do you still have it?"

Estrella chuckled. "As a matter of fact, I do."

"Me too. Along with a lot of other stuff from junior high that I would *never* show anyone."

"Pack rat."

"Maybe."

Estrella regarded her. "I wouldn't have suspected you would have hung on to more than a few Ferraris and a couple of old boyfriends."

"Those never meant as much to me."

"You drive a sports car now. And I've heard you date now and again."

"You listen to too much gossip."

"I'm a single mother of a six-year-old boy. I don't have time in my life for any hobbies other than cleaning and laundry and cooking. My one vice is listening to gossip around the camp." Estrella peered over Maggie's shoulder. "What are you looking for?"

"My mom used to have my name engraved on charms she bought me. In case I ever lost them." Maggie squirted more jewelry cleaner onto the charm. "I was hoping maybe this girl's mother did the same thing."

Gradually the scratches that Maggie had noticed earlier became ordered and uniform.

"That's engraving," Estrella said, "but it's too small to see."

Maggie picked up a magnifying glass and adjusted the distance till it brought the cursive writing into focus. "I've got a name," she said.

>> KETCHUM FARMHOUSE
>> NORTH OF JACKSONVILLE, NORTH CAROLINA
>> 0243 HOURS

"Nita."

Nita turned and saw Will approaching her. Trying to appear casual, she dropped a hand into her coveralls pocket and reached through the opening into her slacks pocket. She pulled out a breath mint and popped it into her mouth.

"Will," she said.

"Can I take a minute?"

Dread filled Nita. Will had his serious face on.

"Depends," she said. "Do you want to delay the autopsy findings?"

"Two minutes isn't going to matter."

Reluctantly, Nita stood her ground. A few feet away, Haskins's corpse was being loaded into a waiting ambulance. The driver had orders to take it to the NCIS lab at Camp Lejeune.

Will stopped just a few feet away and studied her.

Conscious of being under scrutiny, Nita breathed shallowly.

"I'm having a driver take you back to camp," Will said.

Irritation flared through Nita immediately. She started to object.

"Don't," Will said in a tone of command that he'd used with her maybe a handful of times since they'd known each other.

Nita held her anger in check, but only because she felt arguing the point would make things worse.

"You've been drinking," Will said.

"You called me in on my night off."

"You were on call."

"I live on call, Will—24-7. I'm not going to be on call every night without having a life of my own."

"You should have let me know you weren't in any shape to drive out here. You were lucky you weren't stopped."

"I know what I'm doing." Nita knew the argument was weak, but it was all she had. "I know what I can handle."

"If you blow positive for alcohol on your way back, you're going to jail tonight."

Nita couldn't argue that. "Did Shel say something?"

"Shel didn't have to. I talked to you when you first arrived."

She'd forgotten that.

"You don't smoke," Will said, "but I smelled smoke all over you. You pick that up when you're out at a club. Then there's the fact that you're eating breath mints."

Sometimes having a trained investigator for a boss really stank.

"I've got a right to a private life," Nita objected.

"You do. But you could have told me you weren't . . . *ready* to take this assignment."

"I've tried to do that in the past. You always have me come in."

"Then that's my fault," Will said. "I'll be more careful about that in the future. You don't always have to be the ME on-site after hours."

Is that a threat? Nita decided she didn't want to know.

"As soon as the body's in the lab," Will said, "go home. Leave it for tonight."

"I can work," Nita said.

"I don't want you to." Will's gaze was level. "I'll have the driver take you home as soon as the body is taken care of."

Nita knew from experience that arguing with him wouldn't help, but she mounted a final protest anyway. "I can drive myself."

"It's not up for discussion," Will told her. "The driver will take you in your car."

Not trusting herself to speak because she was so angry, Nita only nodded.

"We'll decide how we're going to proceed with the body in the morning," Will said.

"It'll need a face," Nita said. "For comparison purposes. To make sure that body really is Haskins's."

"Okay. Start there in the morning."

"Is that all?" Nita asked.

Will looked at her for a moment. "Are you all right, Nita?"

"I'm fine."

Will touched his face. "It looks like you have a bruise here on your cheekbone."

Nita resisted the impulse to touch her own face. "It's probably dirt."

"It isn't dirt." Will hesitated. "Is everything all right at home?"

For a moment Nita didn't understand what Will was driving at. Then she got it. He actually thought Joe might have struck her.

"Joe didn't do this," she said defensively. "I had an accident in the lab tonight. It hurt for just a moment, but I didn't think it was enough to leave a mark."

Quietly, Will thought a moment, then nodded. "I'll talk to you in the morning."

Nita nodded and turned away from him. She didn't have to salute; she wasn't in the military.

A Marine private was waiting at her car. He opened the passenger door at her approach. Nita slid inside, leaned her head back on the headrest, and closed her eyes. The memory of what had almost happened in Horton's apartment kept rattling through her. Nausea rose at the back of her throat, but she fought it off. She tried to push the memory out of her mind, but to no avail. Horton's face kept looming before her.

>> NCIS COMMAND POST
>> NORTH OF JACKSONVILLE, NORTH CAROLINA
>> 0251 HOURS

The engraving on the tiny silver shoe spelled out *Chloe Ivers*. The name rang no bells for Maggie, but it took Estrella only a moment to pull up the story on the Internet.

"Chloe Ivers was murdered seventeen years ago in Jacksonville," Estrella said, tapping the news story on the computer monitor. Her voice took on a note of sadness. No one could work the jobs they did and remain untouched. "She was sixteen years old. That's too young to die."

Maggie silently agreed. But young people died and were killed every day.

"According to the story, Chloe Ivers was one of the suspected victims of a serial killer named Isaac Allen Lamont."

That name rang a bell for Maggie. "I've heard of Lamont. We touched on him in a class in college." She'd taken a number of courses in deviant behavior.

Estrella's fingers flew, pulling together information. News stories in print and video compiled from dozens of databases as she worked. "I've never heard about this guy."

"Lamont was found guilty in the deaths of nineteen people." Maggie watched the array of pictures quickly downloading. "Not an excessive number if you take killers like John Wayne Gacy, Henry Lee Lucas, or Gary Leon Ridgway into account." She paused. "All of them were monsters."

"I've heard of Gacy." Estrella frowned. "Community clown if I remember right. He killed something like thirty people."

"Thirty-three," Maggie said, looking at the files Estrella's data miners were pulling up. Evidently the death of Chloe Ivers had been well publicized. "And Gacy buried them under his home. That's how the police found out about it."

"The neighbors called in and complained about the stench." Estrella nodded unhappily. "I remember that."

"Henry Lee Lucas was one of the first serial killers that law-enforcement agencies identified and brought into custody. He ultimately confessed to hundreds of deaths, but he lied about most of them. Ridgway was called the Green River Killer."

"I've heard of him, too, just never by name. He operated in Washington State."

"That's right. He killed over fifty prostitutes and teenage runaways."

Estrella brought up police front and profile headshots of Isaac Allen Lamont. The man was moonfaced and looked childlike and slow. Pale blue eyes knitted together as if the act of standing in front of the camera for the photographs had been difficult work. His short blond hair looked soft as baby-chick down. He didn't look like a murderer.

"So what's Lamont's story?" Estrella asked.

"Serial killers fall into one of two categories," Maggie said. "Either they're organized or disorganized killers. Organized killers tend to be selective about their victims, choosing the time and the place when they strike, and they usually bring a favorite weapon with them. Disorganized killers hunt on impulse and use whatever weapon they can find." She nodded at Lamont. "Isaac Allen Lamont was a disorganized killer. He didn't know his victims. In three of the cases, Lamont got into town only a day or so before he killed a woman. Then he was gone the next day."

"He didn't operate out of a specific area?"

"No. And he didn't stay around." Maggie remembered as best she could. "We'll have to check, but I remember that Lamont was a drifter. He worked in places, construction work mostly, got a little money saved back, and then hit the road again. I think he hoboed back and forth between New York and Miami along the railways."

"He passed through Jacksonville long enough to kill this poor girl."

"Apparently so."

"Lamont didn't know Chloe Ivers?" Estrella asked.

"No. She was a victim of opportunity. All of them were."

"Why did he kill them?"

"Nobody knows for sure what pushes these people. It's one of the frustrating things about chasing a serial killer." So far, the NCIS team hadn't had to do that.

"According to the story in the *Washington Post,* Chloe Ivers was abducted from her home and murdered."

Maggie frowned. "That doesn't sound right. From what I remember, Lamont always attacked women in public places. He never went to the homes of any of them. But I could be wrong about that."

Estrella moved the news stories out to separate monitors. "Let's break this down and see what we have."

S  CRIME SCENE  NCIS  C

NAVAL CRIMINAL INVESTIGATIVE SERVICE

14

SCENE  NCIS  CRIME SCEN

NAVAL CRIMINAL INVESTIGATIVE SERVICE

>> KETCHUM FARMHOUSE
>> NORTH OF JACKSONVILLE, NORTH CAROLINA
>> 0255 HOURS

"Maggie says the charm belonged to a young murder victim named Chloe Ivers," Will told Larkin.

They stood in the farmhouse, overseeing the crime-scene investigation. Photographers, video people, and techs moved slowly and surely through the room. When working a crime scene, there was only one hard rule: Get it all, get it right, and get it the first time.

Since no real mystery was involved in the takedown, all they needed to do was collect evidence that would support what had happened. There was plenty of evidence.

"Where's Nita?" Larkin asked.

"I sent her back with the body," Will said, and that was true enough.

"Did she seem a little . . . off to you?" Larkin's voice was flat, without any inflection of blame or suspicion.

Will answered without batting an eye. "She's tired."

Larkin looked as if he was going to say something further, then clamped his jaw shut and looked around.

Will was silently thankful. He didn't condone what Nita had done, showing up at the crime scene in the condition she had, but she was one of his personnel. He would deal with her. No one else would touch her till then. That was how he handled his team. Larkin knew that from past experience.

"Just make sure she's not . . . tired at the next crime scene," Larkin suggested.

"I will."

Larkin moved through the house, stepping around teams pulling bullets out of the wall. "Do you know about the Chloe Ivers case?"

"Until tonight, I didn't remember there was a Chloe Ivers case."

"It's classified as open/unsolved in NCIS files here in Jacksonville. Chloe Ivers is on my cold-case list," Larkin said.

Will had cold-case files too. All the NCIS units did. They usually met once a year to go over them with other teams, hoping for a fresh perspective on old murders and missing-persons cases. He pulled them out from time to time and went through them, but he had yet to close any of those on his list. That was how it went most of the time.

"Why was NCIS investigating?" Will asked. "Chloe wasn't old enough to be military personnel." The possibility that the girl's killer might have been military zoomed into Will's mind.

"Chloe Ivers belongs to us because her mother is a Navy officer. Her stepfather is a member of Congress. Representative Benjamin Swanson. I'm sure you've heard of him."

Swanson was a vocal figure, very supportive of the current president. Lately Swanson had been coming into his own as a media darling, getting photographed overseas with troops in fire zones, helping out along the Gulf coast where rebuilding efforts had gone in after the latest tropical storms. Ben Swanson was popular in a lot of places, but he'd made enemies along the way. Political commentators believed Swanson had his eyes on the Speaker of the House position.

"When the media gets wind of this," Will said, "they're going to have a field day."

"I know." Larkin sighed. "I want this kept away from them as long as we can. I'll pass the word along the chain of command, let them know the troops can talk about what happened here with Bryce Ketchum and the Asian gang. But that's as far as it goes."

"That'll help." With all the violence that had taken place at the farmhouse, the media outlets would be jammed for days.

But an old, unsolved murder of a teen girl who was the stepdaughter of a powerful congressman currently in the limelight will be an even bigger story, Will realized sourly.

"Do you have any idea why Haskins was buried out here?" Larkin asked.

Will took out his iPAQ Pocket PC. Estrella had forwarded USMC Gunnery Sergeant Haskins, George's service record. Using the stylus, Will summoned the report and slid through the information to the facts he'd highlighted.

"This is all preliminary background," he said, "but it does offer something."

Larkin waited.

"Haskins and Ketchum knew each other," Will said. "If Estrella hadn't been looking for past histories together, we wouldn't have known."

"What past history?"

"They were in the service together."

"Ketchum was in the military?" Larkin shook his head in disbelief. The background on Ketchum had primarily focused on his criminal activity of the last nineteen years.

"Ketchum was a Marine, like Haskins," Will answered. "They joined together, pulled boot together at Camp Lejeune, then did stretches together at Camp Pendleton in California, Camp Butler in Okinawa, Camp Smith in Hawaii, and Camp Lemonier in Djibouti, Africa. They weren't always together, but they set it up so they could be from time to time."

"What was Ketchum's service record like?"

"Estrella's still digging into that. All we know at this point is that Haskins and Ketchum knew each other as far back as high school."

"Here in Jacksonville?"

Will nodded.

"Anything in there to suggest whether Ketchum might have killed Haskins?"

"No."

"What about tying Haskins to Chloe Ivers?"

"We'll look for that."

"Where's the girl's charm bracelet?"

"We don't know."

Frustration knotted Larkin's jaw.

"If we push into this thing," Will said, "the media will find out about it."

"I know."

"Seventeen years is a long time."

"It is." Larkin's eyes looked haunted. "But for people who don't have the answers they need to let go, something like this is only as far away as yesterday."

"We could start out working Haskins's murder," Will suggested. "We don't have to mention the charm at all."

"That's how I want it done. For now. We'll have to handle Congressman Swanson with kid gloves. In fact, I don't want him to know we're even looking around."

"All right." Will shifted, feeling fatigue eating into him. Handling the investigation like that was going to be like swimming with his hands tied behind him. But *military* and *sensitive operations* went together like a hand in a glove. "As soon as we find anything worth knowing, I'll tell you."

Larkin nodded. "Good. But, Will?"

"Sir?"

"Let it wait a day. Whether Haskins's murder connects up to Chloe Ivers's death or not, the trail is seventeen years cold. We'll get to it soon enough. Meanwhile, I took you away from your family tonight so you could return a girl to hers. You've accomplished that. Now I want you to do what you planned to with your kids tomorrow. Go sailing."

Will started to object but then thought better of it. He'd given his life to his career, and he'd lost his marriage in the process of defending his country. He didn't want to lose his kids, too.

"Go sailing," Larkin repeated. "Haskins and Chloe Ivers can wait long enough for you to spend some time with your kids."

Will nodded. Leaving Steven and Wren at the basketball game had been costly. "Aye, sir."

>> NCIS COMMAND POST
>> NORTH OF JACKSONVILLE, NORTH CAROLINA
>> 0312 HOURS

Estrella stared at the dead girl's face. She looked so alive, so cheerful, that it was hard to accept that she was dead.

Chloe Ivers looked like a typical sixteen-year-old girl in the picture. Not hard around the edges and frayed the way Amanda Whitcomb looked. Chloe's picture had been taken seventeen years ago. She'd looked hopeful and excited. Things had been different then.

But not that different, Estrella thought bitterly. *People still killed for no reason that anyone else could fathom. And sometimes they killed themselves.*

Sipping a breath, searching for control, Estrella felt the old emotions threatening to cascade within her. Something about the innocence in Chloe Ivers's eyes touched Estrella, made her think things she'd promised herself she'd stop thinking about.

If Chloe Ivers hadn't died, she'd have been four years older than Estrella was now. She would have been a woman of thirty-three, probably married with kids and deep into whatever career she'd chosen for herself.

Instead she lay in a coffin somewhere. Or maybe she'd been cremated. Estrella hadn't come across that information yet.

"How are you doing?"

Estrella tapped the keys again, checking on the download sequences she was running to create the Chloe Ivers database the team needed. She didn't turn her head to look at Maggie. "Good."

"You looked like you were zoning there."

"I'm just tired," Estrella said. But she knew what was bothering her. Thinking about what had happened to Chloe Ivers made her think of her husband. Even at the end, when the man she loved had been crashing on drugs, trying to eke one more hour out of the day and dying by minutes, Estrella remembered the handsome boy Julian had been when they'd been in high school together. That was whom she saw dead on the floor: the boy. Not the man who had hollowed himself out chasing dreams.

"Coffee?" Maggie asked.

"Please."

Maggie retreated to the coffee service on the other side of the RV and filled two cups. She brought Estrella's back to the workstation.

After a few minutes, Estrella couldn't be silent anymore. She had to make her feelings known.

"I think it would be a mistake to reopen the Chloe Ivers case."

Maggie sipped her coffee and didn't say anything.

Estrella wanted to let it go there, but she couldn't. "The girl's been dead for seventeen years. Her parents have let her go."

"You're probably right," Maggie said.

"I know I'm right." Estrella took a deep breath. "When you have pain like that, confusion like that, you're better off if you can just cut it loose."

Maggie considered that for a moment. "Do you think that's what they did?"

"The stepfather evidently got on with his life. He's a successful congressman these days."

Estrella looked at the picture of Benjamin Swanson. It was a stock photo, one of those that showed up in the media when Swanson's name was mentioned.

Swanson was charismatic. He had magnetic blue eyes, sandy hair that had gone white at the temples, and boyish good looks with a slight spattering of freckles.

"What about the mother?" Maggie asked.

"She's still with the Navy. Out in California." Finding USN Commander Laura Ivers had been easy. Her picture filled one of the monitors on the right.

In her fifties now, Commander Ivers had short blonde hair and brown eyes, and she remained beautiful. She looked like an authority figure, somehow regal and invulnerable.

But Estrella knew that was a facade. No one got over losing someone they loved. Pain was just put on hold for a time, and the grieving continued in private.

"I thought Congressman Swanson was single," Maggie said. "I seem to recall he's constantly paired up with women at different events."

"He and the commander—she was only a lieutenant then—got divorced a few years after her daughter's murder."

"Why?"

Estrella shook her head. Maggie's questions were starting to get on her nerves. "It doesn't say," Estrella said a little more crossly than she'd intended, "but generally when you lose a family member, you don't always make it through that. A loss like that can tear families apart."

"Or make them grow stronger," Maggie replied.

After Julian's death, Estrella's family had come to her. They'd taken care of her, then taken care of Dominic until she was able to take care of herself and her son.

But Julian's family? Estrella had never seen them again. It was as if when Julian died, his wife and child had vanished from the face of the earth. Estrella knew they blamed her for their son's death.

Feeling more irritation now, Estrella turned on Maggie. "Have you ever lost somebody?" She felt certain the answer would be no. Estrella sometimes thought that Maggie's police work and her involvement with NCIS were nothing more than slumming, meant to make her affluent father angry.

"I have," Maggie said. "My mother's had several nervous breakdowns. They started when I was six or seven. Not much older than Nicky. She tried to commit suicide twice. Father hired the best doctors he could. Then the best psychiatrists. Mom tried to kill herself again, but she was determined to kill me first."

Estrella listened to the calm way Maggie related the horrifying tale. None of them knew much about each other outside of work. Except for Will. Everybody on the team knew about his divorce and how hard he was working to have a relationship with his son and daughter.

"The maid and the houseman had to restrain her," Maggie went on.

"Father had her committed to a mental institution. She's been there ever since." She paused. "Mom hasn't died. I still get to visit her there. So maybe it's not the same."

Sympathy and shame touched Estrella. "I'm sorry," she said in a quiet voice. "I didn't know."

"It's all right," Maggie replied. "You couldn't have known. It's not something I talk about, and Father has kept it out of the news ever since he first had Mom institutionalized."

Estrella thought for a moment, suddenly feeling the need to be delicate. "This family has made peace with their loss. That's all I'm saying. I don't think that stirring this up all over again is going to be best for them."

"No," Maggie said. "If this does get brought out again, I think it'll be a very hard thing for them to face. But what if they still have questions? Lamont wasn't found guilty of killing their daughter. He wasn't even tried for it. Everyone just assumed he did it."

"Knowing who did it isn't going to bring that girl back."

"No," Maggie agreed. "But maybe it will help take away at least some of the confusion over what happened."

Estrella suddenly couldn't meet Maggie's eyes. It was as if the other woman were talking directly to her. About Julian.

Taking a deep breath, Estrella turned her attention back to the computer monitors. She thought again of how she'd come home that afternoon to find Julian lying in the bathtub. Blood had been everywhere, hours old and already coagulating.

Afterward Estrella had put the pieces together, learning how deeply in debt to the loan sharks Julian had gotten while trying to finish the computer game he was building. Looking at that, at the fact that Julian knew he was going to have to go back into the corporate scene and use his skills to crunch numbers not create worlds, he'd given up and killed himself.

Estrella had come home from the doctor that day, excited to tell him that the baby growing inside her was a boy. She'd never gotten to tell her husband that.

For over six years she'd wondered if getting to tell Julian would have made a difference. Would he still have killed himself if he'd known he had a son on the way?

And if that would have made a difference, why hadn't simply knowing she was there for him made a difference?

Quietly, Estrella fought the private battle she'd been fighting for years. She packed up her husband's memory and the questions she had and put them away once more. Thinking about them wouldn't do any good. That's what Maggie Foley didn't understand.

The pain was going to be there, waiting, no matter what Chloe Ivers's parents discovered. That was one thing Estrella knew from long experience.

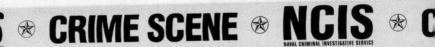

15

SCENE  NCIS  CRIME SCENE

NAVAL CRIMINAL INVESTIGATIVE SERVICE

>> BARRACKS
>> CAMP LEJEUNE, NORTH CAROLINA
>> 0636 HOURS

Will let himself into his quarters as quietly as possible. He still hadn't found proper officer's quarters, though Larkin had been at him to. Except when Steven and Wren stayed with him, he really didn't need the additional space. Without a family constantly around him, a house would feel too big. He'd been used to cramped quarters aboard a Navy ship for years.

His home consisted of a living room with television and computer, a small kitchen and dinette, a bedroom, and a bath. Wren got the bedroom, while Will and Steven bunked in the living room on the sleeper sofa and a folding hammock. Pictures of Steven and Wren hung on the walls along with scenes from famous sea battles.

Steven sat on the edge of the sleeper sofa. His hair was tousled, and he wore only a pair of flannel pajama bottoms. A gold chain glinted around his neck. He held a bowl of cereal in one hand while he watched the local news on television. The cable channel repeated the same news stories over and over until a new show was taped.

"You made it home," Steven said.

Will was conscious of standing there in his doorway wearing combat BDUs and his weapons. Steven hadn't ever seen him like this, fresh from the fight. *I should have cleaned up first.* But he'd been tired and hadn't thought of that.

"Yeah," Will agreed. "Things last night got . . . complicated."

"That's what the news said."

"Have you been up long?"

Steven shrugged. "I slept off and on. Wren was worried about you."

The television was muted, but the images showed scenes of the aftermath from what had taken place out at the Ketchum farm.

"Did she see that?"

Steven nodded.

Anger surfaced in Will, getting away from him before he realized it. "She shouldn't have seen something like that."

"Hey," Steven said sharply. "It's not like I let her. I was taking a shower. How should I know she would watch the news? She *never* watches news. She's all about Cartoon Network."

Will took a breath. "You're right. I apologize." He crossed to the closet and opened the gun safe he had bolted to the wall inside. "I had a long night."

"*All* of us had a long night." Steven used the remote to switch off the television. "Wren kept saying prayers for you. I swear I about wore my knees out before she finally dozed off and stayed asleep."

Will locked the safe. "Did you have any problems getting home?"

"I got lost once, but no problems driving."

"Good."

"That was the first time I ever drove at night."

Will felt the sharp stab of guilt. It was just one more thing he'd missed out on when it came to his son. "You did a good job, Steven. Driving back *and* taking care of your sister."

Steven looked self-conscious. "Thanks." He stared at Will. "Are you okay?"

"I am." Will felt awkward and didn't know what else to say. The fact that Steven had thought to ask touched him.

"The news said a whole bunch of drug dealers were killed and some military guys were injured," Steven said.

Will nodded. "It was a bad situation." He didn't want to talk about last night. He wanted a shower, then about eight hours of sack time. But he knew he wasn't going to get that. "I'm gonna grab a shower."

"Sure." Steven turned his attention away.

Will noticed the hurt look in his son's eyes and didn't know how he could have caused it, but he was sure he had. He started to say something, then realized he didn't know what to say. Instead he went to the bathroom, certain that he was going to mishandle the rest of the day.

❀ ❀ ❀

>> 0641 HOURS

In the bathroom, Will turned the shower up so hot he felt like he was getting scalded. He made himself stand under it, soaping up and willing himself to relax. When he was clean, when he was sure he couldn't take any more of the heat, he turned the water on cold till he couldn't take that.

He dried off, pulled on his Skivvies, and stood in front of the mirror. Using a towel, he cleared away the fog till he could see his reflection. The scar from the bullet he'd taken in Chinhae still looked pink and fresh. Others had joined it over the past year. He'd been lucky.

You look old and tired, he told himself. Then he thought he *should* look that way because he certainly felt it.

Working mechanically, his body trained by years of working on little or no sleep, Will lathered his face and shaved. He felt slightly more awake as he dressed in jeans and a knit shirt.

His mind stayed busy with the investigation. Shel and Remy were supposed to interview Ketchum this morning, after letting the man stew overnight in a cell. Estrella and Maggie were going to dig further into Chloe Ivers's murder. And Nita was going to make certain that the body they'd found actually belonged to USMC Gunnery Sergeant George Haskins.

Will's orders, given by Larkin last night as they'd pulled out of the scene, were to take his kids sailing.

❀ ❀ ❀

>> 0657 HOURS

The smell of coffee filled the living room when Will returned. He was also surprised to see that the sofa sleeper had been neatly folded and put away. Usually he had to mention that to Steven three or four times before it happened.

Steven was in the kitchen, standing by the coffeemaker.

"You know how to make coffee?" Will asked.

Steven frowned. "It's not that hard. The directions are on the coffeemaker and the coffee."

"That wasn't a sarcastic remark." Will went to the pantry and took out waffle mix. "I just didn't know you knew how. Have you had breakfast?"

"I had some cereal."

Will grinned. "Do you still have room for a real breakfast?"

"Sure." Steven reached under the cabinet and took out the electric waffle iron. He plugged it in and got it ready.

Will mixed the waffle batter with a whisk. He glanced at his son from the corner of his eye. This was the first time he could remember Steven helping prepare a meal.

"Pecans or blueberries?" Will asked.

"Pecans," Steven answered. "I had the last of the blueberries with the cereal."

"Did you mark it on the grocery list?"

Steven looked at him for a moment, then went to the refrigerator, took the marker from the cup on top, and wrote *blueberries* on the shopping list.

Will added pecans to the batter, then poured some into the waffle iron and closed the lid.

"Do you want an omelet?" Will asked.

"Yeah."

Will started to reach into the refrigerator.

"I got it." Steven opened the door and brought out the carton of eggs. "We need cheese, onions, peppers, and ham. Anything else?"

"Tomato."

"I don't like tomato."

"Your sister does."

Steven got a tomato out too.

"Sausage or bacon?" Will asked.

"Sausage." Steven grabbed a tube of sausage from the crisper. Again without being asked, he took out the chopping block and started prepping the vegetables.

"You need any help with that?" Will asked.

"Am I doing it right?"

"Yup."

"Then I don't need any help, do I?"

Will bit back a sharp retort. He didn't know what dynamic was in play at the moment, but he didn't want to start a fight.

He cracked eggs in a four-cup measuring cup, added milk and pepper, and whisked them thoroughly. He got out a large skillet and heated it on the stove. Then he took the first of the waffles from the iron and put them on a plate. They could microwave them to bring them back up to temp. Getting the omelets off hot was the most important thing.

When Steven had the vegetables and ham cut up, he held out the cutting board.

Will took it, poured egg into the skillet, and added some veggies.

"Could you have gotten killed last night?" Steven's voice was small.

Will looked at his son. He wanted to lie to Steven when he saw the unexpected worry in the young man's eyes. But Will couldn't lie because whatever was going on this morning between them was fragile.

"Yes," he answered simply.

"Did you know it was going to be like that? All that shooting? When you left us last night?"

"No. I didn't."

Steven searched his face, and Will knew his son was studying him, trying to detect any falsehood. He turned his attention back to the skillet and flipped the omelet, folding it over to hold the vegetables inside.

"Is this what you do?" Steven asked. "Get into stuff like this?"

"Sometimes."

Steven was quiet for a time. "Well," he said finally, "it's a stupid job, if you ask me. And selfish, too."

Will turned to his son, feeling the heat rising in his face.

"Do you know what Wren would do if you got killed like Uncle Frank?" Steven demanded. He answered before Will had a chance to. "She'd freak. That's what she'd do."

Unable to respond to that, not trusting himself to speak coherently at the moment, Will flipped the sausage patties and turned the omelet.

"Good morning, Daddy!"

Running feet slapped against the tile floor. Will had just enough time to turn around and grab Wren as she wrapped her arms around his waist and nearly bowled him over. Her exuberance was overwhelming.

"Hey, kiddo," Will said, stooping long enough to wrap an arm around her and pick her up. She was getting big and heavy, and he knew with a twinge of sadness that he wouldn't be able to hold her like this in just another few years.

"Waffles," Wren said. "Yum!" She hugged Will. "You are the *best* dad in the whole wide world!"

"I'm glad you think so." Will kissed his daughter's cheek.

"I missed you last night," Wren said.

"I missed you." Will smelled the soap on her skin and the herbal shampoo in her hair. "Did you wash your hair?"

"No, silly. Steven did. In the sink." Wren smiled at Will as though he were feebleminded. "He made me stand in a chair."

"I see."

"I thought I was going to break my neck."

"Well, I'm glad you didn't."

"Me too." Wren sighed like that was a big relief. "I looked for you on television last night, but you weren't there."

"I was there. They just didn't take my picture."

Wren looked troubled. "People got hurt."

Will nodded, ignoring the I-told-you-so glance he got from Steven. "Some people did."

"They were bad men."

"They were."

"Did you catch them?"

"Yes."

"Good, because I was worried they might still be out there."

"No, they aren't." That was one thing Will could feel good about.

"Can I watch cartoons?"

"Yes." Will put Wren down and continued making breakfast.

His daughter ran to the living room and switched on Cartoon Network. In just a few minutes, she was laughing.

Steven opened the waffle iron and took out the next batch of waffles. "She worries about you, you know."

"I didn't know." It was hard to know, Will thought, when he spent so much time away from them. Then he realized that he'd spent a whole lot of time away from them even before the divorce. Serving on the aircraft carrier had been the worst. He'd been gone for months at a time then.

"She does."

Will stopped himself short of getting angry. It wouldn't do any good. He knew from experience that Steven could match him ounce for ounce when it came to anger. His son wasn't too far removed from his father.

"Maybe we could just concentrate on getting breakfast ready before we burn it," Will suggested. "Then go sailing."

That seemed to deflect some of Steven's bad mood. "You still feel like going sailing?"

"Yes."

"You haven't had any sleep."

"I'll be fine. Although I may need some extra help with the boat."

Steven nodded. "Okay."

>> DOBROSKY'S BOATYARD
>> OLD BRIDGE STREET
>> JACKSONVILLE, NORTH CAROLINA
>> 0818 HOURS

Will let Steven drive to the boatyard where Will kept the Laser 2000 sailboat he'd bought a few years ago. Steven and Wren both had a high interest in sailing, something that their mother had never developed. During the marriage, Will had seldom gotten to take his son and daughter out in the boat. They'd been on the water more this past year than in any year while they'd lived together as a family.

The day was perfect for sailing—the sun was bright and the skies were clear. According to the radio, the current temperature was forty-nine degrees, and it looked like it might even make it to the expected sixty-two.

After a couple tries, with Wren acting as navigator—"Uh-oh"; "You're too close"; "Try again"—Steven managed to put the pickup in front of the boat trailer.

Together, Will and Steven attached the trailer and connected the electrical and brake hookups.

The sailboat was four inches over fourteen feet in length, featured a fiberglass hull that put her weight at less than three hundred pounds, and was painted blue and silver. She doubled as a family sailboat and a racing craft.

"Hey, Commander."

Recognizing the voice, Will turned and spotted Joe Tomlinson approaching. Joe held Celia's hand.

Joe was dressed in faded jeans and a T-shirt under a Windbreaker. Green-lensed wraparound sunglasses hid his eyes. His shoulder-length blond hair was tousled by the wind and made him look slightly shaggy. Joe was slim, hard muscled, and tanned from being outdoors, and Will knew he turned women's heads.

Celia, Joe and Nita's five-year-old daughter, wore jeans, a sweater, boots, and purple sunglasses shaped like stars. The girl was tall, showing signs of growing as tall as her father, and she looked like him too, all golden hair and bronze skin. She smiled and waved and said hello.

"Don't mean to hold you up," Joe apologized. "I know how hard it is for you or your team to get family time."

"That's all right." Will reintroduced Steven and Wren.

Joe turned to his daughter. "Honey, why don't you go sit in the truck with Wren for a minute. You can show her your new necklace." He looked up at Will. "If that's all right."

Will nodded.

Celia ran to join Wren.

"I just needed a minute of your time." Joe looked uncomfortable. "It's about Nita."

"Is something wrong?"

Will had talked to Nita earlier and knew that she'd gone to the lab to work on positive identification of USMC Gunnery Sergeant George Haskins's remains.

"I don't know. You know she cares a lot about her work."

"Yes."

"But lately Nita seems like she's been under more stress than ever."

Will didn't say anything. The NCIS caseload was considerable, and there were always emotional issues involved, sometimes generated by the team and sometimes just absorbed from the people the team came in contact with.

"Last night I noticed that she'd been drinking." Joe looked flustered. "Usually I don't talk out of school, Commander—"

"Will. Just call me Will."

Joe nodded. "Like I said, I don't talk out of school, and I let my wife handle her own business. Unless I'm invited in. My dad taught me that."

"Smart man."

Joe grinned. "He always said the relationship between a man and a woman is one of the trickiest things you'll ever manage." He glanced out at New River. "The river and the ocean and the wind aren't nearly as hard to figure out."

"I know." Will wondered for a moment how his life might be different if he'd managed his own marriage better.

"Anyway, I'm not trying to pry into Nita's business," Joe said, "but I wondered whether you might just look out for her for a while."

"I will." As Will regarded Joe Tomlinson, he saw that the other man looked stressed out too. It was the first time Will had ever seen that in Joe. Usually Joe was happy-go-lucky, a guy who could find something to be thankful for no matter what the situation.

"I'd appreciate it if you didn't tell Nita I asked you to do that. Or tell her that I was worried."

"I won't."

"I just didn't expect to see you here. Celia and I were picking up some parts I needed for a job I'm doing." Joe offered his hand. "If there's anything I need to do, just let me know."

Will shook Joe's hand.

Joe looked at the sailboat. "Where are you headed?"

"I thought we'd just grab the wind. Sail for a few hours and maybe do a little fishing. Then I thought we'd take a late lunch at Fisherman's Wharf Restaurant."

"Sounds like a plan. I won't take up any more of your time." Joe called Celia to him. Together they crossed the lot and headed toward his pickup.

Will watched Joe go and felt sorry for him. Whatever personal storm Nita was going through clearly threatened her entire family. Will had to wonder if it was going to threaten his team as well.

"Are we ready?"

Will turned to Steven. "Yeah."

"Are you okay?"

Will was surprised at the question and the genuine concern in his son's eyes. "I'm fine. Just worried."

"Is Joe going to be okay?"

Will knew that Joe Tomlinson had left an impression on his son. Steven was at the age where very few grown men impressed him, but Joe had.

"Joe's going to be fine."

"He sounded kind of . . . I don't know. Sad, maybe."

"He's worried about his wife."

"Is there a problem?"

"I don't know."

Steven looked Will in the eye. "Can you help him?"

"I'm going to try."

After giving the trailer hookups one last inspection, Will headed for the truck cab. Steven walked toward the passenger side, giving up the steering wheel without an argument. Driving with a trailer was not allowed by the limitations of his learner's permit.

As he slid behind the wheel, Will thought about Nita, remembering her disheveled appearance and the bruise he'd spotted on her cheek. The possibility that Joe might have put it there came to mind again, but Will immediately dismissed that. Joe would never hurt Nita.

So who had?

That question stayed in Will's mind as he pulled out of the boatyard. He hadn't for a moment bought Nita's explanation that it had been a lab accident. But he knew she wouldn't tell him what had occurred until she was ready.

By then it might be too late.

Will shifted in his seat as he tried to get comfortable. Fatigue chewed at him relentlessly, but a lot of it evaporated when Wren put her arms around his neck from behind and kissed him.

"I'm glad we're going sailing," she said.

Will patted her arm, experiencing again the overpowering love his children inspired in him. "Me too."

CRIME SCENE

NCIS

NAVAL CRIMINAL INVESTIGATIVE SERVICE

16

SCENE  NCIS  CRIME SCENE

NAVAL CRIMINAL INVESTIGATIVE SERVICE

>> NCIS MEDICAL LAB
>> CAMP LEJEUNE, NORTH CAROLINA
>> 0834 HOURS

Nita reached for the coffeepot and stopped when she saw her hand shaking. For a moment she just stared at it, not believing what she was seeing.

It's just a hangover, she told herself. *Not anything to worry about.* She'd been telling herself that for the last hour, since she'd arrived at the lab. The pain between her temples throbbed, matching her pulse.

"Dr. Tomlinson."

Surprised, Nita shoved her hand in her lab-coat pocket and faced the new arrival. "Yes."

"Everything okay?" The lab assistant was young and earnest.

"Everything's fine. Just debating the coffee. The coffee's going to win, though. I need it to stay awake."

The assistant grinned. "Know what you mean." He shifted the cube-shaped box he carried. "One of the guys is about to make a breakfast run into Jacksonville. I can have him pick you up a small thermos of whatever you like."

"Sure." Nita reached into her slacks and took out a twenty-dollar bill. "I'll take a small thermos of anything Colombian that will keep."

The guy set the box he carried on one of the stainless-steel tables, then took out a pad and wrote. "You want cinnamon rolls or anything?"

"Two bagels. Cinnamon." One would be for breakfast and the other would be for lunch. Nita didn't feel like leaving, and she knew Will would want her findings on the corpse as soon as possible. She nodded toward the box. "Is that my head?"

The lab guy finished with the pad and put it away. "It is." He picked up the box and handed it to her. "Cleaned and prepped."

Nita opened the box and peered in. Whoever Will had called in last night had removed the body's head, severing it from the spinal column. They'd also cleaned the skull. Since years in the ground had passed—presumably seventeen years since that was how long George Haskins had been missing—there hadn't been much flesh on the bones.

The skull looked bright and shiny. None of the mildew remained. And the hole in the back of the head looked enormous.

"The note said that all of the skull pieces had been found," the assistant said. "Most of them were inside the skull, but a couple were found at the site and brought in. They've all been cleaned and put in the box."

"Okay. Thanks."

He said he'd deliver her order as soon as it arrived, then left.

Nita turned her full attention to the skull. She felt slightly sick, nauseous. She'd never liked hangovers and usually didn't get them. She wondered if she had suffered a slight concussion during the attack last night.

That episode had haunted her dreams, mixing in with scenes of the recovery of the mildewed corpse till she'd ended up with some kind of weird George Romero–esque nightmare. That wasn't usual either. Normally she slept without waking or remembering anything.

She'd also slept on the couch. When Joe had asked her about that this morning, she'd just told him that she hadn't wanted to wake him.

Nita pushed her problems at home from her mind. She would worry about her marriage some other time and place.

Running her fingertips over the skull, getting to know the structure of the bone intimately, Nita allowed her curiosity to take hold.

"Okay, Gunnery Sergeant George Haskins—if that's what your name is—it's time to fess up and tell me all your secrets. Starting with, are you really George Haskins?"

>> INTERVIEW ROOM B OBSERVATION
>> CAMP LEJEUNE, NORTH CAROLINA
>> 0842 HOURS

Shel stood in the darkness of the observation room and watched Bryce Ketchum sitting at the rectangular table on the other side of the one-way glass. Ketchum appeared bored, but nervous tension showed up as well. He tapped his fingers on the tabletop, playing drums to a song that constantly cycled in his head. His foot danced on the floor, causing the chain between his ankles to clink.

Ketchum wore an orange jumpsuit and looked like he hadn't slept all night. So far he hadn't asked for an attorney. He was experienced enough to know that once he had a lawyer involved any deals he might want to make would be slow in coming. If they came at all.

The observation room door opened, and Remy followed it in. Max recognized the SEAL and got up to meet him, nuzzling his hand briefly to check for treats, then returned to the corner of the room he'd claimed as his own.

"You look like something the cat yakked up," Shel said.

Remy grimaced. "That's what I love about you, gunney. All those positive vibes you throw off."

"That's what I'm here for." Shel looked at Remy. "You solid?"

"I'm good. No double vision. No nausea. Just a headache that feels like somebody shoved a ninety-pound pumpkin inside my head."

"The cat thing—I'm serious about that."

Remy went to the corner where the coffeemaker was and poured a cup. "I'm fine."

"You didn't have to come in today. Will cleared you for a couple days off."

"I'd rather work." Remy faced him. A trace of belligerence showed in his bloodshot eyes. "If that's okay with you."

Shel shrugged. "It's okay with me."

"And it's not like I had really great choices. I could come watch you fumble your way through this interview, or I could watch flesh-eating beetles devour what's left of the guy you dug out of the ground last night."

A smile tugged at Shel's mouth. "If it'd been me that nearly took a round through the gourd, I'd be home watching John Wayne DVDs."

"You can only watch *Sands of Iwo Jima* so many times."

"Not that one. You get shot up, you want to see something uplifting like *Big Jake* or *The War Wagon*. Movies that he didn't die in. Something that makes you feel invincible again."

"I am invincible."

Shel studied Remy. Other than a slight hesitation in his step and the obvious lack of rest, the SEAL looked fine. But Shel knew that Remy didn't care about getting shot as much as anyone else on the team. It wasn't that he was unafraid but that he had a general lack of concern when it came to living or dying.

During the last few months that they'd worked together, Shel had seen that. When he'd talked to Maggie about it, Shel had found that she had noticed the same tendencies. None of them knew where it came from. But Shel was warrior enough and experienced enough to know that someone who didn't recognize fear could be both an asset and a liability. When he'd talked to Will about it, Will had stated only that Remy was a work in progress and that he was on Will's radar.

Remy approached the observation window and sipped his coffee. "Coffee's bad."

"It'll wake you up."

"Has Ketchum said anything?"

"Not yet."

"Have you talked to him?"

"Not yet."

"It's almost 0900, gunney. What have you been doing with yourself?"

"I bagged a couple hours' sleep, got up for my morning ten-mile constitutional, then familiarized myself with the files Maggie pulled on Ketchum over breakfast. I just got here."

"Why isn't Maggie doing the interview?"

"She said that based on the psych profiles she looked at, Ketchum would think having a woman interview him was fun. He wouldn't feel threatened or feel like he didn't have control of the situation."

Remy grinned a little at that. "So we're here to threaten Ketchum and take away any notion he might have that he's in control of what's going on."

"My favorite part of being a crime buster. Rattle the bad guys."

"I'm down with that. Was Ketchum involved with Haskins's murder?"

"We don't know."

"But the corpse was found on Ketchum's land?"

"Right."

"So if Haskins went into the ground about the time that girl—"

"Chloe Ivers," Shel supplied.

"—was kidnapped and murdered, then it stands to reason Ketchum was involved."

"That's the theory we're working with."

"Where was Ketchum when that girl went missing?"

Shel appreciated the questions. Remy had come a long way in a year with the team. One thing Shel had learned about crime-scene investigation was that an education in forensics was an ongoing one. Every year science added or found a new layer of technology that went into their bag of tricks. The hardest part was absorbing all that knowledge.

"Ketchum was up in Raleigh in Central Prison," Shel answered. "He was finishing up a two-year jolt for receivership."

"Nothing heavier than trafficking in stolen goods?"

Shel shook his head. "Ketchum's smart. Anything he does, he lets someone else take the weight for."

Remy thought about that for a moment. "Seems strange that he'd bury a body on his property then. If he was avoiding any long-lasting relationships with the law."

"That's what I was thinking."

"Makes you wonder if he knew that body was there before last night."

"Exactly."

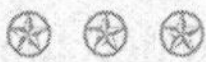

>> NCIS MEDICAL LAB
>> CAMP LEJEUNE, NORTH CAROLINA
>> 0927 HOURS

Placing the skull on the table, Nita picked up a digital camera and took several shots. She uploaded them onto the computer, then accessed the images of USMC Gunnery Sergeant Haskins that Estrella had set up for her.

Using Adobe Photoshop, Nita selected the best Haskins image and the best of the images she'd just taken. It took her a few moments to clean up the image file from Estrella, turn it into a transparency, and make certain the size ratio fit that of the skull photo. Maintaining the integrity of both photographs was important. Any stretching of the photos could result in a missed identification or a mistaken confirmation. Either was bad.

When she was finished with the prep work, she overlaid the transparent skull onto the picture of Haskins when he'd still been wearing his skin.

The process of superimposing a picture of a skull onto a picture of a living person was normally intended to exclude people from a possible identification, but it had been used to positively identify people in the past. The morphological features had to be unique in order to guarantee a positive identification. Forensic anthropologists aiding investigative efforts through their osteopathic expertise used the technique all the time. Bones were the foundation of an individual, and Nita had met forensic anthropologists who could read a skeleton—and sometimes even a single bone—like a book.

Working carefully, Nita examined the nasal bone morphology, the shape of the eye orbits, and the glabella. The glabella was the space between the eyebrows—at least, where the eyebrows *would* have been if there were any face left—and above the nose, joining the superciliary ridges.

All those points on the skull matched the ones in the picture.

But even with that, Nita knew that the possibility still existed that she only had someone who *resembled* George Haskins. She had to be positive.

When—and *if*—Estrella managed to get copies of Haskins's military records that included his dental history, Nita knew they'd be closer to identifying the remains. Haskins had gone missing seventeen years ago, though. Those records might not still exist.

Nita opened another cabinet and took out the facial reconstruction kit she used when she had to put a face on an unidentified skull. She wasn't a forensic artist by trade, but she'd developed a skill at it. She'd gotten into the art through frustration, not wanting to wait on another agency to do a job she needed to get done quickly.

Calmly, confidently, Nita placed the skull on a table in the Frankfort Horizontal position, then pulled up a wheeled stool and started gluing small tissue markers directly onto the bone. The work went quickly because she'd done it before and knew what she was doing.

The tissue markers for race and age were predetermined. Without DNA, she had to guess at the dead man's race and the characteristics that went with it, but with the photographic superimposition going so well, she felt fine about making those assumptions.

Gender and age were easier to determine. The bones belonged to a male; the hip structure and pubic-bone placement and angle confirmed that. Nita had closely examined the xiphoid process, the cartilaginous extension of the lower sternum. By the time an adult human reached his late twenties, the xiphoid process typically fused to the sternum, reinforcing the structure. Based on the state of the xiphoid process in this body, along with other identifiers she had found in the bones, she had determined that the man had been in his late twenties when he died. According to Haskins's file, he'd been twenty-eight when he went missing.

Once she had the markers in place, she checked Haskins's records and found out he'd been brown eyed. She took out a pair of artificial eyes and mounted them in the orbital sockets.

The door opened, and the lab assistant returned carrying a paper bag.

He stopped and stared at the skull with the artificial eyes and the tissue markers sticking out all over it.

"Now that," he said, "creeps me out. It was one thing to bring a skull to you, but now it's starting to look like someone's head."

"It was." Nita pushed the stool back and reached for the bag the guy held.

He gave it to her and told her that her change was inside.

Nita barely had time to thank him before he left. She took out the coffee and the bagels, putting the small, disposable thermos to one side after pouring a cup. She took a vial of analgesics from her purse and popped a couple into her mouth, washing them down with coffee.

She studied the skull for a moment, contemplating what she was going to do. She tore one of the cinnamon bagels into pieces and ate it. Together, the pain relievers, coffee, and warm food slowly dialed down the headache rampaging between her temples.

When half the bagel was finished and she could deny the eagerness to go back to work no longer, Nita sipped the coffee again, then returned to the skull. She opened up blocks of modeling clay and began spreading it over the skull, following the guidelines established by the tissue markers as she started putting a face on the skull.

"Okay, George," Nita whispered, "come to me."

CRIME SCENE NCIS

NAVAL CRIMINAL INVESTIGATIVE SERVICE

17

SCENE  NCIS  CRIME SCENE

NAVAL CRIMINAL INVESTIGATIVE SERVICE

\>> INTERVIEW ROOM B
\>> CAMP LEJEUNE, NORTH CAROLINA
\>> 0931 HOURS

Remy followed Shel into the interview room. They quickly arranged themselves across the rectangular table from Bryce Ketchum.

As he took his seat, Remy felt uncomfortable. He knew the drill well. When he was younger, he'd been on Ketchum's side of the table in handcuffs too many times. He knew what it was like to feel scared and all alone, outnumbered and totally clueless as to what was going to happen to him.

Those memories stirred up the ghost of a fight-or-flight response within him. He squelched it and sat calmly in his chair, as though he had all day to do it and nothing better to do.

Ketchum looked at them with dead eyes. If he was worried or afraid, it didn't show. "I thought you guys forgot about me."

"No." Shel opened the thick folder in front of him, revealing the mug shots of the other times Ketchum had gotten arrested. "We just took time out for a good night's sleep and hit the IHOP for breakfast. How was your night?"

Ketchum cursed. "I slept in this stupid chair as much as I could. People kept coming in, said they were going to ask questions. But they never did."

"Probably got busy."

Ketchum cursed again.

Remy knew that detainees didn't have the same rights in military justice as they did in the civilian world. Ketchum's treatment wasn't unusual; as a former Marine, he should have known that.

Ignoring the invective, Shel switched on the recording unit, turning on audio as well as video feeds. He gave the date and identified himself, Remy, and Ketchum, then stated that they were there pursuant to an investigation of the events of the previous night.

"It was that girl, wasn't it?" Ketchum asked when Shel stopped. "That's what brought you there."

Shel sipped coffee from the Styrofoam cup. "Actually, there were several girls." He pushed a couple photographs of the Chinese women who had been at the site to the middle of the table.

Ketchum frowned. "Not those. The other one. The military brat."

"I don't know what you're talking about," Shel answered.

The official position the NCIS was taking at the moment was that Amanda Whitcomb had never been at the farmhouse. That would become an issue only if the military chose for it to become one. At this point, there was plenty of other probable cause to work the investigation on. As it turned out, two of the men supplying drugs to the camp's civilian population were among those arrested. Other investigations had opened up other avenues as well.

"So that's how it's going to be, huh?" Ketchum grunted. "You guys are just going to cover that up."

"Actually, if that were the case," Shel said in a flat voice, "I think that works out well for you. Contributing to the delinquency of a minor child wouldn't be much more to add to the charges lined up against you, but I guarantee you wouldn't win any sympathy from parents who heard your case."

Ketchum slumped back in his chair.

"So far," Shel went on, looking at the notes on a sheet of yellow legal paper in the file, "we've got you on several drug counts, enough weapons and ammunition to draw the interest of Homeland Security, and human trafficking."

"Then why aren't you charging me with that?"

"We will."

Ketchum cut his eyes to Remy. Despite the throbbing in his head, Remy returned the man's gaze full measure.

"Can I have a cigarette?" Ketchum asked.

"No."

"What about coffee?"

"This isn't a hotel."

Ketchum cursed some more. "All right. What do you want?"

Shel remained impassive. Over the last year, Remy had gotten to watch the big Marine work. Shel McHenry was ponderous, direct, and unforgiving. He took up a tack and stayed on course, plowing through every defense and argument a detainee offered. He reminded Remy a lot of the vice detective who had chased and threatened him during his adolescence.

"I don't want anything," Shel said. "I'm not the one in trouble here."

"Yet here you are. Across the table from me." Ketchum smiled, but Remy could tell it was forced.

"Not by my choice. My commanding officer wanted me here. So here I am. You know how it goes, Ketchum. You used to be a Marine."

"Till I found something better, yeah."

"From where I sit, you don't look like you're doing so good."

"That's because you don't have the view I have."

Remy stayed silent. He didn't have the patience for dealing with others that Shel did. Remy didn't like the lies and double-talk. He had the distinct feeling that Shel didn't care for them either, but he'd learned to be good at it. All Remy had to do was sit there and look threatening, a grim reminder that Ketchum was outnumbered and in hostile territory.

Ketchum leaned back confidently, but the pose was all show. Remy had grown up in New Orleans around bad men who'd acted like they had a lock on more than they could handle. It had always caught up to them.

Just like it caught up to you, chéri, he told himself.

Nonchalant, Ketchum waved a hand. "I've got money. Enough money to get out of this."

"You're a smart guy in some respects," Shel said in that Texas drawl.

Ketchum almost started to smile.

"But don't sell yourself a bill of goods that you wouldn't buy from anybody else. You ain't getting out of this scot-free."

Some of Ketchum's smile went away. "I can hire the best lawyers."

Shel shrugged. "Looking around, I don't see any of them here."

"Looking around, cowboy," Ketchum said with deadly earnestness, "I don't see any cell bars either."

"We'll get you some right up." Shel closed the folder, pushed back from the table, and stood, heading for the door.

Remy followed suit.

"There's something you want," Ketchum called out behind them. "Otherwise you wouldn't have talked to me this morning."

Shel opened the door and looked back. "Nope. Nothing comes to mind."

"What about that body you dug up last night?" Ketchum leaned forward, trying to look confident.

This time it was Remy who had to fake nonchalance, hiding his surprise. *So Ketchum did know the body was there.*

"What about it?" Shel asked.

"Do you know who it is?"

"We'll find out."

"He was a Marine."

Shel didn't say anything.

Remy was confused. Now that Ketchum had admitted knowledge of the body, why wouldn't Shel drill him about it? Remy had thought the whole reason they were talking to Ketchum in the first place was to try to get information about the dead man.

"His name was George Haskins," Ketchum said. "He was a sergeant. I served with him. Check around; there's probably paper on him. He went missing a few years back."

"Okay," Shel said, "if that's important, we'll get back to you." He stepped through the door.

Still confused, Remy followed Shel into the hallway. Shel didn't break stride until they reached the observation room.

"What's going on?" Remy asked when he closed the door behind him. "I thought that was what we were after."

Shel folded his arms across his broad chest. "Uh-uh. Ketchum's playing this card. Not us. Something's off."

"Because Ketchum's giving it up?"

"Yeah."

"Maybe he's hoping somebody'll cut him a break."

"Nope."

"What makes you so sure?"

"You ever play Texas Hold 'Em?"

"No." Remy had been a numbers runner in New Orleans before he'd started stealing cars and moving drugs. Gambling was a fool's dream. The money only flowed one way, and that was into the bookies' pockets. He didn't even like card games between friends.

"Working the pot is an art." Shel looked through the glass at Ketchum, who sat unmoving at the table. "It's how you add to it before the cards are dealt that's important. You don't build the pot when you've got a hot hand, you get a small take. You try to build too much too fast, everybody else knows you're loaded and wired." He nodded at Ketchum. "He just upped the ante when he should have been waiting on us to deal cards."

"By letting us know he knew Haskins was in the ground?"

"Yeah. He's left himself open to additional charges."

"It would have been in his best interest to claim he didn't know Haskins's body was buried on his land."

"Yep."

"So why did he volunteer the information?"

"That's the question, isn't it?"

>> NCIS HEADQUARTERS
>> CAMP LEJEUNE, NORTH CAROLINA
>> 1011 HOURS

In her work space, seated in front of the computer, Maggie stared at the photos of the crime scene where sixteen-year-old Chloe Ivers's body had been recovered. She'd been found by hunters plunging through the brush one night late in October seventeen years ago.

The photos were carefully organized on her desk, moving from the initial shots the CSIs had taken of the girl's body to the close-up work of the injuries she'd suffered.

The coroner's report stated that Chloe Ivers had died of strangulation. Bruises had laced her neck, her larynx had been crushed, and small red blossoms of broken blood vessels had bloomed in her eyes. That condition, known as petechiae, was always present in deaths caused by strangulation or suffocation.

The girl's right leg was broken in three places, her left arm in two. Her skull had been fractured, and she'd suffered a concussion. Lacerations, washed out from the few hours she'd been in the river, showed stark and bloodless on her face. Her left cheekbone had been crushed.

The pictures were horrible. Chloe Ivers had lain there like a mannequin, her pajamas half off. She was exposed and vulnerable, and the photographer hadn't had a choice about taking the pictures any other way.

There was no modesty in death. Maggie knew that from long association with homicide. Even accidental deaths left victims revealed in ways they'd never have accepted in life.

"Hey."

Looking up, Maggie found Estrella standing there. "Hey," she replied.

"You've been quiet for a while," Estrella said. "I thought maybe I'd come over and check on you."

"I'm good." Maggie leaned back in the chair and arched her back. Ergonomic or not, any chair she had to sit in for hours at a time eventually fatigued her.

"Find anything?"

"The NCIS agents who investigated Chloe Ivers's death think she was abducted from her home and killed near New River."

"Have you found anything that says differently?"

"No."

"But you don't think she was killed there."

Maggie sipped her coffee. "I don't know what to think. There was no sign of a struggle in the area. The body—" she resisted the impulse to call the dead girl by name—"was found by hunters."

"Who were probably tanked up on tall boys and moonshine before they even hit the woods."

Maggie nodded. Hunting season brought about accidental shootings involving alcohol and firearms nearly every year. NCIS became involved only when one of the parties was military personnel from the camp. Last deer-hunting season a jealous husband had chosen to "accidentally" kill his wife's current boyfriend. Maggie had helped work that one.

"The girl could have been killed farther upriver," Estrella said.

Maggie didn't take offense. They often played devil's advocate for each other. "I know."

"The body could have drifted a long way before getting hung up in the water."

"I know."

"Did the CSIs search upriver?"

"Yes." Maggie had been through most of the reports, though there were several she'd merely skimmed over, getting a sense of the pertinent information before getting more focused on the details.

"They didn't find anything?"

"No."

Estrella pulled a chair from Shel's desk in the adjoining work space. She sat nearby. "So what has you bothered?"

"The murder." Murder was hard. It was always hard. She'd known that when she entered college and decided to take all the psychology classes that would enable her to become a profiler. She'd intended from the beginning to get into the Federal Bureau of Investigation. Anything that would have taken her away from her father and Boston.

Instead, getting accepted by the FBI hadn't proven as simple as she'd hoped. In the end, she'd applied for the Boston PD, then gotten accepted by one of the outlying towns. She hadn't been able to escape her father's influence.

Not until Director Larkin had offered her the NCIS job at Camp Lejeune. Maggie had never been to North Carolina. And her acceptance of the position had enraged her father, though he'd never lost his composure.

"You don't like the fact that the murder doesn't fit the other homicides committed by Lamont."

"No, I don't."

CRIME SCENE

NCIS
NAVAL CRIMINAL INVESTIGATIVE SERVICE

18

SCENE ✪ NCIS ✪ CRIME SCENE

NAVAL CRIMINAL INVESTIGATIVE SERVICE

>> INTERVIEW ROOM B OBSERVATION
>> CAMP LEJEUNE, NORTH CAROLINA
>> 1024 HOURS

Shel stood watching Bryce Ketchum through the one-way glass. Several minutes had ticked by in silence. Remy stood at Shel's side, sipping coffee and not saying a word.

Ketchum had finally given up waiting and had slumped forward over the table, folding his arms under his head, and—to Shel's best guess—he was now truly asleep.

"If you were Ketchum," Shel said finally, "why would you tell me that you knew George Haskins's body was buried on your property?"

"Because of your eyes," Remy said. "Man, you got pretty blue eyes. Don't know if anyone has ever told you that before."

Shel turned to the SEAL and grimaced. "I'm trying to be serious here."

"Me too."

"Terrific."

"Look," Remy said, "you and I both know the answer to that question. The only reason Ketchum told you that bit about Haskins was to pull your teeth on the upcoming murder accusation. He took that away from you, let you know you didn't have it as a hole card anymore."

"He was locked up when Haskins disappeared."

"Yeah, but it doesn't mean that Haskins went into the ground while Ketchum was away. Ketchum could still have put him there."

"From what Maggie's turned up in Haskins's personal files, there was no reason for him to disappear. He had a wife." Shel checked his notes. "Cindy. And a couple of kids. According to the investigators, she didn't know anything about Haskins's disappearance."

"Haskins didn't choose to disappear," Remy said. "Someone disappeared him. The only hope we have is that Ketchum might know who put Haskins in the ground."

"Even if he does, that's not going to help him. He's still facing charges on everything else."

"But Ketchum *thinks* it's going to help him. Otherwise he wouldn't say anything."

Shel rubbed a big hand over his jaw. "I don't see how it can."

"That's because we don't know everything Ketchum does. Maybe he thinks if he helps solve the murder of a Marine it might buy him some points here. Or maybe he thinks Haskins's death can deflect some of the heat coming down on him. There's only one way we're going to find that out: we're going to have to ask him."

Shel wasn't happy with the turn of events. He'd hoped that telling Ketchum they'd found Haskins's body on his premises might actually undermine the man's confidence. Instead Ketchum had brought up the body first. Remy was right—they had to find out what else Ketchum knew. He might not like it, but he accepted it.

He pulled out his cell phone and dialed Nita Tomlinson. She answered on the third ring.

"Hey Doc, it's Shel."

"I'm kind of busy rebuilding Haskins's face."

"Won't take but a second. Had a wrinkle come up in my interview with Ketchum. I need your help."

"What do you need?"

"Your best guess. Was that George Haskins we turned up last night?"

Nita hesitated. Shel knew that the medical examiner hated guessing. She didn't like being wrong when she said something.

"This is just me and you and Remy, Doc," Shel said. "I'm about to go interview Ketchum again. I've already been blindsided once this morning. I don't want it to happen again."

"My best guess—and that's all it is at this point—is yes, this is Haskins."

"Okay. Thanks, Doc." Shel closed his phone.

"She said yes?"

"She said yes."

Remy stared silently at Ketchum for a short time. "If Ketchum knew Haskins's body was on his property, he could have moved it when he got out. Disposed of the evidence."

"I thought of that."

"He left it there on purpose."

Shel nodded. "Because he thought, at one point or another, he could use it."

"Gonna be fascinating to see how he thinks he can use it."

"Well, let's go find out." Shel led the way out of the room.

>> NCIS HEADQUARTERS
>> CAMP LEJEUNE, NORTH CAROLINA
>> 1028 HOURS

"You told me Lamont was a disorganized killer. So there shouldn't have to be a pattern to his killings, should there?"

In answer to Estrella's question, Maggie touched the keyboard, causing the monitor to flare to life. She'd been making notes, comparing Chloe Ivers's death to the murders Isaac Allen Lamont had been tried for and found guilty of committing.

"How much do you know about Lamont?"

Estrella shook her head. "I've been working on pulling Haskins's records, stories about his disappearance and Chloe Ivers's murder. In addition to helping organize the physical evidence against Bryce Ketchum and his gang in last night's raid. Once I found out there was a lot of information on Lamont, I shelved that and figured you'd tell me if you needed anything."

"Lamont was a disorganized killer." Maggie flipped through the pictures as she spoke. Several showed Lamont in street dress. Maggie thought he looked a little like a cartoon figure because he was overweight and had a round face. "But he killed essentially the same way."

"I thought disorganized killers didn't take weapons with them."

"They don't. Lamont worked on his father's rabbit farm from the time he was eight years old till he was a teenager. Then he killed his first victim, a girl he knew from school, and he caught the first train out of town. He killed the girl by snapping her neck. Grabbing hold of her head and twisting violently till the skull snapped free of the spine."

"And the other eighteen girls were killed the same way?"

"Yes. That's what tied the cases together."

"But not Chloe Ivers."

"Right." Maggie passed over a copy of the coroner's report. "Chloe Ivers's neck wasn't snapped. She was beaten before she was killed. She had multiple breaks in her arm and leg. Her skull was fractured."

"None of Lamont's other victims showed similar injuries?"

"Two of them had experienced broken wrists and ankles. They'd tried to get away. But the damage they'd suffered was understandable in light of their actions."

"Chloe Ivers was also strangled."

"Yes. Not a quick death like he gave the others. And furthermore, Chloe Ivers wasn't raped. All the other victims were."

"Why weren't more of the victims injured? It seems like they would have fought back if they were being raped."

"Lamont is bigger than Shel," Maggie said. "Most of his victims never had a chance. And some of them weren't alive at the time of the rapes."

Maggie felt a familiar unpleasant sensation in her gut at the thought of that, and she was glad. Some investigators grew numb to the horrors they witnessed as part of their job. She hoped she never did. If she ever got to that point, to where such violent actions became just another part of her job, she'd promised herself that she'd quit.

"Maybe the hunters scared Lamont away," Estrella suggested.

"That means that the hunters would have found Chloe Ivers at the crime scene."

"They could have scared Lamont away, and her body could have floated downriver."

"Maybe. But if Lamont had believed he had a chance of remaining hidden, he would have done that. Once the hunters cleared the area without finding Chloe Ivers, he would have returned and finished what he'd started."

Estrella frowned. "I don't even like thinking about that."

"Neither do I. But it's a fact. Also, Lamont left DNA evidence behind at all his other kills."

"So when the police caught him, they had him solid on the other homicides."

"Yes. And Lamont confessed to them when he was asked about the victims. He had trophies he kept from all of them. Key chains. Jewelry. Drivers' licenses. All nineteen."

"But nothing from Chloe Ivers."

Maggie shook her head. "Not one single thing."

"What about her charm bracelet? Was it at the scene?"

"No."

"Maybe it was lost in the river."

"Except for the one charm that was caught in Sergeant Haskins's pants cuff."

"Except for that." Estrella thought for a moment. "Did Lamont admit to killing Chloe Ivers?"

"Throughout the investigation of her death, Lamont maintained his innocence. Her murder wasn't the only one where he was a prime suspect. When a serial killer gets taken down, police departments have a tendency to cull their open/unsolved cases and see if they can close any of them out. For example, Henry Lee Lucas closed out a lot of cases for investigators, especially since he traveled so widely. But they had to go back and reopen several of them because Lucas made false claims. They found that out when what he said didn't add up with the case facts."

"Without DNA evidence to point to Lamont, why did the NCIS investigators think Lamont killed Chloe Ivers?"

"Lamont had killed a woman in Jacksonville two weeks prior to Chloe Ivers's murder."

"He admitted to that one?"

"Yes, and the MO matched the other killings Lamont did."

"So all they had linking Lamont to Chloe Ivers was circumstantial evidence?"

"There was also a witness who claimed she saw Lamont near the Swanson household."

"The stepfather's house. The congressman."

"He wasn't a congressman then."

"Who was the witness?"

Maggie consulted her notes. "A woman named Frieda Hamilton."

"A neighbor?"

"She worked for Swanson as a maid."

"Did anyone talk to her?"

"Yes."

"So what are you thinking?" Estrella asked.

"That I want Will to get Director Larkin to clear me for a visit to speak to Lamont."

Estrella was quiet for a moment. "You still want to dig up that girl's murder again?"

"No, that's not what I want to do."

"Because if you do—" Estrella went on as if she hadn't heard Maggie—"you need to think about all the pain you're going to cause that family. They've buried their dead, and for the last seventeen years, they've moved on."

"Something like this can't be easy to move on from." Maggie watched Estrella curiously. She remembered their conversation in the RV at the crime scene the previous night. *This isn't just the devil's advocate speaking here.* Somehow, she knew, she'd touched a nerve.

"It's *not* easy to move on from. That's why you should let them do it. Whatever few steps they've managed to take from all of this, they're entitled to them. All it would take is one question to bring that all back down on them. They don't need that."

"I know."

"Well, keep knowing that."

"If there was a chance to know who killed Chloe Ivers, don't you think they'd want to know?"

"That's not going to bring her back, is it?" Without another word, Estrella got up and left.

Maggie watched Estrella leave, not knowing what she'd said or what she should say.

19

SCENE  NCIS  CRIME SCEN

NAVAL CRIMINAL INVESTIGATIVE SERVICE

>> INTERVIEW ROOM B
>> CAMP LEJEUNE, NORTH CAROLINA
>> 1036 HOURS

Bryce Ketchum looked up as Shel reentered the room. Without a word, Shel dropped George Haskins's photo from his field-service record and sat at the table. Remy sat on his right.

"The dead guy we dug up was USMC Gunnery Sergeant George Haskins," Shel announced. "Our medical examiner just confirmed that." That was a lie, technically, but legally an investigating officer didn't have to tell the truth. Confessions were obtained through lies and trickery all the time. As long as the lies and trickery were legal, the interrogation would hold up in court.

"Wow," Ketchum said. "You guys are regular Dick Tracys."

Shel deliberately didn't ask Ketchum if he had killed Haskins. Ketchum had to be waiting for that.

"We're going to charge you regarding Haskins's death," Shel said.

Some of the confidence left Ketchum then. "What?"

"You knew that his body was on your land."

"I didn't kill him."

"Doesn't matter. You didn't report the murder."

"Wait a minute! I don't have to report the murder. There's no law anywhere that says I have to report any crime."

That was true. Witnesses came forth of their own volition. Most people believed they had a legal responsibility to come forward, but there was no law regarding that. Even someone who saw a homicide take place in front of them didn't have to come forward. Or even discuss it.

"Since you didn't report the murder," Shel said, "we know you were involved."

"You can't *prove* that I was involved." Ketchum tried to stand.

Shel reached across the table and shoved the man back into his chair.

Ketchum swore violently. "I only knew that Haskins had been buried somewhere on the property. Until you found him last night, I didn't even know where."

"Quiet," Shel advised. "I have to advise you of your rights. You have the right to remain silent—"

"No!" Ketchum roared. "You can't do this."

Shel kept on, finishing the list of rights. No matter what, they were arresting Ketchum anyway.

When Shel finished, Ketchum suddenly ceased cursing and sat quietly. "Are you all finished?" he asked.

Shel didn't say anything.

"I sure hope you are," Ketchum went on. "Because we're done here. I want an attorney." He looked up at the walls, talking directly into the hidden camera. "Do you hear me? I want an attorney. Now!"

Puzzled, Shel picked up Haskins's picture and shoved it back into the folder. Ketchum was right: they were done. At least until Ketchum's attorney arrived and he had a chance to talk to him. Once a person of interest became a suspect and had been apprised of his rights, the law took over.

And the law said that Bryce Ketchum was entitled to an attorney.

Shel left the interview room and told the MPs standing post to take Ketchum to the phone and then to lockup. He and Remy watched as Ketchum was led away.

"He thinks he's won," Remy said.

"I know," Shel said, and that bothered him. A lot. Something was going on, and they hadn't figured out what it was yet.

>> NEW RIVER
>> EAST OF JACKSONVILLE, NORTH CAROLINA
>> 1227 HOURS

"Hang on!" Steven yelled. "I'm going to let her have her head!"

Seated in the bow of the boat beside Wren, Will couldn't help grinning. Every time he was out on the water something inside him came alive. He didn't know if the feeling was inspired by something primitive within him or if it came from all the years he'd spent out on the open water with his own father, by himself, and when he'd been on one ship or another while in the Navy.

Maybe it was something in the elements, just the knowledge that the sea could crush him in an eye blink.

Or maybe it was the feeling of mastering something that was never meant to be tamed.

As promised, Steven brought the Laser 2000 around, cutting smartly through the water, and swung the boom to where it was racing before the wind. The canvas bellied tautly, and the boat reacted like a thoroughbred, leaping forward and crashing through the next swell.

Wren screamed in delight, as fearless in the boat as her brother. She hung on tightly, hugged by her bright orange life jacket.

The Laser felt almost weightless as it was driven before the wind. Steven minded the lines controlling the sails and the rudder. The boat could be piloted by a single person or crewed. Will had taught Steven to do it all.

Will rode out the wild ride, studying his son's face. Steven hadn't looked this alive and joyous since . . . well, since the last time they'd been out on the boat.

We've got to go sailing more often, Will thought.

Over the last few months, there'd been precious few visits from his children, and most of them had occurred during bad weather or when Will's caseload had been nearly impossible.

"Faster, Steven!" Wren yelled. "Go *faster!*"

Without warning, a powerboat zipped past, filled with teenagers and dragging two others behind it in a tube. Wake rolled off the powerboat toward the Laser.

According to the rules—and to common sense—the powerboat should have steered wide of the sailboat. Choppy wake could overturn any craft and often caused accidents among inexperienced sailors. Evidently someone aboard the powerboat hadn't been paying attention.

Or maybe they simply hadn't cared.

Either way, the Laser was in trouble.

"Hold on!" Will told Wren as he stood.

"Dad!" Steven yelled.

"I see it. Do what you can, Steven."

With the Laser running flat out, she was vulnerable. A powerboat could have cut or reversed the engines to reduce speed or even reset the trim—the planes that shoved out from some craft like stuffy airplane wings. The small sailboat had no such measures to prevent overturning.

The Laser came equipped with a removable daggerboard that shoved through the bottom of the hull in a watertight seal. Shaped like a shark's fin, the daggerboard was designed to help stabilize the boat in rough water. Unfortunately, the daggerboard ceased helping if the boat tilted drastically. With twenty feet of mast and canvas above it, the boat could overturn in rough water.

Taking long strides, Will went forward on the starboard side, feeling the boat skate dangerously upward. *She's coming free of the water. No way we're going to stay connected.*

The wind was shoving them forward, leaving no time to bring the boat under control across the wake and no way to drop the sail and manage enough control to handle the chop; they had to go through it.

Will grabbed the rigging and stood out on the prow. He pressed himself against the hull and gripped the lines as the boat heeled hard to port. He leaned backward as the boat came over, till he was standing on the boat's side, no longer in the boat at all.

"Starboard!" Will yelled, realizing that his weight wasn't going to be enough to keep the Laser upright.

Immediately Steven erupted from his seated position, clambered out on the gunwale, and held on as he, too, stood on the boat's side. Even Wren reacted, throwing herself to the starboard and holding on.

Even then Will thought they were going to lose the boat. He wasn't worried about drowning. The life vests would prevent that. The threat was the bitter cold of the water. Hypothermia would be one problem. And there was the chance that another passing boat might hit them while they were in the water. The Laser probably wouldn't sink, but recovering it would be impossible without help. The shore was too far away to reach while swimming with a capsized boat in tow.

Will pulled and strained, watching with pride as Steven did the same. Their backs were only inches above the water. The rope bit into Will's hand. The cold air slammed into him, followed by spray from the waves crashing into the boat's hull. They hung, tipped onto the port side, zipping through the water, airborne for just a moment before slamming down again.

Then the boat tilted reluctantly, coming back down onto the water.

"Back," Will yelled, pulling himself up hand over hand.

Steven did the same, moving immediately in position to handle the sails and the rudder. His face was tight, but he wasn't afraid. If anything, Will saw fierce excitement in his son's eyes. The water brought out Steven's competitive nature.

You are way *too much like your father,* Will thought, but along with the trepidation, there was some pride, too.

Things were precarious for another minute or so. Will remained on the prow, using the lines to throw his weight one way or the other while Steven kept the boat under control with a skilled and steady hand. Finally, they were out of the wake.

Will scanned the river but saw no sign of the offending powerboat.

"Wow," Steven exclaimed. His face was flushed with the cold wind and the adrenaline pumping through him. "That was intense."

"Yeah," Wren said. "Let's do it again."

Will shook his head. "You guys are insane."

"Maybe so," Steven said. "Mom says it's your fault."

Will grinned. "All right. I'll accept that. But it's time to head back."

Steven and Wren both protested.

"Can't be helped," Will said. "You knew we could only be out here for a while. That was the agreement."

Reluctantly they gave in.

Will rejoined them in the boat. He dropped a hand on Steven's shoulder. "That was some really good sailing, skipper."

Steven smiled at him, making the adjustments to the sail and tacking into the wind so they could sail back into Jacksonville. "It was, wasn't it?"

"If you hadn't been really good, we'd have lost her," Will said. "A lot of seasoned guys would have lost a boat in that."

"Thanks."

Will sat in the bow, throwing his arm around Wren when she complained of being cold. He offered to get her another Windbreaker, but she said she only wanted him to hold her. He hugged his daughter and watched his son sail the boat, basking in the pride that was a father's due.

Steven was going to grow up, and—God willing—he was going to be a fine man. Will didn't know what kind of man yet, where Steven's interests might take him, but he knew that voyage—like this one—would be interesting.

But even as he sat there with those thoughts, Will couldn't help thinking about Chloe Ivers and how her parents had never gotten to watch her grow up and to see the kind of woman she was going to be.

⊛ ⊛ ⊛

>> NCIS HEADQUARTERS
>> CAMP LEJEUNE, NORTH CAROLINA
>> 1453 HOURS

Maggie answered the ringing phone on her desk. "Naval Criminal Investigative Service. Special Agent Foley speaking."

"Special Agent Foley, this is Corporal Dawes from the provost marshal's office."

That caught Maggie's attention immediately. One of the primary jobs of the provost marshal's office was camp security.

"What can I do for you, Corporal?"

"I've got a civilian here. A Mr. Thomas Wardell. He says he's an attorney and is going to represent one of the men you've arrested."

After last night, several men were being held that the NCIS had incarcerated. More interesting, though, was the fact that Maggie had heard of Thomas Wardell. He was one of the highest-paid attorneys in North Carolina.

"Did Mr. Wardell mention which man he was representing?"

"No, ma'am. Do you want me to ask?"

Maggie considered that, then rejected it. "There's no need, Corporal. I'll see Mr. Wardell. Have someone bring him here. I want to be notified when he arrives."

"Yes, ma'am."

Leaning back in her chair, Maggie thought quickly. None of the men arrested last night were in the building. All of them were being detained in lockup.

She thought about calling Will, then decided against it. Will hadn't slept at all, and he'd planned on taking his kids out in his boat.

You can handle this, Maggie told herself. In fact, when it came to handling high-powered attorneys with finesse, she'd be better than Will Coburn.

Especially in light of the fact that high-powered attorneys didn't generally have their guards up when they met women.

Reaching under her desk, Maggie grabbed her purse. Then she made a beeline for the nearest bathroom. Her makeup needed freshening if she was going to meet Wardell. It was time to armor up.

20

SCENE  NCIS  CRIME SCEN

NAVAL CRIMINAL INVESTIGATIVE SERVICE

>> FISHERMAN'S WHARF RESTAURANT
>> JACKSONVILLE, NORTH CAROLINA
>> 1518 HOURS

Although he was still damp from the river, Will was no longer dripping. He sat at a back table in the restaurant with Steven and Wren. All of them worked on the meals they'd ordered.

Will had reached the point at which he knew he was going to have to give up and take the rest home. The food was always good at the restaurant, but today it seemed even better than ever. Will didn't know if that was because he hadn't slept or because he'd had such a good time with the kids.

"Can we have dessert?" Wren asked.

"Can you eat dessert?" Will asked.

"Of course. There's always room for dessert." Wren smiled, wrinkling her nose.

"What do you want?"

"Cheesecake. With cherries on top."

Will looked at Steven.

"Key lime pie," his son said.

The waitress returned in short order, and Will gave her the requests. Then Wren and Steven started talking again, looking forward to the next day.

Sitting there, listening to his children, amazed at how happy they were—even Steven, who had been so hard to get along with last night—Will realized how much he'd missed with his family when he'd been out to sea. Months-long tours left a lot of gaps in family life. Missed birthdays. Missed events. Missed crises. He couldn't help thinking that if he'd realized that earlier, maybe he wouldn't have lost his marriage.

You can't think like that, he told himself. *Barbara left for her own reasons. If you hadn't had a career with the Navy, you'd have been working somewhere else and maybe been just as gone.*

That possibility made him wonder about Nita Tomlinson and the problems she currently faced. He didn't know if there was anything he could do, but he knew he had to look into it. Nita was good at what she did as a medical examiner, but she also had responsibilities as a wife and mother. She didn't need to self-destruct at any of those things.

His cell phone rang as the waitress brought Steven's and Wren's desserts.

"Hello."

"Sorry to bother you, Commander," Director Larkin said. "I hadn't intended to. I know you're with your family."

Warning bells went off inside Will's head. "It's no problem."

"We've got a situation that's come up."

Will waited.

"Something leaked concerning the action last night. The media found out that Chloe Ivers's charm was found on Haskins's corpse. They're airing the story already, along with backstories on her murder, Isaac Allan Lamont, and Congressman Ben Swanson."

Will leaned back in his chair and gazed through the windows at New River. The media involvement was complicating the case more than he liked.

"Naturally," Larkin went on, "Commander Ivers is upset."

"She has every right to be upset," Will commented. "Do you want me to try to figure out where the leak came from?"

"That would be a waste of effort. There were dozens of people on scene last night. You can't stop a military grapevine."

Will knew that, but he felt the need to protect his people. "Estrella and Maggie were the ones who identified the charm. But they wouldn't release that information."

"I don't think they would either, but there were plenty of other people involved. It could even have been someone on-site here who handled the communications relay. I'm not going to try to fix that problem. The media already know about the charm. There's no taking that back."

"Yes, sir."

"The problem is that Commander Ivers is on her way here."

That surprised Will. "I thought she was assigned to San Diego."

"She is. She got hardship leave, pulled rank, got aboard a military flight, and headed here. She'll be arriving at the camp at 1800 hours."

Will automatically checked his watch. That was only two and a half hours away. "She moves fast."

"From what I gathered about her, that's how she operates. I need you here when she arrives, Will."

"I don't know what to say to her."

"Neither do I."

"Have you talked to her?"

"Briefly. She's not really communicative at this point. She just called to set up an appointment. I tried to talk to her longer on the phone, hoping to head her off and convince her to stay there while we looked into this thing, but she politely—and firmly—brushed me off."

"Did she say why she's coming?"

"Seventeen years ago, her daughter was brutally murdered. Her murderer was never found. Not officially, anyway, and I understood from the quick response Commander Ivers gave that she's never been a proponent of the Isaac Allen Lamont theory."

"I'll be there," Will promised, then folded his phone and put it away.

"When are you going to be there?" Steven asked. The lightheartedness had dropped from his expression, replaced by suspicion.

"This evening." Will knew there was no way to hide it, and he knew neither of his kids was going to be happy about the change in plans.

"What about cooking out tonight?" Wren asked.

"We'll still cook out."

"Sure we will," Steven said. His voice sounded sarcastic and sour. All the excitement and carefree attitude had drained from him. "Unless the job gets in the way."

That was his mother speaking. Will recognized that. He had to curb the impulse to respond in kind, forcing himself to remember that confrontation remained steadfastly unwinnable. Barbara had used it when she was hurt and angry, and he'd gotten hurt and angry in return. Nothing had ever truly been resolved.

Instead he remained silent and waited for the check. He couldn't justify what he was doing to Steven, and it didn't make any sense to even try.

>> NCIS HEADQUARTERS
>> CAMP LEJEUNE, NORTH CAROLINA
>> 1521 HOURS

Thomas Wardell was in his early sixties, a thin rapier of a man who evidently took care of himself. His white hair was carefully groomed, as was his thin mustache. The suit, Maggie noted, was Italian, but the shoes were Spanish. The teakwood briefcase on the ground beside him was slim and elegant.

In addition to applying fresh makeup, Maggie had retreated to her locker, where she kept changes of clothing. She'd discarded her khaki slacks and green blouse for a business suit intended for running stealth missions through military top-brass gatherings that included politicians and black ties.

Men could throw on a suit and be presentable nearly anywhere. The same wasn't true of women, and men just didn't get that. When a woman dressed for a meeting like this, it was like getting dressed to do battle. All too often, confrontation spun out of power and privilege, and Maggie knew she couldn't afford to start out behind in the game. It took everything she had, beginning with first impressions, just to fight back to level ground.

The business suit wasn't standard NCIS wear, but it was designed to impress people like Wardell. Estrella, upon seeing Maggie pass by, had looked on in shock. She hadn't often seen Maggie cycle through the political movers and shakers. The business suit was even cut to conceal her two holstered weapons.

The attorney stood looking across the work spaces where NCIS agents worked cases on the computers and phones.

"Mr. Wardell," Maggie called.

Wardell turned to regard her. Then he took in her appearance and his eyebrows rose in surprise. "Special Agent Foley?" He stood straighter and squared his shoulders, battening down his own hatches, she realized.

"Yes." Maggie offered her hand. The handshake was a woman's prerogative. Men like Wardell knew that. If she'd refrained, he'd have taken it as a sign of weakness, a hesitation about making physical contact. By offering the handshake, she sent a silent message that she felt in control of herself and the situation.

Wardell took her hand briefly then released it. His attention was locked on Maggie, going from head to toe and back again. "Have we met?"

"No. You'd have remembered." That bit of confidence was also designed to get his attention.

A smile flirted with the attorney's lips but never quite surfaced. "Yes," he agreed. "I suppose I would have."

Maggie pointed to the back of the room. "I arranged for us to have an office. There's more privacy."

"Of course." Wardell scooped up his briefcase and followed her to one of the offices.

Heads of the other agents followed their progress. Estrella sat frozen at her desk.

Inside the room, Maggie pointed to the chairs at the conference table. "Sit wherever you like."

Wardell immediately moved to the head of the table. He placed the briefcase on the table before him, then opened it. "Can I get a cup of coffee?"

"There's a carafe in the corner." Maggie made no move to get the coffee. He'd asked because he'd expected her to get it. If he'd been a guest, she would have. But Wardell was here in an adversarial mode, and both of them knew it.

Wardell made no move toward the coffee either. "Perhaps later." He pulled out a leather-bound legal pad.

"I don't mean to be abrupt, Mr. Wardell," Maggie said, "but is this going to take long?"

That stopped him for just a moment. "Is this not a convenient time?"

"No." Maggie didn't flinch from the answer. "Usually when I see people, it's by appointment. You didn't have one."

"I appreciate your seeing me without one. I hope I haven't inconvenienced you."

"I have a job to do. There are only so many hours in the day. Since you specialize in defense work and told the security officer you were here to meet with a client, I can only presume that we're going to be on opposite sides of the table."

Wardell nodded. "Perhaps you'd like to sit."

"I'm not going to be here that long," Maggie assured him.

Wardell glanced at her again and seemed confused. "We're not going to be too long, I shouldn't think."

"Maybe it would help if you told me why you were here."

"Special Agent *Foley*," Wardell mused thoughtfully, brow wrinkling in thought. "Do I detect a Bostonian accent?"

"You do." Maggie had learned how to get rid of most of that accent, but sometimes—like now—she allowed it to sound faintly in her words.

Wardell's eyebrows rose appreciatively. "Foley as in Harrison Talbot Foley III?"

The fact that the attorney had so quickly made the connection proved to Maggie that Wardell traveled in the highest social circles. The same ones her father traveled in.

"That's right." Maggie nodded.

"I'd heard Harrison had a daughter in the military."

Maggie had no doubt that Wardell knew how incensed her father was over the situation as well.

Wardell grinned. "I've met your father on a number of occasions. He's a good man."

When he wants to be, Maggie thought. *When there's not profit or vengeance or a threat in the mix*. "I'll tell him you said so." She glanced at her watch meaningfully.

"I'm here to see a client," Wardell went on.

"You didn't have to come through this office to do that." The information would have gotten back to the team anyway.

"I thought perhaps I could speak to someone at NCIS regarding the arrests."

"You'll have to go through the proper channels to get information, Mr. Wardell. I would have thought you'd know that."

Wardell smiled. "Since I was going to be involved, I thought maybe an introduction was in order. And maybe we could agree to get around some of the protocol."

Maggie knew what Wardell actually hoped to do was intimidate them. "Actually, it's good to know you're involved in this," she told him.

"Oh, really?" Wardell grinned in amusement.

"Really. If you hadn't shown up, willing to get involved, we might not have looked at the situation quite as deeply. Now we'll know we need to pay extra attention to our investigation."

Wardell's smile faded.

"As far as getting around protocol goes, Commander Coburn is a stickler for it. We prepare criminal cases. Everything depends on how we follow rules and procedures."

"I see." Wardell's lips compressed, as though he'd just bitten into a lemon.

"So if there isn't anything else . . . ?" Maggie arched a brow.

More contrite now, but visibly seething all the same, Wardell closed his briefcase and stood. "No, Miss Foley—"

"Special Agent Foley, Mr. Wardell. You'll need to know correct titles for your reports and for any other times you might feel the need to talk to anyone in this office."

Wardell nodded. "I think we understand each other."

"We do," Maggie agreed. She didn't offer her hand this time.

⊛ ⊛ ⊛

>> 1540 HOURS

Seated at her desk, Estrella watched Maggie escort the man to the doors, turning him over to the Marine MP responsible for shadowing him while he visited the camp.

Maggie stood at the door for a moment, obviously locked in thought. Estrella knew the signs. When she was finished thinking, Maggie walked over to Estrella.

"He looks kind of old for you," Estrella commented.

"That was Thomas Wardell," Maggie said, not responding to the dig. "*Attorney* Thomas Wardell of Wardell, Hackmore, Carter, and Dennison. There's more going on here than we thought."

"What makes you say that?" Estrella was interested. Maggie Foley didn't get flustered easily, and she definitely looked a little flustered now.

"Do you know who Wardell is?"

"I could google him."

"He's a trial attorney."

"Somebody called a lawyer. Once we started the official arrests, we knew that was going to happen."

"Wardell isn't just any trial attorney," Maggie said. "He's one of the big guns. I'm surprised he was here by himself. Usually when he moves a small army moves with him. Unless he was just trying to look harmless."

"He's not harmless?"

"Wardell is expensive," Maggie explained.

"How expensive?"

"Movie stars, the Fortune 500 club, and families with old money would know Wardell. Probably on a first-name basis. And probably through a retainer."

Estrella understood then. "He's one of the guys your dad would play golf with, you mean."

Maggie's nostrils flared just a little.

"Sorry," Estrella said. "Didn't know that was a sensitive subject." Actually she did know. Maggie hadn't made any secret of her bloodline, but she didn't volunteer that information either.

Estrella knew enough about Harrison Talbot Foley III to know that Maggie's dad was definitely old money, a corporate pirate and a political powerhouse. Most of the time it was hard to imagine Maggie growing up in a household like that. Maggie didn't act affluent, and she didn't live affluently.

"It's not a sensitive subject," Maggie said, but the strain in her voice indicated it was.

"So we have a high-caliber attorney showing up to represent one of the gang members we brought in last night," Estrella said. "Do we know who?"

"Wardell told the MP escorting him to take him to Bryce Ketchum."

"Can Ketchum afford Wardell?"

"Maybe. We did find a lot of cash at the farmhouse. But the real question is why Wardell would represent Ketchum."

"For the money?"

Maggie shook her head. "It's not about money for someone like Wardell."

"He turns down money? Isn't that against the lawyer's code or something?"

"Wardell probably has more money than he can ever spend. His representation of Ketchum isn't about money."

"It's always about money," Estrella said. "Money or sex. At least where crime is involved. Unless Wardell just loves his job or has a driving need to see justice done."

"Hardly."

"Didn't think so."

"Do you have Bryce Ketchum's court records?"

Estrella nodded. "Do you want to know if Wardell has ever represented Ketchum before?"

"Wardell or anyone from his office, yes."

Turning her attention to her computer, Estrella accessed the files.

Behind her, Maggie picked up a framed picture of Nicky. "New picture?"

"Yes."

The picture showed Nicky wearing a red jersey and standing on fake grass with his arms crossed and one foot on a soccer ball.

"He's playing soccer now?" Maggie asked.

"His first game was last weekend," Estrella said.

"I would have thought it was too cold."

"Not for soccer, they tell me. I wore a jacket but Nicky seemed fine. The coach had the pictures taken early. He said it was easier to do it that way because the season often got hectic."

Maggie returned the picture to the desk. "He's getting big."

"I know." *And looking more like his father every day.* Estrella concentrated on the files she'd opened, scanning the information. She read through it quickly.

Maggie leaned in over her shoulder.

"I see plenty of other lawyers," Estrella said, "but no Wardell." She ran a quick page search to make certain. The name wasn't on the page. "Ketchum shows a preference for a law firm called James and Conagher based out of Wilmington."

"Can you get the phone records of the detention center?"

"Of course." Estrella called them up.

"See if Wardell's law firm is listed there."

Estrella checked. "Not Wardell. James and Conagher were called this morning."

"Shortly after Shel's interview with Ketchum."

Checking the time frame she'd been building regarding the team's action, Estrella nodded. "Think James and Conagher handed the case off to Wardell?"

"No."

Estrella thought about that. "So you think Ketchum had his attorneys call Wardell?"

"Unless Wardell is using some kind of psychic hotline, there's no way he would have known Ketchum asked for representation."

"But we still don't know why Ketchum would ask for Wardell or why Wardell would accept?"

"No." A troubled look tightened Maggie's face. "Can you get an information packet started regarding Thomas Wardell?"

"Just him? Or the law firm too?"

"Both."

Estrella made a note on a yellow Post-it and stuck it to her monitor. "You'll have it as soon as I can put it together."

S

SERVICE

CRIME SCENE

NCIS

NAVAL CRIMINAL INVESTIGATIVE SERVICE

21

SCENE  NCIS  CRIME SCEN

NAVAL CRIMINAL INVESTIGATIVE SERVICE

>> NCIS HEADQUARTERS
>> CAMP LEJEUNE, NORTH CAROLINA
>> 1817 HOURS

"Commander Coburn, the director will see you now."

Will thanked the office manager and got up and headed for Larkin's office. He'd arrived an hour ago and prepped for the meeting in his office, waiting for Larkin to call him. The director had wanted to meet with Commander Ivers first to scout out the terrain.

Evidently Larkin's fact-finding mission hadn't taken long.

Will didn't know if that was a good sign or a bad one. He let himself through the door.

Larkin's office was clean and neat. He had a place for everything, and everything was in its place. That was probably one of the traits that had made him a good homicide detective in New York.

Law books and military training manuals filled the shelves on one wall. Maps of Camp Lejeune and outlying areas, including the swamps and New River, filled the opposite wall. The wall behind the desk held commendations and medals Larkin had earned while on the job, including two citations given by New York City mayors. A few pictures featuring highlights from Larkin's career were in the mix.

United States Navy Commander Laura Ivers occupied one of the chairs in front of Larkin's desk. Her blonde hair fell to her shoulders, enhancing her striking features. She was in her early fifties, full figured, and fit.

She stood and offered her hand. "Commander Coburn," she said in a crisp voice. "Director Larkin has been telling me a lot of good things about you."

"Commander Ivers." Will took her hand briefly, then waited for her to sit back down before taking his own seat.

"Director Larkin has graciously—and reluctantly—agreed to allow me to handle this briefing," Laura said. "If that's all right with you."

"Of course."

"I suspect you know why I'm here," Laura said.

Will nodded.

"My daughter was brutally killed seventeen years ago, Commander Coburn." Laura's voice caught for just a moment, but she worked through it. "She was only sixteen years old. Too young to die. And she was so innocent. She didn't do anything to deserve what happened to her."

Heart aching, Will listened, not knowing what he was supposed to say.

"I could tell you so much about her." Laura's eyes gleamed with unshed tears. "The Navy took me away from her a lot, but I'm sure you know how that is. You have children?"

"Two."

"A daughter?"

"Seven years old."

Laura smiled. "Keep her close. They grow up entirely too quickly."

"I know."

"I don't know how much you know about me. Or about Chloe."

"I've read the case files," Will said. "They aren't enough."

Laura nodded. "Chloe was my only child. My husband had a son by a previous marriage. He was young when Chloe . . . died."

"Jeff was five."

"That's right. He was five. And he was a troubled child. Jeff had been under a doctor's care for months at the time I met him and his father. He used to have terrible nightmares. Chloe was the one who could settle him down the quickest. They were close."

"Losing your daughter must have been hard on him, too."

"It was. Ben had to have Jeff placed under a doctor's care for months after Chloe . . . after Chloe was taken from us. And after a few years had gone by, our grief had gotten so strong that our marriage couldn't survive the strain. I suppose you know that my ex-husband is a political figure."

"Congressman Benjamin Swanson," Will said.

"Ben has done well for himself. And he's done well by this state." Laura's voice held a note of pride. "I wasn't there when he took office, but I feel good about having helped him get there. At the time of Chloe's death, Ben was working on getting party support. There was just too much stress, too many people watching us. We weren't alone in our grief. I don't know if that would have helped." She shook her head. "My career was taking off, and I was gone from home a lot during those months. In some ways, that helped. But in the end, we went our separate ways."

Larkin sat quietly behind the desk. His eyes were watchful.

"Word got back to me regarding the discovery of Gunnery Sergeant Haskins's body in that raid your team staged last night," Laura said. "I heard about the charm that your team identified." She hesitated. "Do you have it?"

Will reached into his pocket and took out an evidence bag that contained the charm. "I can let you see this, Commander Ivers, but the bag has to stay sealed and it has to stay with me."

"I understand." Laura's eyes were locked on the evidence bag.

Will handed it to her.

Carefully, Laura smoothed the bag and studied the charm inside. Tears spilled from her eyes, rolling down her cheeks. "It's Chloe's," she whispered hoarsely. "It's my daughter's." With an obvious effort, she passed the evidence bag back to Will. Her hand shook.

"I'm sorry," Will told her. He didn't know what else to say.

Larkin handed the commander a handkerchief.

Laura accepted the offer with thanks and wiped her face free of tears. "They tried to say that Chloe was killed by Isaac Allen Lamont."

"I know. I read the reports."

"Do you believe them?"

"I believe the reports were done as best as they could be," Will said, "but there's a profiler on my team, Maggie Foley—"

"I know who she is."

Will was willing to bet there wasn't much Laura didn't know. She'd obviously done her homework before coming to Camp Lejeune. "Maggie doesn't think Lamont killed your daughter," he said.

"Why?"

"Her murder doesn't fit with the techniques Lamont used on his other victims."

"In what respects?"

Will hesitated. "I'd rather not go into that, Commander Ivers."

"But I want you to! I *need* to know what happened to my daughter!"

"That information is confidential," Larkin put in. "Commander Coburn can't go into the details."

"I'm her *mother!*" Laura said. "I have a right to know what happened to my daughter!"

"When we know," Larkin said, "you'll know." Although he looked compassionate, he also looked unswerving. "Give us a chance to do our jobs, Laura."

She turned back to face Will. "For seventeen years, my baby has lain in her grave unavenged. Her killer has been free all that time. I want to know that you'll try to find out who killed my baby."

Will floundered, searching for the right words.

"It's been seventeen years, Laura," Larkin said softly. "That's a long time."

Laura faced Larkin fiercely. "Every time I close my eyes at night, I remember having to go to the morgue to identify Chloe. Every time." She paused. "I want to know that you're not just going to ignore this."

"We're not," Larkin said.

Looking at Will, Laura said, "The director tells me you're an honest man. That if you tell me something, I can bet that it's true."

Will nodded.

"I want you to promise me you'll look for my daughter's killer," Laura said. "I want you to tell me right here, right *now,* that you'll speak for her. That's what you're trained to do, right? Forensics? Speaking for the dead?"

"Yes."

"Then I want you to find my daughter's voice. I want you to tell me that you'll do that."

"I will," Will promised, not knowing if he was going to be able to make good on that promise. But he knew Laura Ivers was not about to leave the room—or allow him to leave it—without that promise being made.

>> BULL RUN COUNTRY CLUB
>> HAYMARKET, VIRGINIA
>> 1842 HOURS

Congressman Benjamin Swanson sat at the bar in the Bull Run Country Club. He sipped his drink, flirted with the young bartender, and tried to ignore the reporters the Secret Service agents were barely able to keep at bay. Ignoring the reporters didn't help. A few of them had managed to trail along behind him and the rest of his foursome as they'd played their customary eighteen holes. The press were as relentless as green bottle flies once they got the smell of carrion in their noses.

Swanson was irritated. The golf course was only fifteen minutes from Washington, D.C. The traffic along Interstate 66 and Route 15 hadn't been relaxing. Usually he could count on the golf and a few drinks to get him unwound from a day spent on the Hill. Saturdays were generally heavy work days for him, filled with meetings with lobbyists and other congressmen, all of them wanting part of some deal or hoping to exchange favors to make things happen.

Normally Swanson lived for that sort of thing. He loved the hustle and flow, loved the brinkmanship involved in putting deals together. Or tearing someone else's deal apart.

But he liked to golf to get away from all of that and recharge his batteries.

That wasn't happening today.

Fifty-five years old four months ago, Swanson was a couple inches over six feet in height. He was weight and health conscious and had stated so on several talk shows, but he'd put on the pounds over the last few years. He was still in good shape, but he was twenty pounds over his best weight. Living well had gotten too easy.

He'd finally given up the golf game at hole thirteen, which had seemed an appropriate place to throw in the towel. He'd been nineteen strokes off his game because he hadn't been able to keep the ball out of the rough. The networks had been airing stories about his stepdaughter all day because of the charm found on George Haskins's body. It was bad enough the press was bringing up all that bad business about Chloe again, but having footage of the worst game he'd shot in ten years just added insult to injury.

So he shelled peanuts, sipped his rum and Coke, and flirted with the bartender.

"Sir. Sir, you can't go over there."

Recognizing the voice of one of the Secret Service agents, Swanson glanced over his shoulder and saw two of them standing in front of another man.

The man was in his fifties and wore an elegant suit that made Swanson wish he could lose the extra twenty pounds he couldn't seem to divest himself of.

"Ben," the man said, shaking his head in sardonic amusement. "You haven't been this hard to approach in a long time."

Swanson waved at the lead security man. "Let him through."

"Yes, sir." The agents stepped aside and let the man through, then closed ranks again.

"You've got quite the entourage," Wesley Humboldt said. He was one of the main lobbyists for a coalition of pharmaceutical companies who wanted Swanson's weight behind their efforts to expand internationally.

"They're a fickle crowd, though," Swanson said. "They get the smell of blood in their nose and they're all over you."

"You get enough jackals," Humboldt said, "and even a lion can be brought down."

So that's what this is about, Swanson thought. Humboldt was on a fact-finding run. The congressman turned to the bartender and ordered two drinks.

"My stepdaughter," Swanson said, "was killed seventeen years ago by a serial killer. Nobody's trying to bring me down."

"They'll get there, though."

Anger ignited within Swanson. "This isn't the place to talk about this."

"No, it's not. But this *is* the time. We need to get a game plan in place. The people I work for—the people you're possibly going to be representing—have got a lot riding on this."

Possibly? Swanson didn't like the sound of that at all. He was counting on Humboldt's connections to help support a large part of his reelection campaign.

Humboldt looked around. "Can you get a room somewhere? So we can talk about this?"

Swanson got up and headed for the back of the club. He didn't like the fact that Humboldt had shown up. A lot of the media knew who the bigger lobbyists were, and Humboldt was one of the biggest.

An uneasy feeling squirmed through Swanson's stomach.

22

SCENE  

 CRIME SCEN

>> NCIS HEADQUARTERS
>> CAMP LEJEUNE, NORTH CAROLINA
>> 1903 HOURS

"Did you know George Haskins?" Will had his iPAQ in his hand, taking notes as he questioned Laura Ivers.

She answered with a calm that showed considerable experience. "No. In fact, until this morning, I'd never heard of him."

"So you don't know if your daughter knew him?"

Anger stained the commander's face, but she made herself answer civilly. "No. But given what I know of Haskins's record, he's not the kind of man my daughter would have known."

"These are questions the media is going to ask," Larkin pointed out. "After the story breaks, there are going to be a lot of indelicate moments."

"My daughter's murder is the most horrible thing I've ever known," Laura replied. "This is going to be hard, but it's not ever going to be as hard as that." She looked at Will, and her gaze softened. "I know you have to ask these questions."

"What can you tell me about the night your daughter went missing?" Will had to distance himself from his own sympathies for the woman. He didn't know if he'd have the strength to face what she was dealing with.

Laura swallowed hard, then spoke in a strained voice. "Chloe called me that night. At 2100 hours. She always called when I was out of the house for the night. I was here in Camp Lejeune prepping training maneuvers that the Navy was going to perform in conjunction with the Marines. Asset recovery. Salvage diving. The Navy goes after a lot of things that the military loses at sea."

Will nodded.

"After we talked, she told me good night. That's . . . the last time I ever spoke to her."

"What did you talk about?" Will didn't ask if Chloe had been upset or had seemed worried. Interviewers who asked questions like that sometimes caused the person being questioned to read more into the memory than had actually been there. An investigator had to learn to ask neutral questions that didn't lead or color the exchange.

"The usual. How her day had been at school. How she'd done on midterms. How Jeff was doing." Laura took a breath. "Jeff was having a tough time of it again. His doctors had changed his meds. Every time they did that, there was always a period of adjustment. Chloe was really good at helping him through those times."

"When did you find out Chloe had been abducted?"

"At 0123 that Wednesday morning." Laura's face lost color. "The police who initially investigated Chloe's death always wondered how I knew the time so precisely." She wiped away a tear in frustration. "But you don't get calls like that, you know? Something like that you remember. I knew from other investigations I'd been aware of that the first forty-eight hours were the most critical. I looked at the clock and marked the time in my log. That's one of the things you do in this job—keep track of time."

"Your husband was in the house at the time?"

"Yes."

"Had he spoken with your daughter?"

"Yes. Chloe had signed for some papers that came for him earlier that day. She let him know they'd arrived."

Will hesitated a moment, thinking how best to move on to the other areas he had to get into.

"You can't take it easy on me, Commander Coburn," Laura said. "If you try to do that, you're not doing your job. Trust me when I tell you I'll be very surprised if you ask me any questions that the civilian and military investigators didn't ask me."

"All right," Will said. "Did you ever have trouble with your daughter?"

"Arguments, you mean?"

"Yes."

"Of course we had arguments. No mother and teenage daughter get through life without having arguments."

Will thought of Steven, who had quietly skulked off when they'd returned to Will's quarters from the restaurant, and silently amended that to include fathers and sons. "What did you argue over?"

"Nothing in particular. We occasionally got on each other's nerves. Curfew times. Nights she could go out. How long she could spend on the phone. Stuff like that."

"Did she use drugs or drink?"

"Not to my knowledge."

That was a good answer. Will knew that most parents believed they knew what their children did all the time, but in reality few of them did. Laura Ivers had evidently thought about the possibility.

"I've spent years thinking about my daughter," Laura said. "You can drive yourself crazy doing that. I could tell you that Chloe never had anything to do with drugs or alcohol, but I don't really know. Sometimes I can think back to a night she came home late or how sluggish she'd been one morning and I second-guess myself. All I can tell you is to the best of my knowledge Chloe never had an interest in any of those things."

"What about boys?"

"She didn't date very often. Ben was a real stickler about that. He didn't think Chloe needed to date one-on-one. When she went out with a boy she was interested in, she had to go with friends."

"Was she all right with that?"

"She didn't like it."

"Did she ever go against your will and date one-on-one anyway?"

Laura shook her head. "Not that I know of. Chloe really was no trouble. She was a *good* daughter."

"Do you know if your daughter had her charm bracelet the night she was taken from your home?"

"We never found it at home. Chloe loved that bracelet."

"But it wasn't found with her either?"

"No. They said that Isaac Allen Lamont always kept souvenirs from his victims, but he wasn't found with the bracelet either. The investigators thought perhaps it was lost in the river." Laura paused. "Haskins had that charm. That's what needs to be explained."

Will slid the stylus back into his iPAQ and looked at Laura. "Reopening the investigation into your daughter's death isn't going to be easy for you."

"Losing her," Laura promised, "was much harder than this is ever going to be." Tears glimmered in her eyes.

Larkin spoke up quietly. "What Will is saying is that the press, if they're given the opportunity—and they will be at some point because we can't contain this—are going to be all over our investigation."

"Not because of Chloe, though," Laura said bitterly. "Or because of me. Or because of some need for justice. But because of my ex-husband and the sensationalism of the death of a congressman's stepdaughter."

Will nodded. That was as succinct and bald as it could have been stated. Congressman Ben Swanson was news. His stepdaughter's death was one more weakness his enemies, and the press, would try to exploit.

>> BULL RUN COUNTRY CLUB
>> HAYMARKET, VIRGINIA
>> 1910 HOURS

"You're vulnerable, Ben. Pure and simple. Your personal life has been, and is, a train wreck."

Swanson sat in an overstuffed chair in the small conference room he'd borrowed at the country club. "Glad to see you so supportive about everything, Wesley."

Humboldt waved the comment away and smiled. "You know I don't mean anything personal by that. You and I are old friends."

"I thought we were," Swanson said. "But you can always spot rats leaving a sinking ship."

"I'm not a rat and you're not sinking."

"Maybe you could be a little more convincing."

"It's not me losing faith in you, Ben." Humboldt's voice took on a hint of anger. "It's the people I'm responsible for."

"What do they say?"

Humboldt looked at Swanson quietly for a moment. "They say that you're in trouble."

Swanson sipped his drink and thought about what that meant for him. His reelection wasn't a slam dunk. He was going to have to work hard to make that happen. And it was going to take a lot of money. Money that he didn't have if his backers pulled up stakes and bailed. His personal life *had* been a train wreck. And he had only himself to blame.

Of course, he also blamed his ex-wife, Laura. She'd left him when he was running for his first reelection. Laura had been good to have in the fold, a female Navy officer who worked on important Navy maneuvers. Whatever those were. He hadn't kept up with her career. But Laura had brought in the women's vote.

Swanson had lost part of that during his years of bachelorhood after the divorce. It seemed the American public hadn't cared for a skirt-chasing congressman nearly as much as they had a president who'd had affairs in the White House.

"Do you think I'm in trouble?" Swanson asked.

"Yes," Humboldt answered without hesitation. "However, I'm also of the opinion that this is fixable. We just need to put the right spin on it. You're a survivor, Ben. You always have been."

"Just hold your people together," Swanson said. "I'll get through this."

"They're getting ready to launch a major campaign to restructure the Medicare guidelines when the new administration comes in."

Swanson knew that. He'd been involved with the push every step of the way, balancing the needs of the pharmacies with the power he had on the House floor.

Pharmaceutical companies spent millions on lobbying efforts. The previous year alone they'd spent over $140 million swaying congressmen and the federal government. There had been almost thirteen hundred registered pharmaceutical lobbyists, outnumbering congressional members two to one. Nearly five hundred of them were ex–federal officials, proving that the pharmaceutical companies took care of those who did well by them even after they were out of office.

Pharmaceuticals were big business, but a lot of the profit hung on leveraging political favor.

"Not everyone can do what I can do," Swanson declared.

"I know," Humboldt agreed. "That's why I'm in your corner. So far I've got the CEOs on three of the corporations to back off and give you time to see this through. But there's not much time. We're all getting squeezed if this thing blows up. Public opinion, because of the administration's handling of the war and the oil crisis, doesn't favor anyone who smacks of the old-boy network in government."

"If it weren't for the old-boy network in the capitol, nothing would get done."

"You and I know that. The American public doesn't. As a group, today's Americans are the least educated and least involved of any who have gone before."

"That's worked in our favor before."

"Not anymore. People are angry. They're feeling an economic crunch that they don't understand, and they're ready to see someone hang for it."

"If your people don't go with me, whom do they plan on going with?" Swanson asked.

Humboldt hesitated. "You don't really want to know."

"Sure I do." Swanson grinned. "You and I both know that no one can deliver like I can. I've got the House Appropriations Committee wired. We don't turn loose of a single dollar that I don't agree to."

That wasn't exactly the truth, but it was true more times than not.

"I've helped your people get government supply contracts domestically and internationally," Swanson went on. "I've gotten two of those corporations onto the stem cell research short list."

"They know that, Ben, and they're grateful. But you know how this works."

Swanson cursed. He *did* know how it worked. "It's not about what you've *done;* it's about what you've done for me *lately.*"

Humboldt nodded. "It's not fair, but that's how it is. And right now the people we're doing business with want the new Medicare package passed."

The package was built around expanding coverage to include new prescriptions and undermining the government's efforts to control cost. Then medical providers, including of the special-interest groups Humboldt represented, could reach even further into Uncle Sam's deep pockets.

"I can deliver," Swanson said with conviction. He was counting on the backing of the pharmaceutical companies, not only for their campaign contributions but also for the vacations and kickbacks they had always arranged. That was how business was done on the Hill. It was all about horse-trading and bartering. And he wasn't prepared to cut loose the affluent lifestyle he had.

And then there was the role of being a congressman. Political power was like a drug. He didn't want to ever let that go.

"Your delivery is incumbent upon your reelection. Everyone knows you can't get the bill passed this term."

"I'll get reelected."

Humboldt sighed, looking incredibly tired. "We've had a good run, you and I."

"It's not over."

"We've weathered a lot of storms. I was there when you won your first election, I was there when you won your last, and I was there every time in between."

"That's not going to change."

"If Chloe—God rest her soul—gets hot in the news again," Humboldt said, "the media is going to take another look at you. They're going to talk about your divorce from Laura. The affairs that you had at the time. The fact that she's here in the area will only give them more material to work with."

That stopped Swanson in his tracks. "What did you say?"

Humboldt looked puzzled. "You didn't know? She was talking to some people at the NCIS earlier today."

"Are you sure?"

"I heard one of the reporters say he saw her there when he was interviewing the NCIS public-information officer. He probably remembered Laura from the newspaper reports."

Swanson thought fast. Laura talking to the NCIS could mean only one thing: she wanted them to reopen Chloe's case. But would they, based on a single charm found on a corpse that had been dead for seventeen years? *They might,* he thought, *if the link to Haskins gives them reason to believe she wasn't murdered by Lamont after all.* He had to get out of here. Had to talk to Laura. Maybe he could convince her not to have the investigation reopened.

"Oprah will crucify you," Humboldt was saying. "*The View* will take you apart. Letterman and Leno will take every shot they can at you."

Swanson stood. "Look," he said, "this is all going to go away. I'll be reelected, and the Medicare bill will pass. Tell your people they have nothing to worry about. Don't bail on me, Wes. I'll get it done."

"You'd better" was Humboldt's reply.

 CRIME SCENE  NCIS 

NAVAL CRIMINAL INVESTIGATIVE SERVICE

23

SCENE NCIS CRIME SCENE

NAVAL CRIMINAL INVESTIGATIVE SERVICE

```
>> NCIS HEADQUARTERS
>> CAMP LEJEUNE, NORTH CAROLINA
>> 1924 HOURS
```

An instant message pinged its arrival in the lower right corner of Maggie's computer monitor. The IM was from Estrella, who was still working as well.

Using the mouse, Maggie opened the instant message.

Wardell's files are in your e-mail.

Maggie typed a quick thanks, then opened her e-mail and accessed the files. It took a few minutes for them to load. Once she had them, she backed them up on her iPAQ so she'd have copies in the field if she needed them.

Then she started going through the files, looking for names.

Most of what Estrella had sent over was court documents, cases that Thomas Wardell had worked on. The majority of the work involved civil matters, but there were several criminal cases as well.

Wardell hadn't been afraid to get his hands dirty. Looking through the records, Maggie found that the attorney didn't handle small infractions of the law. He handled large ones. The cases Wardell took on dealt with a lot of money.

Wardell hadn't won most of his cases, but he had negotiated plea bargains and reduced sentences.

Taking up her iPAQ, Maggie started going through the list, jotting down the names of the people Wardell had represented, looking for a pattern or something she could build on.

Footsteps sounded in the stairwell behind her. She reached for the stainless-steel pen-and-pencil holder, using its mirrorlike surface to look behind her without turning her head and attracting attention. That was why she'd bought the holder. In her father's house, she'd had to learn to observe without being caught observing. It wasn't a skill she was particularly proud of, but it had served her in good stead.

Will and Larkin accompanied a woman Maggie recognized as Commander Laura Ivers. None of them talked much, remaining polite and quiet as they crossed the room and exited.

Maggie had heard that Commander Ivers had arrived, and she'd guessed that the woman would ask Will and Larkin to investigate her daughter's death again.

An IM from Estrella blinked on Maggie's screen.

Snooping?

Maggie felt embarrassed for just an instant. Then the feeling passed. She typed an IM back.

Interested. You?

Maybe you're right. Maybe she does need closure. I'm just not convinced we can give it to her.

Me neither.

Tiredly, Maggie closed the IM and went back to work.

A few minutes later, Will came back in. He got Estrella's and Maggie's attention. He also pulled Shel and Remy in from their workstations, where they'd been churning through paperwork.

"That was Commander Laura Ivers," Will said. "You probably knew she was here."

"Yes," Estrella replied.

"And you can probably guess what she wants."

"Her daughter's case reinvestigated," Maggie said.

"Yes."

"Are we going to do that?" Remy asked.

"We are," Will said. "But the director's orders are to keep this on stealth mode. I don't know if we'll make any headway here or not, but we're at least going to cover some ground on this thing." He looked at Shel and Remy. "On Monday, I want you two to look up some of George Haskins's old buddies. People he worked the black market with. Military personnel he knew. Whatever you can turn up. I want to know what he was involved with seventeen years ago that brought him anywhere close to Chloe Ivers."

"Or Isaac Allen Lamont," Maggie said.

Will looked at her.

"It's possible that Lamont killed Chloe Ivers, then had contact with Haskins."

"All right." Will glanced at Shel and Remy to make sure they had registered the suggestion, then looked back at Maggie. "You're with me. We've got the NCIS files regarding the investigation. We'll talk to the Raleigh PD and see if we can work a little goodwill."

Maggie nodded.

"Estrella, I need you to coordinate whatever we find and keep on top of whatever we need to make Bryce Ketchum and his people go away for a long time."

"Yes, sir."

"Will?" Maggie said.

He looked at her.

"You knew that Ketchum had asked for an attorney?"

"I heard."

"I met his attorney. He came by the offices today. His name is Thomas Wardell."

Will thought for a moment. "I know that name."

"He's a high-powered shark," Maggie replied. "Very expensive."

"Guess Ketchum figures he's in enough trouble that he needs the best," Remy said.

"He is," Shel said, scratching Max's ears. The dog lay at his feet. "We've got him cold."

"Wardell's not an attorney that someone like Ketchum could just hire," Maggie said.

"What are you saying?"

"I don't know yet," Maggie replied. "Just be careful. Wardell doesn't play fair. He plays legal, but he doesn't play fair."

Will glanced at his watch. "We're done here tonight. Get home and get sacked out. I want everybody back at 0800 Monday. Take tomorrow off. It may be the last day you have off for a while."

>> NCIS MEDICAL LAB
>> CAMP LEJEUNE, NORTH CAROLINA
>> 1941 HOURS

Nita held her cell phone in one hand and listened to it ring. Her home number showed on the screen.

You should just turn it off, she told herself. But she didn't. She knew that listening to it ring, demanding her attention—thinking of *Joe and Celia* demanding her attention—would stoke her anger. She needed that anger to set herself free.

Finally, after two more strident rings that echoed in the stillness of the empty lab, her answering service picked up the call.

Nita breathed out a sigh of relief.

"Wrong number?"

Startled, Nita glanced up to find Will standing in the doorway. She'd left the door to the hallway open.

"Yes," she lied. She shoved the phone into her smock pocket.

Will entered the room and walked over to where George Haskins's skull now wore the pseudoflesh she'd modeled from clay. She'd finished the work only a few minutes ago.

After studying the head, Will surveyed the eight-by-ten images Nita had worked from. "Looks like we have a match."

"I think so," Nita agreed. "We'll know more once we get the DNA samples back."

"You found DNA?"

Nita nodded, picking up her Styrofoam cup of lukewarm coffee. "In the marrow. If it hasn't been corrupted. Even with a rush on it, the results will take a week or so for confirmation."

"The DNA is only going to confirm what you're showing here."

"Probably."

Will leaned a hip against the stainless-steel table. "Everything going okay, Nita?"

"Everything's fine. I've got a new morgue assistant who's going to need some experience, but—"

"Not here," Will interrupted. "At home."

Nita stopped speaking and just looked at him for a moment. "Everything at home is none of your business."

"What about that bruise on your face?"

"Back off," Nita said. "This is none of your concern."

"If I thought Joe had done that, I'd have already filed reports," Will said. "But I know Joe. And I know Joe wouldn't do anything like that. So I have to ask: where did you get that bruise?"

"In the lab. I slipped," Nita told Will in a flat voice, letting him know she would keep telling him the same story until he got tired of asking.

Will was silent for a time. Only the whir of the refrigeration units kicking in interrupted the deathly quiet of the room.

"You're losing it, Nita," Will said.

Angry now, Nita demanded, "Do you have a problem with my work?"

"No. Not yet. I'm just worried about you."

"You don't have anything to worry about. My work will always be a hundred percent."

Will's eyes remained locked on hers. "Is there anything I can do?"

Looking into Will's eyes, Nita felt the pull to tell him everything, to tell him about the confusion and the feeling of being trapped that filled her. He had eyes that really looked at her, really saw her, and she knew he could listen. He was a lot like—

Like Joe.

Nita hadn't really noticed it before, but Will had started reminding her more of Joe lately. Something had happened to him during his divorce from Barbara and during that crisis in North Korea last year. He'd . . . *changed* in some way that she couldn't quite identify.

"No," Nita said.

"Look," Will told her quietly, "if you're having a problem—"

"The only problem I'm having is getting people to leave me alone." She put steel in her voice. "I did my job, Commander. I rebuilt Haskins's face. It's done. Now, if there isn't anything else, I'd like to get on with my work."

Will shook his head. "No more work. Not tonight. And not tomorrow. I pulled your sign-in sheets. You haven't taken a day off in over a month."

No! Nita curbed the impulse to yell at Will. *I don't want to go home!* But she didn't say a word.

"I'll see you back here on Monday," Will said. "I'm going to leave orders with the MPs that you're not to enter the premises without my permission till 0800 Monday morning."

Tears stung Nita's eyes. She refused to let them fall. Will didn't know what he was doing, didn't know what he was putting her through. She needed to work. That was her escape.

"And if you're not out of this lab in thirty minutes, I'm going to have MPs put you out."

"You can't do that."

"I can. I am." Will looked at her. "Whatever problem you're dealing with, Nita, it's not here in this lab. Go wherever it is and deal with it."

"Yes, sir." Nita answered only so he would leave.

"Good night, Nita." Without a backward glance, Will left the room.

Nita glanced at her watch. At least she still had thirty minutes before she had to leave. She didn't know what she was going to do, but she knew she wasn't going home.

IS  CRIME SCENE  NCIS 

NAVAL CRIMINAL INVESTIGATIVE SERVICE

24

SCENE  NCIS NAVAL CRIMINAL INVESTIGATIVE SERVICE 

>> INTERSTATE 66
>> HAYMARKET, VIRGINIA
>> 1956 HOURS

In the back of the stretch limousine, Congressman Benjamin Swanson looked at the tiny cell phone in his hand and contemplated calling his ex-wife. They hadn't spoken in years, but he had her numbers—the ones for her home and for the cell phone she carried. He had investigators who kept up with people for him. Laura had been easy because she hadn't been trying to hide.

He wondered how she would take his phone call. Maybe with Chloe's death fresh in her mind, she'd be willing to talk to him. After all, he'd gone through Chloe's loss with her. But Swanson knew he'd also done enough to his ex-wife to ensure that she hated him forever.

Outside the tinted windows, evening was stretching a dark, clawed hand across the stark terrain.

The television built into the overhead showed *FOX News*. As he watched, the previous night's NCIS raid was shown again, covering the discovery of Haskins's body and the small charm found in his pants cuff. "Though no link is yet known to exist between Chloe Ivers and George Haskins, the discovery of the girl's charm has led investigators to make speculations regarding a possible connection between the two deaths, which occurred during roughly the same time period. Chloe Ivers was the daughter of Navy commander Laura Ivers and the stepdaughter of noted U.S. congressman Benjamin Swanson—"

Swanson clicked off the TV.

He picked up the phone again. This time he dialed. Settling into the comfort of the limo's backseat, he listened to the phone ring twice before it was answered.

"Hello?"

Laura's voice still gave Swanson pause. He could remember the first time he'd seen her at one of the political functions in Raleigh that involved military appropriations, on the arm of some young Navy lieutenant.

"Laura," he said, making himself speak, "it's Ben."

"Ben?" In the background, a television muted. "Why are you calling?"

"Look," he said, "I just heard about George Haskins's body being found. And the charm. Chloe's charm."

Laura didn't say anything.

"I know how upsetting this must be for you," he said. "I'm feeling very upset myself."

"Why did you call?"

"I just wanted to check on you."

"I'm fine."

"That's good. But this has to be hard."

"It is." Laura's voice took on a harder edge, but she sounded tired, too. "What do you want, Ben?"

"Can't I just call to make sure you're all right?"

"You could. But you didn't. I've never known a time when you did anything for anybody without wanting something in return."

Swanson thought that was unfair and unkind, but he didn't protest. It was also true. She knew him as well as he knew her.

"So what do you want, Ben?"

Swanson took a deep breath. "I'd also heard you were at Camp Lejeune."

Laura's voice turned cold and distant. "Good-bye, Ben."

"Wait!"

She didn't hang up.

"Laura," Swanson said, putting more force into his words, "you need to think about what you're doing. Everything you're stirring up is going to hurt you all over again."

"It's not going to hurt me all over again," she told him. "I'm still hurt. I've never stopped hurting since the night Chloe died. But you don't understand that, do you?"

"Laura, I understand that the newspeople are—"

Click.

Listening to the white noise coming from the phone, Swanson knew she'd hung up. Irritated, he punched in her number again.

After one ring, he was informed that his call couldn't go through.

She'd blocked his number.

Raging, Swanson closed the phone and barely resisted the impulse to throw it. She was going to be difficult. He'd known that going in.

But Swanson had people on his payroll who handled difficult people. He reached for the phone again. If he couldn't reason with Laura, he could always have her handled.

>> SILHOUETTE CLUB
>> JACKSONVILLE, NORTH CAROLINA
>> 2028 HOURS

The Saturday-night club scene packed the Silhouette Club. It featured country-and-western music and line dances. Pickups filled the gravel parking lot. Neon ringed the club's roof, and the swivel-hipped, winking cowgirl on the sign out front.

Nita sat in her Mustang and listened to country music on her radio. The neon wash glinted off her windshield. She had what was left of a six-pack of beer between the seats and was drinking from a can. She'd swiped beer from her mom and from her mom's boyfriends from the time she was fourteen years old. She'd never gotten caught. And she'd never seen beer poured into a glass until she was eighteen and got into a club with a fake ID.

She smiled a little at that. *Those were the days.* She took a sip of beer. For a moment she closed her eyes and imagined what it would be like inside the club. She'd been in hundreds of them. Smoke filled, loud, and dark. That was how it would be.

And line dancing. She loved line dancing. There was nothing like it. When she line danced, she was able to get out on the floor without a partner, without really sharing the limelight, and strut her stuff for all the cowboys to see. She'd always gloried in the attention she'd gotten from the men.

Tonight she knew she looked as good as she ever had. It would be nothing to walk inside and join a line dance.

Her phone rang.

Caller ID showed her home number.

She watched it ring, then couldn't take the guilt anymore and picked up. "Hello."

"Hey." Joe's voice was soft.

"Hey." Nita watched a pair of long-legged cowboys walk into the club. They had broad-brimmed hats and huge belt buckles.

"Am I calling at a bad time?"

Nita wanted to say yes, but she couldn't bring herself to. "No. Now is okay."

"Celia and I were wondering if you're going to make it home before bedtime tonight."

Nita wanted to say no, that she was busy. But she couldn't. The club looked inviting, but she kept flashing back to the attack the previous night. She couldn't quite get past it.

Fear had kept her inside her car drinking the six-pack she'd picked up at a convenience store. She hated that.

"We're making ice cream," Joe said. "Peach."

Peach ice cream was her favorite. Joe knew that. What he didn't know was that the first ice cream she could remember eating had been peach. She'd been seven years old, living in one of the endless trailer parks her mother had moved through. She'd never told Joe that. She'd never told Joe anything about her life. Except that her parents were dead and she had no siblings.

It was almost the truth. She'd never known her father, and the man probably was dead. And Nita had been her mom's only mistake.

But her mom was still alive, still living in a trailer park, now in Tennessee. Mail still occasionally came to Nita through the military post office. It was the only address her mother had for her. Usually the mail consisted of birthday cards with *Love, Mom* scrawled at the bottom. No note. No questions. No announcement on how her mom was doing.

It was all pretend. Nita knew that. She'd never been fooled. The last time she'd actually spoken to her mom had been seven years ago, shortly before Nita met Joe, before her whole life had changed. Her mom had called and told her she needed money, that she was sick and in the hospital from a beating her latest boyfriend had given her.

Nita had hung up, blocked any further calls, and changed her number the next day to one that was unlisted.

That was her mother: Carol Purdue. At least, that was the name her mother kept going back to every time she got divorced. Nita had given up trying to keep track of the other names. But Purdue was the name her mother had been born with, and it was the name Nita had been born with.

"Are you still there?" Joe asked.

"Yes. Sorry." Why did she say that? She had nothing to be sorry for. It was her life. She'd spend it as she pleased. "Must have hit a bad patch on the cell phone."

"I keep hearing music."

"It's the radio."

"Oh."

Nita gazed longingly at the club doors. They swung open every time someone walked up to them. Everyone was allowed.

"So," Joe said, "are you going to be able to make it?"

Guilt stung Nita, and she hated it. She wasn't a good mom or a good wife. How could she be? She didn't even want to go home.

"Sure," she replied, surprising herself. "I'll be there in twenty minutes."

"Great. I'll tell Celia. Be careful."

Part of Nita resented the excitement she heard in Joe's voice, but part of her was glad it was still there. "I will. See you soon."

Nita folded the phone and dropped it into her purse. She looked at the six-pack. Five remained.

Someone knocked on her window, startling her. She looked through the glass.

A tall cowboy with long blond hair stood beside her door. He grinned and pushed his hat back with a thumb. "You comin' in? Or are you gonna sit out here an' be a wallflower all night?"

His smile was infectious. On another night, Nita knew she'd be tempted. She wanted to be tempted now, but she wasn't.

She picked up the six-pack, rolled down the window, and said, "Merry Christmas."

"I never turn down beer," the cowboy said, taking the carton. "How about comin' in for a dance?" He did a couple steps. "I ain't half bad."

Nita smiled and wished she hadn't told Joe she was coming home. "Another time."

"Well then, happy trails, little lady." The cowboy waved and walked away.

Nita started the car, turned on her lights, and drove away. The neon lights dimmed in her rearview mirror.

S  CRIME SCENE  NCIS  C

NAVAL CRIMINAL INVESTIGATIVE SERVICE

25

SCENE  NCIS  CRIME SCENE

NAVAL CRIMINAL INVESTIGATIVE SERVICE

>> CLUB INFERNO
>> WASHINGTON, D.C.
>> 2122 HOURS

Ben Swanson watched on a security monitor in Mason Craddock's office as Craddock walked through the second floor of his downtown club like a lord in his kingdom.

Six feet four inches tall, Craddock towered over most of the crowd out on the dance floor. He was in his forties, but the way he took care of himself, he was often mistaken for a man ten or fifteen years younger. He spent two hours in the gym every morning, and that dedication to his body showed. Tailored clothes made the most of his broad shoulders and narrow waist. His sandy hair was cut short, maybe a half inch in length all over. His goatee was cut similarly short. He had pale gray wolf's eyes that constantly radiated hunger to those who knew what to look for.

After Craddock had gotten out of the military twenty years ago, he'd shown up at Swanson's office one day offering to obtain information on other politicians and players on the Hill for a fee. Swanson remembered the man on sight—he was several years younger than Swanson, but both had grown up in the same town. Craddock had been young and fast and willing to do anything. Swanson had accepted the offer without hesitation.

Craddock had worked for Swanson for several years, getting black-mail-worthy information by methods Swanson didn't even want to guess at. Swanson paid him well, though Craddock's name didn't come anywhere close to the official payroll. Craddock's main job was information gathering, though occasionally Swanson used him to accomplish other, more sinister tasks.

After a few years, Craddock had struck out on his own. He'd bought small clubs, plowed some of his illegal profits into them, and turned them into moneymakers, then sold them and continued upgrading till he was finally able to buy space and build his own club.

Washington, D.C., had a thriving nightlife, and its citizens loved to party. Craddock had been an overnight success years in the making.

Club Inferno was a palace of sin and decadence, and it was one that only had to open the doors every night to watch the money roll in. Craddock pushed the profits back into the club and into a development fund.

These days Swanson had minimal contact with Craddock. But from time to time their association came in handy. Like now. Swanson didn't enjoy visiting the club, and coming here at all was a risk. As a responsible congressman, he couldn't afford to be seen in a place like this. Still, he couldn't deny the club's success. Craddock clearly was every bit as good a businessman as he had been a criminal.

As Swanson watched, Craddock closed on two men hitting on one of the servers. They'd blocked her way and hemmed her in, not taking no for an answer.

Big mistake, Swanson thought, grinning a little in anticipation. Craddock was a former Navy SEAL. Taking care of a couple of troublemakers would be no problem for him.

Craddock talked to the two men. His body language was polite but firm.

Then one of the men made the mistake of putting his hands out to push Craddock back. Craddock twisted, throwing the man off balance, then sucker punched him in the side of the neck. The man went wobble legged at once. Before he could take more than one staggering step, Craddock followed up with a punch to the stomach.

The man dropped to his knees and threw up.

Craddock knew some kind of martial art. Swanson didn't know which one or ones. And he carried a gun on his person at all times, even though he wasn't authorized to carry one. Years ago Swanson had introduced Craddock to Thomas Wardell, whom Craddock now kept on retainer as an attorney. Wardell kept Craddock out of serious trouble, and the rest of it Craddock simply threw money at till it went away.

The second man found out in a hurry that Craddock had a gun. He stepped back, throwing his hands high. By that time Craddock's black-suited bouncers had descended upon the troublemakers like crows. They forced the two men through the crowd and tossed them. The club patrons hooted and hollered their appreciation.

It was a typical night at Club Inferno.

❂ ❂ ❂

>> 2127 HOURS

By the time Craddock reached the personal office he kept in the club, Swanson was seated in one of the expensive chairs in front of the metal-and-glass desk, drink already in hand.

"Get here in time for the floor show, Congressman?" Craddock poured himself a drink at the built-in bar.

"I did. Seems like you still have the moves."

Craddock smiled and sat behind the desk. "You know it." He drank. "You mentioned on the phone that you had a problem."

"You heard Bryce Ketchum was arrested last night?"

"Who hasn't?"

"It appears that someone buried George Haskins on that farm."

Craddock nodded, his face blank. "I'd heard that too."

Swanson swore. "You should have told me where George's body was."

"What difference would it have made if you'd known?" Craddock asked mildly.

Swanson ignored the question. "One of my stepdaughter's charms was found in Haskins's clothing. If anyone thinks to link me with Haskins's death, things could get ugly."

"Is that going to happen?"

Swanson forced himself to calm down. "After seventeen years, I don't think so. Everyone thinks that Isaac Allen Lamont killed Chloe. If no one found any evidence to the contrary all those years ago, they won't find it now."

"Then what are you worried about?"

"My ex-wife. She never believed that Lamont killed her daughter. She went to the NCIS headquarters today."

"Why?"

"I think she asked them to reopen Chloe's investigation."

Craddock sipped his drink. "Do you think they will?"

"She's a commander in the Navy. And forensics are better than what they were seventeen years ago."

"You think they will find something."

"No." Swanson heaved a sigh. "What I think could happen is that the publicity from this investigation—if there is one—will adversely affect some of the backers I'm depending on for my upcoming reelection."

Craddock swirled his glass. Ice clinked, and the sound was tiny, but it filled the room. Outside, the club was jumping. Lights splashed against the one-way glass. But inside it was so quiet Swanson could almost hear the rapid thump of his heart.

"Well," Craddock said with a smile, "if the reelection doesn't work out for you, I could find a place for you here."

"Not funny," Swanson said. "I came here for solutions, not wisecracks."

"What do you want me to do?"

Swanson thought about that. "I want you to find out whatever you can about the NCIS team. I need information, but if I start asking questions, or if those questions come out of my office, it's going to look bad for me. Like I'm trying to cover something up."

Craddock grinned. "All right." He finished his drink. "What am I supposed to find?"

"Leverage," Swanson said. "The same thing we're always looking for."

"Wouldn't it be better to let these people look and tell your ex-wife that nothing's there?"

"I'm not worried about them. I'm concerned about the media, what they'll turn this into if it grabs the headlines again. I don't want to deal with that."

"All right. I'll let you know when I have something. It shouldn't take long. Nobody in this life gets through without having some kind of skeleton hiding in the closet."

Swanson finished his drink and headed out the back way, the same way he'd come in.

He felt better for having talked to Craddock. When it came to playing dirty, Swanson didn't know anyone more accomplished.

>> GOD'S LITTLE HOUSE CHURCH
>> JACKSONVILLE, NORTH CAROLINA
>> 1057 HOURS

Churches made Nita uncomfortable. Even as a child she hadn't liked them. No matter what trailer park her mother had picked for them to live at, there was always a church nearby. Always. And it was always within walking distance.

Carol Purdue had viewed church as a free babysitting service. Wednesday evenings, Sunday mornings, and Sunday evenings, Nita's mom would dress Nita up in her best clothes and walk her over to the church. Her mom never went inside, unless it was to ask for a handout when she was behind on the rent or the heating bill was out of hand.

Summer brought Vacation Bible School. Not only did Nita have to go to the church she was normally made to attend, but buses ran through the neighborhood to pick up attendees for other Vacation Bible Schools. Her mother made sure Nita went to every one of them she heard about.

Being abandoned at church hadn't been pleasant. If the church people had just left her alone, Nita might not have hated it so much. But all of them had to come by, see how she was doing . . . and ask where her mother was. She'd even heard some of the ladies at different churches complaining about the way Nita's mom just expected them to take care of her daughter.

It had been embarrassing. Worse, it had been demeaning.

Nita had stopped going when she was twelve, finally big enough to scream back at her mother and take getting slapped in the face for it. She hadn't gone again. And her mom had responded by abandoning her there at her own home, sometimes gone for days at a time.

During those times, Nita had learned a whole new way to survive. When she ran out of food, she made sure she got invited somewhere. She'd learned to shoplift at convenience stores, and that had made her feel bad. But she'd gotten by.

Joe had attended the same church all his life. His parents and his grandparents had been married there. Joe and Nita had been married there. He knew everyone, and everyone knew him.

Nita had never gotten comfortable in Joe's church, and she attended as rarely as she could. Already she regretted agreeing to come with Joe and Celia today. At least she'd only agreed to go to the main service, not to Sunday school. Sunday school tended to be too personal, too much like the women who had complained at Nita's mother's absences.

Although she wore a cotton dress like the other women and sat small and contrite, Nita didn't feel like one of them. And she could tell they didn't feel like she was one of them either. Many stared at her as if they didn't know what to say. They tried to be polite, because of Joe, but Nita was conscious of the strain behind the effort.

All through the service, Joe sat quietly and held her hand. Celia sat beside Joe and looked through her Bible storybook.

Nita wanted to bolt from the church, but she didn't have the courage to get up. So she sat without singing, listening to Joe's baritone and Celia's warble.

I don't belong here, she thought. *If I did, God wouldn't make me feel so uncomfortable.*

26

SCENE  NCIS  CRIME SCENE

NAVAL CRIMINAL INVESTIGATIVE SERVICE

>> GOD'S LITTLE HOUSE CHURCH
>> JACKSONVILLE, NORTH CAROLINA
>> 1218 HOURS

After the service, the congregation held a potluck dinner. The preacher's wife had organized and passed out the food sign-ups.

Nita had never seen the list, but Joe had signed up to bring a meat dish. He'd cooked enough meat loaf to feed a small army, which was what the congregation of God's Little House Church amounted to.

The women served the dinners, doling out food to the children and then to the men, who went off to talk hunting or weekend projects or past sporting events they'd played together or against each other.

Joe was helping organize the church's softball league, so a crowd swallowed him up immediately. Celia ran off with her friends to jump rope and run around. The sun was warm and the wind was fair.

Nita sat alone at one of the folding tables the church kept for socials. She'd tried to help the other ladies, but they'd made it clear—*politely* clear—that they could get along without her and, in fact, wanted to do that very thing.

She felt ostracized while her husband and daughter were drawn into the bosom of the church.

She sipped tea and picked at a salad, thinking that she would rather be in the lab. There she was in control of everything. She was needed. She still didn't know why she'd agreed to stay when Joe had told her about the dinner.

"Mrs. Tomlinson."

A thin woman with a severe face stood behind Nita. She wore a dress and a sweater and had two small boys with her. The woman looked like she was in her midtwenties, so she must have had the kids when she was young.

"Yes," Nita said, thinking maybe the church ladies had found something for her to do after all.

"You don't know me," the woman said. "I'm Leslie Horton."

Nita held out a hand, thinking that the woman was probably someone Joe had helped. "It's nice to meet you, Mrs. Horton."

Leslie stared at Nita's hand but made no move to take it.

Not knowing what else to do, Nita withdrew her hand.

"I don't want to start any trouble, Mrs. Tomlinson," Leslie said. "I asked God to make me strong enough not to even talk to you when I saw you here with your husband. But I'm a weak woman and here I am. I'll hit my knees later this afternoon and pray for forgiveness. I'll probably even pray for you. That's just how I am."

"I don't understand," Nita said.

Leslie shook her head in disbelief. "Does the name David Horton ring any bells for you, Mrs. Tomlinson?"

Nita honestly tried to remember but couldn't. "No."

"Last Friday night, Mrs. Tomlinson. Can't you even remember what happened two nights ago? The Extreme Rush Club?"

Then the name hit Nita and she knew. *David Horton. The Navy flier.*

"David Horton is my husband, Mrs. Tomlinson," Leslie said. "He's the father of these two boys."

"He didn't tell me he was married." Nita didn't know what else to say.

"Did you tell David you were married?"

Not wanting any part of the confrontation, Nita turned to go. Leslie grabbed her by the wrist, holding her in a grip of iron. The woman was either so mad or so hurt that her hand shook.

Nita wanted to jerk her hand away, but she didn't want to cause a scene. Some of the church ladies were already watching.

"I don't think you know what it's like trying to hang on to a man," Leslie said. "You got Joe. He's a good man. A God-fearing man who wouldn't hurt anyone." She shook her head. "I don't know what he sees in you, though, because anyone with sense in their head can look at you and know that you aren't anything but trouble."

"Nothing happened."

"Nothing happened? I had to go get my husband at the emergency room that night. He had a concussion and had to have twenty-three staples put in his head. He had blood all over him."

He deserved worse for what he tried to do, Nita thought.

"David tried to lie to me," Leslie went on. "But he had alcohol and perfume all over him."

Nita wanted to be anywhere but here, but the woman still hadn't let go of her wrist.

"I stayed at him, and it took me hours to get the truth out of him. Some of the other military wives know about that apartment. A few of the men rent it out, but other men can borrow it. For a price. It's cheaper and more discreet than a hotel, I suppose."

Not from where Nita was standing.

"It's hard hanging on to a man, Mrs. Tomlinson," Leslie went on. "If I didn't have these two boys, if I didn't love my husband the way I do—though I know he doesn't love me back like that—if I didn't trust God to reach out and turn David away from his wicked ways at some point, I think I'd give up." She took a deep breath. "But the problem is, Mrs. Tomlinson, all those things are before me."

Nita felt the inexorable grip slip from her wrist.

"I did some checking around on you, Mrs. Tomlinson. You're something of a loose woman. If I didn't care about Joe as much as I do, I'd tell him. But I know how much pain you can go through when someone you love betrays you." Leslie shook her head. "I wouldn't wish that on him. So I won't be the one to tell him. Someone else might, though."

Fear thrummed through Nita, electric and alive. It was one thing to think about leaving Joe, but the thought of him confronting her scared her to death. She knew he wouldn't hurt her. He'd never hurt her. But she didn't want to be there to see him hurt that badly.

"But I'm going to tell you this one time and one time only, Mrs. Tomlinson," Leslie went on. "You stay away from my husband. Because if you don't, I'm going to hurt you. There's nowhere in the Bible that says a woman doesn't have the right to protect her family, and I'll do whatever it takes. God strike me dead if I'm lying to you."

There was no doubt in Nita's mind that the woman would do exactly what she promised.

"There's others besides me who have their eyes on you, Mrs. Tomlinson. We know what you are even if your husband doesn't."

At that moment, Joe must have seen that something was going on. He excused himself from the group of men eager to talk about the softball team and headed for Nita.

Leslie Horton saw Joe coming. She took her children by the hands and hurried off.

"What's going on?" Joe asked.

"Nothing." Nita could barely speak. If the problem had been something else, *anything* else, she'd have told Joe. But she couldn't tell him this.

"Wasn't that Leslie Horton?" Joe asked. "Did she say something to upset you?" He started to go after the woman.

Nita caught him by the arm and stopped him. "No. It's nothing. She just wanted to talk to me."

"I know she's having some trouble with her husband," Joe said. "He's a Navy flier. From what I understand, he gets mad and likes to hit. I've never seen any indication of that, but I've heard about it."

"She asked me if I knew him," Nita said. "I told her I didn't." That was mostly true. Friday night didn't count because David Horton hadn't turned out to be anything like she'd thought he would. "Camp Lejeune is a big place. I'm not a flier. He's not a corpse."

Joe looked at her. "Are you sure?"

"I'm sure." Nita wanted to hug him. Actually, she wanted to be hugged by him. But she couldn't do that. Too many of the churchwomen were watching. "Look, I'm going to go home. I've got a headache that might turn into a migraine if I don't do something about it."

"Let me get Celia. We can go with—"

"No. You and Celia stay. Just give me a call when you need to come home."

"It's no problem," Joe said. "Somebody will give us a ride."

"All right."

Joe hugged her then. She felt the strength of him, and part of her knew that she was going to miss that, but it was better to miss it than to tear him to pieces eventually. Then she left, head held high, without a backward glance.

Silently, Nita cursed Will. She needed to work. She needed something that would keep her away from home and give her a chance to figure out what she was doing.

>> RALEIGH POLICE DEPARTMENT
>> 110 S. McDOWELL STREET
>> RALEIGH, NORTH CAROLINA
>> 1012 HOURS

"Did you have a good time with Steven and Wren?"

Will parked his truck in the visitors parking lot at the Raleigh Police Department on Monday morning and switched the engine off. "There were some rough spots," he admitted, "but most of it was good."

Maggie sat in the passenger seat. She was dressed in a business suit that far outclassed the khakis, sweater, and sports coat Will wore. "I'm sure getting called out to talk with Laura Ivers didn't help."

"No." Will grabbed his files and clambered from the truck. They'd taken his vehicle because he didn't comfortably fit into the Crossfire two-seater sports car Maggie was currently driving.

"A divorce is a hard thing to work through, Will," Maggie said. "For the spouses and for the kids. It's almost like having to reinvent the family."

"I know. Even though we're divorced, there's still a relationship there."

"Right."

"And as long as there's a relationship, everything is fixable."

"Or at least adjustable."

Will walked toward the doors. "Let's concentrate on finding out what the Raleigh Police Department was doing when Chloe Ivers was taken seventeen years ago."

"Sure. When are you seeing the kids again?"

"Couple weeks."

"Got anything planned?"

"Thought we'd go sailing again. That seemed to work out well."

"Part of making those adjustments is just being yourself, Will," Maggie said. "You're not an entertainment system for them. Sometimes you need to just be yourself."

"You've never gone sailing with me, have you?"

"No."

Will stopped and looked at her. "When I'm out there, on that water with a good wind at my back, I'm more alive than I've ever been in my life. That's where I'm myself, Maggie. Out on the water. Whether it's the ocean, a lake, or a river. And I see that in my kids, too. When we're in that boat, we're a team."

"Then maybe you should think about an extended cruise along the eastern seaboard," Maggie said.

"Not in that little boat I've got."

"Then get something bigger. Rent it or borrow it." Maggie frowned, as if debating whether she should say anything further. But she did. "You don't have a home, Will. You're living in a shoe box. It's a place where you keep your stuff. Steven and Wren aren't seeing you where you live. They're seeing you where you survive, in the foxhole you've pulled up for yourself. If the sea works for you, then do it right."

Without another word, she turned and left Will standing there. He didn't know if he'd been praised, given direction, or maligned over his choice of living quarters. After a moment, he followed Maggie into the building.

>> ACE WELDING
>> JACKSONVILLE, NORTH CAROLINA
>> 1014 HOURS

"How do you want to do this?" Remy adjusted the do-rag he wore to hide the gauze bandage covering the side of his head. The double vision had finally cleared up, but he was still having headaches bad enough to cause nausea from time to time.

The welding shop was a metal building with a gravel parking lot and a high security fence. Rust showed in places on the building's exterior. Light danced on the paned windows. Double doors in the middle of the building were open to allow the breeze in. Remy didn't figure the conditions inside the building were very cool, but in March they had to be better than they were in July and August.

Seated behind the wheel of his Jeep, Max leaning excitedly over his shoulder from the backseat, Shel opened one of the files Estrella had prepared for them. "Dawson, Ronald Wayne," he read.

Remy recognized the name. He'd studied the files while Shel drove. Of course, Shel had gotten to the office a couple hours before everyone else and familiarized himself with the files. *Probably after a ten-mile run and a session at the shooting range,* Remy thought.

"He was one of George Haskins's black-market contacts outside the military," Remy said.

"That's right. Haskins disappeared before he could be busted for illegal trafficking, but Dawson got nailed. After a seven-year stretch in the penitentiary, he allegedly started cooking meth, though he hasn't been caught doing it yet. He hooked up with a local biker gang—" Shel pointed at the welding business—"which this business is also supposed to be part of."

"We're walking into the middle of a biker shop?"

Shel slipped on his mirrored sunglasses and grinned. "You gotta love chasing the bad guys, Remy. I'm just grateful these guys work for a living part of the time. Most of the criminals I know don't get up till noon, and if you don't know where they live—which you usually don't—you can't just go roust them out of bed."

"Great." Remy reached under his warm-up jacket and loosened his .357 in the shoulder holster. "I haven't even had breakfast yet."

"Shoulda had it before you showed up for work."

"We passed a McDonald's. I distinctly remember suggesting we stop."

"I wanted to get something done today."

"Breakfast is still on my list."

"Maybe we'll stop there on the way back." Shel opened the door and climbed out. Max hopped to the ground and fell into position at his side.

"Breakfast will be over by then," Remy protested.

"Look on the bright side. Maybe we'll go in here, you'll get shot, and you can have your breakfast through an IV at the hospital."

"It doesn't taste the same."

"Strained peas are strained peas, buddy. An IV's just a little more strained; that's all."

"I don't like strained peas," Remy groused. He knew the patter they had between them was part of the technique. Both of them were jazzed on adrenaline and the banter was a way of talking themselves off that ledge a little.

"Is that all you're going to do today?" Shel asked. "Complain?"

Remy ignored the comment and nodded at the welding shop. "What do you plan on doing? Just walk in here and ask, 'Is Dawson around?'"

"Yep."

"A white guy. A black guy. And a dog. And we're not carrying anything inside that needs welding. They're going to make us as cops."

"So?"

"Dawson will run, is so."

"A guilty man flees though no man pursues," Shel said. "Says that somewhere in the Bible."

"Oh, and now I get Scripture in the morning."

"If Dawson runs, we chase him."

"Great plan," Remy said.

"It's an old standby. I like it because it's simple and direct."

"It's a wonder it hasn't gotten you killed."

"Keeps me on my toes."

"If he runs," Remy said, "you're buying me lunch, and I'm picking the spot."

Remy followed Shel and Max into the welding shop. They skipped the office and went directly back to the work area, even though there was signage to customers that they weren't supposed to do that.

The work area was filled with men and metal, flying sparks and the smell of burning steel. The men wore welders' helmets and dark blue uniforms with heavy gloves, leather aprons, and forearm protectors.

One of the men, a grizzled veteran with a full, charred beard and tattoos around his neck, intercepted them. "You ain't supposed to be back here. There's an office up front for customers." He pointed the way.

Shel reached under his leather bomber jacket and brought out his NCIS ID. "Special Agent McHenry. NCIS. I'm supposed to be wherever I want to be."

The man didn't look impressed. "What do you want?"

"Ronald Dawson."

Shrugging, the man said, "I don't think he made it in today."

"He's not at home."

They'd stopped by there earlier. Estrella had included his home address in the file she'd put together.

"Maybe he went to his mom's," the man said.

"Dawson is fifty-six. His mom died in a nursing home four years ago. Dawson hadn't been to see her in eight years. He didn't even take care of her body when she died. County had to bury her."

Well, Shel's ready for the pop quiz, Remy thought. Since he'd been working with NCIS for the last year, Remy had been continually impressed with how much the big Marine researched his caseload.

Shel walked away from the man. "Since you can't help me, I'll find him myself."

"Hey! *Hey!* You can't just walk through here!"

"Yeah," Shel said. "I can." He raised his voice and addressed the welders. All of them were watching the action. "Your helmets. Get 'em up so I can see your faces." Shel mimed lifting the helmets.

Slowly the men lifted the dark welding helmets. Five men back, Ronald Dawson lifted his mask. With all the noise going on, few of the welders could have heard the exchange, but they all saw the badge.

Dawson looked old and withered and used up. Gray whiskers flecked his sallow face. His eyes held equal measures of fear and contempt.

Without a word, Dawson turned and fled toward a door at the back of the shop.

"I told you he was gonna run," Remy growled.

"Stop yapping and get chasing," Shel growled back.

Remy knew he brought out the sense of competition in Shel, but he enjoyed it.

Just not today, Remy thought as he took off in pursuit and felt the headache throb to life between his temples again.

27

SCENE ✪ NCIS ✪ CRIME SCEN

NAVAL CRIMINAL INVESTIGATIVE SERVICE

>> ACE WELDING
>> JACKSONVILLE, NORTH CAROLINA
>> 1027 HOURS

Remy, lighter and faster than Shel, got the early jump on chasing Dawson. He pulled his sidearm because it was better to have it in hand and not need it than to try to draw it when he did need it. He'd learned that on the bad streets of New Orleans, before the SEAL instructor had taught him.

In three long strides, Remy crashed through the back door after Dawson. Dawson ran through the graveled alley, splashing through mud puddles left there by the rain Sunday night.

Fast as Remy was, Max was faster. The Labrador plunged ahead, churning all four paws in pursuit.

Dawson glanced over his shoulder. Fear blanched his face when he saw the dog gaining on him as if he were standing still. He missed a step and careened to the left, slamming through a half dozen trash cans. Noise filled the alley.

"Takedown!" Shel ordered from beside Remy.

In response, Max lunged up immediately, seized Dawson's leather-covered wrist, and put the brakes on. Off balance, Dawson heeled over to the side and dropped to the ground.

Dawson tried to get up, cursing and flailing at Max. The dog moved, keeping tension on the arm constantly, twisting and turning to pull from different directions and keep his adversary on the ground. Dawson screamed and cursed, kicking his feet to try to find purchase only to have his balance yanked away from him each time he attempted to get up.

"Good dog." Shel stopped by Max and patted Max on the head. "Release."

Max's jaws opened.

"I didn't do anything," Dawson whined. He squinted up at the bright morning sun. "You can't arrest me. I didn't do anything."

Shel shook his head. "We didn't come to arrest you. We just came to ask a few questions."

"You're not going to arrest me?" That seemed to surprise Dawson.

"No. Why'd you run?"

Lying flat on his back made it hard for Dawson to shrug, but he did. "I don't know."

"That was stupid."

Remy said nothing. He knew from experience that running was a way of life for people who lived outside the law.

"What do you want?" Dawson asked.

"Just to talk."

Dawson looked suspicious. "What if I don't want to talk?"

"You don't have to."

"Then I don't want to talk to you."

Shel sighed and shook his head. "You want to talk to us."

"No. I don't."

Squatting down beside the man, Max at his side, Shel regarded Dawson. "Yes, you do."

"Forget it."

"Let me tell you why," Shel suggested. "If you don't talk to us, my buddy and I are going to haunt your every waking moment. We'll be there to tuck you into bed at night and hit your snooze bar for you in the morning."

"You can't do that."

"Yes, we can. And we will." Shel's face was hard and implacable behind his amber-tinted aviator glasses.

"I'd listen to the man if I were you," Remy said.

Dawson shifted his gaze to Remy. "Why?"

"Because he's telling you the truth. I mean, does he look like a man with anything else to do? It's just him and that dog."

Max lay there contentedly, pink tongue lolling out as he watched the group of men who had followed the action from the welding shop.

"They got all day to kill," Remy said. "If they weren't haunting you, they'd be out chasing cars."

Dawson looked back at Shel. He licked his lips. "What do you want to talk about?"

"George Haskins."

Confusion twisted Dawson's wrinkled features. "Haskins has been gone a long time."

"He just recently turned up again."

"What do you want to know about Haskins?"

"We've got a few questions."

"Come with us," Remy suggested. "Special Agent McHenry will buy you lunch." He stuck out a hand.

Shel's head tilted slightly, just enough to pull Remy into his view. But he didn't say anything. His lips tightened in a small, ironic smile.

Dawson thought about it for a moment, then grabbed Remy's hand. "Lunch sounds good," Dawson said. "I missed breakfast this morning."

Me too, Remy thought as he pulled Dawson to his feet.

>> RALEIGH POLICE DEPARTMENT
>> RALEIGH, NORTH CAROLINA
>> 1034 HOURS

Detective Mark Broward was a big man. In his midfifties, he was overweight and rumpled. He wore a gunslinger mustache that made him look like a hard case. Judging from the scars on the man's knuckles, the knife scar on the right side of his throat, and the ragged scar that mangled his left eyebrow, it wasn't just a look.

Maggie took in the desk. Most people might have assumed the desk was cluttered because piles sat everywhere. However, when she studied the piles of folders, newspapers, and pictures, she noticed they were all organized.

You're a tidy man, Detective Broward, Maggie thought. *This is just part of your disguise.*

On the right side of the desk blotter was a rectangular calendar with notes and phone numbers scribbled all over it. Newspaper stories about George Haskins's body being recovered draped a small pile of folders.

Will shook hands with Broward; then Maggie did the same.

The detective waved them to two straight-backed chairs in front of the desk. "You didn't say what this was about." Broward took off his suit jacket and hung it over the back of his chair.

"You worked the Chloe Ivers kidnapping seventeen years ago," Will said. "We'd like to talk about that."

Broward's eyes cut to the pile containing the stories about George Haskins. He grinned a little, and Maggie could almost see the wheels turning in the man's mind.

"That's interesting," Broward said.

"Why?" Will asked.

"Nobody's brought up Chloe Ivers in a long time. Now you guys find a charm belonging to her in the cuff of a dead man's pants, and suddenly it seems like she's on everyone's mind." Broward clasped his hands together and leaned forward across the desk.

"You were one of the detectives on her kidnapping and murder."

"That's right. What do you want to know?" Broward asked.

"How tight was the case against Isaac Allen Lamont?"

"Not tight enough to suit the district attorney." Broward shrugged. "Those guys like wins. A cop like me, he just likes putting bad guys away. I take more chances than the DA's office. I want a guy to know I know what he is."

What not *who*. Maggie watched Broward, taking in the personality traits she picked up on. In addition to the neatness of the apparent chaos on the desk, people were neatly distributed in Broward's mental lists according to category. He was a very black-and-white kind of guy. Everything in his world was about balance.

"Did you think Lamont killed that girl?" Will asked.

Broward spread his hands. "What else was there to think?"

Will was silent for a moment. Maggie knew he was frustrated with the interview. He'd expected more cooperation.

"Did you have any other suspects?" Will asked.

"Of course we did."

"Who?"

Broward shifted, leaning back in the chair.

He thinks we're wasting his time, Maggie realized.

"Look, Commander Coburn," Broward said in a bored tone, "I don't know what kind of training you get at NCIS, but we get a lot. If you have a homicide, you look at the family first. That's where you'll find most of the killers. Usually the deceased—that's the dead person—is killed by the person he or she knew best. Someone in the family. You get a wife killed, you look at the husband. You get a husband killed, you look at the wife. Or, if they got one, the boyfriend or girlfriend. Most homicides are abrupt, crimes of passion, brought on by a confluence of events." He smiled.

Will didn't get deterred. Maggie had known he wouldn't.

"You checked into the parents' alibis?" Will asked.

Broward nodded and laced his hands behind his head as though he were completely disinterested. "Of course. Look, I don't know what your schedule looks like there with the NCIS, but mine's pretty jammed. If you just want a rundown of our investigation, I'll be happy to send you my case notes."

Maggie knew they'd never get any notes. Broward was brushing them off. She looked at Will. "He's not going to give us anything unless we give him something in return."

Will didn't take his eyes from Broward. "What about the spirit of cooperation?"

"He figures we need to make the first step. Plus, he's already formed an opinion about what's going on." Maggie leaned forward and picked up the small pile of folders under the news articles about the recovery of George Haskins's body.

"Hey," Broward protested, grabbing the stack.

Maggie didn't release the folders. She met Broward's gaze.

Broward smiled. "You're a pretty smart lady."

"Yes." Maggie waited.

Shrugging, Broward released the folders.

Maggie put them on her side of the desk, pushed the news stories aside, and opened the first folder. It contained pictures of Chloe Ivers.

"I can see you've already put some of it together," Maggie said, "but you don't know everything we know. That must mean you're working off of something else. Maybe something that we don't know; I suggest we trade information. We give you what we know, you give us what you know."

Broward looked back at her contemplatively.

"Anything we tell you," Will said, "is off the record."

Broward grinned. "I get the same deal from you."

"Done."

Standing, Broward hooked his suit jacket from the back of the chair and pulled it on. He took his sidearm from the desk and slid it into a pancake holster on his hip. "Let's take a ride."

CRIME SCENE

28

SCENE NCIS CRIME SCENE

NAVAL CRIMINAL INVESTIGATIVE SERVICE

>> ROSA'S CANTINA
>> JACKSONVILLE, NORTH CAROLINA
>> 1058 HOURS

The restaurant was a small mom-and-pop operation not far from Ace Welding. Painted plywood cutouts in the shape of cacti, a couple of burros, and a Mexican man stood out front. A string of red jalapeño lights framed the windows.

Mexican wasn't Cajun cooking, which would have suited Remy better, but for the moment he was fine with it. The hostess seated them in a corner booth at the back under a rack of sombreros and serapes. Max stayed out in the Jeep with the windows rolled down. No one would touch the vehicle with the dog there.

Heads turned as the regulars took in the new faces. A few of them even called out a greeting to Ronald Dawson.

"They know you here?" Shel asked.

Dawson shrugged. He'd taken off his welding gear and wore a dark blue uniform top and jeans. "I eat here sometimes."

Shel stripped off his jacket, revealing the pistols in the double shoulder holsters.

"Probably not after today," Dawson said morosely.

"Sit down."

Dawson sat at the side of the booth. Shel scooted him over, hemming him in. Remy got in on the other side, across the table.

A pretty server in a black skirt and white blouse came by with setups, placing chips, salsa, and tortillas on the table.

Remy talked to her in Spanish, chatting her up with a quick smile and ordering fajitas. She flirted with him for a moment, then turned her attention to Shel.

Shel ordered the same, also in Spanish, but without the flirting.

Dawson looked at both of them. "I don't speak Spanish."

"It's okay," the server said with a heavy accent. "I speak English."

Dawson ordered a plate of enchiladas.

"Dude," Remy said, "*enchiladas* is Spanish."

Dawson helped himself to the chips and salsa.

"Tell us about George Haskins," Shel said.

"What do you want to know?"

"How did you hook up with him? What did you do for him? When was the last time you saw him?"

Dawson frowned. "I don't want to get myself in trouble."

"In trouble for what?" Shel sounded patient.

"The things I did with Haskins."

"Whatever you did with Haskins is off the table. The statute of limitations has run out for everything but murder."

Dawson ate his chip.

"Did you kill somebody while you were working with Haskins?"

Cautiously, Dawson said, "No."

"Then you don't have any worries."

Narrowing his eyes, Dawson peered from Shel to Remy to Shel again. "Cops lie."

"Cops," Remy said, "also take people who don't answer their questions out into an alley and beat them to a pulp."

Dawson looked at him and choked on a chip.

Remy smiled.

Dawson washed the chip down and wiped his mouth on the back of his arm. "I hooked up with Haskins a couple years before he disappeared. He was running black-market stuff out of Camp Lejeune."

"What kind of stuff?" Shel asked.

"Electronics. Asian and Philippine pornography. Russian weapons. The Berlin wall hadn't fallen then, but everybody knew it was coming. Eastern Europe was having a fire sale on weapons. Haskins's people were bringing them in by the boatload, and we were off-loading them to gangs. I was the connection for the local bikers."

"A black-market pipeline usually goes both ways," Shel said.

Dawson nodded. "It did. The bikers traded cash and drugs for the weapons. We got cash from pawnshops and secondhand stores for the electronics. Finally opened our own place and started a semilegitimate business."

"Seems like it would have been risky."

Dawson shook his shaggy head. "Nah. Haskins had something going with the local cops. They gave the shops a pass as long as we kept the trouble out of there. We did."

"What happened to the shop?"

"NCIS shut it down. They nabbed Bryce Ketchum for illegal trafficking, and he took the fall. That's when they busted him out of the Marines. They almost got Haskins, too."

"How'd they miss?" Shel asked.

"Ketchum wouldn't roll over on Haskins. He took the fall himself. The full weight. Didn't name nobody on the military side of the operation." Dawson shrugged. "They caught a couple guys on some ships, but nobody talked."

"Why?"

"Haskins would have killed anybody who did."

"Is that a fact?" Remy asked, not impressed.

Shel was interested. "Haskins had killed people before?"

Dawson nodded. "Yeah, one time. A guy who was chiseling on the profits. I never saw it myself, but I knew two guys who did."

"Maybe they were lying."

"Maybe, but I don't think so. Haskins was rough as a cob. If you crossed him, you were taking your life in your hands. I think that's one of the reasons Ketchum never gave him up."

The server arrived with plates of food, quickly disbursed them, and retreated.

"When was the last time you saw Haskins?" Shel asked.

"Shortly before he disappeared." Dawson took a bite of enchilada and washed it down with tea. "Didn't even know he was missing for a while."

"Why?"

"Because Haskins had stepped away from the operation on a day-to-day basis. He was letting others run it."

"That seems strange for a guy who was so hands-on," Remy commented.

"Word I got was Haskins had found himself another gig."

"Which was . . . ?" Shel asked.

Dawson shook his head. "He got connected to somebody political. Somebody who needed a backdoor man every so often."

"A backdoor man?" Shel repeated.

Remy smiled. It seemed the Marine's education wasn't complete after all. "That's a Southern term, Tex. A backdoor man is usually an investigator or a blackmailer. Somebody a supposedly honest person doesn't want other people to know they're doing business with. They don't let them in the front door. They let them in the back so that no one sees them."

Shel swiveled his attention back to Dawson. "Haskins was somebody's backdoor man?"

"Yeah."

"Whose?"

Dawson raised his shoulders and dropped them. "That was as big of a secret as what happened to Haskins. All we knew is that when Ketchum went down for the black-market gig, Haskins seemed bulletproof."

"Somebody was protecting him?" Remy asked.

"Don't know. Back then, a few people whispered about it. But nobody knew anything."

"What about Ketchum?" Remy asked. "Did he find out if Haskins had a guardian angel?"

"You'd have to ask him."

"If Ketchum went down while Haskins was being protected, Ketchum could've flipped on Haskins. Cut a deal."

"We all could have," Dawson said. "There were seven of us who took a fall over that." He shook his head. "But wasn't anybody gonna roll over on Haskins."

"Why?"

"He'd have killed whoever did. Like I said, we all knew that. If you crossed Haskins, you could bet you were going on a one-way trip to the morgue, and George Haskins was gonna be there to check your bags."

>> LAKE RALEIGH
>> RALEIGH, NORTH CAROLINA
>> 1102 HOURS

Following Detective Broward's directions, Will drove north from the Raleigh Police Department. He turned off S. McDowell Street onto US-70, then onto I-40 for a short distance. He exited at Gorman Street, then turned right onto Thistledown Drive, which became Crump Road.

When they stopped, they were at the marina at Lake Raleigh.

"I come here when I want to think without people asking what I'm thinking." Broward sat in the backseat of the pickup.

Will watched the detective's eyes in the mirror. Beyond the windshield, several boaters were taking advantage of the fair weather and bright sun. The day seemed too good to spend talking about a dead girl.

But that's what we're here to do. Will turned his attention to Broward, then confirmed the media's story of Chloe Ivers's charm being found in George Haskins's pants cuff. He didn't mention that Laura Ivers had been to the NCIS offices. The only thing that affected Broward's case was the possible connection between Haskins and Chloe Ivers.

Broward settled back in the seat, his hands clasped behind his head. "Do you have anything linking Haskins and the girl other than the charm?"

"Not yet," Maggie said from the passenger seat. "But we will. We don't believe Isaac Allen Lamont killed Chloe Ivers, and there's absolutely no evidence to suggest he killed Haskins. That leaves two murders unsolved here, and there's got to be more evidence somewhere."

"I agree with you about Lamont. It never felt right. Lamont's as cold-blooded a killer as I've ever seen, but you look at his stats. That monster killed young women, but he never killed girls."

"Unless Chloe was the first," Will said.

Broward rubbed his broad chin. "Maybe. But I wouldn't put money on it. His MO was off too. He never did home invasions. For Lamont to have taken the girl from her room, he'd have had to know exactly where it was."

"Lamont didn't stalk his victims that closely," Maggie said.

"That's right. He chose them at random. Whenever the mood struck him. But not without a plan for escape." Broward looked at her more closely. "What do you do at NCIS?"

"Profiler."

Nodding in satisfaction, Broward switched his attention to Will. "All right, let's get down to it. Are you trying to find out who killed George Haskins or who killed Chloe Ivers? Or maybe you're thinking you'll get lucky and it'll be a twofer on the doer?"

"We're going to follow it where it goes."

"Okay. Will you keep me in the loop on this?"

"As much as I can."

Broward rubbed his hands. "If you got a twofer here, the trail leading back to the killer gets twice as tight: you're looking for someone who knew Chloe Ivers *and* George Haskins."

Will listened.

"Those two didn't run in the same crowds," Broward said. "You generate a pool of friends and acquaintances for both of them, then cross-reference them, you're going to end up with a short list."

"If you didn't think that Lamont was the killer, whom did you have in mind?"

"On any murder investigation, you start small."

"The family members."

Broward nodded. "Always the family. In this case, you had three." He counted them off on his fingers. "Mom. Stepdad. And little brother."

"Mom was away from home at the time Chloe was killed."

"Maybe. The coroner's time of death is always an estimate. Laura Ivers was working at Camp Lejeune, but I also found out she was on her own a lot. Let's just say there was a window of opportunity."

"What about a motive?"

Broward shrugged. "We didn't develop that line. But you have a teenage daughter around the house with a stepdad who liked to chase women. . . ."

"Ben Swanson was having affairs while he was married?" Will asked.

"I don't know, but I know he had them after his stepdaughter's death. People talk like it was the wife's fault, that she turned cold after her daughter's death. Maybe that happened. But I've followed the congressman's career. He has a problem with being faithful. All I'm saying is that maybe it didn't start after the stepdaughter's death."

"Do you have any proof to back that up?"

Broward shook his head. "Guesswork. But I wanted to follow up on it back then."

"Why didn't you?"

"I wasn't running primary on the investigation. I was taking orders, not trusted to think for myself. I still take orders today, which is why we're out here talking about this instead of back at the department."

"You've been ordered not to talk about the Chloe Ivers case?" Maggie asked.

"Right. Then and lately."

"Why lately?" Will asked.

"Congressman Swanson is a big deal around here," Broward said. "And he's getting to be more of a big deal up in Washington. He makes magic happen for his district. Funding. Grants. Political appointees. People wanting careers in government are standing around waiting to be touched by lightning. Swanson's got the lightning." He paused. "That's partly the reason the investigation got shut down seventeen years ago."

"What do you mean?" Maggie asked.

"We were two weeks into the murder investigation," Broward said. "It was in all the papers."

Will knew that. He had copies of all of them on DVD from Estrella.

"Everybody was trying to guess what happened to Chloe Ivers." Broward took a deep breath. "I got to the scene where she was found. It was bad. It was the first time I'd ever worked a dead kid. It's hard." His eyes turned cold. "Which is why I've never let this case go. Whoever did this needs to pay."

A group of fishermen walked close to the pickup, carrying rods and coolers. Will wished he could join them out on the water, because the mood inside his pickup had become cold, hard, and desperate.

"Swanson was one of the main forces behind pinning Chloe Ivers's murder on Lamont," Broward said. "Once Swanson found out Lamont had been in the area, he didn't rest until Lamont was apprehended. He got everybody involved—city, county, and state. They even rolled out National Guard units. That's how Lamont was found and brought down. I think the only surprising thing was that they brought Lamont in alive."

"Why?" Maggie asked.

Broward shrugged. "It would have been easier if Lamont was dead. He wouldn't have been protesting his innocence. That's one of the main reasons he was never convicted for the girl's murder. He talked up a storm about the other murders once he was caught and knew he was going away. He even talked about murders he'd committed that prosecutors couldn't tie him to. But he maintains to this day that he didn't kill Chloe Ivers."

"Do you think Laura Ivers killed her daughter?" Maggie asked.

"I don't have a reason to think so, no. From what I'd seen of her, she was a stand-up lady. Real. But she was married to a louse like Swanson, so maybe her objectivity wasn't everything it could have been."

"A lot of people don't think Swanson is a louse," Will said.

"Hey, sorry," Broward said. "If I stepped on any toes there, I didn't mean to."

"No foul," Will said. "I've never met the man. But he has done a lot of good for this state."

"I didn't say that he hadn't. But as a husband and dad, he's left a lot to be desired."

"Could Swanson have killed his stepdaughter?" Maggie asked.

"That's possibility number two. Say there was some hanky-panky going on between stepdad and stepdaughter. Maybe Swanson was afraid Chloe wasn't going to keep her mouth shut. Maybe she wanted a new car and was threatening dear old stepdad."

"Something like that would have killed his political career," Will said.

"You know," Broward said casually, "something like that still might."

"There were no signs of sexual activity in the coroner's report," Maggie said.

"The coroner was looking for *recent* sexual activity," Broward pointed out. "Nobody said whether or not the girl was sexually active."

Sitting there, Will felt dirty, like he was getting buried alive. Some investigations were like that. No matter how hard he tried, he ended up getting covered in the despair and hopelessness of the victims.

"The fact that the girl wasn't molested at the time of the murder is another indicator that Lamont didn't kill her," Broward said. "But let's get away from the really depressing side of this thing. Let's say Chloe Ivers was an innocent. And let's say that she caught her dad in the middle of one of his affairs. Maybe she was going to tell her mom. At the time, Swanson's career as congressman was just getting started, and he was beginning to pick up speed. But something like that would have taken the wind out of his sails. People liked Laura Ivers before the election. They liked her even more when they saw her dealing with her daughter's death."

Will had no problem believing that. Laura Ivers had left an impression on him, too, when he'd met her.

"Then there's possibility number three," Broward continued flatly, as if they were discussing the weather.

"Jeff Swanson?" Maggie said. "But he was only five years old when Chloe was killed."

"Jeff Swanson," Broward said calmly, "was a messed-up kid. Today he's a messed-up adult. Have you looked into him much?"

"No," Will answered.

"Well, you won't find much about him. His father keeps a tight grip on any information about his son. But Jeff Swanson is a head case. He's been on medication since he was three or four."

"Why?"

"Some kind of emotional imbalance or something. That's all I ever heard. Legally, you can't poke around in stuff like that, and Swanson keeps a tight lid on all of it. But if you check with the Washington, D.C., police, you'll see that Jeff Swanson's had several automobile accidents and even—maybe—tried to commit suicide twice. He has a history of violent behavior."

"How does that tie in with Chloe's death?" Maggie asked. "She was strangled. There's no way a five-year-old could have done that."

"I know Chloe was choked to death, but look at all those other injuries she suffered. Broken bones. Lacerations. I didn't think about it then—I was too new on the job—but later, after I saw more deaths that were homicides as well as accidents, I thought about those injuries. They could have been from a fall down a flight of stairs. A five-year-old could push a full-grown man down the stairs if he caught him off guard. A teenage stepsister would be even easier."

Will thought about that. "Can I get a copy of the coroner's file from you? pictures and X-rays?"

"Oh, I couldn't give you something like that," Broward said. "Chloe Ivers's case is technically solved. And Congressman Swanson has given strict orders to my department that no one is supposed to be given access to those files." He reached into his briefcase and took out a thick folder. "So it would be better if, after you look at these, you forget where you got them."

Will took the folder and said thanks.

"Thank me by finding out what happened," Broward said.

Will unlocked the compartment between the seats and slipped the folder inside next to the notebook computer he carried in the truck. "What do you know about George Haskins?"

Broward grinned. "Haskins was an interesting case. I looked into him after he came to Raleigh. His name came up during an investigation into a burglary of Michael Tarlton."

Will shook his head. "I don't know the name."

"You're too young," Broward said. "You were in college or maybe even high school when Tarlton used to be congressman from this district. Tarlton had been in place for two terms, and he was looking at an easy reelection. He was running against Swanson. It looked like Tarlton was going to walk off with the race. Then journalists got wind of Tarlton's affairs. He pulled out of the race before they got made into an issue and before anyone published anything more than hints of it."

"Other careers have weathered hits like that," Will said. "Swanson has held his career together."

"Times have changed somewhat. A certain president of the United States changed the standard on that in the public eye, if you recall. But this was almost two decades ago."

"How was Haskins involved?"

"I busted the guy who broke into Tarlton's house. His name was Clyde Turnbill. Turnbill admitted to stealing some incriminating pictures Tarlton had. He said he gave them to George Haskins. Then Turnbill got to the department and grew a backbone. Asked for an attorney. Two hours after he got released on bail, Clyde Turnbill turned up dead. Somebody shot him right between the eyes."

"Did you talk to Haskins about it?"

"Sure. But I had nothing solid, and Haskins knew it. He told me where to get off. I had no choice. I got off. But I was working some stuff with the Jacksonville police. Kind of following up. I found out about the trouble Haskins was in there. And I also found out Haskins was coming to Raleigh regularly." Broward paused. "Guess who benefited most from Tarlton's files getting stolen?"

"Swanson," Will said.

"Bingo." Broward smiled.

"Could Haskins have been working for Swanson?" Maggie asked. "If so, it's possible that he knew Chloe Ivers."

"Shel and Remy are talking with one of Haskins's old associates, probably as we speak," Will said. "Maybe they'll turn up something."

29

SCENE NCIS CRIME SCEN

NAVAL CRIMINAL INVESTIGATIVE SERVICE

>> NCIS HEADQUARTERS
>> CAMP LEJEUNE, NORTH CAROLINA
>> 0843 HOURS

Will's phone rang as he sat at his desk going over the notes on the raid at the Ketchum farm. He grabbed the receiver and pulled it to his ear. "Coburn."

"Will," Larkin said, "I wanted you to know that Bryce Ketchum just made bail."

Leaning back in his chair, Will felt tired and beaten. The team had spent three days going over the raid and Chloe Ivers's murder. Nothing new had turned up.

The problem was that they had nothing in either case that they could move on. Having Bryce Ketchum in custody at least gave a flicker of hope. The man was looking at prison with no hope of ever getting out. Even if Ketchum couldn't cut a deal, Will had hoped he might talk just to make sure someone else hung along with him.

"How did he get out?" Will asked.

"He had a high-powered attorney," Larkin said.

"Thomas Wardell. Maggie told me about him."

"Even with Wardell pushing to get Ketchum released, Ketchum had to put up a million-dollar bail."

"A bail bondsman fronted that kind of money?"

"No. Wardell brought the money into court. In untraceable bearer bonds from a Swiss bank."

"Where did Ketchum get the money? I thought we'd seized everything." With the drugs involved, they'd been able to do that through other federal agencies.

"We must have missed some."

"You'd think a million dollars would be hard to miss."

"There are people still looking, Will. No matter what, we've hurt his operation."

"Do we have anyone on him?"

"No. With Wardell involved, my superiors didn't want to take the chance with a stalking charge that could mess up the court case. You've got Ketchum, Will. When we get him before a jury, he's not coming back out of prison. No one wants to endanger that."

Will understood. That was the safest course. Bryce Ketchum was free and running for the moment. But there was, theoretically, nowhere for him to go.

"Do we know what the tie is between Wardell and Ketchum?" Larkin asked.

"No. Maggie checked back through the histories of both of them. They've never had dealings with each other."

"Any people in common?"

"None that we've found."

"Has Wardell ever worked for Swanson?"

"No."

Larkin sighed. "We're missing something, Will."

"Yes, sir." Will hesitated. "It's out there, sir. We'll find it." They talked for a few more minutes; then both of them hung up.

Turning, Will gazed out his window at the camp. In the streets below, Marines and sailors went about morning PT and drills. Being in a military environment was reassuring. Everyone had a purpose and a function, and there were things to do every day that mattered.

A knock on the door drew his attention. Maggie stood there. She didn't look happy.

Will waved her in.

Maggie sat in the chair. "Did you know Ketchum was released on bail?"

"I just finished talking with Larkin."

"It doesn't make any sense."

"Wardell's involvement?"

"Yes."

They knew from the camp phone records that Ketchum had called his own attorney, a woman he'd used in several instances before for himself and for people who worked for him. Logic told them that she had called Wardell. But no one knew why she would pass the case on to Wardell or why Wardell would take it on. Especially since it was a slam dunk legally.

"Someone somewhere," Maggie said, "thinks they have something to save."

"Ketchum thinks he's saving his butt. What does Wardell get out of it? Money?"

Maggie shook her head. "Wardell got his money the hard way. He worked for it. Now he can afford to be choosy about whom he represents."

"But if it's not the paycheck, what motivates Wardell to take on a lowlife like Ketchum as a client?"

"That's the question," Maggie said. "There's something here that we're missing. Of course, Wardell isn't representing Ketchum for free. Ketchum has to pay Wardell's fee somehow."

"Which means that Ketchum not only came up with bail, but he also put down a sizable retainer for Wardell."

"A very sizable retainer. But we still have no idea what the connection is between the two."

"Larkin doesn't have anyone on Ketchum," Will said, "and he doesn't want anyone on him. But that doesn't mean we can't talk to other people who know him, to follow up on our own investigation."

Maggie raised an eyebrow. "You mean spy on him?"

Will grinned. "Just a little."

Maggie nodded and stood. "I'll let Shel and Remy know." She left.

Will checked his e-mail quickly before returning to the case files. Wren had sent him a picture she'd drawn. It showed the sailboat with her, Steven, and Will on board. A brief note said she'd "had the best time ever!"

There was nothing from Steven.

Knowing his kids were safe, though, helped him feel more hopeful. Reading about what had happened to Chloe Ivers reminded him that children were at risk every day. Parents were sometimes oblivious to that, but recognizing the fear that was there on a daily basis would have been too heavy to deal with.

Determined, he turned his attention back to the case files.

>> FULCHER LANDING

>> SNEADS FERRY, NORTH CAROLINA

>> 1520 HOURS

Bryce Ketchum sat at a table in a small café not far from the boat slips near Fulcher Landing. His family had lived in North Carolina for generations. Jacksonville and the areas around it were home. They'd always felt that way.

He stared out the window, feeling the chill from New River breezing in against the glass. He tried not to think about leaving Jacksonville, but he had no choice. Things had gotten too big for him to handle.

Thankfully, he'd always saved some of his money. After the first stint in prison, when he'd learned everything could be taken from him with the single fall of a judge's gavel, he'd planned for the day he had to leave.

But he didn't just have money set aside. He also had information. That information was worth a lot to certain people. That information had gotten him Thomas Wardell as his attorney and had freed up a million dollars in bearer bonds to get him out of NCIS holding.

The tricky part was that the information could also get him killed.

Ketchum crushed out his cigarette and lit another. He glanced at his watch. His contact was almost twenty minutes late.

Then the track phone he'd bought that morning rang. He'd only given the number to Wardell. Either the lawyer was calling or the man Ketchum was supposed to meet was.

Ketchum punched the Talk button. "Yeah."

"You ready?" The voice was deep and confident.

Guy's got a right to sound that way, Ketchum thought bitterly. *He's been living off the fat of the land.* "You're late."

"Unavoidable, I'm afraid," the man on the phone said. "Are you coming out?"

"You can see me?" That thought disturbed Ketchum. He thought about how a man with a high-powered rifle would have no problem at all taking him out.

"Tar Heels Windbreaker. Jeans. Tennis shoes."

Ketchum's hands shook a little. *Okay, so he could be seen.* "I just want to make a deal. Something we'll both find beneficial."

"I'm willing to discuss it."

"I don't know how my attorney sounded when she called you," Ketchum said. "But I wasn't threatening you."

"I understand. So let's talk."

"I've never said a thing about anything," Ketchum said. "And I've never leaned on you in seventeen years."

"I know. Like I said, we're simpatico. Just one hand washing the other."

"Yeah. That's it." Only Ketchum hadn't left the other hand any choice about washing his hand.

"Are you coming?"

"Where?"

"There's a Sea Ray out in the river. Gray and blue. She's called *Jilly.*"

Shading his eyes against the midafternoon sunlight, Ketchum looked north toward the river. He spotted the fully dressed twenty-eight-foot yacht cruising into one of the public docks. A man sat at the wheel, and two more sat in back.

"I see it," Ketchum said. "Where are you?"

"In the cabin."

Suspicion filled Ketchum. "Come out where I can see you." He watched the yacht intently.

The two men in the stern leaped out and moored the boat to cleats.

A moment later a man stepped from the yacht's forward cabin and stood by the pilot. He waved. His other hand held a cell phone to his ear. Dressed in a baseball cap and Windbreaker, he looked like a television star trying to go incognito.

"All right. Let's talk," said the voice on the phone. Then the connection went dead.

Years had passed since Ketchum had seen the man in the flesh. He still didn't trust him. The man had always been out for himself.

The two men by the mooring cleats held their positions. They didn't fit in with the fishermen and tourists around them.

A sour bubble burst in Ketchum's gut. A tiny voice in the back of his head told him he should run now while he still could.

But he was greedy.

The NCIS and federal law enforcement agencies were going to take most of his money. His empire, modest as it had been, was in shambles. Even if he got out of prison—and he didn't think the government would give him that deal even if he told them everything he knew—he'd have nothing.

Bryce Ketchum wouldn't live his life destitute. That was unacceptable. He'd worked too hard for too long to get where he was. More than that, he had enemies. Out on the street, without protection, he doubted he'd live more than a month. The Chinese gang he'd been dealing with already held him responsible for what had happened at the farm. Ketchum wouldn't be surprised to learn that a bounty had been placed on his head.

You don't have a choice, he told himself.

For a moment he held on to the business card Wardell had given him. Ketchum honestly didn't think he'd see the lawyer again because he didn't intend to hang around. Either with the help he was trying to arrange or on his own hook, Ketchum was going to shake the dust of North Carolina off and never look back.

There were places in Mexico, the Caribbean, and South America where a guy like him—one willing to do whatever it took—could make a living and stay beyond extradition by the United States. He would be heading in that direction before the sun set.

The man on the boat waved impatiently.

Reluctantly, Ketchum stood up. He left a tip for the tired server and went out.

Cold wind from the river buffeted Ketchum. Still, he liked its bracing nature. He'd lived around New River more than half his life. He'd fished and swam in the river, killed his first man and buried his first body in the swamplands. He felt tied to it in ways that he was certain other people didn't.

Hands in his Windbreaker pockets, his right hand curled around the small Browning .380 semiautomatic there, Ketchum walked to the yacht and stepped aboard. The deck tilted slightly.

Before Ketchum could settle himself, the man he'd come to meet grabbed him by the back of his neck, tripped him, and guided his fall through the narrow, short doorway to the forward cabin.

Ketchum fell hard, landing on the couch/bed that took up most of the forward deck. He hit hard enough to have the wind knocked out of him. Panic set in, fierce and relentless. He tried to pull the .380 from his pocket, but the material trapped his hand, and he lay on top of his arm.

Helpless, feeling the other man's weight on his back, Ketchum struggled but couldn't get away. Cold steel pressed against the back of his neck.

"You should have stayed out of my business," the man told him.

"I had no choice," Ketchum said. "I was going to prison."

"At least you would have lived."

Before Ketchum could say anything else, he felt something slam into the base of his skull. Then he didn't feel anything.

30

SCENE  NCIS  CRIME SCEN

NAVAL CRIMINAL INVESTIGATIVE SERVICE

>> NCIS HEADQUARTERS
>> CAMP LEJEUNE, NORTH CAROLINA
>> 1649 HOURS

Will stared at the television broadcast on Estrella's computer. Commander Laura Ivers stood in front of a Navy building. She wore her uniform and looked tired.

"Commander Ivers, do you still think Isaac Allen Lamont killed your daughter?" The reporter was a slim, Asian female for the local news. She held out a microphone.

Laura's expression hardened. "I *never* believed that."

"Is this live?" Will asked.

Estrella shook her head. "It's not more than ten minutes old, though. They're rerunning it." She glanced at one of the other monitors on her desk. "The story's spreading. It won't be long before our phones start ringing off the hook."

"Did you know Sergeant Haskins?"

"I did not."

Will suspected that only Laura's experience and training as a Navy officer kept her calm in front of the camera. *But it's the mother that keeps her talking,* he thought. The Navy would have liked to stay clear of the situation, especially since it had the potential of snowballing politically.

"Did you know Sergeant Haskins was stationed at Camp Lejeune?" the reporter asked.

"No. I told you that I didn't know Sergeant Haskins."

"Did you know that Sergeant Haskins disappeared shortly after your daughter's murder?"

"No." A flicker of irritation passed through Laura's blue eyes.

"Did your daughter know Sergeant Haskins?"

"No." Laura's voice grew more harsh.

Will didn't blame the woman. In his dealings with news reporters, he'd found most of them weren't very creative when it came to asking questions. The choice tactic tended to be to ask the same questions over and over again, more loudly and with more accusation, till they got a quote that they could use as they saw fit.

"Did you know all your daughter's friends?" the reporter asked.

"No. Of course not."

"Then it is possible that your daughter knew Sergeant Haskins?"

Laura took a deep breath. "Here's your statement, and it's all you're going to get. Only a few days ago, I discovered that the body of a man believed to be George Haskins was found in Jacksonville, North Carolina. He had a charm that's been identified as my daughter's on his person. I know that George Haskins has been missing for seventeen years, almost the same length of time since my daughter's death. I've been assured that the NCIS office at Camp Lejeune is looking into the matter. Commander Will Coburn is in charge of the unit there." She paused. "Now, we're through here."

Stepping back, Laura waved to two Marine MPs standing nearby. Both men moved forward and covered the commander's retreat, interposing their bodies between the television crew and Laura Ivers.

"Well," Will commented drily, "that should ensure our phone lines get busy."

"They already have been," Estrella said. "From the first broadcast. This is going to make it worse."

The reporter didn't give up. "Commander Ivers. Commander Ivers. Just one more question."

Laura kept walking, and the Marines remained where they were.

"Commander Ivers, have you talked to Congressman Ben Swanson about this latest revelation regarding the murder of your daughter? What is your ex-husband going to do about uncovering the truth of your daughter's death?"

"By my count," Estrella said, "that was two questions." She looked up at Will. "What do you want me to do about the media calls?"

"Draft a few agents from another detail. Have them answer the phones. They're to give no comment, but I want them taking notes. Questions the media pose may include information we don't have."

Estrella nodded.

"We have to keep the phone lines open. In case someone does come forward with information."

"Aye, sir."

Will got a fresh cup of coffee and headed back to his office. With the media interest keyed to Swanson's position in the House of Representatives, exposure was about to explode.

>> 1702 HOURS

The phone rang and Will answered.

"It's Larkin."

Frustration chafed at Will. He knew the director wouldn't have called him just about the media coverage of Chloe Ivers's murder. Things had gotten worse. "Yes, sir."

"You've kept up with the news?"

"Yes."

"Did you see the interview with Commander Ivers?"

"I did."

"What do you think?"

Will leaned back in the chair and felt conflicted. Part of him—the father part that totally understood where Laura Ivers was coming from—wanted to defend her. But he'd also been around politics enough to recognize a power play when he saw one. He couldn't help the woman with the pain she had gone through—*is still going through*, he corrected himself—but he couldn't blame her for what she'd done either.

"I think she deliberately said what she did to put pressure on us," Will said. "And on Congressman Swanson."

"I'd say you're right. Swanson can throw more weight this way. And he's going to now that his ex-wife has thrown the gauntlet by agreeing to the interview then refusing to answer questions about him."

Will had figured the situation pretty much the same way.

"In fact," Larkin said, "the congressman's flying down to talk to us in person."

"That's surprising. All it would take is a phone call."

"I got the phone call. From an aide. We're scheduled here in my office for a meeting at 2100 hours."

Will made a note on his iPAQ. "I'll be there. Should we expect members of the press too?"

"No. In fact, the congressman doesn't want anyone to know he's here. We're to meet him at the gate and escort him in. His name can't even be listed on the security logbook."

"Why?"

"The aide didn't say. I knew asking him would be a waste of my time. But my guess is that the congressman knows he and his ex-wife are no longer on the same page. Things might come out now that didn't come out seventeen years ago."

That was the way it happened in a cold case. People once united by passion or economics or fear or a need to be sheltered got divided. Solutions to a lot of cold cases happened because people changed and no longer protected each other.

"This meeting should be interesting," Will replied.

"I think so too."

>> 2057 HOURS

Will stood with Larkin just inside the security post. The guards remained vigilant, occasionally talking among themselves.

"Have we managed to find Bryce Ketchum yet?" Larkin asked.

"No." Ketchum had disappeared within five minutes of making bail and walking out of the Jacksonville courthouse. No one had seen him since.

Larkin sighed. "Choosing not to have him followed might prove to be a mistake."

"We didn't have a choice with Wardell involved."

"I know. But I'd still feel better if Shel or Remy were looking over Ketchum's shoulder right now."

Will silently agreed. "They're searching for him. Ketchum hasn't returned home or to any of his regular retreats. Most of the people he usually hangs with are in lockup. They didn't have Thomas Wardell applying legal pressure to get them out."

Too bad Ketchum's not still in the military, Will thought wryly. Most civilians weren't aware of the differences between the civilian and military court systems. When military personnel were tried in a military court, they were treated as government property. They weren't given any rights except the ones the government decided to give them. Bail could be denied, and a member of the military couldn't refuse to answer a question even if doing so would incriminate him or her.

Now that Ketchum was a civilian, he would be tried in a civilian court, and the trial would be a whole different story. And with the legal might of Thomas Wardell thrown into the mix, all bets were off.

"Do we have a positive ID on Haskins?" Larkin asked.

"Yes. It's Haskins. Nita got his dental records. I sent you an e-mail."

"Haven't seen it yet." Larkin was quiet for a moment. "You know I don't like to interfere with your team, Will. I don't meddle in any of the teams I've got working out in the field."

That was true. During the years that Will had worked with Larkin, the director had tried to maintain a supportive and mentoring posture.

"I know that." With a sinking feeling in his stomach, Will thought he knew what was going on.

"I have to ask about Nita."

"Nita's fine. She got the final results on Haskins as soon as she could."

"It's not her work I'm concerned about."

Will consulted his watch and discovered the congressman was already three minutes late. He hadn't expected Swanson to arrive on time.

"I've heard some things," Larkin said. "Last Friday, when you and your team were at the farmhouse rescuing Amanda Whitcomb, Nita was in a bar getting picked up by a Navy flier."

"I haven't heard anything about that."

"I haven't checked into it. I don't want to. So far no one's asked me to." Larkin sighed. "Nita's work is important. If she becomes compromised, the work the rest of us do here becomes compromised."

Will knew that.

"If Nita needs help, get her some help. Even if she doesn't want it." Larkin paused. "If she's beyond help, we need to get her out."

Standing there in the dark, Will remembered Frank Billings. Since Will had been with NCIS, Frank was the only man—only person—he had ever lost. Losing Nita would be almost as bad.

"I'm depending on you to look into this, Will," Larkin said. "I respect you, and I trust you to do whatever it is that needs doing."

"Yes, sir." There was no other answer.

Larkin's cell phone rang and he answered. "Yes, sir. We're in place, sir." He closed the phone and slid it into his pocket. Then he took a deep breath and nodded at the pair of headlights closing on the security gate checkpoint. "It's showtime."

CRIME SCENE  NCIS

NAVAL CRIMINAL INVESTIGATIVE SERVICE

31

SCENE  NCIS  CRIME SCEN

NAVAL CRIMINAL INVESTIGATIVE SERVICE

>> NCIS HEADQUARTERS
>> CAMP LEJEUNE, NORTH CAROLINA
>> 2123 HOURS

Inside the conference room Larkin had scheduled for the meeting, Will sat on the side of the table with the director and waited. It took all of ten seconds for Congressman Swanson to start asserting his authority.

"Do you even have a clue what you're doing with this investigation?" Swanson demanded. Although he wore an expensive suit, he looked frenzied.

"We've got a good case against Bryce Ketchum and his people." Larkin remained unagitated.

Pacing the length of the floor, Swanson scowled and shook his head. "I'm referring to the murder of my daughter."

"I thought that was already solved," Larkin said.

"To my satisfaction," Swanson said, "my daughter's death has been solved in every way but court."

Will noted that Swanson referred to his stepdaughter as his daughter. But in not naming her, it was almost as though he was stripping Chloe Ivers of her identity, turning her into a possession.

"But my daughter's death hasn't been resolved to my ex-wife's satisfaction," Swanson said.

"I realize that, sir," Larkin said. "It would have been better if Lamont had been tried for your daughter's murder."

Trials, Will had come to find out, brought a sense of closure to families who had lost loved ones. Sometimes the losses came through homicides, but many times they came about through accident. It always seemed better in the latter cases if the family could find someone other than the deceased person to blame.

"It would have been better if he'd been convicted," Swanson said.

"Yes."

"I know my ex-wife has been out here to see you," Swanson said.

Neither Larkin nor Will denied that.

"And I suppose you saw the interview my ex-wife granted this afternoon."

"We did," Larkin replied.

"That interview has caused considerable dismay among my supporters."

"I'm sorry to hear that," Larkin said.

Swanson shot the director a look, as if suspecting the acknowledgment was false. "I have enough aggravation in my job without dealing with this."

"Yes, sir."

Will felt certain that Swanson would have been happier if Haskins's body had remained buried.

"What did Laura want when she visited you?" Swanson demanded.

"She wanted me to reopen her daughter's case."

"Have you?"

"No."

It hasn't been reopened, Will thought, *because it was never closed.*

Larkin's answer seemed to surprise the congressman. "Do you plan to?"

"No," Larkin said.

"What about Haskins?"

"Haskins went missing at about the same time as your daughter." The director kept his face unreadable. "We can assume Lamont killed Haskins and buried him on the Ketchum farm."

Will kept his eyes on the congressman, but he marveled at Larkin. What the director had said wasn't exactly a lie, but it flirted with it. In Will's estimation, anyone who assumed that Lamont somehow kidnapped Chloe Ivers and George Haskins then killed them at his leisure was a fool.

"Do you believe that's what happened?" Swanson asked.

"It's been seventeen years," Larkin said. "It's unlikely that we'll ever know what truly happened."

Swanson cursed. "Maybe we won't know; maybe my ex-wife will never be satisfied. But you can bet that the press will use this against me every chance they can. If they don't, my detractors and my opponent will." He paused. "I appreciate your candor in this, Director Larkin."

"You're welcome, Congressman." Without batting an eye, Larkin went on. "Did your daughter know Gunnery Sergeant George Haskins?"

Suspicion and anger darkened Swanson's eyes. "Why are you asking that?"

"I'm just putting it together in my mind, sir," Larkin said. "I'm sure your ex-wife will call back. I thought perhaps if I could explain it to her, she might not be as willing to talk to the journalists in the future."

"No. My daughter didn't know Haskins."

"Then what do you suppose brought them together to allow Lamont to kidnap and kill them both on the same night?"

"How do you know it was the same night?"

"We have to assume that. The charm from Chloe's bracelet indicates that she and Haskins came into contact with each other."

Will watched the congressman's face, seeking some signal of what was going through the man's mind. But Swanson was too practiced at being in front of an audience. He was a good poker player. Will could read nothing in the congressman's blank expression.

"So we have to wonder why Lamont chose to get the two of them. You're sure you have no idea?"

Swanson shook his head. "How should I know? Lamont is insane."

"Actually," Will said quietly, "Lamont isn't insane. He was tested and judged accountable for his actions." *He just likes to kill people.*

"Maybe Lamont had already killed Haskins," Swanson suggested. "Before he took my daughter. Maybe . . ." He hesitated. "Maybe Haskins and my daughter were kept in the same area—a car trunk or something like that—for a short time. Maybe that's how my daughter's charm ended up in Haskins's clothing."

Will had to admit that it could have happened like that. The scenario would explain the presence of the charm. But he'd checked the coroner's reports and homicide detectives' reports. Nothing of Haskins's had been found with Chloe Ivers. *Her charm bracelet wasn't found either.*

"Then why bury Haskins only to leave your daughter's body in New River?" Will asked.

"I don't know."

"The choice doesn't make sense," Larkin added. "Hiding two bodies wouldn't have been any harder than hiding one."

"Perhaps Chloe was still alive after Lamont killed Haskins," Swanson said.

"Why bother burying Haskins's body at all?" Will asked.

Swanson shrugged. "Maybe there was something about Haskins that could have tied Lamont to the crime."

Larkin nodded. "That could be it."

"Of course that could be it," Swanson said. "What other reason could there be?" He smiled a little. "I don't claim to be a professional crime buster like you gentlemen, but I've seen enough television crime shows to guess at a motive."

"There are a lot of possibilities," Larkin said.

"Of course there are," Swanson agreed. "That's what I'm concerned about. That's why I came here tonight."

Larkin was quiet for a time, breaking the silence just before it got uncomfortable. "What do you want from this office, Congressman Swanson?"

Swanson paced for a moment, then turned to Larkin. "What I want, Director Larkin, is for your investigation *not* to dredge up things that my family buried seventeen years ago." He took a breath. "My ex-wife . . . *Laura* . . . has been hurting all that time. She never got over losing Chloe. This investigation is going to put a fine edge on her pain again. I truly don't want to see that happen. I care about her."

Will tried to keep his face devoid of emotion. His feelings about his own ex-wife were in constant flux. Some days he cared more about Barbara's happiness and well-being than others. There were times when he hoped they would get back together, and there were times when he looked forward to rediscovering his life.

If only Steven and Wren didn't have to get caught up in all the confusion.

"I understand and respect that, Congressman Swanson," Larkin said.

"And I want you to keep me apprised of any developments that might occur."

Larkin nodded and stood. "Some of the avenues of the investigation we're pursuing toward finding out who killed Gunnery Sergeant George Haskins may overlap that old investigation involving your daughter. I need you to understand that."

"Why would it?"

"Because if Lamont killed both Chloe and Haskins, we're going to be covering some of the same ground."

"Do you really think that after seventeen years you're going to find out who murdered Haskins?"

"I don't know. What I do know is we have to try."

"Why? From what I have found out about that man, he was more a disgrace to the military than an asset."

"Yes, sir, but a crime was committed. And at the end, Haskins was still a Marine. We take care of our Marines here at Camp Lejeune."

Swanson shook his head. "Seems like wasted effort if you ask me."

"Yes, sir."

Slipping his jacket back on, Swanson extended his hand and shook Larkin's, then Will's. "Gentlemen, if there's anything I can do for you, please don't hesitate to ask."

"Yes, sir. Thank you, sir."

Swanson headed for the door.

"There is one thing," Larkin said.

Half in and half out the door, Swanson paused.

"Michael Tarlton," Larkin said. "Do you remember him?"

"Yes. He was representative of this area before I was."

"Commander Coburn's preliminary investigation so far has revealed that Haskins was suspected of blackmailing Tarlton. Did you know anything about that?"

Swanson's eyes narrowed. "What do you mean?"

"Did you ever hear anything about that?"

"No, of course not."

"I ask only because if Haskins was instrumental in blackmailing Tarlton, it's possible he may have been intending to blackmail you as well."

"Where did you get this information?"

"It was contained in some of the records of previous NCIS investigators. And there are records of Haskins's frequent travels to Raleigh."

"What are your thoughts?"

Larkin looked grimly earnest. "It's also possible that Haskins was complicit in your daughter's kidnapping."

Swanson remained quiet.

"Lamont had never used kidnapping before," Larkin said. "There was no reason to change his methods. But it is possible that Haskins took your daughter from her room, intending to demand ransom, and Lamont caught him."

Nodding, Swanson said, "That would explain how Chloe's charm was in Haskins's possession."

"It's possible."

"Do you believe that's what happened?"

"We're pursuing that line of investigation," Larkin said.

"Let me know what you find." Swanson still stood in the door. "You know, I was in the house the night my daughter was taken. My son, Jeffrey, was having a bad night of it. He had chronic nightmares when he was little. Still has trouble even today." He pursed his lips. "It continues to bother me. That I was there and didn't know anything, I mean. The guilt hasn't gone away. Even though Laura tried to stay with me and didn't blame me for Chloe's death, I blamed myself."

"Yes, sir."

"Anything you need, gentlemen. Any way I can help. Please don't hesitate."

Larkin said they wouldn't, and then Will followed Larkin and Swanson out the door.

>> 2209 HOURS

Will signed Congressman Swanson's car back through the security gate, watched it drive away, then went back to rejoin Larkin.

"That was interesting," Will commented.

"It was quite a show," Larkin agreed.

"How much of it did you believe?"

Larkin frowned. "About as much as you did." He stroked his jaw absently. "Swanson's hiding something."

Will nodded.

"He came here tonight to let us know he was watching us," Larkin said.

"So if we start watching him, he's going to know."

"Yeah."

"How do you want to handle this?"

"When I was with NYPD, we had cases that sometimes got out of hand like this. Political cases that involved sons and daughters or spouses of moneyed families. They were the tough ones. You had to work harder. You had to wear kid gloves."

"Did you ever deal with a United States congressman before?"

"No," Larkin admitted. "This is a definite upgrade." He paused. "We're going to pursue Chloe Ivers's murderer, but we're going to run a layered investigation. Haskins's death buys us into every aspect of this investigation. Even if the murderer or murderers turn out to be civilians, we have a right to find out who killed Haskins and Chloe Ivers. She was under the protection of the United States Navy when she went down. She was one of our family members. On the surface, we'll be chasing Haskins's murderer—"

"All we'll have to hope is that the two murders are connected."

"We don't have to hope. They're connected. We just need to figure out how."

32

SCENE  NCIS 

>> NCIS MEDICAL LAB
>> CAMP LEJEUNE, NORTH CAROLINA
>> 0851 HOURS

Nita stared at George Haskins's face modeled in clay, thinking about the skull that served as the foundation for the image she'd constructed. She wondered about the man briefly, curious about the twists and turns in his life that had led him to being buried on the Ketchum farm.

She usually didn't think about things like this. She didn't like that she was thinking about it now. The work she did was scientific, weighing and measuring, with no degree of personal involvement. She preferred that, and that distance was something that had drawn her to the work.

The headache from her hangover after last night's drinking throbbed between her temples. Opening a drawer, she reached into her purse and took out two analgesics.

"Feeling okay?" Will stood in the door with a tray of coffees and a bag from a doughnut shop.

"Headache." Nita was instantly suspicious of what had brought Will to the lab. Nothing she was working on at present was on any kind of deadline.

"Did you have breakfast?"

"No." When she'd left home this morning, Nita had actually felt a little nauseous. She'd worked late, avoiding most of the evening with her husband and daughter, arriving home in time to see the gingerbread house Joe and Celia had made for some church function they were attending Saturday.

"I've got extra." Will placed the bag on one of the tables next to the body of a young sailor who'd died in a training exercise the previous day. Such things didn't happen often, but with things heating up in the Middle East, training had intensified, and occasionally mistakes were made.

Nita rummaged through the bag and took out a powdered sugar–covered beignet. She leaned a hip against the table and took a bite. "Aren't you going to eat?"

Will glanced at the sheet-covered body on the stainless-steel table. "I think I'll wait."

Nita washed the beignet down with coffee. "You didn't come here to bring me breakfast."

Will looked a little uncomfortable. "We need to talk."

Anger flared inside Nita. "About what?"

"About you."

"Do you have a problem with my work, Commander?"

"No."

"Then I don't see that we have anything to talk about."

"Do you know a Navy flier named David Horton?"

Nita hesitated only a moment. Will wouldn't have come to her, wouldn't have asked that question, if he didn't already know the answer. "Yes," she said. "We've met."

"There's a rumor going around that you're responsible for his emergency room visit Friday night."

Nita had no sympathy for the lieutenant. Ever since that night, she'd had dreams of his attack on her.

"Were you?" Will asked.

"Lieutenant Horton brought that on himself."

"Does Joe know?"

That stopped Nita for a moment. She covered by sipping coffee. "No. Is Horton talking about it?"

"I haven't talked to him."

"Are you going to?"

"I'm not planning on it. I'm not Horton's superior officer."

"But you're mine, right? That's what you're here for?"

Will's eyes narrowed slightly.

Nita knew she'd pushed too hard. Despite Will's easygoing nature, he was still a United States naval officer. There was a chain of command. And he *was* her superior.

"Yes," Will said. "That's what I'm here for."

"What are you going to do?"

"Try to help."

"Is Horton pressing charges?"

"Not that I know of. Should he?"

"Not unless he's stupid."

"Horton had his pride hurt," Will pointed out. "He could get stupid before this is over."

For a moment, Nita's confidence wavered. She liked her job. She was good at it. Horton's complaints and the resulting complications could threaten it.

"Horton tried to rape me," she said. She folded her arms across herself, not liking how vulnerable she suddenly felt. "I defended myself."

"At a club?"

"We weren't at a club. We were at an apartment."

"His apartment?"

"At the time I thought it was his apartment. As it turned out, the apartment belonged to a friend of his."

"What were you doing there?"

Nita chose not to answer that.

Will suddenly understood. Crimson touched his cheeks for just a moment.

That bit of embarrassment, that touch of the Boy Scout, made Nita feel safer around Will and at the same time sharpened her shame.

"Things aren't going so well at home," she said lamely.

Will waited.

"I'm tired of being married," Nita said. "And I'm tired of being a mom."

"Have you tried talking to a counselor?"

"No. I'm not big on counseling. And I'm really not thrilled with discussing my life with strangers."

"You could talk to Maggie."

"No." That would be worse. Nita seriously didn't feel like being judged by Maggie. "I'm tired of feeling trapped, Will. No matter what I do, I can't seem to do enough." Tears burned at the back of her eyes but she kept them from falling. "I never planned on getting married. I never planned on having Celia. I met Joe. He swept me off my feet. The next thing I knew, I was married. It was almost like it happened before I knew what was going on."

"Have you talked to Joe about this?"

"I can't. Joe is too . . . innocent." Nita knew that was exactly the word to describe her husband. "He's all wrapped up in his faith. It's like he's got blinders on about the real world."

"I don't think that's true."

"You're not married to him," Nita said angrily. "He goes to church, and he reads the Bible. The answer to every question and problem in life is in those places."

"I don't think that's a fair assessment."

"Joe wouldn't understand. Trust me."

"There's nothing wrong with faith, Nita."

"Church has never worked for me, Will. Even when I was little. People there are too judgmental. They always want to tell you how to run your life."

"I'm not talking about a church environment," Will said. "I'm talking about belief. I know Joe is heavily involved in your church—"

"*His* church. Trust me on that. Those people there don't care if I'm around. In fact, I think they prefer it when I'm not."

"It might help if you talked to Joe. Let him know how you feel."

"Joe is the problem," Nita said. "No matter what I do, I can't measure up to him. I can't be what he wants." *Or what he deserves.* "I'm just really tired of trying."

"Joe could have gotten married a long time ago if that's what he'd wanted. Instead, he waited till you came along."

Several times over the years of her marriage, Nita had considered that. She couldn't understand why Joe had waited to marry until he'd met her. Any woman in the church would have been happy to have his attentions. So why hadn't one of them turned his head and captured him?

"Joe thinks he can convert me into the perfect wife," Nita said.

"How?"

Nita felt flustered. "He wants me to be with him all the time."

"He wants you to quit your job?"

"No."

"Does he complain about your hours?"

"No."

"Joe," Will said, "is one of the most complete men I think I've ever met."

Nita sighed when she heard the approval in Will's voice. No one had a bad word to say about Joe Tomlinson. But they didn't live with him.

"What about Joe makes you unhappy?" Will asked.

Nita thought about that for a moment, working through the anger and pain she felt. "I just can't measure up, Will." She was surprised at the hoarseness in her voice. "I can't be the kind of wife he wants—and deserves. And I've never been a good mother."

"From what I've seen, I think you are."

"Do you know anything about me, Will?"

Will looked at her and took the question seriously. "I know you're one of the smartest people I've ever met. You're dedicated and unflagging and—"

"I grew up in a single-parent household," Nita interrupted. "My mother dragged us through every trailer park from Florida to Tennessee. I never knew who my father was. I don't even know if my mother knew." Her voice tightened but she worked her way through it. "I grew up alone. My mother drank and partied. From the time I was old enough to feed myself, she'd stay gone for a day or two at a time. Once she was gone for eight days straight. I thought she was dead. For a while, I wished she were dead. Because she abandoned me. I had to crawl through a back window to avoid child protective services. The day she got back, we moved in with a truck driver she'd met and had gone out on the road with."

Will looked away.

"That's the kind of childhood I had," Nita stated vehemently. "Do you really think I can ever be the wife Joe deserves or the mother Celia needs?"

Will didn't answer.

"I need to get out before I hurt them," Nita whispered

"Leaving them is going to hurt them."

"Every day I stay, every day I let them believe everything is going to be all right, is going to make it hurt worse." Nita took a deep breath. "The best I can hope for is to make a clean break."

For a moment they were both silent.

"I think," Will said slowly, "that you and Joe could talk this out and find some way to work through it."

"The way that you and Barbara did?" Nita knew at once that she'd hurt Will. She saw it in his eyes. Her immediate impulse was to apologize, but she knew it would undermine what she was trying to drive home to him. "There are some things that you can't fix. It only makes it worse when you try."

"Maybe you're right." Will looked at his watch. "I've got to go. Bryce Ketchum is scheduled for a hearing at ten-thirty. I need to be there to help the district attorney in case there are any questions."

Nita took another bite of her beignet. She didn't have an appetite, not really, but she'd learned to eat even when she didn't feel like it. The analgesics had already blunted some of the sharp edges of the pain in her head.

"I appreciate the effort, Will," Nita said.

"Joe's a good man. You'll find a lot of David Hortons in the world, but Joe is special. He's one of a kind."

"I know. That's why he deserves someone other than me."

"I don't think he'll understand that."

"He will. In time." *He'll have to.*

"Let me know if I can help," Will said.

"Thank you."

"But at the same time," Will went on, "I'll expect you to handle your job. If you lose control of yourself, if you fumble an investigation, I won't cover for you."

"I know that, too." Nita watched him hesitate, hoping he would simply leave it at that.

Thankfully, Will did. He said a final good-bye and left the lab.

Turning back to the body on the stainless-steel table, Nita looked at how calm the young man's features were. Death looked easy compared to trying to live. Some days, like today, the idea of being dead was almost attractive.

>> NCIS HEADQUARTERS
>> CAMP LEJEUNE, NORTH CAROLINA
>> 0913 HOURS

Will felt unsettled when he returned to his office after talking to Nita. He tried to work but ended up staring out the window and thinking about his kids.

And Barbara.

There was no getting around thinking about his ex-wife when he thought about Steven and Wren. He wished he knew what to do to help Nita, and at the same time he wished he knew if anything could even be done.

Sometimes marriages ended. He'd seen that happen firsthand. It wasn't his place to try to fix Nita's family problems. He hadn't been trained for anything like that.

The futility of the situation weighed on him. Families were hard to handle. What advice could he possibly give Nita or Joe? He didn't even know what he was going to do about his own family. Still, the need to do something pushed at him.

Abruptly he shifted gears. He still needed to prepare for Bryce Ketchum's hearing. Whatever was going on with Nita would have to wait.

33

SCENE  NCIS  CRIME SCEN

NAVAL CRIMINAL INVESTIGATIVE SERVICE

>> BODYMAP
>> JACKSONVILLE, NORTH CAROLINA
>> 0921 HOURS

"We do this fast and hard," Shel said. "Once we go through the door, we're nobody's friends."

"Okay." Remy moved at his side, light and quick on his feet. Max was on the other side, working now, head down and ears pricked.

"You up to this?" Shel asked. Adrenaline was hitting him constantly. The thrill of the hunt excited him and made him feel more alive. He'd never found anything else in the world like it.

"Yeah."

"We could have called for backup."

"And given Morris a chance to disappear again?" Remy shook his head. "We've been chasing this guy for two days. He's been in the wind. Let's put him down."

Frank Morris had slipped under the sweep at the farmhouse. Several of the men who had been with Ketchum had gotten away that night, but none of the others had been part of Ketchum's organization for as long as Morris. The two men went back at least twenty-one years, when they'd both been arrested on a drunk-and-disorderly charge. Back then, Ketchum had been serving with the Marines. Morris hadn't served in the military. He'd been an outlaw all his life, chiefly with motorcycle gangs.

BodyMap was a tattoo parlor that opened early and closed late. The business was located between a submarine-sandwich shop and a video-rental enterprise. Morning traffic was heavy. There weren't many parking areas in front of any of the shops.

Shel reached under his Windbreaker and drew one of the Mark 23 Mod 0 SOCOM .45-caliber combat pistols from his shoulder holsters. Keeping the pistol at his side, covering it with his leg as much as he could, he put his hand on the door and went through.

The shop was packed with reference materials—magazines and books. Pictures, presumably of past customers happy with the designs they'd chosen for themselves, covered the walls. Risqué T-shirts hung on freestanding circle racks. Displays held body piercings.

A young peroxide blonde stood behind the counter. She looked all of fifteen, dressed in hip-huggers and a crop top that showed tattooing covering her arms from shoulder to wrist. The theme was primarily Japanese, featuring fish and dragons. She was bored and inattentive, watching MTV on the letterbox HDTV monitor hanging from the ceiling.

Her head swiveled to Shel. "Hey. What can I do for—?" She stopped speaking when she saw the pistol in Shel's hand. She reached for the phone.

Shel covered her hand with his. "No," he said gently.

"Who—?"

Remy showed her his ID and badge.

"Cops," the girl snarled, not impressed. She acted tough, but Shel was of the opinion that she hadn't had any real trouble with police officers in the past. There wasn't enough fear in her.

Shel nodded and read her name off her tag. "Talk softly, Monica."

Monica glared at him. "What do you want?"

"We're looking for a guy."

The buzz of electric tattoo needles remained constant in the back, mixing in with hard rock music.

"Frank Morris," Shel said.

Remy put a playing card–size picture of Morris on the countertop. Morris was in his fifties and looked ten or fifteen years older. His face was a wrinkled smudge of scars and hard times. Iron gray hair hung past his shoulders, held in place by a turquoise headband.

"Why—?" Monica began.

"Where is he?" Shel demanded.

"Do I have to talk to you?"

"If you don't want to go downtown with us, yeah."

The young woman pouted. "Second floor. They've got rooms up there."

Shel knew from the information Estrella had given him that the owners lived above the shop. "How do I get there?"

"Stairs in the back."

"How many people are here?"

"Two customers. Then there's Sal and Irondog. They're back there working. Maybe a couple of their friends."

"Maybe?"

Monica acted a little belligerent, as if testing what was acceptable. "I get here in the morning. I don't know who stayed over through the night. Sometimes there's a party and people crash here."

Shel gave her a hard look and watched her wilt back from him. "If you stay put and don't get involved, you'll get to stay here when we leave. Interfere and I'll arrest you along with Morris and anyone else who tries to stop us."

She hesitated. "Sal and Irondog own the place." She bit her lip. "They're holding."

Drugs on the premises meant the charges were going to be more severe. Everyone who knew about the drugs was going to be interested in getting away.

"Stay out of the way," Shel said, "and you won't be arrested."

Monica nodded.

Shel unplugged the phone and stripped the end of the cord so it couldn't simply be plugged back in. He took Monica's cell phone before she could stop him, disconnected the battery for a second—long enough to discharge it and render it momentarily useless—then handed it back.

He took the lead with Max at his side and Remy behind him. Stepping into the back room, Shel lifted the pistol in a short-armed Weaver stance, his arms crooked to make the legs of the triangle.

Four barber's chairs occupied the center of the back room, able to fully recline while customers were worked on. Chemical odors hung in the still air. Two of the chairs held young male clients stripped to the waist.

One of the guys inking was young, in his midtwenties, wearing a beanie and a sleeveless black concert T-shirt. He was smoking a marijuana cigarette. The other was in his forties or fifties, balding, with a goatee and dressed in a Hawaiian shirt.

None of the four men were Frank Morris.

"Naval Criminal Investigative Service," Shel said, stepping to the left so Remy could fill in to his right. "Nobody moves, nobody gets hurt."

He spoke in a tone of command, but not frenzy. Too many police officers went in yelling and scared the guys they were after into an immediate hostile reaction. There was a time and place for that, but this wasn't the time or the place.

The older man lifted his hands immediately. "Be cool, brother."

The younger man froze. His right hand started to drift behind his back.

"Don't do anything stupid, Gerry," the older guy ordered. His eyes never left Shel.

Shel put the sights of his pistol over Gerry's heart. "Play it smart, Gerry. The guys in the movies get to go home after the director yells 'cut.' You won't."

Cursing, Gerry slowly took the cigarette from his mouth and crushed it out in a nearby glass ashtray. He lifted his hands.

"I got 'em," Shel said.

"Okay." Remy leathered his pistol and reached for one of the disposable cuffs at the back of his belt. He crossed behind Shel, staying out of the Marine's field of fire.

"We're looking for Frank Morris," Shel said.

"Upstairs," the older man said.

"What's your name?"

"Sal."

That left Gerry as Irondog. As Remy cuffed the young man, Shel spotted the iron-jawed pit bull on Gerry's upper arm.

"What's Frank doing upstairs?" Shel asked.

"Last time I saw him, he was sleeping," Sal answered.

"Does he have company?"

"He's got a couple guys up there with him."

"Who are they?"

"Couple of his boys he's been working with."

"They were all out at the Ketchum farm Friday night?"

"Probably."

Remy moved over to Sal and cuffed him as well.

"Do they have weapons?" Shel asked.

"Yeah."

That was trouble. Frank Morris was known to be violent. He'd already taken two falls. A third was going to put him behind bars for years. He'd be motivated to stay free and moving.

The two customers protested about being taken into custody. They may have been clean, but Shel wasn't going to leave anyone loose behind them.

When Remy had them secure, Shel took point and started up the switchback stairs leading to the second floor. The steps creaked. Shel regretted that because it sounded incredibly loud in the stairwell. He kept his feet at the edges of the steps where the treads had less chance of bowing.

A shotgun barrel emerged from the door when Shel reached the landing.

"*Gun!*" Shel roared, swinging back and down.

The shotgun detonation filled the narrow stairwell with explosive thunder. Double-ought buckshot ripped into the Sheetrock walls, spreading nearly a foot across to leave a yawning opening.

Partially deafened by the shotgun blast, Shel took aim and fired, punching rounds into the doorframe where the shotgun barrel was thrust through. The bullets splintered the wood. The shotgun retreated at once.

Shel replaced the partially expended magazine with a fresh one and freed his other pistol. He went up quickly, both .45s level before him. *"Naval Criminal Investigative Service! Put down your weapons!"*

The hallway was almost flush with the door, providing little shelter. The guy with the shotgun had fled the living room and taken up position in the next doorway to the left. The shotgun swung up.

Shel fired without hesitation, triggering both pistols three times. The .45-caliber rounds chopped through the Sheetrock the shooter had thought would defend him. He staggered and fell back, firing as he went down. The shotgun blast slammed into the television set in the living room, turning it into a twisted mass of smoking electronics.

"I got one down," Shel told Remy.

"Roger that. How many left?"

"Unconfirmed." Shel went forward. His ears rang with the explosions of the gunshots.

The man in the doorway tried to get up, then shivered and went still.

Two doors were on opposite walls of the living room. One led to the kitchen/dining room, and the other led to the bedroom.

"Clear!" Remy called from the bedroom.

Wind pulled at the drapes covering an open window in the dining area. After kicking the shotgun away from the man he'd shot, Shel used one of his pistols to pull the drapes aside and peer out. Max took up a guard position on the fallen man.

The window opened over an alley. Below, two men ran toward the nearest street.

"Runners," Shel called out, holstering the pistol in his left hand.

"Roger that."

Shoving through the window, Shel dropped to the alley, landing on bent legs. Max followed him through, landing with a growl only a few feet away and rolling till he got his feet under him again. He shook himself irritably. The Labrador didn't care much for heights.

Shel raced in pursuit of the two men. One of them was Frank Morris. Both of them were armed. Neither of them was as quick as Shel or Max.

Running for all he was worth, not wanting to lose either of the men, Shel gained ground quickly. The twenty-foot head start they'd had dropped to five by the time they reached the street.

The young man turned around and lifted his pistol, pointing it at Max. Shel took aim, but there were pedestrians on the other side of the street. He didn't have a clear field of fire.

Max attacked, vaulting up from the ground and going for the gunman's arm as he'd been trained to. The Labrador's jaws closed around the man's wrist; then his full weight crashed into the man, knocking him back and down in front of an SUV that barely braked in time. Rubber shrilled.

"I got him! I got him!" Remy yelled from behind. "Get Morris."

Shel ran, gaining on Morris with every step now. A car slid to a halt in front of Morris, who put his hands out to steady himself, twisting his head to peer back over his shoulder.

Without breaking stride, Shel hurled himself at Morris, going chest to chest with the big man and levering his left arm up between them. Shel closed his empty fist on Morris's clothing, taking a firm hold. Even though he was prepared for it, the impact drove the air from Shel's lungs. It also drove Morris up and over the car, knocking his pistol away.

Shel stayed on top of the man as they slid across the hood and dropped into the street. Twisted during the fall, Shel landed hard on his right elbow. His pistol skittered away. He lunged for the weapon but missed as Morris got to his feet.

The man lifted a foot and tried to smash it into Shel's face. Blocking the blow with one arm, Shel rolled and got to his feet, but the .45 remained out of reach. Before Shel could reach for his second pistol, Morris growled an oath and closed on him, evidently intending to put him down before making his escape. The man pulled something out of his pocket. Shel saw it was a blackjack—a leather bag filled with lead shot and attached to a handle.

Morris swung the weapon at Shel's head. Shel knew that if the blackjack hit him in the face, his cheek, chin, or temples—possibly even his skull—would shatter like an eggshell.

Stepping into the swing, Shel caught Morris's right arm in his left, hooking over the top of the elbow to control the swing. Twisting his hips to add power to the blow, Shel struck Morris in the stomach with a bunched fist, driving the air out of the man in an explosive gust. Roping a hand behind Morris's neck, Shel brought his opponent's head down and a knee up. Morris's nose broke with a loud pop.

The big man went backward. Shel plucked the blackjack from Morris's hand. Rubber legged, Morris collapsed and fell to his back. His eyes fluttered once; then he was unconscious.

Breathing hard, Shel drew his second pistol and surveyed the street. Stalled cars blocked the intersection. A few impatient drivers honked their horns. Remy had the other man handcuffed and on his feet, moving him toward Shel in a come-along grip that had the prisoner moving fast. Max trotted nearby.

"Is that Frank Morris?" Remy asked when he got to where Shel stood over the unconscious man.

"Yeah. When he comes to, maybe he'll know more about where Bryce Ketchum disappeared to. If not, maybe he'll know about George Haskins. Morris was working with Ketchum back then."

Remy stayed with the prisoners while Shel retrieved his Jeep from around the corner and drove it back. Remy guided his prisoner to the backseat and secured him inside, then helped Shel carry the still-unconscious Morris to the other side.

"We still need to check out the other couple guys at the tattoo shop," Shel said. "Don't know if they're connected to this or are innocent bystanders."

Remy nodded.

In the distance, police sirens sounded.

"We need to call the PD," Shel said. "Let them know what they're dealing with before they get here, guns blazing. And call Will. He'll want to be here for this."

S CRIME SCENE  NCIS 

NAVAL CRIMINAL INVESTIGATIVE SERVICE

34

SCENE  NCIS  CRIME SCEN

NAVAL CRIMINAL INVESTIGATIVE SERVICE

>> ONSLOW COUNTY COURTHOUSE
>> 625 COURT STREET
>> JACKSONVILLE, NORTH CAROLINA
>> 1029 HOURS

The Onslow County Courthouse was a two-story, redbrick building that dispensed justice and was a historic monument to the city.

Estrella had grown up in Chicago, a metropolitan area several times the size of Jacksonville. When she'd first gone into the courthouse, she'd been put off by the small stature, but something about the history seemed to permeate the whole structure. It was a building and an institution that had been through a lot of changes, a lot of hardship.

There was also something pure and true about it.

Estrella sat quietly in the back of the courtroom. Will had been on his way to the hearing when Remy called, summoning him to a crime scene across town. Will had asked her to cover the court proceedings in his stead. He hadn't been too explicit about what was going on with Shel and Remy, but she knew they were all right. Maggie was on her way back from Raleigh.

Usually the courtroom would have only a few attendees. Today there was a full house. Most of the people in the audience were reporters. Camera crews had staked claims in the parking lot. All of it was fallout from the Chloe Ivers murder.

But it's not for the girl, Estrella thought sadly. *It's because of Ben Swanson.*

Checking her watch, Estrella saw that they were getting started two minutes late. The bailiff came out. Glancing at the defendant's table, Estrella spotted Thomas Wardell sitting there with what looked like two junior attorneys. It was a heavy showing for an arraignment. Then again, Bryce Ketchum had a lot of grief aimed his way.

"All rise," the bailiff called out, then introduced the judge, Vernon Tate.

The judge sat and banged his gavel.

"Be seated."

Everyone sat.

Estrella looked at the empty defendant's chair.

The bailiff called for Bryce Ketchum.

Wardell stood. "If it please Your Honor, Mr. Ketchum has not yet made an appearance."

Judge Tate frowned. "Is your client coming, Counselor?"

"Yes, Your Honor. I'm sure he must just be running late. The traffic can be—"

"The traffic can be accounted for," the judge said. "Your client has had all morning to get here."

"Yes, Your Honor."

Everyone waited. The silence in the courtroom grew deafening.

Three minutes passed.

"Counselor," the judge said, "I assume you have a phone number where your client can be reached."

"Yes, Your Honor." Wardell was nervous and clearly off his game.

"Perhaps you might call Mr. Ketchum and find out if he intends to be here this morning."

"Yes, Your Honor." One of the junior attorneys handed Wardell a cell phone. The attorney checked his notes, then placed the call.

Estrella knew the call wasn't going to be answered.

It wasn't.

Weakly, Wardell closed the phone after trying twice more. "It appears that Mr. Ketchum isn't answering his phone."

The judge flipped through the notes in front of him. "When was the last time you saw your client?"

"Yesterday."

"When he was released from jail?"

"Yes."

"Didn't you set up a preliminary meeting between your client and yourself before you stepped into my courtroom?"

"Yes, Your Honor."

"And?"

Wardell's shoulders slumped. "He didn't show up, Your Honor."

"When were you supposed to meet?"

"Last night, Your Honor."

The judge took a deep breath. "You didn't notify the police or my court?"

"I didn't see the need, Your Honor. I assumed my client—"

"We'll talk about what you assumed at a later date, Mr. Wardell," the judge interrupted. He addressed the bailiff. "Put out a bench warrant on Mr. Ketchum. His bail has been rescinded."

Estrella left the courtroom. She fished her cell phone from her purse and pressed speed-dial for Will Coburn. Reporters left the courtroom as well, talking among themselves, trying to figure out their next angle of attack for the story.

"Coburn."

"It's Estrella." She walked to the front door. "Ketchum was a no-show."

Sirens sounded in the background as Will sighed. "Okay. Get back to headquarters and open lines of communication with the local law enforcement. I want to be in the loop with the Jacksonville PD and the Onslow Sheriff's Office. Talk to people we know in the outlying counties too. And the state people."

"I will." Estrella knew why: Will already figured they weren't looking for Bryce Ketchum anymore. They were looking for his corpse.

>> OUTSIDE THE BODYMAP TATTOO PARLOR
>> JACKSONVILLE, NORTH CAROLINA
>> 1128 HOURS

Sorting everything out at the crime scene took time. Since bullets had been fired, they had to be found. Will called in additional manpower from NCIS and let the Jacksonville forensics crew work with them. Building goodwill, especially in a city often torn apart by the disparity between civilian and military jurisdiction, remained important.

When he was satisfied that everything that could be done was being done, Will returned to the prisoners. They sat in the back of separate Hummers brought by the NCIS special agents he'd called in.

Director Larkin stood near one of the Hummers, dressed in a suit and wearing dark sunglasses. For the first time, Will noticed the news trucks and vans that sat beyond the perimeter created by the crime-scene tape and sawhorses. Cameras captured his every move.

"This has turned into a circus." Larkin wasn't happy.

"Yes, sir."

When Larkin spoke, he covered his mouth with a clipboard. It was too easy to read lips these days. Even head football coaches and baseball pitchers couldn't avoid the scrutiny of a long-lensed camera.

"I heard Ketchum didn't show for court."

"No, sir." Will covered his lower face with his NCIS cap.

"We should have followed him."

"Hindsight, sir. The judge that turned Ketchum loose has got to be feeling worse than we do."

"Yeah, but Ketchum's in the wind."

"Maybe. He got away from us. Doesn't mean he got away from everybody."

"No one would kill him for what went down at the farmhouse." Larkin shifted.

"No, sir. Everybody connected to that had their own trouble to deal with."

"If he was killed, it was to hide something else."

Will silently agreed.

Larkin switched his attention to the Hummer. "Shel and Remy got Morris."

"Yes, sir."

"Have you talked to him?"

"Not yet."

"Why don't we do that now."

Will fell in step with the director. Morris sat in the back, sweltering in the heat of the enclosed Hummer. Will slid behind the wheel, and Larkin took the passenger seat.

Blood streaked Morris' face. His nose was swollen to twice its original size and made his eyes look like they were too close together. Insolence clung to him as tight as varnish.

"We've got you on drug charges," Will said.

Morris broke eye contact and looked away. He hadn't asked for an attorney yet. Will knew that the man was open to a deal, if one could be made. Otherwise he'd have lawyered up.

"We also know you were at Ketchum's farmhouse a week ago," Will went on.

"You can't prove that."

The argument was token resistance. "We have the meth you were carrying. We can match it up to the meth Ketchum had on hand that night."

Every meth cooker had his own recipe for making the drug, and each batch turned out chemically unique because of the cooking process and the chemical process. No meth cook could turn out the same exact product time after time.

"Doesn't mean I was there Friday night," Morris said.

"Being there Friday night means that you could take a fall on kidnapping charges," Larkin said. "There was an underage girl being held against her will at the farmhouse."

A flicker of recognition burned in Morris's eyes. "I didn't kidnap her."

"Doesn't matter," Larkin said. "If we decide to press the issue, you all go down for it. Kidnapping carries a life sentence. For the moment, the girl and the family don't want to be involved. That could change. It might be in your best interest if we didn't look too deeply into Friday night. That means cooperating with us now."

Morris's left eye twitched. Sweat trickled down his temple and turned bloody at the jawline. "I got cigarettes in my shirt pocket."

Will reached back and took the pack out. He put one between Morris's lips and lit it with the lighter he habitually carried.

Morris took a deep drag, held it, then let it out and coughed for a moment. He squinted at Will and Larkin through the smoke. "What do you want?"

"Ketchum didn't show up for court today."

"So?"

"We want to know where Ketchum is," Will said.

"I don't know."

"You've been with him a long time," Larkin said.

"We weren't exactly linked at the hip."

"Did you know George Haskins?"

Morris considered. "What am I getting out of this?"

"Our goodwill."

Morris cursed.

"You're going to jail," Larkin said. "That's going to happen. You've been in the system before. You know how bad it can be. What I'm prepared to offer you is your choice of prisons. You can be with friends when you go back inside. Or I can throw some weight and get you transferred somewhere that will be a little less friendly."

"That's what you've got to offer?"

"Yeah." Larkin's gaze didn't flinch.

"It's not much."

"You dug yourself in pretty deep."

After a moment, Morris nodded. "All right. What I've got isn't much. I don't know where Ketchum is. We were supposed to meet last night. Talk over some business."

"He didn't show?" Will asked.

Morris shook his head, then obviously regretted the movement. "No."

"What were you going to talk about?"

"Bryce figured he had a way out."

"Out of what?"

Morris shrugged. "Everything, man. He planned to be long gone. Down to Mexico. South America. Someplace where money would last longer and there wasn't no extradition for the death penalty."

"We took his cash assets," Will pointed out.

"He figured on getting more money somewhere else."

"Where?"

"He didn't say."

"How did he get Wardell to represent him?"

"I don't know."

"Did Ketchum know Wardell?" Will asked.

Morris snorted. "Are you kidding? That guy don't even breathe the same air we do."

"Get back to George Haskins," Larkin suggested.

Taking another drag on the cigarette, Morris let the smoke go through his clenched teeth. Nothing was coming through his swollen nose. "I knew George Haskins."

"Let's talk about that."

35

SCENE  NCIS  CRIME SCENE

NAVAL CRIMINAL INVESTIGATIVE SERVICE

>> OUTSIDE THE BODYMAP TATTOO PARLOR
>> JACKSONVILLE, NORTH CAROLINA
>> 1142 HOURS

"George and Bryce were friends since grade school," Frank Morris said. "When George signed up for the Marines, Bryce followed him in. He didn't know what else to do with himself."

"Haskins and Ketchum went to grade school together?" Will made a note on his iPAQ. This was new information. He knew that the two men had attended the same high school, but it was very interesting that their association went back even further. That hadn't been covered in the background material Estrella had put together on the two men.

"Yeah." Morris seemed surprised. "I thought you would know that. They grew up in some little town in Kentucky. They ended up at Camp Lejeune. That's where I met them."

"Ketchum's grandfather and great-grandfather owned the farmhouse outside of Jacksonville."

"Bryce was born here, but he went to live with his mama in Kentucky after his parents got divorced. He didn't make it back to Jacksonville till he was seventeen. By the time Bryce's father died, he was the only heir left for the farm."

"You were part of the black-market operation they ran." Will was aware of the activity outside the Hummer. Inside the vehicle, the temperature climbed as the sunny day continued to heat up.

Morris nodded. "Didn't take either of them long to get into the business."

Will's phone vibrated for attention. He flipped it open. "Coburn."

"Commander, this is Detective Stilson. If you're done with the crime scene, we'll release it and get traffic going again."

"Let me call you right back." Will broke the connection, called Remy, and found out the forensics team had everything buttoned down outside the tattoo parlor. He called Stilson back and released the scene.

Using the keys in the ignition, Will pulled the Hummer out of the way and parked in the shade against the curb.

"Haskins and Ketchum were in business together," Larkin said.

"Yeah," said Morris. "Even when Bryce got busted out of the Marines and later got sent away, Haskins made sure he got his cut. That's how it was between those two. Always looking out for each other."

"You knew Haskins went missing."

"Of course I did. Everybody who ran with him knew he did."

"But you didn't know he was dead."

Morris shook his head. "Not till that body turned up and you people identified it."

"Didn't anyone look for Haskins?" Larkin asked.

"Why would we? We thought he was still alive and had run off with a big score he'd made."

"Why would you think that?"

Morris stuck his chin up. "You wanna crush that butt for me?"

Will took the cigarette and dropped it into a nearly empty bottle of water between the seats.

"Haskins was working a big score?" Larkin asked.

"Yeah, but we didn't know what it was. He was gone a lot the last few years. He wasn't around to finesse things. That's why Bryce got caught and run out of the Marine Corps. He just wasn't very good at handling the details."

"Did Ketchum know what happened to Haskins?"

"I don't know. He never said."

"But Ketchum didn't know what Haskins was working on?"

Morris shook his head. "If Bryce knew, he wasn't telling no one. The problem was, everything Bryce did eventually led back to George. That's how come George was about to get kicked from the Marines. Or arrested and throwed in the brig."

"Then Haskins just disappeared?"Larkin asked.

"Yeah."

"Was that before or after the Chloe Ivers murder?"

"I seen all that stuff on the television," Morris said. "I know there's some of the reporters trying to link them because of that charm that George was supposed to have. I've thought about it, trying to get it right in my mind, but I can't. I don't know which one happened first. But if you think about it, that girl had to have gone missing first. Otherwise, how would George have had that charm?"

He has a point, Will thought. "Did Ketchum ever mention Chloe Ivers?"

"You mean before yesterday?"

Will nodded.

"Not that I can recall."

"What did he say about her yesterday?"

"Not much. That girl's problems were over nearly twenty years ago. Bryce, he was stuck smack-dab in the middle of his. He was more concerned about his own neck."

"Was the money he put up as bail his?" Larkin asked.

"I don't know."

"How did he get Wardell to represent him?"

Morris shrugged.

"Did Ketchum say he was leaving town?"

"Why would he stick around? With everything you guys had on him, he was going away. He knew that." Morris leaned back against the seat and tried to get comfortable with his hands cuffed behind him. "Bryce was greedy and he was cocksure of himself, but he wasn't stupid. You want to know what I think, I think he was getting out of Dodge."

Will thought so too.

S
CRIME SCENE
NCIS
NAVAL CRIMINAL INVESTIGATIVE SERVICE

36

SCENE  NCIS  CRIME SCENE

NAVAL CRIMINAL INVESTIGATIVE SERVICE

>> JACKSONVILLE, NORTH CAROLINA
>> 0218 HOURS

Nita parked under the carport beside Joe's pickup and sat quietly for a while. Her head buzzed with the wine she'd drunk. Instead of a club, she'd gone to a small bar to drink. No one had bothered her, and she'd quietly tried not to think from eleven o'clock till two when the bar closed. Sitting in the car, she listened to the radio and blearily tried to remember what she had to do in the morning.

Finally she gave up. It didn't matter. Whatever she had to do would wait on her.

Then she remembered that she'd talked to Joe earlier in the evening and told him she'd be home in time for dinner. Cursing, she fumbled in her purse for her phone and pulled it out.

The bright light on the display stabbed into her eyes. She had to blink a few times to focus against the painful brightness.

There were three missed calls. All of them were from home. Evidently Joe had called right before seven, then again at seven-thirty and eight.

Nita had been posting some overflow work from the Middle East, two young Marines who had fallen prey to improvised explosive devices. The IEDs had made horrible wreckage of both. She'd worked to put them back together as best she could and confirmed both identities.

The bodies weren't due to be shipped back to the families till Monday, so she hadn't needed to do the work tonight. But she hadn't wanted to go home. She'd immersed herself in her work.

There were no phone calls after eight. There were also no messages. Evidently Joe hadn't figured a message would be worth leaving.

Cursing again, hating having other people's expectations put on her, Nita dropped the phone back into her purse, then opened the Mustang's door and got out. The movement made her light-headed. Her senses swam. She leaned against the side of the car till she felt like she could function.

As she crossed to the front door, she smelled the odor of freshly mowed grass. Evidently Joe had cut the lawn today. The small garden in front of the house held a variety of flowering plants and shrubs. Celia didn't exactly have a plan in mind when she put her garden together. Anything that caught her eye had gone into the mix.

At the door, Nita fumbled for her keys. Then the door opened.

Joe stood there, barefoot and clad in jean cutoffs and a muscle T-shirt. He looked tired and worried.

Guilt flooded Nita. She knew she was the reason Joe felt the way he did. *That's not your fault,* she told herself. *You're not responsible for his feelings. He's not responsible for yours.*

"Hi." Joe's voice was quiet.

"You're up late." Nita returned her keys to her purse and entered the house.

"I was worried."

Nita listened for any accusation in his voice. There wasn't any. But she did hear relief.

"I should have called." Nita was irritated with herself for automatically accepting blame. She had a job to do. Joe had known that when he married her.

"I tried to hold dinner."

Nita walked into the living room and sat in one of the easy chairs. She wanted to sit on the couch, but she was afraid that might encourage Joe to sit with her. More than anything, she wanted a drink.

"I've told you never to hold dinner," Nita said. She knew she had an edge in her voice.

Joe sat in the chair across the coffee table from her. His family Bible lay on the arm of the chair. A reading lamp shone over one tanned shoulder and lit gold fire in his hair.

He looked like he'd looked on several occasions, Nita thought. Angelic. That was the thing that had drawn her to him first. She'd seen plenty of handsome men. They were a dime a dozen. But Joe was the most at-peace man she'd ever met in her life.

They'd met on New River. One of Nita's friends had been out sailing with a local guy. Nita had gone to meet the guy's buddy, but the buddy hadn't shown. When the boat had broken down, Joe was the one who'd shown up to work on it.

Joe had been calm and friendly, and he'd had the boat running again in less than an hour. During that time, Nita had assisted him, handing him tools like one of the assistants in her lab would. To her it had been as natural as breathing. She'd always had a curious mind, and she'd discovered that a combustion engine was as deftly put together as any organ in the human body.

The weird thing was, she had talked. All Joe had done was listen. He'd smiled at her stories and laughed at her jokes. And he'd never once told her anything about himself.

He was, she'd realized at the time, the most mysterious man she'd ever met. Later, after the boat was running, she'd asked him about himself. He told her he ran a boat-repair business and had lived in Jacksonville all his life.

When he talked about the river, he'd come alive, describing some of the things he'd seen, the people he'd met. And during that all-too-short hour when he'd drunk a soft drink and talked to her while the other couple stayed busy driving the boat to make sure the repairs were going to hold up, Nita had become infatuated with him.

He hadn't come after her. He hadn't even asked where she worked. Instead, she'd been the one to pursue him, dropping by his work on the pretense of thinking about buying a boat.

In a few weeks, she'd fallen head over heels for him because he was so complete and so undemanding. His friends said he didn't date much, but there were plenty of women who were interested. Joe had his work, his friends, and his church. He stayed busy.

While trying to date him, Nita had discovered there were very few idle minutes in Joe's life. In fact, the first few "dates" had consisted of helping Joe help someone else. He'd always apologized, but later he'd admitted that he hadn't known she was interested in dating, just in getting to know him.

A few weeks after that, Nita had captured Joe's attention enough that he started asking her on dates. Their romance kindled quickly, and Joe asked her to marry him three months later. Caught up in the bliss of the new relationship, Nita had said yes without thinking. If only she'd known what it would mean. If she'd turned Joe down then, her life would be so different now.

She'd always had her life in control. From the time she entered junior high, when she'd realized that she really would survive living with her mother and get a chance at her own life, she'd focused on her studies and getting scholastic grants to go to college, then medical school. She'd interned at Camp Lejeune, then moved quickly into her position as medical examiner because she learned fast and was willing to work almost around the clock. The NCIS needed someone like her, and they'd rewarded her commitment.

Joe looked at her hesitantly, as if unsure what to say. "I'm concerned about you."

Nita thought about letting the comment pass or simply thanking him for his concern. But she couldn't. Something inside her felt challenged. "Why?" she asked. "I worked late. I've always worked late."

"It isn't the working late that concerns me."

"Then what?" But Nita knew what he was going to say.

"Your drinking concerns me."

"My drinking is *my* concern," Nita replied. The arguments she'd heard as a child in her mother's house came back to her in a rush. Suddenly she was right back there, cowering in the bedroom or the bathroom, knowing her mom was about to have another fight with whoever had been the latest man in her life.

"It's not your concern when you're driving." Joe didn't get mad. He just stated a fact. "You can hurt other people when you're on the road, Nita."

"I'm not going to hurt anyone else."

"You don't know that."

"I *do* know that." Nita stood up, no longer wanting to sit and argue. Her brain seemed to flip inside her skull, and for a split second she was disoriented. "I know the human body like you know boats, Joe. And I know my body most of all. I know what my tolerances are."

"You weren't in any condition to drive home tonight."

"Don't you dare try to tell me what my condition is, mister," Nita snarled. The anger and vehemence surprised her. She hadn't known how close they lay to the surface. But now they were naked and bared. "I know what my limitations are." She swayed.

Joe was quiet for a moment. "You can barely stand."

"I'm standing just fine." Nita knew she wasn't. She didn't know where the dizziness had come from. She hadn't noticed it before.

"This isn't just about you," Joe said. "There are other people out there. Even though you don't want to, you could hurt them."

"I'm not going to hurt anyone."

"You don't know that, Nita. You don't know that at all." For the first time, steel rang in Joe's voice.

That stopped Nita dead in her tracks for a moment. Joe had never raised his voice to her. She'd never heard him raise his voice around *anyone*.

"Don't tell me what I know and don't know."

Joe stood and said quietly, "This was a mistake. I apologize. Maybe we can talk in the morning. I'm glad you're safe. I'm glad you're home." He turned and started to walk away.

"No." Not knowing what compelled her, Nita stepped in front of Joe and cut off his retreat to the bedroom. "You're not just going to walk away from this."

Joe looked at her. "I don't want to fight."

"Maybe I do."

"I see that, but this isn't a good time."

"Why? Because you think I'm drunk?"

"You've had too much to drink."

"Maybe it's better this way. I can say what I need to this way."

"All right," Joe said. "What do you need to say?"

Nita took a breath. *You're stifling me. You're weighing me down with your needs and expectations.* All those things were on the tip of her tongue.

But instead she said, "You don't know what I had to see this evening."

"No. You're right. I don't."

"Then I'll tell you. I had to post two young men, a nineteen-year-old and a twenty-year-old. Both of them barely out of high school. They hadn't even had a chance to live life yet. They came back in body bags. I had to put them back together the best that I could. Their families still aren't going to be able to have an open-coffin service when they bury them."

"I'll pray for their families."

Nita was exasperated. "Prayer isn't going to fix those soldiers. And it's not going to help those families."

"I believe it will, Nita." His light hazel eyes held hers. The lamplight made them glow.

"Prayer isn't the answer for all things."

"We'll have to disagree."

"Disagree all you want to," Nita said, leaning into him, wishing she could shake that aggravating self-righteousness that he carried like armor. "All you have to do to know that prayer doesn't work is open the newspaper. War. Murder. Rape. Suicide. Violence. It's on every page, Joe. If prayer worked, if God worked, those things wouldn't happen."

"Those things happen because of people." Joe's voice was calm and steady—and utterly convinced. "When you open the newspaper, you don't generally get the stories of the people prayer has saved. Or at least helped. A miracle cure gets attributed to a doctor or a pharmaceutical company.

Someone lost at sea when his boat goes down who gets saved by the Coast Guard? It's luck that he's found, not God's hand. But the reality is that God is everywhere, working all the time."

"It's not that simple."

"Sure it is. You just have to open your eyes."

Fury gripped Nita. She didn't know how to proceed with her argument. Joe was wrong. He was so wrapped up in his blind faith that he didn't have a clue about the real world.

"Mom." Celia's tiny voice entered the tense silence. "Dad."

Although she didn't want to, Nita looked and saw her daughter standing in the doorway of her bedroom.

Celia wore Little Mermaid pajamas and stood partially hidden by the door. Fear widened her eyes.

"It's okay, Celia," Joe said.

"Are you fighting?"

"We're just disagreeing," Joe told her. "Way too loudly. We'll stop." He glanced at Nita, and his voice sounded a little more forceful. "We'll stop . . . now."

Nita almost blew up again. It was in her to do that. But she remembered all the nights when she had hidden and cried, listening to the angry voices, the slaps and punches, the cries of pain and—finally—the slamming doors.

You don't want that for her, Nita told herself. *No matter what else you want, you don't want that for Celia. That's why you're getting out of this relationship.*

"We're through disagreeing, Celia. You can go back to bed."

"I want to be tucked in," Celia said.

Reluctantly, Nita turned to her daughter. "All right."

"Not you," Celia said. "I want Daddy to do it."

Even in the state she was in, Nita realized how badly that simple declaration hurt. She didn't know what to say.

Without a word, Joe went to their daughter and picked her up. They disappeared inside Celia's room.

Overcome by drink and strong emotion, Nita walked back to the couch. She heard Celia's soft voice saying her prayers, heard Joe telling her to pray for her mom.

Dizzy, hurting, and confused, Nita lay down on the couch and was asleep in minutes. It was not a restful slumber.

37

SCENE  NCIS  CRIME SCENE

NAVAL CRIMINAL INVESTIGATIVE SERVICE

>> NEW RIVER
>> SNEADS FERRY, NORTH CAROLINA
>> 0320 HOURS

Gary Dover hugged the coastline in the little bass boat his grandfather had given him. Thirteen years old, Gary was a natural-born sailor and fisherman. Everyone had always said so. Even though his mom pretended that she didn't like the idea and that schoolwork was more important, Gary knew even she was proud of his ability. He'd come from a long line of fishermen.

That was why he was out on the water after curfew. He was fishing, looking for Mr. Whiskers, the legendary catfish that lived in the river channel. Although he'd been after the scar-faced, one-eyed catfish for five years and had heard about the fish as far back as he could remember, Gary had never before tried fishing this late at night—or early in the morning, depending on how a person looked at it—for Mr. Whiskers.

"We need to go back," Ricky whined.

Ricky was Gary's little brother. With a headful of shaggy brown hair and brown eyes, Ricky looked a lot like Gary. Ricky was nine.

"We don't need to go back," Gary said.

"We're going to get in trouble."

"Only if we get caught, and we're not going to get caught. Unless somebody hears you whining."

Ricky stared at the dark woods that lined the river. "There's stuff in the woods, Gary. I heard 'em."

"'Course you did. That's where they live."

"Who?"

"Animals. Critters." Gary had to admit that when he didn't take care, he got a little creeped himself. But he'd learned the night could do that to a person—just weird them out for no reason at all.

"Snakes?"

"There aren't any snakes out at this time of night," Gary lied. He didn't really know because he hadn't been out this late before. On the other times when he'd been out almost as late, he hadn't noticed any snakes. Well, at least most of the time he hadn't noticed any.

"Cory says snakes like to climb trees and drop on people at night."

That was definitely a creepy thought. Gary fought the urge to look up. Ricky wanted him to look up because then he'd win. And if Gary looked, Ricky wouldn't shut up about going back home until they were safe in their beds.

"Cory tells you all kinds of lies. Remember when he told you he had Martians living next door?"

"They could have been Martians."

Gary dropped anchor on the boat. "They weren't Martians."

"How do you know?"

"Because they didn't eat Martian food." Cory had been behind that fact-finding mission. All three of them had been caught rummaging through the neighbors' trash cans. Gary and Ricky got grounded for two weeks. Cory's parents had believed Cory when he'd claimed it was all Gary's fault.

"It could have been a disguise," Ricky said.

"It wasn't a disguise. They were human. And snakes don't climb trees."

"There's lots of snakes in trees in South America. Remember that show we watched on Discovery Channel?"

"This isn't South America." Gary baited a hook with stink bait and dropped it into the water. Then he settled down to wait. The boat drifted slightly on the river, falling into line behind the anchor.

Now all he had to do was be patient.

Ricky, of course, fell back on his primary defense against his older brother. "You don't know everything, Gary."

Gary sighed. "I know that if I'd been a little quieter getting out of the house, I wouldn't have to put up with you."

"You're not that sneaky."

But he'd *tried* to be. It wasn't his fault Ricky was such a light sleeper.

"Shhhh," Gary said. "You're going to scare Mr. Whiskers away."

"Do you think we can really catch him?"

"No, I just thought maybe I could give up sleeping tonight and take a chance on Mom grounding me for a month so I could come sit out in the boat with my pesky little brother."

"Oh."

For a while, Ricky was quiet. But Gary knew it wouldn't last long.

"Gary?"

"What?"

"I'm cold."

Grumbling to himself loud enough for his little brother to hear, Gary grabbed the blanket he'd brought in their fishing gear and handed it to Ricky. Ricky pulled the blanket around himself.

Then something bumped up against the boat.

Gary almost jumped out of his skin. Whatever had hit them had been big.

"What was that?" Ricky asked.

"I don't know." Gary laid the fishing pole aside and picked up the flashlight.

"I'm scared."

"You're always scared." Gary held the flashlight but didn't turn it on. There was a possibility the light might draw whatever it was back to them. He wasn't sure he wanted that. In fact, with something that big, he was pretty sure he didn't.

"Cory said alligators have been known to take people out of boats."

"I never heard that." Gary had seen the alligators, though. That was another reason his mom was going to kill him if she found out he'd gone out on the river at night. Especially with Ricky.

The boat got bumped again. This time whatever had hit it stayed underneath, causing the boat to list to port.

"What is it?" Ricky whispered as he grabbed Gary's arm.

"How should I know?" Gary tried to free himself from Ricky's hands but couldn't. When nothing climbed over the side of the boat, his curiosity outweighed his fear, but it was a close-run race.

Switching the flashlight on, Gary peered over the boat's side into the murky water.

Illuminated by the flashlight, the pale oval of the dead man's face—mouth yawning like a fish's—floated only a few inches beneath the river's surface.

Ricky started screaming. A moment later, when his heart slammed back into motion, Gary joined him.

CRIME SCENE

38

SCENE  NCIS  CRIME SCEN

NAVAL CRIMINAL INVESTIGATIVE SERVICE

>> NEW RIVER
>> SNEADS FERRY, NORTH CAROLINA
>> 0443 HOURS

"Who else is out here?" Will stood in the prow of the United States Coast Guard river-patrol boat as it powered across the sluggish current. He had to talk loudly over the throbbing engines.

The phone call from the Coast Guard officer had woken Will from a restless slumber. He'd called Remy but let the rest of the team sleep. After he'd picked Remy up, they'd driven to Sneads Ferry to join the Coast Guard.

Ahead, a cluster of lights marked the spot where the two boys had found Bryce Ketchum's body. At least a half dozen crafts had converged on the area.

"Sneads Ferry patrol guys showed up first," said the Coast Guard lieutenant driving the craft. "Then we got the squeal. The Onslow Sheriff's Office and some Marine security guys watching the Camp Lejeune side of the river followed. I guess it's a boring night. Except for this." The lieutenant stared straight ahead through the gloom. "Sneads Ferry guys wanted to claim the body. But they're not prepared to handle a murder like this. Besides that, you people wanted Ketchum."

"Yes, we did," Will said. He scanned the water and tried to feel hopeful despite the difficulty presented by the scene. Underwater crime scenes provided any number of problems for investigators. The murky water and time of day added to those problems.

Two small boys sat huddled in one of the Sneads Ferry patrol boats.

"The Sneads Ferry people were first on the scene?" Will asked.

"Yeah. The boys who found the body hightailed it for town and got caught by one of the fishermen getting his boat ready. The fisherman called the Sneads Ferry guys. They called us."

"Why you? Why not Camp Lejeune?"

"The locals have a better working relationship with the Coast Guard. We're just here trying to keep everybody safe, not keep 'em out of lands and water they figure are prime for hunting and fishing."

That was part of the ongoing friction between the military and civilians in the area. Of course, the camp's location also helped out the local economies.

"They wanted to pull the corpse out of the water," the lieutenant said. "We arrived here just as they were about to do that."

"Did they touch the body?"

"Yeah. They had hold of it with a fishing gaff. The guys working the Sneads Ferry call-outs tonight aren't experienced in recovering bodies."

"I'll need that gaff, and I'll need to talk to the guys who tried to bring the body in."

"I got their names. And I got the gaff in custody. Figured you'd want to see it."

The Coast Guard pilot reversed the engines and guided the craft near the point where the other boats had gathered. Will shone his flashlight over the water.

"Once I saw who the dead guy was—recognized him from the warrant the court put out—I figured I'd call you," the lieutenant said.

"You're sure it's Ketchum."

The Coast Guard lieutenant nodded. "You're lucky the gators haven't gotten to him."

Will stared into the water. Ketchum's body was hard to see because of all the light hitting the surface. Looking at the pallid features blunted by the water, Will felt bad for the two boys who had discovered it. The sight wasn't one they were going to forget anytime soon.

Nearby one of the Sneads Ferry patrolmen stood in a short outboard sporting a life vest and a revolver on his hip.

"Has anyone been down there?" Will asked.

"We didn't have a chance before that lieutenant pulled rank on us," the patrolman said. "We'd have had him up out of there for you if the lieutenant hadn't ordered us out of the water."

"On a crime scene like this," Will said, "you'll find that most investigators prefer that the body stay in the water until they're ready to pull it out."

The man looked away. "That ain't the way we handle it with drowning victims."

"I don't think this one is a drowning victim," Will said.

>> 0511 HOURS

Dressed in scuba gear, Remy sat on the edge of the Coast Guard boat, tucked the mouthpiece between his teeth, and blew air into his mask to get the seal right. The weight of the air tank on his back was familiar. As a SEAL, he'd done a lot of underwater missions in practice as well as on ops.

Will handed him the underwater digital camera. "Be careful down there."

Remy gave Will a thumbs-up. He'd seen the alligators that lived in New River. They were few in number and tended not to be overly interested in humans, but that was above the water—not in it.

And water wasn't Remy's natural environment. Alligators had the edge. Still, the SEAL had been trained to be a deadly predator in the water.

When everything was checked and ready, Remy flipped backward over the gunwale and slipped into the water. Bubbles rose all around him for a moment as he sank toward the bottom. He breathed easily, naturally. That was one of the key skills to diving.

Just before he touched bottom, barely visible even with the underwater halogen lights he wore on either side of his head, Remy turned and gracefully flicked his flippers. He carried the digital camera in one hand and a CO_2-powered speargun in the other. He also wore a Randall survival knife strapped to his right calf.

He swam toward the lights centered on Ketchum's corpse. The man had been in the water for a while. Gases had built up inside the corpse, ballooning the midsection and turning the skin to the texture of prunes.

Even after everything he'd seen, the sight bothered Remy a bit. There was no mistaking who it was, though. Even with the bites taken out of the features by fish and crawdads, Bryce Ketchum was recognizable. A few more days in the water—especially if the alligators found him—and that wouldn't have been true.

Remy brought the camera up and took pictures, shooting several of them from all angles. The lights, his included, created a canopy against the surface of the river, sharply dividing the area above and below. He felt alone in the river. The sound of the scuba gear and his own heart filled his ears.

The mask pressed tightly against his temples, causing a little painful throbbing from his injury. A week had passed, and it had nearly healed. He'd taken the stitches out himself on Wednesday.

Ketchum's jacket weighed heavily on one side.

Peering into the pocket, Remy spotted a pistol. He took pictures of the weapon as well but left it in place. He didn't think fingerprints would be possible on any part of the gun. The river water would have destroyed the oils left behind by prints. But there was a chance that some part of the weapon might have been watertight enough to preserve a clue. He'd seen the magic the team worked in the lab.

Remy wasn't sure how Bryce Ketchum had died. There were no bullet wounds. The neck and the spine seemed intact. There was no bruising of the face. Other than the assorted bites, nothing appeared wrong with the man.

However, someone had chained Ketchum to a small boat anchor. The length of chain around Ketchum's right leg didn't allow him to quite reach the surface. If the river hadn't been so shallow in the area, he probably would have gone unnoticed.

Taking up the camera again, Remy photographed the chain and the anchor. He'd only been with the NCIS for the last year, but Will and the others had drilled the importance of gathering everything they could at a crime scene.

Locard's Principle, the fundamental rule behind all crime-scene investigations, stated that anyone who entered a crime scene left something behind and took something with them. In every case that Remy had worked with the team, that had been true.

The chain wasn't tied or knotted. It was secured at both ends with padlocks.

Remy got closer to the body and shot pictures of the hands. The fingerprints looked intact. As he shone the light on the corpse, a crawdad almost as big as his hand scuttled out from under Ketchum's jacket and shot away.

Remy didn't even flinch.

He took a few more pictures of Ketchum's hands. There was no bruising, and all the fingernails were in place.

He was dead when he went into the water. If Ketchum had been alive, drowning at the end of the chain, he would have bruised his hands and torn his fingernails off trying to get free. Remy had seen instances of that.

Once the team had recovered the body of a woman who'd been locked in the trunk of a car by her lover, a Marine who'd gotten jealous enough to kill her. The Marine had driven the car into a lake, then got out in time to save himself. The woman was dead when they found her, but Remy would never forget the damage she'd done to her hands trying to get free of the trunk while underwater.

That death had bothered him, haunted his sleep for days. The young woman had been only twenty.

Finished, Remy swam up and rejoined Will.

"It's Ketchum." Remy handed the camera up.

Will flipped through the digital images. "This isn't the crime scene."

"No." Remy held on to the boat and floated in the river. "The body is secured to that boat anchor. It's not heavy enough to keep him down. I don't think it was supposed to."

"Whoever killed Ketchum and dumped his body wanted him to stay underwater but hoped that the river would carry him out to the Atlantic."

New River emptied into the ocean. That was one of the reasons the Coast Guard was posted there.

"Why didn't whoever killed him just take him out there and dump him directly into the ocean?" Remy asked.

"The Coast Guard and the Marines maintain an active presence on the river," Will said, continuing to flip through the pictures. "Whoever killed Ketchum didn't want to take a chance on getting caught with his body. They killed him and dumped him immediately."

The cold seeped into Remy through the neoprene wet suit.

"Ketchum was armed?" Will studied the camera display.

"Unless whoever killed him shoved the pistol into his pocket. Maybe the murderer wanted to tie Ketchum to something else. Personally, I think Ketchum was carrying because he didn't trust whoever it was he was meeting."

"But he had no choice about meeting that person."

"Yeah."

"Were any shots fired from the pistol?"

"I don't know. I didn't touch it. The jacket pocket was intact."

"No rips or tears?"

"None that I can see."

"He didn't even have a chance to go for the pistol," Will said.

Remy shook his head. "There's no obvious cause of death, but it looks to me like whoever killed him killed him quick."

"Ketchum was a liability to someone. They were afraid he couldn't run far enough or fast enough."

"What do you want to do with the body?"

"Nita's on her way. We'll wait."

❁ ❁ ❁

>> JACKSONVILLE, NORTH CAROLINA

>> 0523 HOURS

When Nita stepped out of the shower, Joe stood at the door, his arms folded across his chest. She didn't know what to say. She hadn't expected him to be awake. Her cell phone had been set on vibrate when Will's call came in.

"You're leaving?" Joe asked.

Nita had to curb the sarcastic remark that instantly flew to the tip of her tongue. She wrapped a towel around herself and felt uncomfortable.

"Will called," she said. "They just found Bryce Ketchum's body. He wants me out there. He'll probably want me to post him this morning too."

"I can drive you."

"I can drive myself."

Joe frowned. "I don't think that's a good idea. You're not in any shape to—"

"I'm fine." Nita knew that she was. Despite the hangover throbbing at her temples and the overall fatigue, she was sober. It wasn't a good feeling.

"Nita, I care about you."

"I care about you too." The words were out of Nita's mouth before she realized it. But they came automatically, and she regretted them the instant she realized what she'd said. "I can drive myself."

"You've barely slept."

"I'm fine. There's no sense in both of us losing sleep. And there's really no sense in waking Celia to drag her off to watch a body being hauled out of the river. I don't want her around something like that."

Joe sighed. "Neither do I."

"Look. It'll be fine. I've had about three hours of sleep. I got by on less than that when I was an intern."

Joe didn't move.

"I've got to go," Nita said. "There are people waiting."

"I know. I just want us . . . to be able to talk about this."

"Later." But Nita had no intention of talking about it. There was nothing to talk about. And if she did say what was on her mind, Joe wasn't going to like it. "I *have* to go."

Reluctantly, Joe stepped away. "I'm taking Celia to work with me today."

Nita had to think for a moment to remember that it was Saturday. "All right."

"If you need anything, we'll be there."

"Okay."

Tentatively, Joe leaned in and kissed her.

For a moment Nita forgot herself and forgot the anger she felt at him. She kissed him back, reaching out and sliding a hand behind his neck, pulling him to her. It was so easy to be with him when it was just the two of them and she didn't have to think about tomorrow.

But this was a trap. The best and worst trap she had ever fallen into. There had to be more to life than just Joe and Celia, but if she settled for them, she'd lose herself.

It was all so confusing.

She broke the kiss. Hot tears brushed the backs of her eyes. She looked away before he saw them. "I've *really* got to go."

"I know." Joe stepped back.

Nita dressed in the bedroom while Joe went into the kitchen. She pulled on jeans and hiking boots because the recovery site was at New River and she knew what conditions there were like.

By the time she was ready, Joe had packed a thermos of coffee and two scrambled-egg-and-sausage burritos. He'd scrambled the eggs and fried the sausage while she'd been in the shower. He usually kept fresh vegetables on hand, so the onion, peppers, and tomatoes were already chopped.

"Breakfast," he said. "Save you the time of stopping for something, and it's fresh."

"Thanks." Nita took the food, hesitated, then kissed him again. He smelled good, clean, and she wished that he didn't because then she wouldn't have to feel like everything going wrong was all her fault.

Even if it is me, she told herself, *it's only because I'm not the person Joe wants me to be. I'm me. And I need to be me.*

She kissed Celia good-bye without waking her, then headed for the door, hoping that Bryce Ketchum's body would occupy her day and fill her thoughts so she wouldn't have to deal with all the confusion inside her.

S  CRIME SCENE  NCIS  C

NAVAL CRIMINAL INVESTIGATIVE SERVICE

39

SCENE  NCIS  CRIME SCEN

NAVAL CRIMINAL INVESTIGATIVE SERVICE

\>> NEW RIVER
\>> SNEADS FERRY, NORTH CAROLINA
\>> 0632 HOURS

Gold-and-pink daylight streaked the eastern sky. Morning had come to Sneads Ferry. Since many of the inhabitants were fishermen, they'd been up and gone in the small hours of the morning, giving the crime-scene boats a wide berth on their way downriver. But several of the weekend sailors and tourists had turned out to watch what was going on.

Before it was done, Will was glad so many other law enforcement agencies had turned up at the site. It took all of them—and reinforcements—to keep the gawkers away from the scene.

Nita knelt on the prow of the Coast Guard vessel and reached into the water. Surgical gloves covered her hands.

Remy was in the water again. He floated near the body.

"We can get him up out of the water now," Nita said.

Until she'd arrived to take possession of the body at the scene, the corpse wasn't supposed to be moved. Remy had had to secure the boat anchor so the body wouldn't continue to drift.

Seagulls lined the banks and the trees, all watching for the flotsam left by the fishermen and boaters. The media had arrived as well, standing in neatly ordered groups as the camcorder operators tried to get shots of the corpse. Several of the reporters yelled questions across the river.

Will looked at the reporters with growing distaste. He knew they had jobs to do, but he needed to be able to do *his* job without distraction.

And if it were an ordinary murder, it wouldn't have drawn as much attention as this one did. Speculation on the murder was going wild, much of it tying back to Congressman Swanson.

Larkin had already contacted Will to let him know that Swanson's office had been calling. Obviously the congressman wasn't happy with the turn of events.

On the surface it appeared that Swanson was every bit as surprised by the murder as anyone else. But Will still felt sure the man was hiding something. As a politician with years of experience, Swanson was a consummate actor.

One of the Coast Guard divers joined Remy in the water. Together, using an underwater torch, they cut Ketchum's body free of the chain.

"Get that blanket up," Will directed.

Two NCIS special agents held up a blanket to block the view of the body. Groans erupted from the crowd.

Will helped pull the corpse aboard the Coast Guard boat. The Coast Guard lieutenant Will had spoken to earlier had got clearance to escort the body and the NCIS team to a rendezvous point that would leave the reporters behind.

"Bag his hands," Nita said. "I doubt there's any tissue under his fingernails. He doesn't look like he got a chance to put up a fight. Still, you never know."

Will used one of the paper bags she handed him. They used paper so the hands could dry. Plastic often stuck to tissue and ripped it away, and it promoted bacterial growth. When he had the hand bagged, he taped it on.

Nita did the same with the other hand.

Remy and the Coast Guard diver brought up the chain and boat anchor.

"Can you determine the cause of death?" Will asked.

Nita remained on her knees by the body and began a quick examination. She put a hand under Ketchum's head and rolled it. "Spine's intact. His neck wasn't broken. There are no ligature marks. Hold his head and let me check his mouth."

Will held the dead man's head as Nita withdrew her hand. Both of them saw the blood on her surgical glove at the same time.

"Roll him over," Nita said.

Handling two hundred plus pounds of deadweight was hard, but they managed. Remy came over to join them. Shouted questions from the onlookers floated across the water, mixing in with the sound of the engines.

Nita combed her fingers through Ketchum's hair at the back of his head. She didn't find the bullet hole at the base of the dead man's skull till the third pass.

With the heart no longer beating, blood tended to stay inside the body. What blood remained had congealed so much that very little exited the small, round wound in the hair.

"He was shot in the back of the head." Nita held the hair out of the way.

"Looks like a .22 round," Remy said. "Probably silenced. There are burn marks."

Will looked closer and saw where the flesh had been seared. When a weapon discharged, superheated gases—especially when trapped against flesh—warmed the metal enough to burn skin.

Nita took forceps from her pocket. She probed the flesh, lifting it enough to reveal the small, short rips. "The killer held the pistol against Ketchum's head when it was fired."

Will nodded. Stellate rips occurred when the explosion of gases followed the bullet into flesh and tore free. A revolver would have allowed them to escape around the cylinder. The killer had to have used a semiautomatic pistol. That would have allowed the use of a silencer; a revolver didn't. A semiautomatic pistol was an enclosed system.

"There's no exit wound." Nita examined the dead man's head. "The bullet's still inside."

"If it was a .22, you're not going to recover anything usable," Remy said. "The bullet would have bounced around inside Ketchum's head, shredding his brain but also falling to pieces."

Nita looked at him.

Remy grinned awkwardly. "Sorry. You're the medical examiner. I guess you knew that."

"I am and I did." Nita stood and stripped off her gloves. "Let's get him back to the lab. If I can't give you the bullet, let's see what I *can* give you."

Will helped Remy and the other Coast Guard sailors lift the corpse into a body bag.

"Remy and I are going to stay here and see if we can find the original crime scene," Will told Nita. "Leave us your keys and we'll drive your car back."

Nita took her keys from her pocket and handed them over.

Will took her arm and walked her a few steps away. "Remy wasn't trying to tell you how to do your job," he said. "He was just thinking out loud. Remember, he's still figuring out everything we already know."

"I know." Nita sighed. "I didn't get very much sleep last night. I'll apologize to him later. After I've had more coffee."

Will nodded. "You feel up to this?"

Nita glanced at the body bag. "I know how to do this, Will. This may be the only thing I know how to do for certain right now, at this point in my life. I'll get it done as soon as I can."

Leaving her with the body bag, Will went to gather Remy. He didn't look forward to the search. The boat-rental agencies in Sneads Ferry were going to do great business if the media followed along.

>> NCIS HEADQUARTERS
>> CAMP LEJEUNE, NORTH CAROLINA
>> 0830 HOURS

Maggie's cell phone chirped and rattled on her desk. She picked it up and checked the caller ID. The call was from her father.

Her phone was one of the few that her father didn't mask his number from, but he usually called from an exchange, so even if she called back on the number that showed, she didn't get through.

Maggie truly didn't want to deal with her father this morning. Harrison Talbot Foley III never called just to pass the time of day. Anytime he called there was a deal in the works, and he was going to get something he wanted out of it.

Years ago Maggie's mother had been institutionalized after trying to commit suicide, and Maggie's father had sole authority over her visitors. He was the only one who could allow Maggie in to see her mother. Without that leverage over her, Maggie wouldn't have been quite so docile or compliant around her father. Harrison Foley was the most controlling person she knew. If she deliberately slighted him, Maggie knew she wouldn't get to see her mother for months.

Maggie flicked the phone open and said hello.

"Hello, Margaret. Did I catch you at a good time?"

Maggie took a breath, her mind racing. No one unnerved her more than her father. He always called her by her given name. It had been his mother's name.

"Now is fine, Father." She always called him Father, never Dad. Father was all he would allow.

"Good. I'm glad. I hate calling so unexpectedly."

Anytime Harrison Foley called was unexpected. Except on Maggie's birthday. He always called her then. Precisely at 7 a.m. before he got his business day under way. The chat never lasted more than five minutes.

"It's all right."

"Did I catch you at home?" Her father's clipped Bostonian accent was in rarefied form.

"Actually, I'm working."

"Well, that's fortuitous. I wanted to discuss your work with you."

"Is Mother all right?"

"Your mother is fine." A trace of irritation sounded in her father's words. He didn't like talking about her. "I'm watching the news right now, Margaret."

Maggie glanced at the monitor displaying the CNN footage. She knew her father was watching that channel. The television displayed yet another story about Congressman Benjamin Swanson and the possible connection between his stepdaughter and George Haskins.

"Have you met Ben Swanson?" Maggie's father asked.

"No." It didn't surprise Maggie that her father talked about the congressman like they were old friends. They had probably done business somewhere together, either in corporations or on the floor of the House.

"Oh, surely you must have met him. You once accompanied me on many of my engagements."

That had been at his request, not because Maggie had wanted to take part in her father's business. "If I did, I don't remember it."

An annoyed tone entered his voice. "It would do you well to remember your friends and acquaintances, Margaret. Otherwise you'll miss out on a lot of opportunities."

Maggie waited, knowing her father would get around to what he wanted to say when he was ready.

"I almost called you days ago, when this thing with Ben first started," her father said.

"Why?"

"To speak on his behalf, of course."

"Does Congressman Swanson feel like he needs you to speak on his behalf?"

Displeasure resonated in her father's words. "Don't play at being coy, Margaret. You've never been very good at it."

His words stung. The only thing that kept Maggie from hanging up was the certain knowledge that he wouldn't allow her to visit her mother in the mental-health facility. Mother's Day was coming up soon. Maggie couldn't imagine not being there for that.

She never went home for Father's Day, but that was mostly because Father's Day usually fell during the week when Harrison Talbot Foley III entertained himself with an annual retreat to the country of his choice. With whichever starlet or heiress was appropriate and in need of a boost to her career or public image.

"Did you hear me?" her father asked.

"Yes, Father."

"Good. For a moment there I thought the connection had been severed."

"No. The connection is fine."

"I won't take up much more of your time. I've got a pressing engagement at this end. But I would ask you to do something for me."

Maggie was so shocked she didn't know what to say. Her father never asked her for anything except obedience.

"Tell your boss or commanding officer or whatever he is that Ben Swanson has any number of friends who will come to his defense. I'm proud to count myself among them. Coburn should tread carefully before making any outlandish accusations if he wants to continue his career."

That, Maggie realized, *is a definite threat.*

"Furthermore, you might tell Coburn that he'd best step lightly around Ben. Be respectful. Otherwise, someone might come along and slap him for being impertinent. Coburn is out of his league on this one. Ben has a lot of highly placed friends who look out for him."

Maggie's immediate response was to warn her father off. If he'd called another NCIS special agent, his thinly sheathed commentary wouldn't have gone unchallenged.

But that's why you called me, isn't it? You knew I wouldn't argue with you.

"You will tell Coburn, won't you?" he asked.

"All right." Maggie didn't have a choice. She'd have to tell Will about the call for several reasons. But she hated how her father had forced her into the position of go-between.

"Well, if there isn't anything else," her father said, "I've got something I need to get back to."

"Of course."

Her father said good-bye and hung up.

Worn and frazzled, Maggie slumped back in her chair and tried to figure out exactly how she was going to tell Will Coburn that her father had just threatened him and the investigation.

⊛⊛⊛

>> NCIS MEDICAL LAB
>> CAMP LEJEUNE, NORTH CAROLINA
>> 0927 HOURS

Nita meticulously shaved the back of the dead man's head. The diener, a young lab assistant named Craig, held a paper bag to catch the hair as it fell. The hair would have to be tested as well. Clues could come from anywhere.

As Nita worked, she talked into the microphone hanging overhead. She described the entrance wound she found, measured it, and announced her findings. Then she took the camera and photographed the area.

"Help me turn him back over."

Craig helped her turn Ketchum's body. The corpse smelled like the river, but it also stank from decomposition. Nature tended to clean up her losses in a hurry.

"The body is in flaccid rigor," Nita stated.

Rigor mortis, the stiffening and contracting of dead muscle tissue, usually started two hours after death and first showed up in the small muscles of the face and neck. Rigor generally moved down, from head to toe. After twelve hours, the body became fully stiff and remained so for another eighteen hours before starting to relax again.

"With rigid rigor well past, I believe the victim has been dead at least thirty-six hours and probably no more than forty-eight." Nita consulted her laptop, bringing up the files Estrella had put together on the case.

Bryce Ketchum had been released from jail at eight-thirty Thursday morning.

You didn't live long after that, did you? Nita thought. Despite his criminal nature and the fact that he'd been responsible for a lot of misery, she couldn't help feeling a little sorry for him. *Somebody wanted you out of the way.*

She paused long enough to call Will and give him the estimated time of death. It was safe to assume Ketchum had gone into the water shortly after that.

Taking a penlight from her lab coat, Nita approached the body again. She pushed the eyelids back and examined the eyes. "Craig."

"Yes."

"I'm going to need you to take the body to X-ray. When you do, point this out to the tech." Nita shone the flashlight on the right eye.

The pupil was dilated so large that it totally eclipsed the iris.

"Do you know what caused that?" Nita asked.

"A concussion?"

"Good guess, but not quite." Concussions—bruising of the brain—sometimes resulted in mismatched pupil sizes. But nothing as severe as what was showing in the dead man's eye. "Tell the tech I think he's going to find the bullet behind the right eye. But if it's a .22, it will have fragmented. I need to know where as many of the recoverable pieces are as he can spot. They'll probably be scattered throughout the brain. Some of them may have traveled down into the diaphragm or the neck. Bullets don't always end up where you think they will once they're trapped inside a body. Have him do a full-body scan."

"All right."

"Stay with the body. When X-ray is done with it, I want it back. Beep me when you have it."

Craig nodded, kicked the brakes loose on the gurney, and wheeled it out of the room.

Nita switched the recording program off. She rubbed her temples and wished the headache she'd had all morning would finally subside. She took another analgesic even though she knew it was going to thin her blood more than she should have allowed.

She picked up the phone and called Maggie at her desk.

"Special Agent Foley," Maggie answered.

"It's Nita. Tell me you have coffee."

"I have coffee. I also have Danish."

"I'll be right there."

"I was about to call you to let you know you have a guest."

"A guest?" At first Nita was afraid Maggie was going to tell her Joe was there. Then she realized that Maggie would simply have told her it was Joe. This was someone else.

"His name is Daniel Wilkins. He says you know him."

Nita's stomach tightened. Daniel Wilkins was the minister of Joe's church. The throbbing in her head suddenly increased in tempo. Whatever Pastor Wilkins was doing there, it couldn't be good.

40

SCENE  NCIS  CRIME SCEN

NAVAL CRIMINAL INVESTIGATIVE SERVICE

>> JOSIE'S CAFÉ
>> SNEADS FERRY, NORTH CAROLINA
>> 0938 HOURS

A law enforcement officer's daily life wasn't much different from that of a commander aboard an aircraft carrier. Will had discovered that early in his career at NCIS. As executive officer serving under the captain of USS *John F. Kennedy,* most of Will's day had been occupied with day-to-day responsibilities. The XO kept the ship running smoothly while the captain dealt with the brass.

Will had been a good XO, detail oriented. He'd loved the sea and enjoyed training enlisted men and officers. Those skills stood him in good stead in the NCIS.

Most investigations, like most shipboard functions, depended on checking up on procedure, adhering to a set action plan. In police work, when there were no other definite clues at a crime scene, investigators turned to the tried-and-true method of detection: they knocked on doors and asked questions.

Knowing they wouldn't get anything off the river, Will had organized Remy and the special agents to talk to the local businesses. They went door-to-door, talking to shop owners and fishermen—anyone who might have been around when Bryce Ketchum had dropped into town.

Assuming that he'd been dead two days, going by Nita's estimate, that meant someone had killed Ketchum Thursday, shortly after he'd made bail. Will doubted that Ketchum had floated all the way from Jacksonville, and Camp Lejeune Marines patrolled the rest of New River. Sneads Ferry was the closest upriver access point to where the body had been found.

Ketchum's body had obviously been dumped into the river from a boat, but Will still didn't know for sure whether Ketchum had been killed on a boat or on land. Either way, Sneads Ferry made the most sense as the place where Ketchum had been either killed or picked up by a boat.

The searchers got lucky—twice. The first time was when one of the agents found a rental car that turned out to be in Ketchum's name. The leasing agency wasn't far from the jail, and a phone call from Will confirmed that Ketchum had rented the car on Thursday.

The NCIS took the car into custody. Will doubted they'd get any of the killer's prints from the vehicle, but every avenue had to be explored.

Redefining the search, keying off the vehicle, they discovered that Ketchum had been in Josie's Café Thursday afternoon. Fred Blake, the owner, was also the morning short-order cook.

Blake was a big man in his late sixties. Balding and soft featured, he wore glasses, shorts, and a Tar Heels T-shirt that reminded Will of the game he'd taken Wren and Steven to that had been interrupted. If everything went right, he'd have them again next weekend.

"Yeah, he was in here." Blake tapped the picture of Ketchum that Will had placed before him. "I saw him. A coffee drinker. He didn't eat. You get a lot of those in here in the afternoon."

At the moment, Josie's Café was packed with the morning crowd.

Blake worked the grill with alacrity. "Mornings aren't usually this busy. Now we got all these newspeople here. And the rubberneckers."

Will was painfully conscious of being the center of attention at the moment. "Was the man in that picture alone?"

"Yeah. He sat over there at that table." Blake pointed with a greasy spatula.

"Did he talk on the phone?" Will had already gotten Ketchum's phone records. Ketchum hadn't made a call on any of them since his arrest.

Blake nodded and flipped pancakes. "Not very long. Then he got up and went to meet the boat."

"What boat?"

"A powerboat. You could call it a yacht, I suppose. It was big enough." Blake threw a bar towel over his shoulder, hoisted the coffeepot, and refilled Will's cup.

"Did you get the name of the boat?"

Blake leaned on the table a moment. A young waitress took the spatula from him and tended the grill while he was distracted. He looked out at the river, frowning. "My mind isn't what it used to be. Or maybe it was never that good."

"Just take your time," Will suggested.

The frown cleared up. "It was gray and blue. A Sea Ray. She had her name painted in red on the back. *Jilly.*"

And that, Will knew, was the trifecta of clues. It was a red-letter day.

>> NCIS HEADQUARTERS
>> CAMP LEJEUNE, NORTH CAROLINA
>> 0944 HOURS

"Where is he?"

Maggie glanced at Nita and immediately knew she wasn't happy. "Mr. Wilkins?"

"Yes." Nita poured coffee from the nearby pot.

"I put him in Interview Room A. I told him it might take you a little while to get here from the lab. In case you were in up to your elbows."

"Okay. Thanks."

"I gather this wasn't an expected meeting."

"Since no one expected to find Bryce Ketchum's body this morning and I thought I had the day off, it would have been hard to schedule this, wouldn't it?"

"Hey, don't shoot the messenger."

Nita grimaced. "Sorry. I don't know what he wants, and I don't know if I'm ready to deal with whatever it is he's got on his mind."

Maggie leaned back in her chair to stretch fatigued back muscles. News footage of the search at Sneads Ferry was now being carried on the local networks, CNN, and FOX News. With all the attention drawn to Congressman Swanson, it would have taken a flare-up in the Middle East to pull the media away. The ante had been upped with the discovery of Ketchum's body. Speculation was rampant.

Maggie was watching and recording all of it. Both screens carried footage shot by different cameramen in Sneads Ferry.

Noticing how haggard Nita looked, Maggie said, "You don't have to talk to him right now."

Nita looked at her.

"You're tired," Maggie said. "You've been up for hours dealing with this. You've got an autopsy to do. If this is going to be a lot of grief, you don't need to deal. I'll run interference—tell him you got tied up and send him packing."

Nita sipped her coffee.

"It wouldn't be a problem," Maggie said.

"Wilkins is the pastor of Joe's church."

Maggie didn't know what to say to that. When she realized that Nita wasn't going to say anything, she said, "I gather he's not here about raffle tickets."

"No." Nita sighed. "I'd better go talk to him." She walked away.

"If you need me to come rescue you, just call."

"I will. Thanks."

Maggie turned back to the monitors. The footage was going out live. As she watched, Will stepped out of Josie's Café. Reporters followed him. The reporter covering the story announced that he believed Commander Will Coburn of the NCIS had just gotten new information on the investigation.

The phone rang.

"Special Agent Foley."

"It's me." Will sounded irritable.

"I heard you just got new information on your investigation."

"Who told you that?"

"It's on the news."

"Terrific. Look, I need some information as quick as you can get it."

"Okay."

"I need to know where a boat named *Jilly* is kept."

"Jilly?"

Will spelled it.

Maggie pulled up boat registration quickly and did a name search. The computer spit out the results in just a few seconds.

"I've got a listing in Holly Ridge. Out on Morris Landing. The owner of record is Lester Bridges."

"Get me directions to that marina," Will said, "and all the information you have on Lester Bridges."

Maggie did. "I'm sending it to your iPAQ now."

"Thanks. I'll be in touch."

"Do you need me out there?" Maggie hated sitting at the desk.

"If I do, I'll let you know."

"Will, there's something else you should know about."

"What is it?"

"I got a call from my father this morning. He . . ." Maggie paused, wondering how best to phrase her father's message. "Well, he basically told me to tell you not to make any accusations against Congressman Swanson if you know what's good for you."

"Your father called to have you tell me to watch my step?" Will sounded incredulous.

"Yes, in a nutshell." Maggie felt blood rush to her face as she recalled the conversation that morning.

"Anything else?"

"No."

"Why is your father taking an interest in this?" Will asked.

"The only reason my father would take an interest in this is because Swanson means something to him."

"As a friend?"

"No. It'll tie back to business somewhere. That's all my father is interested in."

"Does Larkin know?"

"I thought maybe you could tell him."

Will sighed. "Okay, I'll handle it. Thanks for the info." He ended the call.

Maggie sat back in her chair and sighed heavily. It appeared that nobody was happy this morning.

CRIME SCENE
NCIS
NAVAL CRIMINAL INVESTIGATIVE SERVICE

41

SCENE  NCIS  CRIME SCEN

NAVAL CRIMINAL INVESTIGATIVE SERVICE

>> INTERVIEW ROOM A
>> NCIS HEADQUARTERS
>> 0958 HOURS

Nita went next door to the observation room and watched Pastor Daniel Wilkins. The preacher was a soft-spoken man in his late fifties. He wore a dark blue suit and glasses and carried a book bag rather than a briefcase.

Wilkins delivered great oratory, and he knew the Bible. He'd raised his children and helped with three grandchildren. He played Santa for the orphanage every year and made sure the church stayed active in the Big Brothers Big Sisters program. By his own admission, he had a weakness for anything chocolate, herbal tea—he always carried a thermos with him—and Raymond Chandler novels.

Calm and relaxed inside the interview room, Wilkins sipped tea and made notes. Nita assumed the preacher was preparing for Sunday's sermon.

Angry, knowing she wanted to put off speaking to the man but knowing at the same time that it would stick in her mind if she didn't, Nita went next door.

Wilkins stood to greet her. "Mrs. Tomlinson."

"*Dr.* Tomlinson," Nita corrected before she had time to think about it. She'd worked hard to achieve that degree, and she wasn't going to let anyone casually strip it from her.

"Of course. I forgot. I don't usually deal with many doctors."

And you haven't seen me enough in church to remember, Nita thought, feeling a little guilty. But that only served to fuel the anger.

She waved to the chair, choosing to take command of the encounter. "Have a seat."

"Thank you." Wilkins held up his thermos. "Would you like some tea? I've brought plenty."

"No, thank you."

Wilkins sat and studied Nita for a moment. "I hope I haven't come at a bad time."

"It's a busy day, but I have a few minutes. If I get buzzed, I'll need to go. I have an autopsy to do."

Wilkins nodded. "I heard about the body that was pulled out of New River near Sneads Ferry. That's getting a lot of attention."

Nita rubbed her forehead. So far the analgesics she'd taken hadn't fazed the headache.

"I don't usually drop in unannounced," Wilkins said. "I want to apologize for that."

Nita nodded. Making small talk would only impede finding out why Wilkins was here.

"I saw Joe this morning," Wilkins said.

The anger tightened inside Nita. She couldn't believe Joe would go to the preacher with their problems. Then she realized she was being naive. *Whom else would he have gone to?*

"Joe mentioned . . . that there was strain in the family," Wilkins said.

"It really helps that he goes around talking about it," Nita said sarcastically.

"He didn't bring it up. I did." Wilkins pursed his lips. "Well, I inadvertently did. I went by the boat shop this morning, just to thank Joe for some of the work he's done on the church's stage."

Nita hadn't even known Joe was working on the church. If he'd told her—and he probably had—she'd promptly forgotten it.

"I couldn't help noticing Joe didn't look well rested," Wilkins said. "Or happy." He spread his hands. "That's really not like Joe."

Everybody notices when Joe's unhappy, but they don't notice when I am.

"I asked Joe about it," Wilkins continued, "thinking maybe he was sick or worried about something. Then Celia told me you and Joe had a fight last night."

"It wasn't a fight."

"Disagreement, then."

Nita didn't say anything.

"Celia said there had been several disagreements lately. Joe asked her to go play, but I could tell that . . . *whatever* is going on is also affecting her."

"Joe and I will work this out."

Wilkins looked uncomfortable. "I wish I was as sure about that as you sound."

"I would think," Nita said in a measured tone, "that as church pastor you would have more to do than meddle in the lives of your parishioners."

"I don't consider it meddling."

"Did Joe invite you into this? Because if he did, you can talk to him. Not me." Nita stood.

"Joe didn't invite me in." Wilkins's voice was harder than Nita had ever heard it. "Mrs. Horton did."

Nita's stomach flipped. Sour bile burst at the back of her throat. She thought for a moment that her legs weren't going to hold her.

"Mrs. Horton said she talked to you," Wilkins went on.

Nita refused to comment.

"Mrs. Horton is under a great deal of stress. She has a new baby on the way, and her husband is . . . less than committed to their relationship. What she's dealing with is very difficult. Without it being added to."

"I didn't know her husband—" Nita stopped. "I didn't know he was married."

"But you are, Dr. Tomlinson. To one of the finest men I've ever known." Wilkins's tone was the epitome of cool reproach.

"That," Nita said, "is none of your business."

"I disagree. When my parishioners are in pain, I consider it my duty to serve in whatever capacity I may."

"Mrs. Horton was in pain long before I arrived on the scene," Nita said. "Her husband is a jerk. I should have pressed charges that night."

"I wasn't talking about her."

"Does Joe know about this?"

"Not from me."

"Then I would suggest you not tell him. Let us work this out on our own." Nita struggled to keep her voice calm, but panic washed over her. She couldn't help worrying about how long it was going to take for Joe to learn about David Horton.

"I wasn't talking about Joe either, Dr. Tomlinson. I was talking about you."

Nita stared at him in disbelief.

"Joe and Celia and Mrs. Horton are all tending to their needs by talking to people," Wilkins said. "They're praying and seeking God's guidance in this. I was concerned that you needed someone to talk to."

For a moment, Nita was inarticulate.

"I don't think this is normal behavior for you, Dr. Tomlinson. I haven't seen this trouble in your family before. I just wondered if you'd tried prayer. If you want, I could pray with you." Wilkins held out his hands.

"No," Nita replied. "I don't think so."

After a short time, Wilkins let his hands drop. "I'd really like to help."

"Then stay out of this and let us handle it," Nita told him. "You can find your own way out. Don't come here again." Without another word, she turned and left.

Sickness bubbled and boiled in her stomach. Earlier that morning, after she'd first stepped into the lab and the strong chemical odor had hit her, she'd had to go to the bathroom and throw up. The episode had left her weak and shaking.

She forced herself to keep walking until she rounded the next corner. Then she had to lean against the wall while her knees threatened to buckle. She pushed the air out of her lungs, trying to combat the light-headedness that assailed her.

Gradually it passed.

Nerves, she told herself. *It's just nerves.*

After a few minutes, the nausea left her as inexplicably as it had struck. But the fear over what Joe would do when he found out about David Horton didn't leave her.

She knew she had to do something. She was all out of time.

Her cell phone vibrated for attention. A quick glance told her that the call was coming from the lab extension. Craig was back with Bryce Ketchum's body. She took a final breath, squared her shoulders, and set off for the lab.

>> MORRIS LANDING
>> HOLLY RIDGE, NORTH CAROLINA
>> 1022 HOURS

Holding the binoculars steady, Will scanned the yacht moored in its registered slip. Several other boats were in the area, some setting sail and others returning from morning activities. When the weather was good, sailors were always out. Engines spat and snorted all around them.

"According to the info Maggie turned up," Remy said at Will's side, "*Jilly* is registered to Dr. Lester Bridges, a local dentist. Dr. Bridges is currently out of the country on vacation. Maggie got that from the doctor's office manager."

"Someone borrowed his boat." Will capped the binoculars and put them back inside his truck. He'd parked up the slight incline from New River, behind the trees that lined the marina. "Let's hope whoever it was left something behind."

Drawing his sidearm, Will led the way. His senses keyed up. Ever since they'd found Ketchum's body, he'd felt certain they were on the heels of the murderer.

Remy followed him. Marine sharpshooters occupied positions along the marina that gave them clear, overlapping fields of fire. Shel and Max were already in place on the dock.

It was *not,* Will couldn't help thinking, the stealthiest intercept he'd ever executed.

He wore elbow and knee pads, protective glasses, and a Kevlar vest under his *Special Agent* Windbreaker. Boaters passed by him with concerned glances as he strode along the dock toward Shel. Others remained in their boats or on the shore.

The cover wasn't on the boat, leaving the deck open to see. No true boater would have left a vessel unprotected. Pedestrians who weren't boaters used boats as trash receptacles, and raccoons and other varmints sometimes crept out of the woods or the water to forage for food that might have been left aboard.

The only thing Will hadn't been able to examine was the forward cabin. Below the boat, the lift stayed submerged. Whoever had brought *Jilly* back hadn't bothered to moor her properly. They'd just tied her to the cleats and left.

"Ready?" Will asked.

"I got you." Remy stood behind a pylon that would provide partial cover. He held his .357 in both hands, aiming at the closed cabin door.

Shel stood, weapon at the ready, on the other side of the slip, out of view of the cabin door. The Marine and his Labrador were poised to jump onto the deck at the first sign of trouble.

Will stepped onto the yacht, then down into it. When nothing happened, he went forward. Holstering his weapon, he studied the door, taking time with it rather than just pulling it open.

Whoever took the boat had to know there was a good chance it would be seen. If it was found, he or they would know it would be treated as a crime scene.

Will cracked open the door, then reached into his chest pack and took out a fiber-optic cable connected to a handheld viewer. He slid the cable between the door and the frame and turned it on. Under the Windbreaker and the Kevlar vest, he was sweating.

The view screen displayed color images. Slowly, carefully, Will moved the cable around, twisting the fish-eye lens to take in the cabin's interior.

Blood covered the bed. Enough of it that Will felt certain Bryce Ketchum—or someone—had been murdered there. It had dried and turned black.

He also spotted a gray-white block about the size of both his fists put together lying on the floor in front of the entrance. Electrical wires connected to the door.

Will's breath died in his lungs. During the course of his NCIS career, he'd encountered a few bombs. He slid the fiber-optic cable back around the jamb and crossed the boat cautiously. The fact that the bomb hadn't gone off when the boat had jarred against the slip was somewhat reassuring. And he'd seen no sign of a timer.

"The door's wired," Will told Remy when he reached the dock. "We need a bomb unit. There's enough of what looks like C-4 in there to take out this whole landing." He motioned to Shel to join them.

"Whoever did this knew we'd find the boat," Remy said.

"They knew someone would. Or maybe that someone who knew Bridges was out of town would come by to check on it."

"Either way the crime scene would be destroyed," Shel said.

Will nodded. "Let's get this area secured."

42

SCENE    CRIME SCEN

>> NCIS MEDICAL LAB
>> CAMP LEJEUNE, NORTH CAROLINA
>> 1031 HOURS

"X-ray said to tell you they found an extra bullet."

Her curiosity aroused by the announcement and thankful for the diversion from her thoughts about Joe and Pastor Wilkins, Nita took the X-rays from Craig and walked over to the viewer. "Where?"

"They found the fragments of the .22 in the deceased's head like you thought they would," Craig told her. "Nearly all the fragments are there, but there is one that made its way down into the soft palate. The other bullet is above the deceased's left hip. In front of the kidney."

With two of the X-rays of Ketchum's midsection on the viewer, Nita flipped on the light. Sure enough, she could clearly see a white spot on the film. It was definitely metal, and it certainly looked like a bullet. The foreign body had the familiar mushroomed deformity a bullet would have after striking bone.

Sorting through the X-rays, Nita found another view of Ketchum's abdomen. This one was from his left side. She placed it on the viewer.

With the new angle she spotted the divot the bullet had cut across the ilium, the portion of the hip bone that was also called the wing. Faint fracture lines showed in the bone as well. The bullet had hit the ilium with solid force, but it hadn't penetrated. Instead it had ricocheted and lodged in front of the kidney.

Returning to the dead man, Nita examined his left side. She switched the recording equipment on. "The X-rays show the presence of a foreign body near the subject's left kidney. It resembles a bullet, probably a .45-caliber round. There is some structural damage to the ilium. I'm going to attempt recovery when I perform the autopsy. There are blemishes on the subject's skin that suggest a puncture wound, but the scar tissue looks old."

She paused the recording and picked up the digital camera. Working quickly, she took pictures of the scarring and uploaded them to the case file she'd designated as Ketchum's. Then she switched the recorder back on and laid the camera aside.

"Question: Has subject ever suffered a gunshot wound in this area? Aside to Estrella: That'll be for you to ferret out. There is evidence of a GSW here, so you'll have to find out if it's important.

"The .22-caliber round fired into the back of the subject's neck just under the skull was the cause of death. The subject probably lived for a short time afterward. Submersion in the river for hours probably washed most of the blood from his clothing, but the crime scene, unless it was the river, should be bloody."

Craig lifted the cover off the surgical-instrument tray.

"You're going to assist today. Will is going to want answers as quickly as we can get them." Nita picked up a scalpel. "I want you to pop the skull, and let's recover what we can of that .22 round. I'll deal with the torso." Leaning forward, she thrust the scalpel into Ketchum's chest and began cutting.

>> NCIS MEDICAL LAB
>> CAMP LEJEUNE, NORTH CAROLINA
>> 1412 HOURS

Will picked up his desk phone. He'd just gotten back from Holly Ridge after watching the bomb unit disable the explosive device left on *Jilly*. Remy and Shel had stayed with the boat while it was brought to an NCIS garage, where they could go over the evidence. "Coburn."

"It's Nita. I have something you might want to come take a look at."

Will stood and headed for the lab.

Nita opened the door. She held up a plastic envelope that held a mushroomed bullet. Ketchum's body lay in disarray on the table behind her. Will was glad not to have to go in.

"What's this?" Will took the bullet, but he studied Nita. She looked totally fatigued and used up. Her features were pallid, and her eyes looked feverish.

"It's not the .22 round that killed Ketchum," Nita said. "That is a .45-caliber bullet. My guess is that it was an underpowered ACP cartridge."

"That round is usually fired from a silenced pistol." Will looked more closely at the bullet.

"That's right. Ketchum has been carrying it inside his body for probably fifteen to twenty years, judging from the damage to his ilium and the scar tissue on his kidney. I can think of only one reason he suffered with keeping that bullet inside his body."

"He couldn't go to a doctor because a doctor would call the police."

"Right. I thought maybe you could run it through IBIS."

The Integrated Ballistics Identification System was a program started and maintained by the Bureau of Alcohol, Tobacco and Firearms. The BATF kept digital records of all bullets used in violent crimes, creating a database that could be accessed nationwide. Since the program had started, law enforcement departments had been able to tie cases together and close them out.

Unfortunately, IBIS hadn't gotten going until 1992. But the FBI had their own database on bullets and casings called DRUGFIRE that had started up in 1989. That gave another three years' coverage.

"That bullet may not have anything to do with what we're working on now," Nita said, "but since Ketchum is tied to Haskins and Haskins is tied to a seventeen-year-old murder, you never know."

Will agreed. He slid the bullet back into the evidence bag to send to the ballistics department. "What about Ketchum?"

"One bullet to the base of the skull. Just like we thought."

"Could you recover that bullet?"

"Yes, but it's in pieces. The round shattered inside Ketchum's skull when it bounced around. If we get anything more from it than GRCs, I'll be surprised."

General rifling characteristics were good only for profiling a bullet, not for making it unique and tying it to a weapon or other crimes.

"Do you need anything?" Will asked.

"No."

"You don't look like you feel well."

"Eight hours of sleep," Nita said. "That I could use."

We all could, Will thought tiredly.

❀ ❀ ❀

>> CAMP LEJEUNE, NORTH CAROLINA
>> 1807 HOURS

Nita sat in her car in the NCIS parking area and listened to the music as the air-conditioning cycled and cooled the interior. Groups of Marines and sailors jogged by in sweats, putting in their PT requirements.

Finally, when she knew she couldn't put it off any longer, she called Joe.

"Tomlinson's Boat Repair," Joe answered. The house phone was set to forward calls to the shop when no one was home.

"It's me." Nervous frustration filled Nita. What she had to say wasn't going to be easy.

"Hey." Joe's tone was friendly but cautious.

"You're still at work."

"I figured you'd be working late when I heard about the body being found this morning."

"Actually," Nita said, "I'm off."

Joe was quiet for a moment. Nita heard Celia talking to someone in the background.

"I was just marking time here," Joe said. "There's no rush on this project. Celia and I can probably be home about the time you get there."

Nita forced herself to be numb and say what she had to say. "I'm not coming home, Joe."

There was more silence. "I thought you said you were off work."

"I am. But I'm not coming home."

"May I ask why?"

"Things there aren't working out between us," Nita said. "All we do is fight and argue these days."

"We're just going through a bad patch; that's all."

"No, Joe," Nita said. She felt tears well up in her eyes, and she grew mad at herself. "I'm not happy." Her voice almost broke. "I haven't been happy for a long time."

"I don't know what to say," Joe told her quietly. His words sounded fragile and too soft. Not like Joe's words at all. "I love you. You know that."

Nita felt like her heart was breaking, but she knew she couldn't go back to feeling trapped or to waiting for the time when she would let Joe and Celia down. She wanted her life back—the happy, self-contained life she'd known for too short a time after she'd gotten away from her mother's influence.

"I know that," she whispered. "I just . . . I just don't want to come home tonight." *Or ever again.* But somehow she couldn't bring herself to say that even though she felt Joe deserved to know the truth.

"Is there anything I can do to help you?"

"No," she said. "This is just how I feel."

"If there's something I've done—"

"It's nothing you've done, Joe." *It's everything you've done. I can't be what you need. I'm just not that good. Can't you understand that?*

"There must be something I can—"

"No!" Nita's voice exploded out of her. "Just give me some time. Let me think. I haven't slept well in days." She took a breath. "Just . . . just give me tonight."

"All right."

Nita hated Joe's calmness at this moment. She was leaving him. He was supposed to fight and argue. That's what her mother's boyfriends had always done. Joe's behavior wasn't normal.

"Pastor Wilkins came by today," she went on. It wasn't fair that Joe didn't think at least some of this was his responsibility. She couldn't bear the pressure of its being all her fault.

"I'm sorry about that. I asked him not to."

"Telling people about our problems probably isn't the best thing you could do," Nita said. That sounded right. Her mother had always pointed out the things her boyfriends had done wrong.

"I know. I didn't want to say anything."

"Then you shouldn't have."

Joe was silent for a time, then said, "I love you, Nita. No matter what else you think, remember that."

The tears fell then, streaming hotly down her cheeks. She wiped them away helplessly, hating the weakness she felt. Desperately, she hardened her heart, remembering how trapped and unhappy she'd felt the last year and more.

"I've got to go," she said. She closed the phone and tossed it into the passenger seat. Laying her head back, she breathed deeply till she was once more in control of her emotions.

She kept expecting Joe to call back, either to plead or to yell at her. That was what her mother's boyfriends had always done.

The phone continued its silence.

But not Joe Tomlinson, she thought angrily. *Oh no. You're too holier-than-thou to plead or get involved in a shouting match.*

Anger ignited in Nita again. She used it to turn off the tears. Then she put the car in gear and started forward.

This is the first day of the rest of your life. Let's see where it takes you.

⊛ ⊛ ⊛

>> NCIS HEADQUARTERS
>> 1822 HOURS

"The blood in the boat is Bryce Ketchum's. We've found some hairs and fibers, but they could belong to the dentist and his wife. Maybe guests they've had on the boat."

Will held the phone to his ear as he listened to Remy's report. "We'll get someone out to Dr. Bridges's house and take samples. When are they supposed to be home?" He knew he had it in his notes somewhere, but he couldn't remember off the top of his head.

"Sunday night."

"Tomorrow?"

"A week from tomorrow."

Will sighed. *Cases usually get solved by grinding through them. Nothing comes fast.* But this one needed to hurry along. The media still had their teeth in the story, and every new wrinkle added fuel to the fire. Congressman Ben Swanson's name and Chloe Ivers's murder were staying in the public view.

"We'll work on canvassing Holly Ridge tomorrow," Will said. "Maybe we'll get lucky and get a description on whoever stole the boat."

"I wouldn't count on getting that lucky," Remy said.

Will thanked Remy for the report and hung up the phone at the same time Maggie appeared at his doorway. He waved her in.

"It took some time," she said, "but we got a hit on the bullet that Nita took out of Bryce Ketchum."

"The .22?"

"The .45."

Will looked at her. "I'm not going to like this, am I?"

"The bullet matched two other bullets that were recovered from a carjacking victim nineteen years ago."

Will waited, knowing that the other shoe hadn't yet dropped.

"The carjacking victim was Deanna Swanson," Maggie said. "Congressman Ben Swanson's first wife."

43

SCENE NCIS CRIME SCENE

NAVAL CRIMINAL INVESTIGATIVE SERVICE

>> NCIS HEADQUARTERS
>> CAMP LEJEUNE, NORTH CAROLINA
>> 1917 HOURS

Director Larkin grimaced at the bullet in the plastic evidence bag lying on his desk. "Tell me about Deanna Swanson."

Seated on the other side of the desk, Will said, "I've sent you a link to the page Maggie set up regarding the carjacking."

Larkin abandoned his chair and gestured to the computer. "Be my guest."

Will came around the desk, sat at the computer, and brought the Web page up. He wrote the pass code down on a Post-it for Larkin to have later if he needed it, then entered it in the Web page.

"Deanna Akehurst was married to Swanson for five and a half years before her murder," Will said.

The screen showed a pretty brunette in her late twenties. She held a small boy in her arms.

"She was heir to Solomon Akehurst," Will went on.

"That's old Raleigh money," Larkin said.

"Yes." The Akehurst family had been prosperous back around the turn of the twentieth century and had eventually stepped back from running the actual businesses Solomon Akehurst had created—including land development, television, radio, and electronics companies—to live off a managed estate that was handed down through the generations. "Deanna and her brother, Zachary, were the last of the line."

"Who got the Akehurst money when she died?"

"Her son by Swanson." Will nodded at the child in the woman's arms. "Jeffrey Swanson."

"But Congressman Swanson managed the estate until Jeffrey came of age?"

"Jeffrey still isn't of age," Will said. "According to what Maggie was able to find out through her connections, Jeffrey Swanson doesn't gain control over the estate until he reaches age twenty-five. He's only twenty-three now."

"Interesting, but that doesn't put the bullet into Bryce Ketchum."

Will moved on through the Web page, stopping when he reached the news stories of Deanna Swanson's brutal death. "Nineteen years ago in November, Deanna Swanson was carjacked. Witnesses say there were two men, both masked. They approached her at a red light, pulled a gun on her, and talked to her briefly, then shot her, pulled her body out into the street, and drove off."

"She didn't try to get out of the car when they told her to?"

"Apparently not."

Larkin frowned. "That doesn't make sense. With the money she had, replacing the car wouldn't be a problem."

"Maybe she froze and the carjackers panicked." Will shook his head. "We're not going to know everything that happened."

"Okay. If the bullets that were recovered from that crime scene matched the one Nita took from Bryce Ketchum, that can only mean Ketchum was at the crime scene."

"As one of the two carjackers," Will agreed. "Witness testimony always has to be taken with a grain of salt, but in this case most of those who talked to police investigators agreed that there were *four* shots fired. One ended up in Deanna Swanson's chest. The second one stopped in the driver's seat after it passed through the victim's neck. The third one was in the passenger seat."

"I take it the car was recovered."

"It was." Will went on down to the pictures of the Mercedes coupe Deanna Swanson had been driving that morning. Police investigators had taken several pictures, and Maggie had somehow obtained digital copies of the photos. They were equally divided between the exterior and interior of the Mercedes.

The luxury car's interior was bathed in blood.

"Where was the car found?" Larkin asked.

"A few miles out of Raleigh off Highway 64 near Beaver Dam Lake."

"Abandoned?"

"Yes."

"They didn't try to hide it?"

"The detectives Maggie spoke to said they believed the carjackers panicked. Maybe they killed Deanna Swanson in anger, or they were on drugs and didn't know what they were doing until it was too late. They ran."

"And one of them might have been Bryce Ketchum."

Will nodded. The guesswork felt right.

"It's possible that Ketchum was shot at a later date by the carjacker." Larkin played devil's advocate, forcing Will to defend his re-creation of events. "Or that the gun ended up in someone else's hands later."

"The gun was never used again. At least not in the commission of a crime involving shots fired. And witnesses claimed that *four* shots were fired at the carjacking. Not three."

"So how did the fourth bullet end up in Ketchum's hip?"

"Who knows? Assume for the moment it was an accident. Somehow in the excitement and confusion the gun goes off while pointed at Ketchum, and he gets shot. The important thing is, it puts him at the scene."

Larkin nodded. "So we can tie Ketchum to the weapon that killed Deanna Swanson nineteen years ago. We know that Ben Swanson married Laura Ivers a little over a year later and that Laura already had Chloe Ivers. We can tie George Haskins to Chloe Ivers through the charm."

"And we can tie Haskins and Ketchum together through school records, military service, and interviews we've given."

"Even spread out as it is, that bullet brings everything tighter."

Will nodded. "There's also the possibility that Haskins removed one of Swanson's chief rivals for election as congressman for his first term."

"Hearsay," Larkin objected.

"Let's say for a moment that it's a fact we can't substantiate. But if it's true, it shows that Haskins had an interest in Swanson."

"What interest?"

"There's the Akehurst fortune," Will pointed out. "Maybe the carjacking wasn't a carjacking. Maybe it was a kidnapping attempt that went wrong."

"Then a year later, Haskins takes out the guy standing between Swanson and a seat in the House of Representatives? And then after the election kidnaps the new congressman's stepdaughter?"

"Maybe. It fits what we know and what we have to guess at."

Larkin sat on the edge of his desk. "You know this means we're going to need to talk to Swanson again."

"I know. And I'll bet he isn't as friendly and giving this time."

"No. He won't be."

"There's another wrinkle," Will said. "Maggie's father called today."

Larkin grimaced. Will knew the director didn't approve of Harrison Talbot Foley III, but Larkin had never held Maggie's paternity against her. On occasion, Maggie's family connections had worked out for them.

"What did he want?" Larkin asked.

"To let us know he was looking out for Congressman Swanson's interests."

"Great," Larkin commented drily. He glared at the computer screen, then at the bullet. "I'll see if I can get a meeting set up with Swanson."

"Do you think you can make that happen?"

"I'll point out to him that he'd rather talk to us about this than have us canvassing witnesses from that carjacking nineteen years ago and getting all that stirred up again. Especially now." Larkin looked grimly confident. "I'll make it happen."

>> SLEEPYTIME MOTEL
>> JACKSONVILLE, NORTH CAROLINA
>> 0716 HOURS

Nita's cell phone woke her with a series of strident rings that she thought might explode her head. Glancing at the time on the clock radio by the bed, she fumbled on the bedside table for the phone. Reflexes took over as she hit the Talk button and said, "Hello."

"Mommy?"

Celia's voice caught Nita off guard. She'd been expecting a call from Will.

"Celia?"

"Hi, Mommy. I was worried about you. So I called." Celia was talking in hushed tones.

Nita glanced around the motel room. It was small and unadorned, an uninspired collection of bed, tiny desk, nightstand, and portable television on a scarred chest of drawers.

A gallon of wine sat beside the television. Nita had picked it up right before she'd checked into the motel. She'd been so tired that she hadn't even opened it. Looking down, she discovered she was still wearing her clothes. She couldn't even remember her head hitting the pillow.

All night, though, she'd dreamed of her mother. Nita had been trapped in an endless stream of trailer parks, looking for her mother but never finding her.

Nausea bubbled and broke at the back of her throat.

"Mommy?" Celia said.

"Wait just a minute, sweetie." Nita put the phone down and went into the bathroom to throw up. When she was finished, she felt weak and empty. She washed her face and returned to the phone, hoping that was the last of it.

"Mommy, are you sick?"

"No," Nita lied. "I just had to go to the bathroom." She didn't want Celia worried about her.

"You didn't come home last night."

"No, I didn't."

"Were you working?"

Nita hated lying to her daughter, but she forced herself to. "Yes, I was."

"Are you done now? Can you come home?"

"Not right now." Nita sat on the edge of the bed and held her head in her hands.

"How come?"

"I've got a lot to do."

"Work?"

"Yes." Suspicion filled Nita's mind. "Did your daddy ask you to call?"

"No. I called all by myself. All I had to do was find your picture."

Joe's phone was programmed to display faces instead of numbers. He'd bought it like that so Celia could easily use it.

"I miss you, Mommy."

"I miss you too. Where's Daddy?"

Celia's voice softened. "He's asleep."

"Can I talk to him?"

"Sure."

Nita heard the sound of her daughter's feet padding through Joe's house. Celia woke Joe and quickly told him she had Mommy on the phone.

"Nita?" Concern edged Joe's voice. "Is anything wrong?"

"No. Celia called. I was trying to sleep."

"So was I."

Nita took a deep breath. "Look, Joe, I can't have Celia calling me like this. Not for a little while."

Silence filled the line.

"You don't want her to call?" Joe's voice was harder than she'd ever heard it.

"Not for a while. Not until I get some things figured out."

"I'm going to tell you something, Nita. If you have a problem with her calling or a problem with me calling to interrupt whatever it is you think you're doing, then you're one of the most selfish people I know."

Nita got angry then. "I'm trying to figure out what I'm going to do."

"It isn't just about you," Joe said in that cold, distant voice. "Celia cried herself to sleep last night because you didn't come home."

"I don't need to be guilted over that."

"Then who's supposed to feel guilty? Everything you do affects *us*. Celia and me. I can deal with this better than she can. But it's hard for me to handle my feelings *and* hers."

Nita couldn't believe Joe was being so direct. And she really couldn't believe that he blamed her. He hadn't been happy with the way things were going either. He couldn't have been.

"You go do whatever it is you think you need to do, Nita," Joe told her. "But you need to remember that we've got feelings too. In fact, until you figure out whatever it is you're trying to figure out, I want you to stay away from us. If you need clothes or anything, I'll make sure you get them. Whatever it is. But don't come around this house just to appear and disappear whenever you want to. Celia deserves better than that. And frankly, so do I."

Nita tried to think of something to say, but the phone went dead in her hand before she could. Joe had hung up on her. During their whole marriage, he'd never done anything like that.

Anger almost pushed her into calling and unloading on him. She stopped herself just short of punching in the numbers.

Instead she called Will's cell phone, hating it because she was certain she was going to wake him as well. But he answered on the first ring, not exactly cheerful but coherent nonetheless.

"It's Nita." Her stomach turned over threateningly.

"Are you okay?"

"Yeah. I'm fine." Nita took a breath. "Look, I need some time off. Just a few days. I've got some things I need to take care of."

"This case we're working on is pretty important."

"You don't have anything more for me to do right now. Unless you produce a new corpse."

"We're not planning on that."

"Then give me a few days. I've never asked you before."

"All right. Is there anything I can help with?"

"Not yet. If something comes up, I'll let you know."

"Are you going to have your phone with you?"

"Yes."

"I'll square it with the director. You've got enough comp time that you don't have to worry about pay."

"Thanks, Will."

"If you need anything, call."

"I will." Nita closed the phone and sat on the edge of the bed. Eyeing the gallon of wine, she was surprised to discover she had no taste for it. What she really wanted was a shower.

Taking her keys, including the room key, Nita went out to her car. She always carried a packed bag in the trunk so she was ready to go at a moment's notice.

As she was getting the bag out of the car, she jostled a shoe box filled with papers from work. She would eventually get around to filing the articles and reports that she found interesting.

A small envelope tumbled to the bottom of the trunk. Nita recognized it at once. It was the latest birthday card from her mother. The return address was written in the upper-left corner.

As if hypnotized, Nita picked up the envelope and carried it into the motel room with her.

S CRIME SCENE NCIS C
NAVAL CRIMINAL INVESTIGATIVE SERVICE

44

CENE  NCIS   CRIME SCENE

NAVAL CRIMINAL INVESTIGATIVE SERVICE

>> SILVER SPRING, MARYLAND
>> 0927 HOURS

Congressman Ben Swanson agreed to meet Larkin, Will, and Maggie on Tuesday morning. The congressman hadn't been happy about the situation, Larkin told Will, but in the end, faced with the question about the bullet, Swanson hadn't had much choice.

Swanson maintained a home in Raleigh, as was required, but he'd bought a large mansion in Silver Spring, Maryland, within easy commuting distance of the Capitol. They landed at Ronald Reagan Washington National Airport. An NCIS agent awaited them there with a rental car.

Larkin drove. Will sat in the passenger seat.

An armed security guard checked them through the heavy gates at the estate. As Larkin drove toward the large, Tudor-style manor house, Will surveyed the landscaped grounds. *Swanson didn't afford this on a congressman's salary.*

Swanson's majordomo, an efficient-looking young man who was also armed, met them at the door and ushered them into the congressman's den.

The den was lavishly decorated in a subdued but distinctly masculine style, filled with books and pictures spanning Swanson's political career that provided a brief study in his success for anyone who wasn't already aware of it. It was all carefully designed with Swanson's antique desk as the crown jewel.

The congressman sat on the corner of the desk and talked to two men who were already there. Will knew one of them.

Harrison Talbot Foley III looked regal. At sixty years old, he was slim and fit. His Italian suit was carefully tailored. He had ash-blond hair and a tanned complexion that stopped somewhere just short of George Hamilton's.

His presence surprised Will. He could tell it caught Larkin off guard as well. Maggie must have been the one most impacted, but if he hadn't known her and worked closely with her for years, Will didn't think he would have noticed the way her lips compressed in dread.

"Ah, you've arrived." Swanson stood and offered his hand.

Will politely took the hand, as did Larkin and Maggie.

"I take it you know Harrison Foley," Swanson said.

"Father," Maggie said.

"Margaret." Her father inclined his head a little but showed no sign of being pleased to see her. She made no physical contact with her father, and he didn't offer it.

"We've never met," Will said.

"I've heard a lot about you, though," Foley said, and the announcement sounded threatening.

"It's a pleasure to meet you, sir," Larkin said. "I've enjoyed working with your daughter. She's a very talented agent."

"I will defer to your judgment in such matters," Foley said. "What you people do is unfamiliar to me."

Will thought Foley also believed what they did was beneath him and possibly an affront.

"I do hope," Foley said, "that you can dispense with whatever business you have with Ben in short order. He's a busy man with important things to do. His time shouldn't be needlessly wasted."

"I think they know that, Harrison," Swanson said.

If they hadn't before then, Foley's comment had definitely made it clear.

"This is Carlton Bledsoe." Swanson waved to the other man. He was in his fifties or sixties, portly and officious. His suit didn't fit him as well as Foley's, but it was close. "Carlton is my attorney. He'll be advising me today."

"I just want you to know, Director Larkin," Bledsoe said, "that I don't approve of the bullying tactics you employed to get Congressman Swanson's attention."

Larkin regarded Swanson. "I wasn't aware that you felt bullied."

Swanson smiled. "Carlton is somewhat overly protective, I'm afraid.

Laura's comments in the press and the nature of this investigation haven't set well with him."

"I particularly don't like the way you've taken the liberty of switching the focus of the investigation from that dead sergeant to the appalling murder of Congressman Swanson's daughter nearly two decades ago," Bledsoe commented.

"We have to examine the possibility that whoever killed Chloe Ivers might have killed Gunnery Sergeant George Haskins."

"There's also the possibility that neither murder has anything to do with the other."

"The evidence we've found suggests otherwise." Larkin was polite, but he didn't give an inch. "Either Haskins was involved in Chloe Ivers's murder, or the person who killed him was. We're only looking into the matter to figure out who killed Haskins."

"According to the materials I've seen, Haskins was nothing more than a criminal in uniform. I don't see why the NCIS would be interested in the murder of such a man. Criminals are murdered by their own ilk every day. The newspapers and media are filled with it. I don't see law enforcement agencies striving to catch their murderers."

"I can't speak for other law enforcement agencies," Larkin said. "I can only speak for my own. We want to know who killed George Haskins."

"Carlton," Foley said in a well-modulated voice, "I think it's safe to assume we're working at cross-purposes here."

"With all due respect, sir," Will said, "we're not. We're conducting an investigation into the murder of a member of the United States military. We didn't put the connections there." Foley's arrogant manner grated on Will's nerves.

"Ah yes," Foley said, smiling mirthlessly, "*connections*. I find it hard to believe that yet another *connection* has turned up to Ben's family."

"Probably not as hard to believe as we find it, Father," Maggie said. Her chin was tilted up and defiant.

Foley turned his attention to his daughter. "What are you suggesting?"

"What we're suggesting," Will said, "is that Haskins has been more involved in Congressman Swanson's life for far longer than we'd believed. The possibility exists that Haskins tried to kidnap Deanna Swanson and ended up killing her. Only to repeat the same thing with Chloe Ivers a few years later."

"You think Haskins was stalking Congressman Swanson?" Bledsoe asked.

"That is a possibility," Larkin said.

"Then you believe that the congressman was a victim in all this?"

"Haskins was involved in Chloe Ivers's abduction and murder," Will said. "A known associate of Haskins, someone who had been in his life for years, was found with a bullet in him that matches those taken from the carjacking that claimed Deanna's life." He paused. "Maybe the congressman's bad luck with family members hasn't been bad luck at all."

"If you know all that, then why are we here?" Bledsoe demanded.

"Someone executed Bryce Ketchum," Larkin said. "It's quite possible that the threat to the congressman hasn't ended."

"You're here to protect his interests?"

"We're here," Larkin said, "to get information that may lead us to the murderer of George Haskins. It's possible that effort might remove an existing threat directed at Congressman Swanson."

"It's been seventeen years," Swanson said. "Whatever threat there was at that time has surely gone away."

"But we don't know that, sir," Larkin said. "And I still have a dead sergeant to answer for."

"All right," Swanson said. "We've all got our own agendas, but maybe I could just answer whatever questions these agents have, and we could all get back to work."

Bledsoe reluctantly nodded. "You know I still don't support this interview, Ben."

Swanson waved them to comfortable chairs in front of the desk, then offered them something to drink. They all declined.

"What do you want to know?" Swanson asked.

Will pulled out his iPAQ and brought up the questions he'd prepared for the meeting. Beside him, Maggie did the same. Neither of them needed to. The effort was for show.

Swanson sat behind the desk, and Bledsoe stood at his side like a trained hound. Foley stood to one side, arms across his chest, and observed. Will had no doubt the man would step in whenever he wanted to.

Will took Swanson back over the events that led up to the carjacking. Swanson had seen his wife that morning over breakfast. She'd seemed normal, animated as always.

"She'd gone into the city that day to take Jeffrey to the pediatrician," Swanson said. "There was some shot he needed."

"Jeffrey is your son?" Will asked.

"Yes."

"Where was he that morning?"

Swanson hesitated. Up until this moment, there'd been no hesitation. "He was with me. I was doing some paperwork at home. Deanna had asked if I could watch him."

"I thought she was taking him to the pediatrician," Maggie said.

"She was. But she had some shopping she wanted to do first. She didn't want to be encumbered with Jeffrey, so she asked me if could watch him for a little while. I did."

"Didn't you have a live-in nanny?"

"Yes. But she was off that morning."

Will continued with the questioning, going over the phone call Swanson had gotten from the Raleigh Police Department and the subsequent visit to the morgue. Finally there were no more questions to ask.

Bledsoe shook his head in disdain. "If you ask me, this has all been a waste of time."

"Nonsense, Carlton," Swanson said. "They're just trying to do their job." He sighed. "At least we know that the men who murdered poor Deanna didn't get away with it." He stood, signaling an end to the interview.

"Do you know who killed my mother?" The voice sounded young and strident.

Turning, Will saw a young man standing in the doorway of the den.

"Jeffrey," Swanson said. "I didn't know you were up."

Jeffrey Swanson was several inches shorter than his father. Long dark hair framed his thin, pale face, and his dark brown eyes looked like they'd been punched into his skull. Dozens of tattoos covered his bare arms and legs. He apparently hadn't shaved in days.

Will remembered from the background information he'd read that Jeff Swanson had been under a psychiatrist's care since he was a child. That information had also included a number of arrests for violent behavior that his father's attorneys had struggled to get him out of. His file was a road map of self-destruction. In addition to the legal meds he took on a daily basis, Jeff had been arrested for possession and intent to distribute.

Judging from the history Will had read, it was a wonder that Jeff hadn't overdosed and died. He'd been through at least three dry-out sessions in rehab clinics for drug abuse and alcoholism.

"Do you know who killed my mother?" Jeff repeated.

"We think so." Will took pictures of Haskins and Ketchum from the file he'd carried in. "We believe these two men did it."

Jeff walked over to him. He stank of cigarettes, marijuana, and body odor. Obviously personal grooming wasn't something he cared about. He took the pictures Will offered, then stared at them myopically.

"Ben," Bledsoe said quietly, "Jeff shouldn't be here."

"Do you recognize either of those men?" Will asked.

"No." Jeff's voice was hoarse. His hands shook. He blinked and tried to focus again. "I don't know."

"Jeff," Swanson said softly, "you couldn't possibly recognize those men. You were barely three when your mother died. Besides that, you never saw them. They ambushed your mother in the city." He paused. "Neither of us had ever seen them." Gently, he took the pictures from his son and gave them back to Will.

Jeff looked at Will. The young man's pupils were tiny pinpricks, letting Will know he was under the influence of something.

"Where are these guys?" Jeff asked.

"They're dead," Will answered.

Jeff thought about that for a moment; then he nodded. "Good. Murderers shouldn't go free. It's not right."

"No," Will agreed. "It's not." As he looked at the young man, he thought about Steven. He hoped his son never faced the kinds of problems that Jeff Swanson obviously dealt with on a daily basis.

"They were evil," Jeff said. "Killing Mom like that—it wasn't an accident."

Will thought that was an odd turn of phrase but didn't know what he could say in response.

"You shouldn't be here, Jeff," Swanson said. "You should rest. Go upstairs and lie down."

"Sure." Jeff turned to go, then paused and looked at Will. "I'm glad the men that killed my mom are dead. I still miss her."

Will nodded.

"We all do," Swanson said. He put a hand on Jeff's shoulder and pushed him gently into motion, guiding him out of the room. "Carlton, why don't you show my guests out while I put Jeff to bed."

"Happily," Bledsoe replied.

Will noted that Harrison Talbot Foley III delivered only a perfunctory good-bye to Maggie. Will felt bad for her, only now glimpsing what her childhood must have been like. Then he realized that it probably hadn't been much different from Jeff Swanson's.

Except for the murdered mother and stepsister.

45

SCENE  NCIS  CRIME SCENE

NAVAL CRIMINAL INVESTIGATIVE SERVICE

>> 114 APPLEGATE ROAD
>> RALEIGH, NORTH CAROLINA
>> 0917 HOURS

Will knocked on the door of the rambling two-story house and stepped back. Maggie, Estrella, Remy, Shel, and a dozen of the best forensics investigators Larkin could spare from their caseloads stood behind him. They all wore navy Windbreakers that had *Special Agent* across the back in yellow block letters that could be easily seen.

A handful of neighbors peered through the windows of their houses or stood in their yards.

Not exactly a stealth moment here, Will thought. But that suited him fine. He'd wanted to attract attention.

An older woman answered the door. She was heavyset and wore thick glasses, slacks, and a sweater. "Yes?"

"Abbie Parker?"

"Yes."

"I'm Commander Will Coburn of the Naval Criminal Investigative Service, ma'am," Will said. "I talked to you on the phone." He showed her his ID.

She smiled a little uncertainly. "I remember." She looked past Will at the rest of the NCIS team. "You all want to come in?"

"Yes, ma'am. If we could."

The woman stepped back and the NCIS team filed in. Will's eyes went to the stairs across the room and on the right.

"I didn't know there were going to be so many of you," Abbie said.

"We want to get this done quickly if we can," Will said. "I don't want to be in your way long."

"Just take whatever time you need, Commander." A short, older man walked toward them from the den on the right. "If this is going to help bring peace to that poor family, we're happy to help."

Yesterday, after the meeting with Ben Swanson, Will had considered his options concerning the investigation. At the moment, everything had stalled out.

Will had decided to create pressure. Swanson had sold the house that the family had lived in when Chloe Ivers was killed. Will had asked the current owners if he could bring an NCIS team onto the premises.

"I hope it helps too," Will said sincerely. Then he split the team into groups and they got to work.

>> 0942 HOURS

Will applied fluorescein to the stairs. Nita's interpretation of the injuries Chloe Ivers had sustained prior to her death suggested she'd fallen down a flight of stairs. The stairs he was working on were the only ones in the house.

Normally luminol was used when searching for bloodstains that couldn't be seen with the naked eye. Made of the same chemicals that created a firefly's glowing tail, luminol reacted with even a millionth part of blood in an area. However an area that was cleaned with chlorine bleach often negated that necessary chemical reaction.

The Swanson household had been searched thoroughly after Chloe's disappearance. Suspicious bloodstains would have been noticed. Therefore, if there were any, they'd have been cleaned up.

In order to counteract seventeen years' worth of cleanings, Will had chosen to use fluorescein instead of luminol. Fluorescein didn't have the same vulnerabilities to bleach that luminol did, and it was thicker, so it could be sprayed on walls and doors and didn't drip as much.

The windows of the house had been covered, darkening the rooms so the chemical reactions could be seen. So far they hadn't found anything substantial on the stairs.

Will's cell phone rang. He straightened up and answered it. "Coburn."

"You're on television," Larkin told him.

"What channels?" Will walked down the stairs, passing Maggie, and went to the den, where the Parkers were.

The couple sat on the couch and watched their house on television on a live report.

"The local channels so far," Larkin said, "but I'm willing to bet that CNN and FOX News get involved before long. They'll either send someone down here or pick up a stringer who can shoot video for them."

"Good." Will had hoped the media would get involved. "This will add to the pressure that's going around."

"I haven't gotten a call from Swanson or his attorney yet, but I'm expecting that to happen at any minute."

"Are you regretting agreeing to this?"

"Not yet. I'm a little antsy though." Larkin let out a breath. "But I think you're right, Will. This was the only thing you could do to launch an offensive against whoever is covering their tracks on this thing."

"Laura Ivers deserves to know what happened to her daughter," Will said.

"I know. That's why I put my head on the chopping block with yours. Get back to work and find something."

"Yes, sir." Will closed the phone and put it away. For a moment he watched the reporter standing in front of the Parker house recapping Chloe Ivers's murder and speculating on what the NCIS team hoped to find here. Everything was happening the way he'd hoped it would. Now all they had to do was come up with a solid lead.

>> SILVER SPRING, MARYLAND
>> 1005 HOURS

"Ben?"

Sitting in his den, going over the speech he had to deliver the next day, Swanson cradled the phone against his head. He'd recognized the number as belonging to Harrison Talbot Foley III. The multimillionaire was one of the few people he was taking phone calls from today.

"Hello, Harrison." Swanson leaned back in his chair.

"It appears your house is on television," Foley said.

"It's the stupid reporters." Swanson had seen them earlier when he'd checked the grounds over the security system. Reporters had sat outside his gates for days, trying to get a quote from him regarding the investigations the NCIS had launched. So far he'd avoided them.

"Not your house in Maryland," Foley said. "Your old house in Raleigh."

"What?" Swanson dug the remote control from inside the desk and pressed the Power button. Panels on the wall to his right slid open to reveal a plasma-screen television. He flicked through the channels and found a local Raleigh station that was showing footage of the old house on Applegate.

"Apparently my daughter and her compatriots don't take guidance—or warnings—too well," Foley said.

The banner at the bottom of the television broadcast read *NCIS investigates U.S. congressman Swanson's home.*

"What are they looking for?" Swanson asked.

"I wouldn't know," Foley said.

Swanson stared in disbelief. Panic gnawed at his reserve. "It's been seventeen years. They can't hope to find anything in that house."

"I would hope there's nothing there for them to find."

"There's not." But the panic in the back of Swanson's mind was growing.

"Maybe you should give Carlton a call," Foley suggested. "Perhaps there's something he could do about this matter."

"I'll do that. Thanks, Harrison."

The phone clicked dead in Swanson's ear.

Cursing, unable to sit quietly in his chair, Swanson took the cordless handset and paced. When he passed through the living room, he saw Jeff sitting on the couch watching the broadcast.

Jeff had his own home to go to, but when he was doing badly—as he had been since the investigation into Chloe's death had begun—he returned to his father's home.

Swanson usually let his son stay for a few days, but if Jeff didn't get better and leave—or if things got worse—he shipped him back to the rehab center. It looked like he was going to have to do that again. In fact, he knew he should probably do it today. Having Jeff show up during the meeting with the NCIS people had been a near disaster.

"Dad." Jeff looked at Swanson. Tears ran down the young man's face. "The police are at our house."

"That's not our house anymore, Jeff."

"They're going to find out, Dad." Hysteria edged Jeff's words. "They're going to find out what happened to Chloe."

"No, they're not," Swanson assured him. "Nobody's going to find out a thing."

Carlton Bledsoe answered the phone on the first ring. "Ben, I was just about to call you. Do you know what's going on at your house? Your old house, I mean?"

"Yes. I just found out myself." Swanson returned to his den. *I should have burned that house. I knew I should have burned that house.* He'd known even then how good the police forensics efforts were getting. But burning the house would have been too suspicious. "Is there anything we can do to stop them?"

"They didn't go in there with a court order," Bledsoe said.

"How did they get permission to conduct an investigation?" Swanson watched the footage roll. The camera focused on the NCIS vehicles for a time, then went back to the house.

"They asked the owners."

"They *asked* the owners?"

"That's what I was told by one of the people I do business with in the local news."

Swanson couldn't believe it. "They can't find anything. It's been seventeen years."

"Even if they do," the lawyer said, "I'll have it thrown out. There's no way they can find anything conclusive in that house that they can bring against you."

Swanson felt a little better. "I need to take care of Jeff. Stay on top of this."

"I will."

Swanson hung up the phone and returned to the living room. He'd drive Jeff to the rehab center himself.

But when he got to the living room, Jeff was gone. The house phone rang and Swanson answered it. It was the security guard at the gate.

"Congressman Swanson, your son just left in your Cadillac, sir. We thought it was you. We didn't notice till he sped through that it wasn't."

Swanson cursed. Jeff didn't have a license. It had been taken away when he was twenty. "Well, find him," he roared into the phone. "And find him quick. He's not well."

He threw the phone across the room and tried to calm himself. But he felt like everything was starting to come unraveled.

>> 114 APPLEGATE ROAD

>> RALEIGH, NORTH CAROLINA

>> 1013 HOURS

"Will, you want to come look at this?"

Abandoning his efforts on the landing at the top of the stairs, still not finding anything, Will joined Shel. The big Marine led him into the den.

With sheets over the windows, the room was dark. The glowing blue light in the center of the hardwood floor stood out immediately.

"I don't know who it was," Shel said solemnly, "but somebody lost a lot of blood in this room."

Will stared at the evidence before him. Not only was there a huge pool of light, but streak marks showed where a body had been pulled away.

"Get pictures and video," Will ordered. "Let's see what we can do with this." When he turned around, he found the Parkers standing in the doorway with anguished faces.

"Was she killed in here?" Abbie Parker asked in a hoarse voice. "Was that little girl killed in here?"

"No," Will replied. Chloe Ivers had been strangled and hadn't suffered any major blood loss. "But I think someone was."

46

SCENE  NCIS  CRIME SCENE

NAVAL CRIMINAL INVESTIGATIVE SERVICE

>> ANGEL'S TRAILER COURT
>> MURFREESBORO, TENNESSEE
>> 1028 HOURS

Nita sat in her car down the street from lot 49, where her mother lived. After leaving Jacksonville Sunday afternoon, Nita had spent Monday and part of Tuesday driving to Murfreesboro.

Carol Purdue's last birthday card had come from Murfreesboro, Tennessee. Specifically, from lot 49.

Of course, the previous year's card had come from another residence. That one had been a house. Nita knew that because she'd returned to her NCIS office long enough to get the haphazard file of birthday cards she'd gotten from her mother over the last few years. She still didn't know why she'd kept them. All they represented were a lot of unfulfilled promises and pain.

Nita had spent the night in a chain hotel. She'd thought about drinking but somehow didn't have the stomach for it. For the last four mornings, she'd woken and gone straight to the bathroom to throw up. It was either a virus or nerves.

She couldn't think straight, and her emotions were raw. She wanted to be mad and cry at the same time. When she thought about Joe and Celia, she missed them, but at the same time she was relieved they weren't around. She wanted company, and she wanted to be alone, and she didn't know what she wanted at all.

In all her life, Nita could never remember feeling so lost.

Murfreesboro, Tennessee, was colder than Jacksonville in March. Nita sat in her car and occasionally had to start it and run the heater to stay warm. She drank from a big cup of convenience-store coffee as she watched lot 49 for any sign of her mother. When the coffee cup ran empty, she went over a few blocks and got another.

It figured that Carol Purdue wasn't at home. That fit with the fact that she'd been gone from Nita's life most of the time.

When she'd first arrived the night before, Nita thought she might have missed her mother because she worked evenings and nights. She'd often had two jobs, usually as a server or stocker or checkout clerk. None of them had ever paid well. When she had a job that paid well, Carol usually messed it up by dating one of the married bosses or making two of them jealous.

Finally, with the last of the big cup of coffee gone again, Nita got her nerve up and got out of the car. Crossing the street, she walked to the trailer next to her mother's, climbed the rickety wooden steps, and knocked on the door.

She stood and waited, feeling the bite of the cold increase the sour sickness rolling in her stomach. Just standing there huddled inside her coat brought back a torrent of memories Nita had tried to forget. Images filled her head: the yellow school buses, dozens of kids dressed as raggedly as she'd been and just as clueless about how little they'd truly had, sheriff's deputies knocking on doors to serve eviction notices, and Department of Human Services workers asking questions about how her mom treated her.

Paper fluttered on a small table beside a lawn chair on the tiny porch. A sun-bleached copy of *Reader's Digest* sat on the table. It was two months old. The subscriber address label listed Geraldine Wallace and lot 51.

A woman's voice came from the other side of the door. "Who is it?"

She's afraid, Nita realized. "I just wanted to ask you some questions about your neighbor over in number forty-nine."

"I don't know anything about her."

"I won't take more than a few minutes, Mrs. Wallace."

"How do you know my name?"

"It was in my notes."

"What notes? Who would keep notes on me?"

Paranoia was a staple of the poverty-stricken. Some days Nita wondered if she'd ever grown out of it. *You did,* she reminded herself. *As soon as you got the medical license, you changed. You became somebody.* But she'd never lost sight of the fact that she'd hadn't always been who she was now.

“It was in the file on Mrs. Purdue,” Nita replied.

“Why are you keeping a file on Carol?”

“Mrs. Purdue filed an application for a government job. A background check is part of it.”

“You’re here about a job?”

“Yes.” Jobs meant hope. Especially a “government” job that came with medical insurance, a pension, and rules against employers taking advantage of employees.

Nita suddenly realized that she’d been following the same pattern when she’d applied at military bases for her first job. Hospitals were privately owned. Doctors could be released, or their pay could be cut. But working for a military installation meant stability. Even though private practice offered the potential for more pay, a government job had offered a solid future.

“Is it a good job?” the woman asked.

“Yes, ma’am.”

“Who’s it with?”

“I don’t know. Mrs. Purdue’s name has been accepted into a pool. After I complete the background check they’ll make that determination.”

The door opened slightly. A pale blue, rheumy eye peered out. “Do you have any identification?” She hurried on in an apologetic voice. “At the senior center, they tell us to always ask to see identification.”

For a moment Nita didn’t know what to do. Then she reached into her purse and pulled out her NCIS badge case. She doubted the woman’s eyes were good enough to read everything there. But the badge would be plain enough.

The door opened wider. “Do you want to come in?”

“That’s all right, Mrs. Wallace. I won’t take up much of your time.” In actuality, Nita didn’t think she could stand entering the claustrophobic confines of the trailer.

“Anything I can do to help Carol,” the old woman offered. She smiled. “She’s been a good neighbor. Last year when I was having problems with my hip, she came over and took care of me. Cleaned my house and cooked for me. That’s how we met, actually. She saw that I was having trouble being on my own.”

That surprised Nita. She hadn’t ever known her mother to do anything for anybody.

“How long have you lived here, Mrs. Wallace?”

“Ten months.”

“Do you know Mrs. Purdue well?”

“As well as anybody here, I suppose.”

"How long has she lived here?"

"A year or so. Maybe a little longer."

"She lives by herself?" That was an important question. Nita didn't know yet if she wanted to face her mother—she didn't know *what* she was doing here, only that she had to come—but she knew she didn't want to try to talk to her if there was a man living with her.

"Yes." The old woman shrugged. "She has boyfriends from time to time. She's a good-looking woman, so I say more power to her." She smiled.

Nita smiled back even though she didn't feel like it. "Do you know when I could catch her at home? I went over to her house but she doesn't seem to be home now."

"She's not home. She took off a few days from her job down at the truck stop to go off with her boyfriend. He's a trucker."

Fourteen years since she'd left home, and Nita felt like nothing had changed. "Do you know when she's supposed to be back?"

"This is Wednesday, right?"

Nita nodded.

"Well then, she'll be home tonight. Probably around eight o'clock."

"All right," Nita said. "I'll try to come back then." She thanked the old woman for her time, then walked back to her car. Her heart beat fast, and she felt nervous and sick to her stomach.

As she slid behind her steering wheel, she didn't know if she would come back or not, but she suspected that she would. Something had drawn her here at a time when she had no clue about what she was supposed to do with her life. Still, the fear of seeing her mother again almost devoured whatever it was that had pulled her to Murfreesboro.

>> NCIS HEADQUARTERS

>> CAMP LEJEUNE, NORTH CAROLINA

>> 1129 HOURS

After the discovery of the remnants of blood in the den, Will had the Parkers moved to an upstairs room that had already been cleared. Then he started processing the crime scene.

Will called Larkin to update him. "We've got a kill site here, sir."

Larkin was quiet for a moment, thinking. "You're sure?"

"Yes, sir. Someone had cleaned it up, but blood was everywhere. Way too much to be an accident."

"The girl was strangled."

"Yes, sir."

"That can't be her blood."

"No."

"And we can't establish when that blood got there."

"No, sir. But we should be able to type it, which will narrow the field. And we may be able to determine the uniqueness of the RBCs through PGM."

RBCs—red blood cells—contained more information than the simple A, B, O, and AB typing. By analyzing the proteins and antigens, a serologist could also identify intracellular enzymes. Those enzymes contained adenylate kinase, erythrocyte acid phosphatase, and phosphoglucomutase. The last, PGM for short, showed up as several different isoenzymes. PGM also wasn't dependent on blood typing and helped make the RBCs even more identifiable. By using both the typing and the PGM breakdown, the unknown RBC donor could be narrowed down to a particular suspect or possible victim.

"You have a likely candidate in mind?"

"I'm still wondering where Gunnery Sergeant Haskins was murdered."

"And why," Larkin agreed. "Well, you wanted to apply pressure, Will. It looks like your long shot came through."

"I know." Will hadn't really been expecting anything other than increased attention on Swanson. Whether the man was involved or not, Will felt he was key to the investigation.

"Just to keep you in the loop, I also received a call from Commander Ivers. She wanted you to know that she appreciated your efforts today."

"*Our* efforts," Will corrected. Call waiting beeped. Glancing at the caller ID, he saw that the call was coming from NCIS. "Hold on a minute. I'm getting a call from headquarters." He pressed the Flash button and picked up on the other line. "Coburn."

"Commander, this is Special Agent Banks at the field office. I've got a caller on the other line who insists on talking to you."

"Who is it?"

"Jeff Swanson."

Surprise thrilled through Will. "What does he want?"

"To talk to you."

"Where is he?"

"He says he's in Washington, D.C."

Not at his father's house. That was interesting. "Put him through."

"Yes, sir."

The phone clicked again, and Will said hello.

"Commander Coburn?"

Will recognized the young man's voice. It sounded tense and thready. "Yes," Will replied.

"I need to talk to you," Jeff said.

"All right. I can probably see you tomorrow. I'm busy right now."

"I know. You're at my house. My old house. Where Chloe died."

Where Chloe died? Will's attention locked in. "I'm listening."

"I have to talk to you. Now. My dad, he's not going to like that I'm talking to you. He told me not to. If he finds out, he's going to put me away."

"Put you away where?"

"In rehab. He always puts me in rehab when he doesn't like what I'm doing. Right now he can't find me. I left the car—his car—and took a cab. I walked for a few blocks from there. I paid cash for the hotel room. I know not to use the credit cards. He gives me those just so he can find me. But I've gotten good at hiding from him. I need to talk to you. Before he finds me. No matter how good I hide, he always finds me. We may not have much time."

"What do you want to talk about?"

"I know who killed Chloe. I need to tell you."

"Who killed Chloe?"

Jeff started crying. His voice broke and turned hoarse. "I did. I killed her. But I didn't mean to. It was an accident."

47

SCENE  NCIS  CRIME SCEN

NAVAL CRIMINAL INVESTIGATIVE SERVICE

>> CLUB INFERNO
>> WASHINGTON, D.C.
>> 1150 HOURS

"Calm down, Ben."

Swanson bit back an angry retort and stared at Mason Craddock. "Jeff is out there somewhere. You don't know what he's like when he gets like this." He sat in front of Craddock's large desk.

"We'll find him," Craddock said calmly. "You've got people out there looking for him. So do I. We'll find him."

Swanson wanted to believe that. Jeff had disappeared in the past, gotten into trouble, gotten paranoid and depressed, and Swanson's people had always found him.

"He's gotten better at disappearing," Swanson said.

"What set him off?" Craddock asked.

"This whole investigation. As soon as Chloe's name started getting mentioned on television, he started getting tense. The second night after the story broke, he came back home and started living at my house again."

"Maybe he'll come back on his own."

"If he does, I'm putting him back in rehab."

Craddock sipped his drink. "He's weak."

Swanson took exception to that and glared at Craddock.

Unfazed, Craddock just sat quietly behind the desk. "You may not like it, Ben, but you have to deal with the truth. Jeff is weak, and he knows too much."

"A lot has happened to him," Swanson said.

Craddock swirled his drink in his glass. "One of the things that has always linked us—something that George Haskins never quite understood—is we've always been smart enough to know when to cut our losses. We're the only people important to ourselves." He paused. "You and me. No one else."

"This can be handled," Swanson said. "Jeff can be handled. I can do it."

Craddock sipped his drink. "If you can't, he's going to be the death of you. I can promise you that."

Swanson felt like he'd been slapped. Craddock's prediction smacked of a thinly veiled threat. "We just need to find Jeff," Swanson said. "I can take care of everything from then on."

"We know where he left your car," Craddock said. "I've got men searching the area, and I've also got some checking the taxi companies. We'll find him."

Swanson trusted that. Although the club was a legitimate business that was making Craddock a fortune, he still maintained an interface with gangs in the city and had his fingers in the illicit-drug business that flowed through the nation's capital. Beyond that, Craddock maintained a line of call girls with whom he managed to work some enterprising blackmail from time to time. Craddock was very connected, and that was what Swanson had been counting on.

"The sooner we find him, the better."

"Do you think he'll tell what he knows?"

Swanson considered that. "He might. His psychiatrist believes the guilt of what Jeff did to Chloe that night is what's tearing him apart."

"Maybe letting Jeff confess wouldn't be such a bad thing," Craddock suggested.

"He'd be locked away," Swanson said.

"He'd be safe there. Look at how many times he's tried to kill himself. Freedom isn't working out for him."

"You might be right." Swanson thought about it. "If Jeff confesses, it would close the case."

"Except for how a five-year-old boy managed to carry his stepsister's body out of the house."

Swanson thought desperately. "We could give them Haskins. We'd planned on giving them Haskins anyway. We still have Laura's gun locked away. At first we got lucky that Isaac Allen Lamont killed that girl the same week Chloe . . . had her accident. After Haskins got greedy—"

"Desperate," Craddock interrupted. "He knew he was about to get locked up by the military."

Nodding, Swanson remembered. Haskins had been desperate that night. Killing him had become necessary.

"If worse comes to worst, you can at least muddy the waters with that," Craddock said. "After all, it's been seventeen years. It'll be your word against your ex-wife's."

"And her fingerprints are the ones on the gun," Swanson said. He felt a little better. Craddock had always helped him see through his problems. He took a deep breath and let it out. All they had to do was find Jeff.

>> 18,000 FEET OVER VIRGINIA
>> 1323 HOURS

Seated in a comfortable chair in the back of the private plane the NCIS kept for ferrying agents around, Will kept an eye on the horizon. The cloud layer was low enough that they passed through wisps of it from time to time. Far below he saw the gray-green waters of Chesapeake Bay winking in the sunlight.

Will had left the forensics team in place at the Parker house, then loaded his team up and headed for MCAS/McCutcheon Field, where the plane was kept. Larkin had ordered the plane prepped, and it was ready to go when they arrived. They'd gotten immediate clearance.

Across the small aisle, Maggie finally put her cell phone down and slumped back, looking exhausted. She'd been talking nonstop to Jeff Swanson since the young man had agreed to speak with her. Will had figured her profiling skills would help her deal with Jeff.

"What's wrong?" Will asked.

"His phone went dead. It had been beeping for the last ten minutes. I tried to get him to call me from the hotel's landline, but he was afraid his father would find out."

"He'd have to give the front desk a credit card, and they'd run it."

"Right. And I can't call the hotel switchboard from my NCIS phone without potentially raising suspicion."

Will glanced at his watch and did a quick estimation. "We're still forty minutes from Ronald Reagan. If he's not talking to us, is he going to be all right?"

"I don't know." Maggie massaged the back of her neck. "He's in full-blown paranoia right now. He thinks his father is going to lock him up and throw away the key. He's feeling intense guilt over killing his stepsister. His mind, his thinking—" she sighed—"it's all a mess, Will. The meds he's been receiving have probably helped him deal with everything, but he's not on them now. Even worse, he's been using other drugs to keep himself more or less sedated. He exhibits all the signs of posttraumatic stress syndrome. Paranoia. Depression. Hostility. Uncertainty about what he's doing."

"Do you think he's suicidal?"

"Yes."

"We could call the D.C. police department and have them pick him up."

"He's armed. He told me he has a gun. If the police arrive, he could start shooting. Someone would get hurt or killed. We're just going to have to trust that Jeff can hold it together long enough for us to arrive. I gave him our ETA. He should be able to focus on that. As long as we're there by that time, I think he will be too."

Will hoped so. Even though Jeff's guilt in Chloe Ivers's death wasn't what he had been hoping for, it was still closure.

Unfortunately, they were no closer to solving their primary case. The question of who killed Gunnery Sergeant George Haskins remained.

>> THE RYDER HOTEL
>> WASHINGTON, D.C.
>> 1439 HOURS

The Ryder Hotel had seen better days. When it was built during the 1930s, the three-story structure had probably been a nice place to stay while in the capital. But the neighborhood had changed, becoming harder and seedier.

Located off the main streets, the hotel was surrounded by a few small shops and private homes that looked hard-pressed to survive too. Dilapidated cars sat at the curbs, and litter covered the grounds.

It was, Will thought, the perfect neighborhood for a junkie looking to score.

The two unmarked black Suburbans Larkin had had delivered to the airfield for their use stood out immediately. They looked like federal agents when they rolled into the neighborhood and parked at the hotel.

Will slid out from behind the wheel. Maggie and Estrella had ridden with him. Shel and Remy had taken the other vehicle.

A Cadillac with gold rims rolled slowly by. Loud, offensive rap music streamed from concert-ready speakers. The car was packed with young black men. The smell of reefer hung in the air.

Shel settled a sports bag over one broad shoulder and slid his sunglasses into place with a forefinger. Max was at his side, ears pricked and alert. Remy, also carrying a sports bag, stood nearby.

At first Will had thought the sports bags—loaded with weapons because that was the way Shel and Remy liked to do things—were over the top. Looking at the combat zone around him, he no longer felt that way.

He led the way while Shel held their six.

>> 1444 HOURS

With Shel and Remy in the third-floor hallway, taking up positions at both ends, Will stood in front of the door to room 3C and knocked.

There was no answer.

Will knocked again. "Jeff? It's Will Coburn."

A moment later, the locks unlatched. Jeff Swanson stood bare chested and barefoot in jeans. He looked pale and wan, way underweight. An old scar that looked like a bullet burn ran a stripe down his right side.

Behind him, the room was a shell containing mismatched furniture. A television with a rolling screen sat on a cheap chest of drawers.

"You came," Jeff whispered.

"I told you I would," Will said.

"Yeah." Jeff ran a hand through his tangled hair. His tiny pupils and slurred speech gave away the fact that he was under the influence.

"Why don't you come with us?" Will suggested.

Suspicion pinched Jeff's face. He took a step back. "I want to stay here."

Coached by Maggie on what to say, Will said, "We could go somewhere safer than here. You said you were afraid your father might find you here."

Jeff nodded, looking lost and forlorn. "He might. He'll be mad that I took his car. I don't have a license."

"We can go to a safe place," Will said. "We can talk about Chloe there."

Anguish twisted Jeff's face. He spoke in a tortured whisper. "I killed Chloe. I pushed her down the stairs." He shook his head. "I was only five. I didn't know what I was doing."

"It'll be okay," Will soothed. "We'll get away from here, and we'll get it all sorted out."

Jeff hesitated just a moment. "Okay. Okay. Just let me get my stuff." He turned and went back to the chest of drawers, then started raking the handful of pills scattered across the top into his cupped palm.

The curtain fluttered in the partially open glass door that looked out over the neighborhood. Movement on top of the derelict office building next door caught Will's attention.

By the time he realized that what he saw was a man with a rifle on top of the building, Will was already in motion. He ran at Jeff, startling the young man and causing him to step to the side. That was probably what saved his life, because the glass in the sliding door suddenly exploded inward.

Before the sound of the shot reached the hotel room, Will had dragged Jeff—screaming and fighting to get away—to the stained carpet.

SCENE  NCIS ✪ CRIME SCENE

NAVAL CRIMINAL INVESTIGATIVE SERVICE

>> THE RYDER HOTEL
>> WASHINGTON, D.C.
>> 1448 HOURS

Two more shots thundered into the room, punching through what remained of the sliding glass door and digging into the wall.

Will lay on top of Jeff Swanson, holding the young man down. Reaching under his jacket, Will drew his Springfield XD-40 and flipped the safety off.

"Sniper!" Will yelled.

"Stay down," Remy yelled back. "I'm going for a shot."

Two more shots tore through the room; then Remy rolled into view around the doorway. He pulled a Mini-14 Ranch Rifle to his shoulder in one fluid motion and looked through the scope. The hunting rifle was chambered in 7.62 mm and was short enough to be concealed in the sports bag.

Remy fired twice, quickly but deliberately, staying on target. Then he lowered the weapon and looked at Will. "Clear."

Jeff was crying out in fear, both hands wrapped around his head.

Getting to his feet, Will took hold of one of the young man's arms with his free hand, pulling him upright and tugging Jeff's arm across his shoulders. "Come on, Jeff," he said calmly. "Stay with me."

"Okay," Jeff replied. "I'm okay."

Will kept the young man moving, through the doorway and down the hall.

"Here," Shel called from the east-end landing. He had an H&K MP5 submachine gun in both his big fists.

"Did you see who shot at us?" Will asked Remy.

"No. He was black and he had a sniper rifle. That's all I can tell you."

Estrella had her pistol in hand. Maggie held both her Berettas at the ready.

Will went down the stairs as quickly as he could. It was awkward because Jeff Swanson didn't seem in control of his feet. He kept missing steps and nearly sending them sprawling.

Ahead, Shel went to ground, dropping beside the stairwell railing as he yelled, "Down!"

Automatic-weapons fire suddenly rattled through the stairwell, tearing splinters from the wooden railing and striking sparks from the wrought iron. The noise trapped inside the enclosed space was incredible.

"Popping smoke!" Shel pulled the pin on a grenade and tossed it down to the lower-floor landing.

"Grenade!" someone below bellowed. Running feet echoed.

The *bamf* of the grenade detonating seemed anticlimactic, but Will knew it was because it was a smoke grenade, not an antipersonnel one filled with shrapnel or high explosives.

Shel stood and went rapidly down the stairs, his MP5 leading the way. A thick cloud of scarlet smoke that looked like bloody air filled the stairwell.

Autofire ripped behind and above Will. As he turned the corner on the landing to follow Shel, Will saw that Remy was now carrying an MP5 as well.

"Company," Remy said, unleashing another quick tri-burst. "They're coming up the other stairwell."

Will half carried and half dragged Jeff with him into the smoke. "Hold your breath till we're through the smoke," he said.

"Okay."

The smoke grenade hadn't been laced with pepper like one designed for crowd dispersal would have been. This type was used more for obscuring targets on the battlefield or marking targets and landing zones for aircraft.

Maggie and Estrella followed.

Two black men stood in the exit. They fired handguns at Shel but were wide of the mark. The Marine fired back, knocking both gunners down. After changing magazines, he went through the doorway over their bodies.

"Maggie," Will called.

"Yes." Maggie moved into position beside him. She kept her pistols moving, covering them.

"You're driving." Will had made sure she had the extra set of keys to the Suburban. They habitually all had keys to vehicles used out in the field.

"All right."

Outside the hotel, the street had turned into a war zone.

The innocents had cleared the streets.

Shel broke cover and ran for the Suburban he'd driven in. Bullets chased him. Then Maggie and Estrella waded in, returning fire. Remy unleashed the MP5's full voice and laid down a heavy cover.

Just before Shel reached the Suburban, an SUV roared in from the street and came at him. The driver had to brake in order to keep from hitting the low retaining wall in front of the hotel, but it was obvious he intended to run the big Marine down.

Leaping, Shel slid across the Suburban's hood, holding the machine pistol out and firing on full-auto. The bullets chopped through the windshield and into the men on the other side.

Then Shel was on his feet again. In three long strides, he was at the Suburban, clawing the door open as bullets struck the bulletproof armor and glass. He reversed the vehicle and parked sideways behind the other Suburban, blocking it from the street and providing cover.

"Go!" Will yelled. He surged up, yanking Jeff with him, dragging the young man into a stumbling run toward the Suburban.

Maggie ran ahead, heading for the driver's-side door. The sound of bullets drumming against Shel's vehicle echoed all around them.

Estrella caught Jeff's other arm and helped Will hurry him to the Suburban. Maggie unlocked the rear doors from inside. Swinging the doors open, Will and Estrella shoved Jeff into the rear compartment and clambered in.

Will closed the door behind them. "You're going to be okay." He looked at Estrella. "Stay with him."

Estrella nodded and started talking to Jeff in a calm voice.

Climbing through the seats, Will dropped into the passenger seat as Remy joined Shel in the other vehicle and Maggie shoved the gear selector into reverse. She also put the Suburban into four-wheel-drive mode.

Seeing that they were safe and ready, Shel backed away, clearing the rear bumper so Maggie could back out. She did, burning rubber the whole way. Bullets slapped the back windows, not penetrating the glass but sending fracture patterns across it.

"Where to?" Maggie cut the wheel hard, hit the brake to throw the vehicle into a controlled drift, and shoved the transmission into drive. As soon as the nose came around and was pointed down the street, she hit the gas.

"National Naval Medical Center," Will said. The medical center was also known as the flagship of naval medicine. It was located in Bethesda and was no more than twenty minutes away. "We can get Jeff medical help if he needs it, and there are plenty of Marines there."

Maggie nodded. She kept her foot heavy on the accelerator, and they rocketed through the neighborhood.

Looking back, Will saw that Shel was only a short distance behind. However, an SUV was drawing even beside him. Gunmen leaned out the windows and took aim at Shel's tires. They were run-flats, filled with self-sealing foam that wouldn't let them deflate unless they were shredded.

But it looked like they were about to be shredded.

>> 1453 HOURS

Despite the danger and the threat of sudden death or injury, United States Marine Corps Gunnery Sergeant Shel McHenry felt more alive than he had in days. This was what he was made for. He knew Remy felt the same way.

He looked out his window and watched the SUV drawing even with the Suburban. Two gunmen with assault rifles leaned out the windows. Both of them wore heavy gold chains and had gold-capped teeth.

"They're going for our tires," Remy warned. He sat in the passenger seat and reloaded their weapons from spare clips in the sports bags.

"I see that. Do you have those weps ready?"

"Affirmative."

"Good deal. Then grab hold of something." Shel turned the wheel sharply, pulling the Suburban into the SUV. Tortured metal screamed. The two gunners ducked back inside the SUV.

Fully armored and outfitted, the Suburban was—for all practical applications—an urban tank that weighed several hundred pounds more than it should have. With the extra weight, it easily outclassed the SUV, dominating the other vehicle in a head-to-head matchup.

The SUV driver realized what was going on and tried to pull away and slow down.

Shel had no mercy in his heart. Whoever the men were, they were stone killers, probably drug dealers, and just as much an enemy of the country Shel loved as any terrorist he'd ever been up against.

He slowed and stayed with the attack vehicle. No others had closed the distance, all of them staying well back. The SUV driver tried again to get away, but Shel hung with him and swerved, muscling the SUV over and into a derelict Volkswagen Microbus up on blocks.

Shel peeled off at the last minute, then immediately hit the brakes and slewed the Suburban around.

The SUV tried to plow through the Microbus, pushing it for several yards before finally coming to a halt half off the street and into the yard of an abandoned house.

Shel stuck a hand out. Remy shoved an MP5 into it. Easing forward, Shel parked even with the SUV. The driver lay slumped over the steering wheel. The passenger had burst through the windshield and was supine across the SUV's crunched hood.

"We need one guy," Shel said.

"The guy on the hood's breathing," Remy replied.

"All right."

One of the men in the back raised his assault rifle as Shel approached. The Marine squeezed off a three-round burst that blew the man backward. The driver didn't move. When Shel got closer, he saw the man's forehead had been caved in.

The black man on the hood wore blue-inked tats that looked like gang markings.

Together, Shel and Remy yanked the semiconscious man from the SUV's hood and loaded him into the back of the Suburban. Remy climbed on top of him and secured his hands behind his back with disposable cuffs, then secured the cuffs to the D ring mounted on the cargo floor.

By that time, Shel was behind the steering wheel again. He put the big vehicle in gear and closed the distance between himself and the other Suburban.

>> NATIONAL NAVAL MEDICAL CENTER
>> BETHESDA, MARYLAND
>> EAST RIXEY
>> 1607 HOURS

Will stood outside Jeff Swanson's hospital room and talked to Larkin on his cell phone.

"The media is all over this thing," Larkin was saying. "Someone in the Washington police department tipped off the local news services that you were involved in that dustup at the Ryder Hotel. They also released Jeff Swanson's name."

"That's going to bring Congressman Swanson down on top of us," Will said.

Two armed Marines stood guard over the room.

"You can probably expect him at any time," Larkin agreed. "The story broke on the local channels about ten minutes ago. CNN is picking it up now. FOX News won't be far behind. Did you get a chance to interview Jeff Swanson?"

"No. By the time we reached the Ryder Hotel, he had overdosed on tranquilizers. The doctors here couldn't believe he was conscious when we brought him in. They had to pump his stomach, and the meds they put him on to counteract the tranquilizers put him out."

"But he did tell you that he killed Chloe Ivers?"

"Yes, sir. He told Maggie and me that he had pushed her down the steps, and Chloe was dead by the time she hit bottom. Maggie recorded her conversation with him, so we have an electronic file. He was prone to sleepwalking when he was a child. Probably still is. Maggie confirmed that with Commander Ivers only a short time ago. We thought we'd better tell her what happened before she heard about it on the news."

"Jeff Swanson did sleepwalk?"

"Yes, sir. He was also violent during those times. He'd been known to hit family members."

"Does she believe his story about pushing his sister down the stairs?"

"She came up with the same problem with it that we have," Will said.

"Who moved her body if the fall did kill her?"

"Yes, sir." They still had no answer for that; nor did Jeff's admission explain the strangulation marks the coroner had found on her neck.

"Why did he confess?"

"Maggie believes that Jeff Swanson has been struggling with guilt for years. She thinks that the story about his sister's murder coming back out in the public eye again pushed Jeff over the edge."

"He had to confess to feel better."

"Yes, sir."

"Did his father know?"

"He didn't say, but I'd think it was safe to assume that Congressman Swanson did know."

"Maybe you can ask Congressman Swanson about that when he gets there."

Will smiled a little at that. "Yes, sir. I'm actually kind of looking forward to that."

"Did you find out anything about the men who attacked you? From the news reports I'm getting, they're all gangbangers."

"Shel and Remy captured one of them and interviewed him. He was reluctant to answer, but after Shel explained how bad military prisons were and offered to drop all military charges against him in exchange for cooperation, he was a little more forthcoming."

"I assume Shel didn't point out that civilians aren't tried in military courts, therefore there were no military charges."

"No, he didn't. As far as our prisoner is concerned, he just avoided Leavenworth."

"What did he tell you?"

"Only that word spread through the grapevine that someone wanted Jeff Swanson dead. And anyone who was with him."

"Do you think Swanson would put out a hit on his own son?"

"I don't know about that," Will answered. "What I have a problem with is how Congressman Swanson would be able to interface with enough gang members to find his son that quickly."

"Someone else is involved."

"There has to be. And it has to be someone who's involved more in the criminal scene than the congressman is."

"Haskins and Ketchum were both involved with criminals."

"But they're both dead."

"What I was suggesting is that you might be looking for someone connected to them rather than someone connected to Congressman Swanson. Or possibly someone connected to all three."

"Yes, sir. But this thing eventually goes back to everything that happened seventeen years ago. At least to Chloe Ivers's murder. Maybe even back to Deanna Swanson's."

"That should limit the possibilities then."

"It also makes them harder to find. Whoever it is has had seventeen years or more to disappear."

A commotion drew Will's attention to the other end of the hallway. Marines came through, and in their midst was Ben Swanson.

"I've got to go, sir," Will said. "The congressman has just arrived."

"Let me know how it goes. I can be up there in a couple hours if you need me."

Will said that he would, then folded the phone and put it in his jacket pocket. He awaited the congressman's arrival. The attorney, Carlton Bledsoe, was with him.

"Coburn," Swanson growled, "where's my son?"

"In my custody," Will replied. "Maybe we could go somewhere more private to discuss this. A lot of what we're doing seems to end up in the media."

"No," Swanson said. "I want to see my son."

"You can't. He's in custody. If you want to get him an attorney, by all means, get him an attorney."

"Why are you holding Jeff Swanson?" Bledsoe demanded.

"Because he confessed to killing his stepsister by pushing her down the stairs."

"He confessed?"

"Yes," Will replied.

"You can't take his confession," Bledsoe said.

"And why is that?"

"Because Jeff Swanson was declared mentally incompetent at age seventeen." Bledsoe opened his satchel and pulled out several sheets of paper.

Glancing through the papers, Will saw that the attorney was right. Jeff Swanson had been declared incompetent by a judge.

"Congressman Swanson is his parent," Bledsoe went on. "Anything you want to discuss with Jeff is going to have to go through him. I'm afraid your *confession* is null and void, Commander. Now, I want Jeff Swanson released to us immediately, or I shall contact the district attorney's office and start pressing charges on behalf of Congressman Swanson."

Just like that, Will knew everything the confession had netted him had just been stripped away.

49

SCENE    CRIME SCEN

>> ANGEL'S TRAILER COURT
>> MURFREESBORO, TENNESSEE
>> 2017 HOURS

A fully dressed Ford F-150 pickup stopped in front of lot 49, and Carol Purdue got out on the passenger side.

Sitting across the street in her car, Nita was shocked by her mother's appearance. So much time had passed that she'd expected some changes. Instead, the last time she'd seen her could have been yesterday.

It had been fourteen years since Nita had seen her mother. They had argued over the fact that her mother hadn't come to her high school graduation. Nita had graduated as valedictorian. After that Nita had headed out, lived with a couple of girlfriends until she could finally afford her own place, and never looked back.

They hadn't spoken in six years. Her mother didn't even know she was a grandmother.

Carol Purdue was beautiful in a too-thin, used-up way. Fourteen years ago, Nita's mother had had a two-pack-a-day habit, drunk whenever someone else was buying, and lain out in the sun to maintain a tan that she was convinced all men desired. Yet she still looked like she could be Nita's older sister rather than her mom.

Nita saw that her mother still wore her jeans one size too small. She also wore a low-cut blouse, showing off the enhancements a particularly well-off past lover had purchased for her. Nita had heard her mother tell one of her friends that plastic surgery was one gift from a man that a woman should always accept, because once the relationship was over, a man couldn't just take it back.

Nita saw in the bright illumination from the truck's ground-effects lights that her mother's hair was peroxide blonde, just as she remembered. She supposed it would be the same color the day she died even if she lived to be a hundred. Her lipstick would be dark red, though Nita couldn't see it in the night, and she would smell like the flea-market knockoff of whatever the most fashionable perfume was.

That was her mother. That was always her mother.

Nita sat and watched and thought about leaving and was puzzled why she couldn't.

Carol talked with the truck driver—a big, bulky man with a bushy beard and long hair who wore a Willie Nelson T-shirt—for a little while, then kissed him good-bye and walked to her trailer while he drove off. She never looked back.

He's married, Nita thought. *Otherwise he would have spent the night.* She knew that from watching her mother's involvement with men. Her mother had always claimed her affairs with married men were just from boredom. When she couldn't be in love herself, it was nice if someone was in love with her.

Lights went on in the trailer.

Nita watched her mother through the windows, wishing she could just leave. But if she did, all the confusion she had locked up inside her wouldn't be dealt with. There was some reason she'd been unhappy for the last year, some reason she couldn't be a wife or a mother—or just be happy getting back to being on her own.

Taking a deep breath, she opened the Mustang's door and got out. She'd taken the dome light out earlier so it wouldn't come on and she wouldn't be seen. She carried the darkness with her to her mother's doorstep and wondered as she stood there how much of it she had carried away with her fourteen years ago.

Nausea washed through her as she lifted her hand to knock. She was afraid she was going to throw up; then it passed.

She knocked.

"Who is it?" Her mother didn't open the door. She never did after dark once she was inside.

Nita had to try twice before her voice came out. "It's Nita."

The door remained shut for a time. Nita started to think that her mother wasn't going to open it.

Then the chain slipped back and the door opened.

Her mother glowered at her, took a hit off her cigarette, and squinted through the smoke. "What do you want?"

Nita stood on the steps, tears burning her eyes and anger knotting her throat. "I . . . I don't know."

"You don't know?"

Although she wanted to scream at her mother in answer to the question, Nita couldn't speak. Her knees quivered.

Her mother looked outside the door. "Are you alone?"

"Yes." Nita's voice was a whisper.

"Come in."

Nita didn't move. Even though she'd never been in the trailer, she knew what every room would look like. She knew what pictures would be on the walls, which paperback authors would be on the shelves, and that the shower screen would look Hawaiian.

Her mom looked at her again, then flicked ashes outside the door and looked irritated. "You coming in or not? It costs money to heat the house, and it still gets cold at night." Her face hardened and her red lipstick looked stark against her face. "Truck-stop waitresses don't make as much money as doctors."

The attack loosened Nita up. She was used to those. When she'd started growing up and becoming her own person, her mother had fought with her over clothes and the way she wore them, over boys she saw and didn't see, and even over the way she chose to wear her hair.

Nita entered the trailer. The feeling of dread of ever returning to her mother's house—something that had motivated her all through college and medical school—rattled through her.

"I'm having a beer," her mother said. "Want one?"

"Yes."

Nita's mother walked into the small kitchen and took a can of beer—not a bottle—out of the refrigerator. She pressed it into Nita's hand. "Do you want to sit?"

"I don't know."

"Sit." Her mother waved her to the frayed couch while she took the fake-leather armchair. A nineteen-inch television set with rabbit ears sat atop a milk crate against the wall.

Nita sat. She looked around the room. It wasn't much different from all the other trailer living rooms she'd grown up in. In fact, it was better than most. But it still felt small and closed in.

"What are you running from?" her mother asked.

"Nothing." Nita resented the question.

Her mother lit up a fresh cigarette and moved an overflowing four-leaf-clover ashtray on the end table closer to her. She pulled in a long draw, then released it. Smoke wreathed her head. "If you came to see me, you're running from something. It has to be something bad to bring you to a hole like this."

I'm not running, Nita thought vehemently. But she still didn't know what had brought her in search of her mother. "I just wanted to see you." She'd thought she was telling a lie, but it felt so much like the truth that she was certain she'd fooled herself.

"Why?"

"I don't know."

Her mother sipped beer and regarded her. She shook her head. "For a girl that's been to college, there sure is a lot you don't know."

With difficulty, Nita ignored the gibe. She cracked her beer and took a sip. It was too bitter and she knew she couldn't drink it.

"How'd you find me?" her mother asked.

"The birthday cards."

Her mother smiled. "I figured you'd thrown those away."

"I wanted to."

"I guess I can't blame you."

"How did you find me?"

"I went to the library. One of my friends does genealogy. She knows how to use the computers. She put your name in—Nita Purdue—and found some news stories about some murders you helped solve."

"That's what I do," Nita said.

"I watch them do that on the TV. It looks like interesting work."

"It is. I love it."

"That's good," her mother said. "It's good to have work that you love. You always had a good mind, Nita."

"You didn't think so when I was younger."

Her mother's face hardened. "When you were younger, you faulted me for everything I did."

"I did not," Nita objected.

"You didn't like the men I dated—"

"Most of them—*all* of them—were no good," Nita said.

"—the way I dressed—"

"You didn't dress like a mother," Nita accused.

"—or the way I acted."

"I had to lie for you, Mom," Nita said. "I had to lie to everybody I knew. I lied about why I didn't have a father; I told people he'd been killed in the war. I lied to the men you cheated on. I lied to the people you owed money to for rent and bad checks. I lied to DHS workers and told them you took care of me and loved me."

Her mother's hard face cracked a little at that. "I did love you, baby girl."

Tears blurred Nita's vision. Her breathing was ragged and burned the back of her throat, which suddenly felt raw. She felt the tears on her face and brushed them away.

"When . . . ," Nita asked in a soft voice when she felt like she needed to be screaming, "when did you stop loving me, Mom?"

Her mother just stared at her for a moment. Then she took another hit on her cigarette and shook her long blonde tresses. "Well now, if we're gonna get into this, beer ain't gonna be strong enough."

She got up from the chair and walked to the kitchen again. This time she took down a bottle of Johnnie Walker Black from behind boxes of Ding Dongs and microwave macaroni and cheese.

Her mother's idea of food hadn't changed either.

Carol poured a tall glass of the amber-colored whiskey. "You want some?"

Nita did, but she didn't trust her stomach. "No."

"Are you sure? Because if we're gonna talk about this, it's gonna hurt." Her mother drank the whiskey down as if it were Kool-Aid.

Nita didn't answer.

"You know what, Nita, you were always an ungrateful little snot. From the time you were born, you were always whining about something. You always had an opinion."

"I still do."

Her mother carried her glass back into the living room and sat down. "I didn't ask for you, you know. Being a single mom raising a kid ain't no picnic. Do you know how old I was when I had you?"

Nita had always known, but she'd never really thought about it. Now, with the question before her, that fact weighed heavily.

"I was *sixteen,* Nita. *Sixteen* years old. I wasn't more'n a baby myself. I had you, and my dad kicked me out of the house. Said he wasn't gonna raise my brats. And the man I thought loved me, who swore to me he loved me like he loved nobody else, was as gone as a man could get after I told him I was pregnant."

As she sat in that all-too-familiar living room, Nita remembered all the arguments her mother had had with the men who had tramped through her life. All the cursing, the crying, the hitting, the slapping, the pain. Pain for both of them.

"I had to drop out of school to work so I could stay at a halfway house for unwed mothers. Then when I got to be eighteen, I found a man I thought I could trust, but he couldn't stand raising somebody else's kid either. So he left me high and dry. With bills I couldn't pay and no job because he wanted me home waiting for him when he got off at the factory."

Nita tried to imagine what that had been like. She'd felt like the bottom had dropped out of her world when she found out she was pregnant with Celia, but she'd had a good job. *More than a good job. I had a career.* And Joe had never left her side. He had never faltered or fallen behind.

"I looked you up in the papers every now and again. I got more news about you from that Camp Lejeune Web site. I found out about investigations you'd worked on, and I found out you got your name changed. So I'm assuming you got married."

"I did." Nita had an unexplainable impulse to tell her mother about Celia, but she didn't. She didn't want to share her life with her mother. Carol Purdue didn't deserve any of that.

"You got that fancy college degree and became a doctor," her mother said bitterly. "And then you got married. I look at your clothes and the way you're made up, and I know you ain't been living a hard life. You got more'n I ever had."

"What you had and didn't have isn't my fault," Nita said.

"Then whose fault was it? Huh?" Her mother glared at her, and the expression was so like everything Nita remembered about growing up around her mother that she shivered. "I didn't plan on my life being like this. Living in dumps like this. Or did you think that's what I always wanted for myself?"

"I don't know."

"You don't know? Who in their right mind would choose to live like this? like some desperate animal in a tin can on the next block over from Nowhere?"

Nita cried even though she didn't want to.

"I see you sitting there, Nita—all wrapped up in your Oprah best and blaming every bad thing that ever happened to you on your stupid, backward mother—and I have to wonder what it is in your own life that made you come find me just to blame me for it."

"Is that what you think I'm doing? Blaming you?"

"Trust me—from the things you been saying, I know you didn't come all this way to give me a pat on the head for the way I raised you."

"No, I didn't." Nita held on to her anger. "Do you know that no matter what I do, you're always there?"

Her mother just stared at her.

"You are," Nita said. "I finished high school, college, and medical school. I became a professional. More than that, I became an expert in my field. Other professionals around the world have called me to talk about what I do. *I've* been around the world. Sometimes to give seminars on things I do. But no matter what I do, no matter what I become, you're still there. Lurking inside me. Because I know I can't escape what you bred into me and how you raised me."

"Don't blame that on—"

"I know I'll never be as good a wife as my husband deserves, and I'll never be the mother my daughter needs. *Because I don't know how.*"

Nita's mother looked at her with tears brimming in her eyes. "I have a granddaughter?" she whispered.

"No," Nita said. "*I* have a *daughter*. But I can't be a mother to her." Overcome by emotion, torn between anger and fear and confusion, she stood. "Coming here was a mistake."

Nita let herself out, clomped down the stairs, and headed for her Mustang. Tears ran down her cheeks. She was shaking all over.

"Nita!"

She heard her mother coming after her.

"Nita, honey! Come back. I want to talk to you. Nita!"

A loud V-8 engine snorted to sudden life. Headlights flared from an old Chevy parked at the side of the street.

"Carol Purdue!" a woman screamed. "You ain't gonna get away with stealin' my husband!"

Rubber shrilled.

Startled, Nita turned around and saw her mother pinned in the bright glare of the car's headlights. Her mother stood in the center of the street. The car screamed straight for her.

"No," Nita whispered, realizing what was about to happen. She started back toward her mother. "Move! Get out of there!"

But it was too late. Before Carol could move, the car hit her. She folded over the car, rolling onto the hood, then smashing against the windshield before finally being thrown over the top and landing in an unmoving heap. The car kept going.

Horrified, not believing what she'd just witnessed, Nita ran toward her mother, knowing the woman had to be dead.

S  CRIME SCENE  NCIS  C

SERVICE

NAVAL CRIMINAL INVESTIGATIVE SERVICE

50

SCENE    CRIME SCEN

NCIS

NAVAL CRIMINAL INVESTIGATIVE SERVICE

>> NCIS HEADQUARTERS
>> WASHINGTON, D.C.
>> 2100 HOURS

"I don't believe Jeff hurt Chloe," Laura Ivers said. "That's not something he would do, intentionally or by accident. Jeff loved her."

Seated at his borrowed desk in the NCIS offices, Will thumbed through Jeff Swanson's court cases as he talked with Commander Ivers over the phone. She'd called after the news stories about the attack on Jeff had aired. Will hadn't been able to talk to her until now.

The largest number of charges filed against Jeff Swanson centered on possession of controlled substances, but there were also several assault-and-battery charges. Jeff hadn't won every fight he'd fought, but he'd apparently fought a lot. Many of the criminal cases were cross-referenced with civil cases. Congressman Swanson had spent a small fortune to settle judgments against his son in civil court.

"Jeff has probably changed a lot since you were his mom," Will said.

"I know." Laura drew a breath and sounded incredibly tired. "But I remember the scared little boy I helped raise for six years. And that's when we're talking about. Those years, Commander Coburn. Jeff wouldn't have hurt Chloe."

"Jeff said he was sleepwalking when he pushed Chloe down the steps."

"Something like that—" Laura stopped and took a deep breath—"something like that he would have told me about."

Will hated asking Laura Ivers all these questions while she was vulnerable. From the sound of her voice, the last few days with all their twists and turns had left her emotionally bereft.

"He might not have remembered at the time," Will pointed out. "According to the court reports I've gone over regarding Jeff's fights with other people, he sometimes can't remember what he did until days or even weeks or months later."

"That's because of the meds he's taking. He had night terrors as a child. His doctor tried to suppress the dreams. As a result, the treatment caused some temporary memory loss."

"The attack on your daughter, whether intentional or not, could be something that Jeff's only recently remembered," Will said. "He said he's been forgetting his meds frequently over the past few months."

"Even if Jeff hurt his sister all those years ago, he was only five. There was no way he could move her . . . her . . . no way he could move her."

"I know," Will said. "We still don't have the full story."

"If Ben has his way," Laura replied, "you never will."

Will considered telling her about the blood pattern that had been found in the house. So far the Parkers had kept their word that they wouldn't tell anyone, but it was only a matter of time till the story was out.

In the end he elected not to. He believed Laura Ivers was an innocent. She had enough on her plate to worry about.

Director Larkin appeared in the doorway.

Will waved him inside the office. He excused himself from the phone, telling Laura that he would stay in touch as new developments came up.

"You decided to come up," Will said to Larkin.

Larkin nodded. "I figured you could use the moral support."

"I appreciate that."

"Where's the team?"

"They're regrouping while we see what develops. With Jeff Swanson's confession off the table, we're at an impasse."

Larkin smiled. "Not anymore. Not only did I show up for moral support, but I come bearing gifts." He placed his briefcase on the desk and opened the coded locks. Reaching inside, he took out a sheaf of papers and handed them to Will.

It was an arrest warrant. And it was made out with Congressman Swanson's name.

"How did you get this?" Will asked.

"The lab got the results back on the blood recovered at the house in Raleigh. I asked them to compare it to the mitochondrial DNA Nita recovered from George Haskins's body."

Mitochondrial DNA came from small organelles in the mitochondria, which created energy within the cell. Although not as unique as nuclear DNA, the type gathered by serologists from fluids and other nucleated cells, mitochondrial DNA was unique enough to identify a victim or a perpetrator.

Tough and resistant, mitochondrial DNA could be harvested from teeth and bones of old skeletons and burn victims. Normally hair follicles, the bulbs of hair strands that rooted inside the flesh, were the only portion of hair that contained nucleated DNA. However mitochondrial DNA sometimes existed within the rest of the hair.

Passed down and unchanging through the matriarchal line in a family, so that sons and daughters could be matched to mothers, grandmothers, and beyond, mitochondrial DNA was also used to discover family members in mass graves so the bodies could be sorted out.

"The mitochondrial DNA matched?" Will said.

"It was Haskins's blood that got cleaned off that floor."

Will laid the warrant on the desk. "There is a problem."

"I know. We're not going to really be able to arrest the congressman."

Will nodded. "As a member of Congress, Swanson has congressional immunity. All he has to do is say he's on his way to a congressional session or working on official congressional business, and we can't touch him."

Larkin grinned mirthlessly. "True. But we can still rattle his cage and see if we can't shake some of that complacency he's wrapped himself up in. You in?"

"Yes, sir." Will pushed back from the desk and retrieved his sidearm from the drawer. "I'm in."

>> ANGEL'S TRAILER COURT
>> MURFREESBORO, TENNESSEE
>> 2107 HOURS

Nita raced to her mother's side and dropped to her knees. Blood covered Carol Purdue's face, neck, and hands, and more continued to leak out of various lacerations that Nita immediately identified.

Amazingly, her mother's chest rose and fell almost imperceptibly. She was alive.

Nita hesitated, trying to control the fear that threatened to swallow her. *You're a doctor! Act like one!*

After medical school, she'd spent her internship in Atlanta, Georgia, working in the emergency room at Georgia Baptist Medical Center. There had always been a steady line of patients in the downtown area, and they'd run the gamut of accidents and intended homicides.

But that was a long time ago. Now Nita was used to working with corpses or pieces of corpses, not living people. As a medical examiner, there was always pressure to get a body posted, but it was nothing like the frantic pace in the ER. Lives were saved there on a nightly basis. Nita had helped save them once.

"Carol." Nita forced her voice to be calm. If a patient picked up on an attending physician's fear or uncertainty, the patient could lose hope.

Her mother lay in the shadows of the street. Her right leg lay at an improbable angle. *It's broken. Please don't let it be shattered. Please don't let it cut the femoral artery.*

If a jagged piece of bone had nicked the artery, her mother would bleed out in seconds.

Nita's hands shook as she reached into her purse. She carried a Mini Maglite there. A nail file. Antibacterial wipes that she carried out of habit for Celia. A box of Flintstones Band-Aids for boo-boos.

It wasn't enough. She felt inadequate and unprepared.

How do you prep for something like this?

Nita flicked the Mini Maglite on and shone it into her mother's eyes.

Her mother. That thought didn't leave her.

Nita took the vitals. Her mother's respiration was labored—*She just got hit by a car*—and her pulse was thready—*She just got hit by a car*—and her color wasn't good.

Peeling back her mother's eyelids, Nita shone the Mini Maglite beam into them again. Her pupils were no longer the same size. The left one almost filled the iris.

Concussion, Nita thought. It wasn't surprising. What was surprising was that her mother was still alive.

Nita fumbled for her cell phone as she played the flashlight over her mother. Dialing 911 one-handed, she hit the Speaker function and placed the phone on the ground to free up her other hand.

Blood streamed profusely from her mother's right hand, leaking into a growing pool that spread across the uneven street. Closer inspection revealed that the last two fingers had almost been severed. Her ring finger hung by a few shreds of flesh. White-gray fat cells and ivory bone were visible in the wound.

Breathe, Nita told herself. *Stay calm. You can do this. This is the one thing you're good at.*

"911 operator. State your emergency." The voice of the man working dispatch for the emergency service was too cool, so laid-back that he didn't sound concerned.

"I'm Dr. Nita Tomlinson of Jacksonville, North Carolina." Nita knew she had to stanch the blood pouring from her mother's hand. If she lost too much blood, she was going to go into shock. Nita reached for her purse and unfastened the strap. It felt flexible enough. "I need an ambulance at Angel's Trailer Court. Lot 49. Do you know where that is?"

"I do, Dr. Tomlinson. What's the nature of your emergency?"

My mother was hit by a car!

"I'm working on a hit-and-run victim," Nita said. "She's—" she had to stop and do the math—"forty-eight years old. In decent health but poor overall physical condition. Five feet seven. One hundred ten to one hundred twenty pounds. She's a lifelong smoker and drinker. Her name is Carol Purdue. Check around and see which hospital she's been to before. See if you can find out if she has a physician."

Looking at the blood covering her mother's hand, Nita hesitated. Her mother had a history of frequent unprotected sex, which had caused several pregnancy scares and fights with boyfriends, and sharing drugs, which had started several other fights over who had used up whose stash.

Nita didn't have any surgical gloves. Treating her mother meant risking contracting AIDS or hepatitis B or some other blood-borne, sexually transmitted disease. Ever since she'd been in medical school she'd been trained not to incur that risk.

But this wasn't some unknown patient who'd come in through the ER. This was her mother.

"Dr. Tomlinson, could you tell me more about the injuries?" the dispatch officer requested.

"She's got a broken leg," Nita said. "Two of her fingers on her right hand have almost been ripped off. I'm using a tourniquet on the arm now. A concussion. Probably broken ribs. Multiple lacerations and contusions."

It was a laundry list of bad things that could be done to the human body. Usually Nita saw them on bodies of people who were no longer around to care about pain and permanent disability.

"The tourniquet might not be—"

Cursing, Nita raised her voice and knew that the hysteria she was feeling was communicated in her words. "Get that ambulance here now!" She closed the phone and set to work.

Wrapping the purse strap just above her mother's elbow, Nita pulled it tight. The bleeding from her mother's torn fingers halted almost immediately. Applying a tourniquet to the forearm, especially with the makeshift material she had to work with, might not have been effective. The tissue immediately above the elbow was softer and not as densely packed with muscle, and the artery could be squeezed against the bone to shut down the flow.

"God, help us. Poor Carol."

Glancing up, Nita saw Geraldine Wallace, her mother's neighbor, standing there, leaning on a three-footed cane. She had one hand to her mouth. Beyond her, other people from the trailer park had started to gather as well. None of them came forward to offer assistance.

As far back as Nita could remember, it had always been like that. People in hard situations usually helped each other only when helping was easy and they thought they might eventually want something in return for it.

"Mrs. Wallace, I need help." Nita kept pressure on the purse strap till she felt certain it would hold.

"Is she going to be all right?" Geraldine stared at the fallen woman.

"Mrs. Wallace." Nita made her voice sharper. "Stay with me, Mrs. Wallace. I need your help. *Carol* needs your help."

"What can I do?"

"How long will it take for the ambulance to get here?"

"Probably ten or fifteen minutes."

Nita felt trapped and helpless. She wanted to scream. Ten or fifteen minutes could be a lifetime.

Adapt, Nita ordered herself. *That's what you have to do in a life-or-death situation. That's what you always have to do.*

"Mrs. Wallace, I need a blanket. Something to keep Carol warm. As badly hurt as she is, she's probably going to go into shock any minute now."

The old woman stood frozen, staring at Nita's mother.

"Mrs. Wallace," Nita ordered more firmly and with calmness she didn't feel. "Look at me."

Struggling, Geraldine looked at her. "What can I do to help?"

"I need a blanket. An afghan. Something to keep her warm."

"I'll get one." Geraldine limped off.

Nita continued assessing her mother's injuries. "Carol, can you hear me?"

Her mother was going to need stitches in her face and chin. Swelling along her lower left jawbone and her cheek, as well as the deep purple discoloration, indicated possible fracture. She might need facial reconstruction. Her broken leg would need to be set.

She's going to be in the hospital for a long time.

Using one of the antibacterial wipes, Nita started cleaning her mother's face. The wounds would need to be cleaned and disinfected in the ER. Whatever Nita could do here would save time then. Blood matted the peroxide blonde hair.

As she looked at her mother, Nita couldn't believe Carol Purdue looked so small. All her life her mother had loomed gigantically. She had been a force and a prison warden, a great, uncaring anchor that had held Nita back from a better life.

Now she just looked . . . hurt. And small. And fragile.

Her mother's eyelids fluttered. She rolled her head, and her lips parted.

"Mom?" Nita said. "Mom, can you hear me? It's Nita, Mom. I'm here. I need you to stay with me."

Without warning, the air left her mother's lungs in a quiet, bubbling rush—and she stopped breathing.

S  CRIME SCENE  NCIS  C

NAVAL CRIMINAL INVESTIGATIVE SERVICE

51

SCENE  NCIS  CRIME SCENE

NAVAL CRIMINAL INVESTIGATIVE SERVICE

>> ANGEL'S TRAILER COURT
>> MURFREESBORO, TENNESSEE
>> 2115 HOURS

Panic flooded Nita's neural passages. Her body pumped straight adrenaline, filling her with razor-edged awareness. The world was suddenly filled with colors and sounds that were too vibrant and too loud.

"No!" Nita said. "Mom! Mom!" She laid her fingers against her mother's neck, searching for a pulse that wasn't there.

"She's not breathing," someone in the crowd around Nita and her mother said.

"She's dead."

"That's horrible."

"Did anyone see what happened?"

"Buddy LeFevre's old lady ran her down."

"She's the one who's been datin' Buddy LeFevre behind Gloria's back?"

Nita picked up her Mini Maglite and opened her mother's mouth. Remembering all her ER training, Nita went by the numbers. That was all anyone had time to do in the ER: react. React to blood, burned flesh, pieces of victims coming in separately, pain, and fear. Thinking came later. If the patient survived.

Four minutes without oxygen and the brain starts dying.

There was no obstruction in her mother's throat, no tooth that had been dislodged, and the tongue was where it was supposed to be.

Nita put her purse under her mother's neck to elevate her head and tilt her chin back so the breathing passages opened naturally. Opening her mother's mouth, feeling the sickening looseness of the jaw, Nita performed mouth-to-mouth resuscitation, filling her mother's lungs with air.

Then she placed her hands on her mother's sternum and shoved. She felt broken ribs grate. When CPR was administered correctly—vigorously—ribs sometimes broke. But her mother's ribs were starting out broken.

She counted off for herself, then went back and breathed for her mother again. She was conscious of the stares of the crowd, angry that none of them came forward to help and scared that no matter what she could do for her mother it was already too late.

Geraldine Wallace came back and stared at her. "What's happening?"

"That lady stopped breathin'," someone said.

The pace began to wear Nita out. She hadn't been feeling well the last few days anyway, and the stress of leaving Joe and Celia, then the long drive from Jacksonville, had left her utterly exhausted. But she continued, wondering how many minutes had passed since the 911 call and how soon help would arrive.

Kneeling on the road beside Nita and her mother, Geraldine bowed her head and began to pray. "God, you see us here tonight needing you, needing your power and your love. I know you know Carol Purdue ain't always walked on your right side, but so few of us ever do."

Nita couldn't believe it. "You're praying?" she asked as she finished breathing then went back to start CPR again. "Praying isn't going to do any good. I need *help*."

We need a miracle.

Geraldine continued without responding. "Right now Carol needs your forgiveness and understanding, dear Lord. More than that, God, she needs your help. Reach down with your healing touch and show her your love. In Jesus' beautiful name we pray. Amen."

Several of the onlookers said amen as well.

Nita wanted to yell at them. She'd given up believing in praying when she was a little girl, after all the prayers about being adopted into a new family or her mother finding a man who would really be a father to her. All she'd ever gotten was disappointment.

She breathed into her mother's lungs again, then did more chest compressions.

Come on, she thought desperately. *Don't be gone. Don't do this to me. You still haven't met your granddaughter.* She moved back to breathe more air, wishing someone would help her. *If prayers really work, God, now would be the time.*

When she'd walked out of her mother's house fourteen years ago, Nita hadn't cared if she ever saw her again. When she'd walked out of her mother's house only a few minutes ago, she'd intended never to see her again.

Now, if her mother didn't start breathing, Nita knew she'd *never* see her again. Not in this lifetime. And probably not in the next.

The thought chilled her.

Even when she'd left home, Nita had never thought in terms of *forever.* But seeing her now, seeing her mother *die* right in front of her eyes—that was too much. Too final.

Oh, God, Nita thought helplessly as tears blurred her vision and her shoulders ached from the repetitive motion of trying to get her mother's heart started. *Oh, God.*

She knew in that moment why desperate people called on God in their darkest hour. There was simply nowhere else to go, nothing else to do. For some insane reason, Nita remembered one of the few Sunday mornings when she'd attended church with Joe. The pastor had been on a tear and had sounded angry as he'd vented about people who called on God as a last resort when all else failed.

"God isn't supposed to be a last-ditch effort," Pastor Wilkins had said. *"Even when you're dialing 911, God should be the first call you make. And you don't have to go looking. God's right there. He's always right there."*

Nita breathed air into her mother, then forced herself back to the chest compressions. *Breathe! Breathe!*

She thought about Joe, about the way he prayed and asked God's grace even over a task he knew he could do. One day she'd asked him why he did that. He'd told her that God's help was always appreciated, and that God should know that. It had been a child-simple answer. Most of the really hard questions, Joe had insisted, were that simple.

Nita leaned into her efforts, shoving against her mother, striving to restart her stopped heart. Her mother's heart. The one that Nita had always felt was so cold and distant and uncaring and selfish. She wanted that heart beating.

God, I want to talk to my mother again. I don't want the last time I spoke to her to be a shouting argument. I don't want—I don't want to lose her. I'm not ready yet. Please.

Drawing back, Nita went to her mother's head and took a deep breath. In the distance—too far in the distance—she heard sirens approaching.

They're never going to get here in time. She's already dead.

She opened her mother's mouth yet again and leaned in to try once more to breathe life into her mother's smoke-scarred lungs. Then she stopped. She sagged back. She was too exhausted to continue. It was over. Her mother was dead.

Nita tried to accept that her mother was gone, that there were questions that would never be resolved. She tried to identify the emotions inside her at the death of this woman whom she had both loved and hated for so long.

And then Carol Purdue sucked in a ragged breath.

Nita held her mother's head in her hands and watched in disbelief. *She breathed.* Not daring to move, Nita stared in dread as her mother breathed out, certain she would not have the strength to breathe in on her own again.

The sirens grew closer, louder.

Her mother's chest rose, not strongly, not evenly, but alone and unaided.

Tears cascaded down Nita's face. She wiped them away, trying to regain her lost composure. Her emotions were beyond her control.

Her mother breathed again, and it was one of the most wondrous things Nita had ever seen. She pressed her fingers against her mother's neck. A pulse was there, thin and weak, but steady.

"She's breathin' again!"

"Look, that woman brought her back!"

"She's alive!"

Not understanding what had just happened, Nita looked up at Geraldine Wallace. "She was dead. I know she was dead. I saw her."

The old woman smiled. "I know, child, but now she's not."

"I thought I couldn't bring her back. She wasn't responding to any of the CPR. I'd done everything I could do." Nita knew it hadn't been her efforts that had brought her mother back. "She was dead."

"I know, child."

At the end of the street, the ambulance skidded around the corner. The neighborhood reverberated with the sound of the sirens. The flashing light bar strobed the darkness and shredded the shadows. The crowd parted, making way for the emergency vehicle.

"Was it God?" Nita needed to know.

Geraldine looked at her with rheumy eyes. Then the old woman smiled. "Of course it was. What did you think?"

The ambulance stopped only a few feet away. EMTs, one male and one female, carried equipment bags to Carol Purdue's side.

"We've got it now, miss," one of the EMTs announced, shouldering Nita aside. "Move out of the way. Let us deal with this."

Nita resented being dismissed so casually, but she was exhausted and she knew it. She'd used up everything she'd had to give. And it hadn't been enough. She knew that. She hadn't saved her mother's life. That had been in someone else's hands.

>> SILVER SPRING, MARYLAND
>> 2133 HOURS

"I apologize for the inconvenience, sir," a polite male voice announced over the security gate's intercom system, "but Congressman Swanson has no further appointments scheduled this evening. Please contact his public-relations office for assistance. Thank you."

In the passenger seat of the Suburban, Will stared up at the big house. Most of the lights were off, but every now and again a motion detector flared to life and a bright cone of light stabbed through the shadows filling the landscaped yards.

In the night, behind the high security wall and the armed guards, Ben Swanson's home was a fortress. No one got in or out without the proper magic. Fortunately, they had that.

Larkin, behind the steering wheel, leaned out the window and stabbed the button with a forefinger again.

This time the monitor flared to life, showing the no-nonsense face of an experienced security guard. "Sir, I've already told you Congressman Swanson isn't—"

"I'm Director Michael Larkin of the Naval Criminal Investigative Services," Larkin announced loud enough for the reporters across the street to hear. "I'm here to serve the congressman with a warrant for his immediate arrest."

"That should bring the fans out of the cheap seats," Remy commented from the backseat.

A second Suburban carrying Maggie, Estrella, Shel, and Max pulled in behind them.

The reporters amassed on the other side of the street bolted from their vehicles and brought cameras to life. The story about Jeff Swanson nearly getting killed in the Washington, D.C., streets had reignited interest in the story. With Washington politics and a possible cover-up in the works, a cold-case investigation of a girl who'd been believed the victim of a convicted serial killer who claimed he hadn't killed her, and gun battles in the streets that had resulted in a dozen deaths, America was tuning in and staying with the story.

In seconds the reporters had mounted an offensive that threatened to violate the integrity of Swanson's fortress.

"If you further impede me," Larkin continued in that flat, hard voice of his, "I'm going to arrest you and everyone else in that little security tower for interference and obstruction. Do you copy that?"

"Yes, sir." The security guard's voice changed immediately. "I need just a second to—"

"Get that gate open," Larkin commanded.

The gate rumbled back into its housing within the stone-and-mortar wall.

"I'll let Congressman Swanson know you're coming."

"You do that." Larkin drove through as the security monitor went blank.

Several reporters ran for the gate as it closed again. Armed security guards came out of the towers and started repelling the would-be invaders, shoving them back into the street.

Larkin parked the Suburban in front of the big house, and they went in. The director led the group as the houseman met them at the door.

"This way, Director Larkin." The young majordomo looked at the rest of the NCIS group. "Perhaps your colleagues could wait out—"

"They're coming with me," Larkin said. "Is Swanson in his den?"

The majordomo didn't look pleased. "Congressman Swanson is in his *office,* sir."

Larkin brushed by the man.

Will followed, trailed by Maggie, Estrella, Shel, Max, and Remy. It was a show of force and solidarity. All of them knew that they didn't have any direct leverage over Swanson.

"Director," the man protested, "you can't bring the dog into—"

"The dog's working," Shel warned. "Stay out of his way."

Swanson's attorney, Carlton Bledsoe, met Larkin at the doorway to the den. He didn't look happy.

"I'd like to see that warrant, Director Larkin." Bledsoe stuck out a hand. "And trust me when I say that if every *i* isn't dotted and every *t* crossed, I'm going to file so many lawsuits it'll make your head spin."

Larkin ignored the threat, looking over Bledsoe's shoulder to where Swanson sat behind the desk.

"You're arresting Congressman Swanson for the murder of George Haskins?" Bledsoe sounded like he couldn't believe it. "On what evidence?"

"We found evidence of a murder at the house on 114 Applegate," Larkin said. "Crime-scene tests have matched blood recovered at that scene to George Haskins's DNA. Haskins disappeared seventeen years ago. When

Haskins's body was recovered, his clothing contained a charm from the jewelry that went missing the night Chloe Ivers was taken from her home. I don't think—and the judge agreed with me—that it was likely Haskins knowingly hung on to evidence that would lock him up for murder. Or that he went very long without changing clothes. That means he was killed shortly after Chloe Ivers went missing." He paused. "By his own admission, and according to testimony given, Congressman Swanson was there that night."

"I can't believe you'd find a judge crass enough or foolish enough to grant such a warrant based on this evidence," Bledsoe said.

The evidence, Will knew, was thin, but it was solid. Enough for an indictment.

"There are a lot of judges who still believe in justice," Larkin said. "I happen to know a few of them."

"I'm not impressed." Bledsoe handed the warrant back. "You may have that, but you can't execute it. You should know that Congressman Swanson is protected while working on congressional business. He has immunity from legal repercussions."

"That wasn't what they were after, Carlton," Swanson called from inside the den. "Come in, gentlemen."

Obviously not liking the idea, Bledsoe stepped back into the den.

Swanson waved them in.

He's acting like he has every card in the deck, Will thought. But he also realized that as a politician, Congressman Swanson was a trained showman. Furthermore, if he was guity of murdering George Haskins, he'd been lying this particular lie for the last seventeen years. In his mind, it might have even become the truth.

"They knew they couldn't get me when they came here. This is what they were after." Swanson waved toward the wall as panels slid apart to reveal the plasma-screen TV.

On the screen, a FOX News reporter stood in front of the security gates that sealed off Swanson's home. ". . . the director from the NCIS showed up with an arrest warrant at the congressman's home and—"

Swanson switched the television off.

Looking at Larkin, Swanson said, "You came out here tonight to put on a show that would stir up the media again. Well, since you've whetted their appetites with your arrest warrant that can't be served, let's go tell them how George Haskins was killed." He stood, totally in command. "And who did it." A smile curled his lips. "I think you'll enjoy this. But I don't think you're going to get the results you expected."

S CRIME SCENE  

 C

52

SCENE  NCIS  CRIME SCEN

NAVAL CRIMINAL INVESTIGATIVE SERVICE

>> ANGEL'S TRAILER COURT
>> MURFREESBORO, TENNESSEE
>> 2142 HOURS

Nita felt stunned and vaguely faint as she watched the EMTs work on her mother. They got her stabilized and started an IV to replace lost blood, wrapped her maimed hand in gauze for transportation, and placed her on a gurney. Her mother never woke, but she did keep breathing.

Nita focused on the slow rise and fall of her mother's chest and tried not to think about all the other damage. That could be repaired.

She'd been dead. Her mother had been dead.

While serving as an intern in Atlanta, Nita had seen people come back. She'd witnessed a five-year-old who had come back after accidentally drowning and being clinically dead for seven minutes—with no lasting damage. An elderly woman who'd been mugged had expired on the table and resuscitated just when Nita had been about to call the time of death. A sixty-year-old man whose heart had given out came back long enough to spend another three days in the hospital while his family had time to gather. There were others.

But none of them had felt as dead as her mother had. Until the time she started breathing on her own again.

The EMTs lifted the gurney and headed toward the ambulance. Police officers held the perimeter of the accident. A fire truck overshadowed the whole scene. All the whirling lights slashed the shadows to ribbons and caused Nita's eyes to throb.

Nita went over to the ambulance. "Where are you taking her?"

"Middle Tennessee Medical Center," the EMT said. "Over on North Highland Avenue. Can't miss it. It's the only hospital in town."

Nita thanked him and walked to her car.

A uniformed police officer stepped in her way. "Miss."

"Doctor. It's Doctor. Nita Tomlinson." Nita took her keys from her purse, noticing the blood—*her mother's blood*—on one corner.

"Dr. Tomlinson, what can you tell me about the accident?"

"It wasn't an accident. A woman deliberately ran my mother down."

"Excuse me. Did you just say the victim is your mother?"

Nita hesitated for just a moment. She hadn't intended to say that, but it was out of her mouth before she knew it. Angry with herself for her momentary weakness, she opened her door and slid behind the steering wheel. Geraldine Wallace stood nearby.

"You saw what happened?" the policeman asked.

"Yes." Nita pulled the door shut.

"You can't just leave," the policeman said.

"Yes, I can, and I am." Nita started the car.

"I need to get a statement before you go."

Nita glared at him, feeling the anger tightening up inside her and wanting to vent. "What you need and what I'm required to do are two different things. I'm not required by any law to offer a statement about anything." Despite being in the lab, she picked up a lot of the legal technicalities that the other special agents worked with. "Now get out of my way."

Reluctantly, lips pursed in anger, the police officer stepped back.

Nita put the Mustang in gear and pulled onto the street, following the ambulance. *Everything's going to be all right,* she told herself. But she didn't want to be alone with her fear. She wanted someone with her. *All it'll take is one call.*

She reached for her purse and took out her cell phone. Opening the phone, she started to enter Joe's number on speed-dial. Then she stopped herself. Calling Joe might make her feel better, but it wouldn't be fair to him. She'd only be using him.

And it would be confusing to Celia. Nita didn't want her daughter to grow up the way she had. It was better to make a clean break and stay out of their lives.

That was what she wanted, wasn't it?

Then Nita thought about her mother, run down in front of her own home by a jealous wife. That was where she had come from. That was what she was.

With a trembling hand, feeling more scared than she had since she'd been small and living in her mother's home, Nita put the phone back into the purse. She was alone.

❂ ❂ ❂

>> SILVER SPRING, MARYLAND

>> 2300 HOURS

"I'm not sure we should stay here for the unveiling," Larkin said.

"If we don't, we'll have to learn about it later," Will said.

The NCIS director frowned. "This is definitely his party, though."

Will silently agreed. The congressman was in his element. His ease showed in the way he calmly directed the setup and chatted with the different reporters he knew.

It had taken Swanson's security people almost an hour to move the reporters into the house from outside the estate. The media people grouped around their cameras in the huge living room. In addition to the security lights, other lights had been set up in the area. House staff served drinks and appetizers.

"Eleven o'clock at night and this guy has enough food and kitchen staff on hand to handle this crowd," Remy said. "What kind of guy does that?"

"A man who's prepared," Maggie stated quietly. "My father has done things like this." She nodded at Swanson. "He knew we were coming."

Will considered that, not liking where his thoughts immediately went. "Someone in the judge's office let Swanson know we had a warrant for him and that we were going to serve it."

"It's always nice to have a congressman's favor." Maggie didn't sound pleased. "Politics runs on favors. I should know."

"Something else to think about," Shel said. "If Swanson knew we were coming up here to make him look bad in the media, there's only one reason he'd hang around."

"To trap the trappers," Estrella said. "Computer-security people design honeypots—artificial sites and programs—to snare computer crackers trying to break in. By watching the crackers work, they learn their attacks and build safeguards around other areas they're really trying to defend."

"We're in it now," Larkin said unhappily. "Let's let it play. If we walk out before Swanson has a chance to run the river on this thing, we'll take a worse hit in the media."

Will knew Larkin was right.

"In the meantime," Larkin growled, "let's hope that arrogant jerk trips over his own ego and gives us something to work with."

Swanson circulated among his guests for a few minutes more, then stepped in front of the massive fireplace that Will could tell had been intentionally chosen as center stage. None of the tables bearing food or drink had been set up in the area.

It was all choreographed before we got here, Will realized. He glanced at his watch. At three minutes after eleven, the late news shows had just begun. *Plenty of time for them to go live.* He wondered if Swanson would have set up a morning address if they had gotten there any later.

"Ladies and gentlemen, if I could have your attention, please." Smiling benignly, Swanson held up his hands.

The crowd quieted. A few of them stepped forward with video cameras rolling, delivering short setups as the cameras went live.

"Many of you know, and those of you who don't are about to find out, that I've been served with an arrest warrant," Swanson said. "NCIS special agents are in my home at this minute. They've accused me of murdering George Haskins, a man they believe had something to do with my daughter's death seventeen years ago."

He's speaking in sound bites. Will knew then that the congressman's speech had been scripted. He didn't look at anyone on his team, but he suspected they had also figured out what was going on.

"If George Haskins did murder my daughter," Swanson went on, "I don't think anyone could find it in their heart to blame me." He paused dramatically, sweeping the audience with his eyes. "I think that any parent who killed the murderer of her child would be forgiven of that crime."

Her? Will had a bad feeling that he knew where Swanson was going. And there was nothing he could do to stop it.

"I just this evening learned why the NCIS believes I'm guilty of killing George Haskins, the suspected murderer of my daughter," Swanson said. "NCIS crime-scene investigators found a murder scene at the house I once occupied in Raleigh, North Carolina. They matched blood found there with DNA from George Haskins's body."

Will remained steadfast, knowing some of the cameras were now turned in the direction of the NCIS team. The look came from hours in drills spent at parade rest.

"What I'm about to show you," Swanson said, "is going to exonerate me but will bring to light a crime that I hope you—and the court system—will forgive. I have spent years in denial about this."

Bledsoe handed Swanson a file folder.

"This document contains the report given to me by a private investigator I retained seventeen years ago," Swanson said. "In it, along with photographs, is evidence of my then wife's affair with George Haskins. There's proof that he was inside our home. He had opportunity to know the layout of our home and where he could find Chloe the night he abducted her. Judging from Haskins's criminal file, kidnapping would have fit in with everything else he was doing."

Will pushed his breath out. Haskins kidnapping Chloe Ivers was an easy call after the charm had been found in his pants cuff.

"When I got this file, I didn't want to destroy my marriage. Being a politician's wife is hard. I wasn't home much. Laura obviously needed companionship I wasn't there to provide." Swanson's voice took on a soft timbre. "Our marriage survived for years after the death of our daughter." He paused. "I can only hope that she can forgive me what I reveal here tonight."

"Man," Shel whispered, "he's good."

"It's why he's a congressman," Remy whispered back.

"This," Estrella pointed out, "is a possibility we hadn't considered."

Will knew it was true. They'd never seriously looked at Laura Ivers as a suspect in her daughter's death. She'd been at Camp Lejeune that night—*But she could have gotten away*—and didn't have a motive—*We don't have a motive for Swanson either*—for killing her daughter.

"A few days after my daughter's funeral, I was called to Washington for a series of important meetings," Swanson said. "When I got back, I found the carpet in my den had been replaced. At my wife's request. She said she'd wanted to surprise me." He opened the file and took out a piece of paper. "This is the receipt for the carpet my wife had replaced in our house. According to the note here, the old carpet was severely damaged. The carpet company was given instructions to dump it."

"Is that what happened to it?" a reporter asked.

Swanson held up a hand. "Please refrain from questions. We don't have time for that at this point. I'm issuing a statement at this juncture." He took out another piece of paper. "This is another document I hung on to. Primarily to keep it out of the hands of the police. I wanted to protect my wife. It's a receipt for the purchase of a Colt Model 1911 .45 semiautomatic pistol. It's the same caliber weapon that the NCIS believe killed George Haskins."

Only the hum of the electronic equipment could be heard in the massive room.

"And finally, here's a contract for a safe-deposit box at American National Bank in Raleigh." Swanson held up another piece of paper. "I don't know what's in the safe-deposit box there. I've never asked. My name isn't on that contract." Swanson put all the papers back in the file and handed it to his attorney. "I didn't put all of this together until a few days ago."

It was, Will had to admit, a compelling story. And one that spun things out in a direction they hadn't considered.

"I believed my wife had bought the new carpet for my den to surprise me," Swanson said. "Whenever Laura got in a slump, whenever she was frustrated in some area of her life, she would redecorate. I didn't think anything of the new carpet. Losing our daughter hurt Laura terribly. I found out about the pistol and the safe-deposit box in the month that followed. I managed the family finances."

Why would Laura buy a pistol? Will wondered. As a naval officer, she already had one.

"I believe that pistol Laura purchased was used to kill George Haskins," Swanson said. "I also believe that pistol is in that safe-deposit box." He paused. "At the time, I didn't know George Haskins was dead. I thought he'd simply disappeared. Laura was despondent over Chloe's death. She didn't continue her affair with him. I . . . I . . ." His voice broke, and for a moment he bowed his head as if struggling for composure. "I tried to help Laura get through her grief. In the end, our marriage didn't survive. But even if I had known that Laura had killed the man who killed our daughter back then, I wouldn't have come forward. Under the Constitution of our great nation, I didn't have to. I was her spouse. The Bill of Rights guarantees that a spouse doesn't have to offer testimony against the other spouse."

Swanson pointed at the NCIS team.

All the cameras followed his accusing finger.

"The only reason I'm coming forward tonight is because the NCIS suspects me of killing the man who murdered my daughter," Swanson declared. "Even if I'd killed him, I think juries would find it in their hearts to be lenient to me. Given the circumstances, I would ask one favor."

The cameras moved back to the congressman, and he waited on them.

"I would ask that leniency be shown to Laura," Swanson said. "Maybe what she did is a crime in the letter of the law, but what she did—avenging her daughter—was justice that the law enforcement agencies involved in the investigation of my daughter's death could not deliver." He took a deep breath. "Laura, just know that I'm sorry it came to this. But if the truth has to come out, know that I will support you. Whatever I can do to help, I'm here."

"He's not just trying to exonerate himself," Larkin whispered in grim disbelief. "That creep is planning on using this as his platform for reelection."

Will's phone vibrated in his pocket. When he took it out, caller ID identified the caller as Laura Ivers. He pressed the Talk button and held the handset to his ear.

"Everything," Laura told Will in a voice shot through with anger and barely under control, "*everything* that monster is telling you is a lie!"

S  CRIME SCENE NCIS 

VE SERVICE

NAVAL CRIMINAL INVESTIGATIVE SERVICE

53

SCENE  NCIS  CRIME SCENE

NAVAL CRIMINAL INVESTIGATIVE SERVICE

>> ER WAITING ROOM
>> MIDDLE TENNESSEE MEDICAL CENTER
>> MURFREESBORO, TENNESSEE
>> 2316 HOURS

Nita sat in the waiting room. The cup of coffee in her hands had turned cold. She didn't feel like drinking it, but she didn't want to put it down because then her hands would have nothing to do.

The room wasn't properly designed for waiting. It was harshly lit and inelegant, filled with uncomfortable chairs, two televisions that hung from the ceiling, and a table and toys for kids. Nita thought of Celia, and in that moment, she was weak. She wanted to hold her daughter. To kiss her and smell her hair and listen to whatever strange deduction Celia had made about life today.

Nita steeled herself, telling herself that she didn't want her daughter to end up where she was tonight, sitting in a chair waiting to find out if the mother she wasn't sure if she loved or hated was going to live or die.

Because that's what would happen, Nita told herself fiercely. *You're not good enough for Joe or Celia. In the end, you'll fail. Even if you want to succeed, you're going to fail them.*

Other people sat in chairs around the room No one talked much to the other people waiting. The waiting room was a transitory place. No one there wanted to take on anyone else's problems.

Looking at her watch, Nita saw that only four minutes had passed since the last time she'd glanced at it. Her mother had been in surgery for the last thirty minutes. The attending physician had called in a specialist to reattach her mother's severed fingers. Dr. Jacobsen had been hopeful that they could be saved.

Nita leaned her head back against the wall and closed her eyes. She just wanted to go to sleep. Or to not care. Or to know which way she was supposed to feel.

It was all too confusing.

No one should have a life this hard.

"Nita."

Opening her eyes, Nita saw Geraldine Wallace standing before her. The old woman leaned on her cane and carried a large bag under her other arm.

"You feeling okay?" Geraldine asked.

"I'm all right," Nita said.

"Heard anything about your mama?"

Nita looked at her.

"I heard what you said to the policeman," Geraldine said. "I guess you weren't here doing a background check after all."

"No."

"You come all this way to see your mama?"

"Look," Nita said brusquely, "this isn't any of your concern."

Geraldine hesitated. "Carol's my friend. She's my concern."

Nita didn't say anything.

"And you're her daughter," the old woman went on, "so I guess you're my concern too." She pointed at the empty chair next to Nita. "Now . . . can I sit down?"

"I don't want company."

Ignoring her, Geraldine sat down. She rummaged in her bag. "Have they told you about your mama? how she's doing?"

Irritated, Nita didn't look at Geraldine. "She's in surgery. They've got a surgeon in attaching her fingers."

"Is she going to be all right?"

"They think so." Nita wanted to shut up, but she couldn't. "She drinks to excess, uses drugs, smokes, and doesn't take care of herself. Anything can happen."

"She's in God's hands now. That's the best place for anybody to be."

"God hasn't been very good to her so far."

"Maybe that's because your mama hasn't asked God to be."

Like that would make a difference, Nita thought. Before she could stop herself, she said, "If God knows my mother, even he wouldn't help her."

"You don't think so?"

"No. I'm really sure about that."

"Why?"

Nita hesitated, then talked because she wanted to remember why she didn't like her mother. It was hard to focus on that when she kept seeing her mother bent and broken in the street. "My mother," she said in a strained voice, "is not a good person."

"She has been to me."

Nita glared at the woman. "She got run down in the street by a woman whose husband she was cheating with."

"I didn't say your mama didn't have her problems. Everybody does."

"That's not an excuse."

"No, but maybe you might remember that a person is more than one thing."

Nita didn't say anything.

"Your mama was young when she had you," Geraldine said. "I know that because she told me about you."

"Why would she do that?"

"Women talk about their children, Nita. Their hopes, their dreams . . . and their problems with them. It's part of being a mother."

Nita said nothing. She avoided talking about Celia with other people who had kids because it seemed like all she ever had to talk about was one of the hundred ways she'd failed her family.

"She loved you, you know," Geraldine said.

"No," Nita whispered. "No, she didn't. We fought all the time. She was never there. She made . . . so many mistakes."

"Parents make mistakes. That's how they learn." The old woman shrugged. "If they do everything right, without making mistakes, how do they learn anything? How do their children?"

"She should have known how to love me. She should have known how to take care of me."

"Do you have a child?"

Nita didn't say anything.

"You do, don't you?"

"I don't want to talk about my daughter."

"We don't have to talk about her. But let me ask you a question. Did you know how to love her and take care of her?"

Nita looked away. The old woman's questions were hitting too close to home.

"You went to college and became a doctor," Geraldine said. "Why did you do that?"

"I knew that in order to take care of myself, I needed a job that paid well. I didn't want to live like my mother."

"Then perhaps she taught you something."

"I learned by her mistakes." Nita looked at the old woman. "But she's still making the same mistakes she always has."

Geraldine thought for a moment. "Did your mama ever have any close friends?"

Nita thought back, then shook her head. "No. There were people she used. People who used her. But no real friends."

"I'm her friend," the old woman said. "And she's my friend. She's helped me when I didn't have anyone else. And I've been there for her as much as I can be. She tries to be independent . . . but she hasn't learned how." She paused. "She's just not strong enough on her own. She hasn't learned what you have."

Nita closed her eyes and took a deep breath. *And I haven't learned enough.*

"She learned how to give up, and you learned how to push yourself to get somewhere."

"If you want something, you learn how to get it."

"Your mama," Geraldine said, "has been lost for a long time. Ever since her daddy kicked her out of the house when she was pregnant with you. She fought to just stay alive. She didn't know what she wanted or even what she was supposed to expect. She let that first boy she was with, your daddy, hurt her in ways that no one should allow another person to hurt them."

"What do you mean?" Nita found herself asking.

"She allowed your daddy, to convince her that she wasn't worth anything. She never got over that. All she knew was that kind of boy. And she chased him all these years. Right now, that boy is Buddy LeFevre, whose wife ran your mama down in front of her own home tonight."

Nita's eyes burned, and she looked away from the old woman, no longer able to bear the weight of her stare.

"Some people," Geraldine said, "spend their whole lives living out their foolish youth. Never learning anything. They just get caught up in it and don't know how to move on from there." She smiled. "Luckily, some of us finally learn and get out of it."

Closing her eyes, Nita said, "Look, I'm really tired. I'm afraid I don't feel much like talking."

"Then let me talk," Geraldine said, "and you just listen. Let me show you something."

"I don't mean to be rude, but—"

Geraldine lifted a book from her big bag. "Your mama and me go to bingo every now and again. Sometimes one of us wins a little. Not much and not often. If we win, we usually go out to eat. The winner buys. Then we usually buy a half gallon of ice cream to celebrate at home later." She patted the book. "But we do scrapbooking, too. In fact, I helped your mama make this one. It's the only one she's ever made."

Nita stared at the scrapbook. The picture on the front was her as a baby. When she left, she hadn't taken any pictures of herself. She hadn't wanted to remember anything. Celia sometimes asked for pictures of her mother as a child. Nita had told Joe that all the pictures had been lost in the same house fire that killed her parents.

"She made it for you," Geraldine said. "She wanted to give it to you when she was finished with it." She shook her head. "She claimed she wasn't finished with it, but she hasn't added anything in months. She's finished, but she was afraid to send it to you."

Although she didn't want to, Nita reached for the scrapbook and began leafing through it. Her past was on every page.

Looking back through the faded photographs, Nita saw her mother, saw her with the abusive men she'd been with, dressed in too-tight clothing and wearing black eyes and bruises on her wrists and neck, and saw her drinking at parties with other men and women who were just like her. In all the pictures, one thing kept leaping out at her.

"She was so young," Nita whispered.

"She was," Geraldine agreed.

"She's younger than I am in all of these pictures."

"She said she had you when she was sixteen."

Nita nodded, turning pages and watching herself grow up.

"And through it all," Geraldine said, "she never once gave you up. She didn't let the DHS have you and didn't just abandon you. It had to have been hard on her."

"I know," Nita said, thinking how lost she'd have been trying to deal with raising Celia by herself. Joe took to raising their daughter so easily, never seeming to find her a challenge, always finding time in his day for her.

Not once had Nita's mother had anyone, not a man or a parent, to help her.

Nita realized she was crying, tears streaming down her face for her mother as she had been and for her mother and herself as they were now. Geraldine held her and told her everything was going to be all right. But Nita didn't think so. She had ruined too many things.

CRIME SCENE

54

SCENE  NCIS  CRIME SCENE

NAVAL CRIMINAL INVESTIGATIVE SERVICE

>> RALEIGH-DURHAM AIRPORT
>> RALEIGH, NORTH CAROLINA
>> 0719 HOURS

Even dressed in khakis and a green blouse, Laura Ivers carried herself with the purposeful stride of a career soldier. To Will's trained eye, the woman stood out from the other airport passengers around her.

During the phone call last night, while watching the story that Swanson had spun out, Laura had stated that she was coming to Camp Lejeune. She'd even asked if she needed to surrender herself to arrest at the local NCIS offices in San Diego. Larkin had declined.

"Commander," Will called, stepping out from the wall.

Laura turned to face him, shifted her duffel, and offered her hand.

Will took it, feeling the confident strength in her grip. "Have a good flight?"

"I wasn't really paying attention to the flight, Commander."

"Call me Will. May I take your bag?"

She hesitated for a moment, then nodded and slid it from her shoulder. Will led and she followed.

"You didn't have to come pick me up," Laura said. "I'm sure you could have used the sleep."

"You didn't have to come to Camp Lejeune."

"I'd been accused of murder. I'm surprised I wasn't arrested."

"We don't have any evidence that you killed anyone."

"You will." Laura frowned. "Ben doesn't leave much to chance when he starts weaving his magic. This thing will be sealed with a kiss when you open it up."

Will didn't doubt that. Congressman Ben Swanson had impressed him in other ways that were less than favorable.

"He gave you an out," Will said. "Painted you as a heroic mother who got her gun and dealt out justice. The public is going to eat that up."

Laura sighed. "I know. My assistant told me calls have already come in from *Larry King Live, 60 Minutes,* and *The View.*"

"How are you holding up?" Will thought she looked strong and motivated, but she had been through a lot lately.

"I'm good. I'm mad now."

"Not scared?"

"I'm not going to let myself be scared. I didn't kill George Haskins. I never even met the man. Despite the fact that his blood was all over my house."

"I thought we'd stop for breakfast." Will walked past the souvenir shops.

"Shouldn't we get to Camp Lejeune? It's a three-hour trip."

"We have time for breakfast. My team has to try to check out the information that Swanson told the press last night. They'll have a shot at the carpet supplier and the gun shop. They're both still in business."

"What about the private investigator?"

"He was shot six years ago."

"Doesn't that sound suspicious to you?"

"He had set up a wife with a male prostitute, made it look like she was having an affair. The husband wanted out of the alimony situation the divorce was going to trigger. On the day the PI was supposed to deliver testimony, the wife shot him dead in front of the courthouse. She almost got the soon-to-be ex-husband, too."

"I take it the private investigator's reports about my affair with Haskins could be questionable?"

"Yes," Will said. "But they did exist seventeen years ago. I had a documents specialist review the papers. The congressman let us see the originals."

"That was generous."

"Suspiciously so."

Laura smiled a little. "One of the things you'll learn about the congressman: he's thorough."

"Something I learned in crime-scene investigation," Will told her. "When it comes to murder, no one is ever thorough enough. We'll find something. My team is good."

>> ROOM 110
>> MIDDLE TENNESSEE MEDICAL CENTER
>> MURFREESBORO, TENNESSEE
>> 0749 HOURS

Nita woke with the feeling that someone was watching her. And with the familiar gnawing sickness in her stomach that she'd woken up with for over a week. She swallowed and hoped she wouldn't throw up. It would be nice not to have to face that.

She tried to go back to sleep, but rest eluded her. The hospital smells around her seemed stronger than they had the night before, when she'd taken the cot the nurses had offered in her mother's room.

Finally, pushed further by protesting kidneys, she sat up. Dizziness played Ping-Pong inside her skull for a moment. Her stomach rolled.

"I didn't expect you here," a weak voice said.

Nita looked over at her mother on the bed. She looked worse this morning. Gauze and bandages covered her skin. Staples gleamed along her left temple. Her right hand was suspended and heavily bandaged, and her broken leg was in a cast.

"They offered me a bed," Nita said.

Her mother swallowed. "You didn't have to take it."

Anger sparked inside Nita. "Look, I don't have to stay. I knew this was a mistake. I'll go." She stood and picked up her coat and purse. The scrapbook fell to the floor.

The moment was awkward. Did she acknowledge the scrapbook? Or did she just walk out on her past—complete with pictures—again?

Nita picked up the scrapbook and placed it on the cot. She walked toward the door.

"I made that scrapbook for you," her mother said. "But I understand if you don't want it." She closed her eyes.

Get out! Leave! Nita knew now was her chance. The meds in her mother's system were probably so strong that she'd never even remember talking to her.

But she couldn't leave, not with her mother looking so small and frail on the bed.

"Do you need anything?" she asked.

"A cigarette," her mother said. She opened her eyes and smiled at Nita. "But I can't get one in here, can I?"

"No."

"I could use a drink."

"A shot and a chaser?" Nita couldn't resist the streak of meanness that rose up in her. The sickness swirled at the back of her throat.

"Water," her mother said, taking no offense.

Crossing to the table beside the bed, Nita dropped her coat and purse back on the cot. She picked up the carafe and poured a half glass of water. Gently, she lifted her mother's head and helped her drink.

Her mother managed only a few sips. "Thank you."

"You're welcome."

They were silent for a while. Even though the door was closed, they could still hear the hospital coming to life around them.

"I don't suppose a good-looking man has been by to check on me?" her mother asked. "His name is Buddy."

"No."

"Seems about my luck." Her mother sighed. "How bad is it?"

"What do you remember?"

"Just that car hitting me. Did they find out who it was?"

"It was Buddy LeFevre's wife, Mom." Nita shook her head in disgust. "Haven't you learned by now not to mess around with married men?" *And what about you?* she asked herself. *It wasn't that long ago that you almost wound up in the hospital from messing around with a married man yourself.*

Her mother grimaced. "That hag. If she hadn't run me down with the car like that, I could've whipped her."

Despite the situation, Nita couldn't help but smile. It was sad, but it was funny, too. That was how it had sometimes been with her mother. She'd forgotten that.

"What happened to my hand?" her mother asked.

"You almost lost two fingers. The ring finger and the pinkie. They had a specialist in to reattach them. Both of them still had blood circulating through them."

"That's a good thing?"

"A very good thing." Calmly and confidently, Nita laid out the rest of her mother's injuries.

"Everything's going to be okay?" her mother asked when she was finished.

"It will," Nita said. "It'll just take time."

Her mother was quiet for a while. "I'm gonna lose my job," she whispered. "My place. My car. All of it's gonna be gone." She swallowed hard. "I'm just so tired, Nita. I'm tired of losing everything I ever cared about."

Nita felt sorry for her mother. She didn't know what to say.

Tears leaked from her mother's eyes. She cursed. "I hate when I cry. I hate being weak." She wiped her tears away with her good hand. "I keep telling myself that I can't let myself care about anything. No matter what it is, as soon as I start caring about it, it's taken away from me. Or it walks out the door." Her voice broke. "You'd think by now I'd know not to expect anything to go right for me."

Barely holding back tears of her own, Nita pulled tissues from the box by the bed and handed them to her mother.

"Thank you," her mother said.

"You're welcome." Another wave of nausea swept over Nita. She went to the bathroom and threw up. Afterward, she splashed water on her face, feeling weak and washed-out.

"Are you coming down with something?" her mother asked when she returned to the room.

"I think it's just nerves," Nita said. "I've had a lot of stress at . . . at work lately."

They didn't have anything to say after that, and a little while later Nita's mother was asleep again. Nita thought about leaving. Instead, she lay back down on the cot, wrapped up in the blanket, and watched her mother sleep.

Was what her mother felt true? Was she doomed to lose everything? Had that passed on to her? Nita didn't know, but she thought about it until she went back to sleep.

>> PERKINS FAMILY RESTAURANT
>> RALEIGH, NORTH CAROLINA
>> 0837 HOURS

"Let's say that Swanson is trying to frame you," Will said. He kept his voice low enough that the morning restaurant crowd couldn't hear him.

Most of the patrons appeared to be regulars, talking to each other about familiar subjects. With the restaurant located only a short distance from 440, the loop around Raleigh, out-of-towners often ate there and were ignored by the locals.

"He is." Laura bit into a piece of toast.

Will stirred his sunny-side-up eggs, sliding pieces of breakfast sausage through the yolk before popping them into his mouth. "In that case, I see only two plausible motives," he said. "Swanson either killed Haskins himself or is trying to protect whoever did."

"But whom would he be trying to protect?"

"His son?"

Laura shook her head. "Jeff's not under suspicion for killing Haskins. And I still don't believe Jeff killed my daughter. He was only a child."

"If Swanson killed Haskins," Will mused, "we still have the question of motive."

"Retaliation for Chloe's murder?"

"Maybe. But if that was true, why would he go to all the trouble to frame you? As much as I hate to say it, I think what the congressman said during his little speech last night is true: no one would blame a parent—or a stepparent—for killing the man who murdered his child."

"Then there must be some other reason."

"I do have a tentative link between the two men," Will said. "Haskins may have blackmailed an incumbent state representative to step out of the election that resulted in Swanson's election to the House."

"How tentative?"

"I can't make it stick," Will admitted. "But I've got it on good authority that Haskins had been investigated regarding that blackmail."

"Even if you can place Haskins with Ben, where does that get you?"

"Nowhere by itself. But Haskins also knew a man named Bryce Ketchum."

"That's the man who owned the farm where Haskins's body turned up?"

Will nodded. "Haskins and Ketchum knew each other. They grew up together in Kentucky before they moved to Jacksonville."

Laura seemed surprised. "Kentucky? Where in Kentucky?"

Will took out his iPAQ and checked his notes. "Hopkinsville. Why?"

"Didn't you do a background check on Ben?"

"Of course."

"Then you should have known."

"Known what?"

"Ben grew up in Kentucky before he moved to North Carolina. He graduated from high school in Hopkinsville, Kentucky."

Will took out his phone and called Estrella. "Do you have Swanson's file?"

"I can pull it up," Estrella said.

Will's mind worked furiously. A case had to be solid and they were nowhere near close enough, but things were starting to add up.

"Okay," Estrella said, "what am I looking for?"

"Where did Congressman Swanson graduate high school?"

Estrella paused. "Hopkinsville, Kentucky."

"Where was he born?"

A slight pause passed again. "The same place. Will, isn't that where George Haskins and Bryce Ketchum were from?"

"Yes, it is," Will said.

"That means they could have all known each other."

"Yes, it does. How did we miss that?"

"We weren't looking for a tie that went that far back," Estrella admitted. "And we weren't necessarily looking for connections between all three of them."

"Now we are. See what else you can dig up through that link. See if these guys grew up together. Geography binds people almost as much as blood." Will closed the phone, noticing that Laura had finished her meal. "There's one other thing I need to ask you. And it's going to be hard."

"All of this is hard."

Will knew there was no way he could soft sell what he needed to ask. "I want to exhume Chloe's body."

Laura closed her eyes. "Will, I buried my baby seventeen years ago. It was the second-hardest thing I've ever had to do. The hardest was picking up and keeping on with my life."

"I know," Will said. He still felt that way over his divorce. "But it's possible that the medical examiner missed something seventeen years ago."

"How?"

"They were looking for validation that Isaac Allen Lamont killed her. With all the injuries Chloe had suffered, I think they just confirmed that she'd been strangled. They didn't look for anything else."

"What should they have looked for?"

Will shook his head. "I don't know. That's why I want the team medical examiner, Nita Tomlinson, to have a look. But only if you say so."

Tears filmed Laura's eyes, and she leaned back in the booth. "I don't know if I can do this again. I don't know if I can bury her twice."

Will hesitated, trying to find the right words. "Seventeen years ago you buried Chloe not believing Isaac Allen Lamont was her killer. Give me a chance—give *yourself* a chance—to do it right. Swanson is hiding something."

"Jeff didn't kill Chloe."

"But somebody did. Haskins was killed for a reason, in the house where your daughter was taken. This starts with Chloe's death. We need another look."

After a long time, Laura nodded, unable to speak.

"All right," Will said. "Thank you." He just hoped that he could—that *Nita* could—find something so that everything he was putting Laura Ivers through would be justified. To do that, though, he was going to have to find Nita and get her back to the NCIS lab.

55

SCENE  NCIS  CRIME SCENE

NAVAL CRIMINAL INVESTIGATIVE SERVICE

>> ROOM 110
>> MIDDLE TENNESSEE MEDICAL CENTER
>> MURFREESBORO, TENNESSEE
>> 1209 HOURS

When lunch came, Nita watched her mother try to feed herself. She wasn't successful. With her right hand incapacitated and in her weakened state, she couldn't do it. She grew frustrated quickly.

Feeling trapped by circumstances, Nita stood and said, "Let me help you."

Her mother looked at her for a long time. Then, almost grudgingly, she gave up the spoon.

"Mashed potatoes or chicken salad?" Nita asked.

"Potatoes."

Nita scooped up some potatoes.

"Make sure you get some of that gravy on them. I don't think I could choke down these instant potatoes without gravy. You'd think hospital food would be better."

Nita spooned food into her mother's mouth. It reminded her of times when she'd fed Celia.

"I remember when I used to do this for you," her mother said.

"I don't," Nita said, hoping to break the conversation. They'd been talking too much as it was. She wanted to leave and didn't know why she didn't. Maybe it would have been easier if she'd known where to go.

"Feeding you was always fun," her mother said. "You'd end up with food everywhere. I wasn't very good at it."

There were a lot of things you weren't very good at.

"But I just kept at it," her mother said. "I didn't have a choice. If I hadn't fed you, you would have starved."

"Maybe we could do this without the trip down memory lane," Nita suggested.

Her mother chewed chicken salad and swallowed. "I know you hate me, Nita. I get that. Maybe those years were horrible for you, but there were some good times in there for me. I just didn't know it till one day you went from being this baby to being eleven years old and faulting me for everything I did."

"I had reason to."

"I know."

Nita thought maybe it was the painkillers running through her mother's system that made her so talkative. There was no other excuse.

"Some days, baby girl," her mother said, "you were the only bright spot in my whole day."

"Then maybe you should have spent more time at home."

"I couldn't. I had work to do. And somewhere in there I was supposed to find a man. My mama always told me a woman wasn't nothin' without a man."

"That's stupid." Nita had never known her grandparents. She didn't even know if they were still alive.

"Maybe," her mother said. "But that's what she told me. That's why she stayed with Daddy, and he was the meanest drunk in all of Murfreesboro."

That shocked Nita. "Your parents live here?"

"They did. They died a while back. After I left home, Daddy never let me come back. I never saw either of them again. I've got a brother that lives up in Nashville, but I haven't seen him either."

"Why did you come back here?"

Her mother laughed a little. "I was kind of shocked when I ended up here too. But where else was I gonna go? I'd been thrown out everywhere. Nobody wanted me." She took a deep breath. "I thought I was just gonna stay a few weeks, but then I met Geraldine, and she needed help. I ended up staying longer than I should have. If I'd had any sense, I'd have picked up and left as soon as Buddy LeFevre looked at me twice. But I'd always had a crush on him in high school. I guess it was just an itch I had to scratch. I didn't know he was married until last night." She shook her head and smiled sadly. "I shoulda known it was too good to be true, him being interested in me for me instead of what I was willing to give him. You want to know the really sad part?"

"What?"

"I broke it off with him last night. Told him I'd found out he was married and I didn't want to see him again. His wife didn't have to run me over with her car. Now she's probably gonna go to jail, and I'm sure running over me didn't help the looks of her car." Her mother laughed as though it was one of the biggest jokes she'd ever heard.

Despite herself, Nita laughed too. She felt sad and happy and mad all at the same time, and it was confusing. But talking to her mother was easier than she'd expected, and when lunch was over and the stories kept coming, Nita didn't stop them.

>> NCIS HEADQUARTERS
>> CAMP LEJEUNE, NORTH CAROLINA
>> 1453 HOURS

"How bad is it?" Larkin asked. He sat across from Will in Will's office. He didn't look any more rested than Will felt.

With all the traveling he'd been doing, Will hadn't slept at all the night before, but he'd managed a couple hours in his office chair after he'd arrived back with Laura Ivers.

"The notes the private investigator gave Swanson look legitimate," Will said. "I had our forensic document examiners look over the papers the congressman gave us. The papers all have the same chemical signatures."

When he'd first started at NCIS, Will had been surprised to learn that paper manufacturing differed from company to company and from run to run. It was simple to find out if the papers were all from the same batch and time period by comparing their chemical characteristics. Some papers had watermarks, and forged watermarks tended to have fewer fibers than the rest of the page.

"What about the ink?"

"They compared it, too. It was all from the same printer."

"The ink was the same on all the pages?"

Will nodded. Microspectrophotometry assured them that the ink on all the pages was from the same source and at the same time. Thin-layer chromatography measured the distances that ink molecules migrated when applied to paper.

Document forgers had gotten so good that most ink manufacturers had started mixing in fluorescent-dye tags to identify their products. They changed the tags on a yearly basis, so it was even roughly possible to identify what year a document was printed. Unless a forger used old ink.

Larkin thought for a moment. "*All* the papers were printed at the same time?"

Will nodded. "The paper and inks are aged, and they have the same consistency throughout."

"How long was this private eye supposedly watching Commander Ivers?"

Will checked his notes. "Six weeks."

"And in that time, this guy never changed reams of paper or an ink cartridge or ribbon?"

For a moment, Will didn't get what Larkin was driving at. Then it clicked into place. *I must be tired. I've been looking at this too closely—couldn't see the forest for the trees.* "The reports should have been generated at different times. There should have been differences in the paper and ink."

"Yeah," Larkin said. "There should have been."

"I missed that."

"If I hadn't had a case similar to that in New York while I was on the force, I wouldn't have known about it, Will. This is a field where we get an education in psychology, sociology, and a half dozen hard sciences every day."

"Swanson must have had the reports generated all at one time. Therefore they can't be legit."

"What about pictures?"

"Very few. In some of them you can't identify Haskins, and in others you can't identify Laura."

"No one picture of them together where they're both identifiable?"

"No."

"I suppose Swanson could say the guy wasn't good at camera work."

"He could say that," Will agreed, "but I'd like to see him try to explain how the guy he hired was a lousy photographer *and* never once changed the paper or ink in his printer in six weeks."

"What about the carpet supplier and the gun-shop owner?"

"Both of them picked Laura out of the six-pack Shel and Remy showed them." A six-pack was a photographic lineup consisting of a suspect and five other people.

"I'll argue that the only reason those people fingered Laura Ivers's picture is that her face has been in the press so much recently. There's no way they can remember what she looked like seventeen years ago. All Swanson would have had to do was hire a stand-in. What about the pistol in the bank box?"

"The Raleigh Police Department claimed the safe-deposit box this morning. I haven't heard anything from them."

"All right," Larkin said. "I'll see what I can do about getting an information exchange set up. How are we doing on the exhumation?"

"Maggie's working on it. So far, even though Laura has given her consent, I haven't gotten a judge willing to sign off on it."

"Swanson casts a long shadow."

"That's what Maggie said. A lot of judges like to have a political favor or two in their pocket. This one is an easy one to give: all they have to do is nothing." Will frowned. "Maggie also thinks her father has added his weight to the situation. But she thinks she can find a judge. Not everyone cares for Swanson."

"Or Maggie's father," Larkin said. "Have you reached Nita?"

"Not yet. She's not picking up her phone."

"Do you know where she is?"

"No, sir."

Larkin clearly wasn't happy about that. "This is a bad time for her to be gone."

"Yes, sir," Will agreed. "But I haven't got the exhumation papers yet either. She's not needed yet."

"I'll get back to you once I hear from the Raleigh PD," Larkin said. "In the meantime, find Nita."

>> ROOM 110
>> MIDDLE TENNESSEE MEDICAL CENTER
>> MURFREESBORO, TENNESSEE
>> 1505 HOURS

Geraldine Wallace arrived in the afternoon to visit. She carried a small vase of flowers with a single *Get Well* helium balloon tied to it.

"Well, good afternoon," Geraldine said.

"Good afternoon to you, too, Geraldine." Carol Purdue's eyes widened at the flowers. "You didn't have to do that."

Nita got up, took the vase from the old woman, and put it on the table near the window.

"I know I didn't have to," Geraldine said.

"They're too expensive."

"I had a little bingo money put back. I'm all right." Geraldine sat in one of the chairs by the bed. She looked at Nita. "So. Are the two of you getting along?"

Carol looked at Nita and smiled a little. "I guess we are. She's a doctor, you know. She coulda pulled the plug on me before now."

Geraldine laughed at that. "Well, I've got some good news for you."

"I could use some good news."

"It appears that you're tougher than Gloria LeFevre's car. After she hit you with it, she didn't make it fifteen blocks before that thing went to pieces." The old woman cackled.

Carol joined in, and the laughter was so real and infectious that Nita joined in before she knew it.

"I guess next time Gloria better get a bigger car," Carol said.

And that set off another wave of laughter.

Listening to her mother, Nita remembered what it was like to hear her laugh. Looking back on everything, especially thumbing through the scrapbook while her mother dozed off and on, not all the memories had been bad. There had been some good times in there.

"Well, Gloria's not very happy," Geraldine said. "She's sitting in jail right now."

"Do tell?"

Nita sat back and listened to the two women gossip about the news going through the trailer court. After a while, her mother drifted off to sleep.

Geraldine turned to her. "It's good, you being here. I think it's helping your mama."

Cold dread seized Nita's heart. "I'm not staying." *At least not if I can figure out what I'm supposed to do.*

"I know. But you being here right now, that's a good thing. My, my, but don't the Lord work in mysterious ways? If you hadn't been here when you were, I think we mighta lost your mama."

"If I hadn't been here, she wouldn't have followed me out into the street," Nita reminded her. She'd been telling herself all day not to feel guilty about that.

Geraldine waved that away. "If Gloria hadn't got her last night, she'd have waited. Would have got her some other night. And it woulda been when you wasn't there to save her."

Nita shook her head and didn't know what to say.

"Have you told your mama yet?" Geraldine asked.

"Told her what?"

"What you come all this way to say?"

Nita thought about that. "I don't know. I thought I had before I left her house last night. I told her as plain as I could that it was her fault I've got the trouble I've got."

"What trouble is that, honey?"

At first Nita wasn't going to say anything. Then, in the quiet of the hospital, hundreds of miles from Joe and Celia, missing them more than she'd thought she ever could, she talked to a stranger about how she thought she'd never be good enough to be a mother and a wife.

When she was finished, Nita was surprised to find that she'd been crying. Geraldine had pressed tissues into her hands, and now Nita was holding a sodden mess that she didn't know what to do with.

"Honey," Geraldine said, "I'm gonna tell you something, and you take it to your heart. Two things, actually."

Nita looked at the old woman, not knowing if she wanted to hear what Geraldine had to say.

"Number one—and I believe this with everything in me—the Lord wouldn't have given you that baby and that man if he hadn't figured you could all do each other some good. And number two, there's not a woman alive worth her salt that hasn't been afraid of not being good enough for a good man and a child she loved." Geraldine nodded toward Carol. "Your mama, she's fought with those same fears all your life. She just wasn't able to get up on top of them. But you, Nita, you're different. Being raised up by your mama like you were has made you a different woman. You got strength in you that you ain't even used yet. My hand on a stack of Bibles to that."

Even though Nita thought she was all cried out, she still found a few more tears. "I've messed everything up," she whispered. "I ran. Just like I ran when I got old enough to leave Mom. I'm afraid of failing. I'm afraid of not being good enough."

"What you're afraid of," Carol said quietly, "is being your mama."

Nita hadn't realized her mother had woken up. Ashamed, she looked at the broken woman on the bed. "Yes," she whispered.

"Baby girl," her mother said, "you ain't never been like me. Not since you drew your first breath of air. Your mind works different from mine. You're smart. You're curious. More than that, you didn't let your circumstances keep you down. You got out, Nita, and you made something of yourself. There's nobody trying to take that away from you but your own fears."

Geraldine put one of her shaking hands on Nita's hand. "Whenever I get scared, honey, I just pray to the Lord. I ask him for the strength that I don't have. And you know what?"

Nita looked at the old woman and shook her head.

"There has never been a time when God didn't give me enough strength to do what I set out to do if I really wanted to do something. When you get scared and need help, call on the Lord and let him guide you."

"You're not me, Nita," her mother whispered from the bed. "You'll never be me. I've been glad about that every day of my life."

Nita put her face in her hands and rocked herself, letting the tears come.

56

SCENE ⊛ NCIS ⊛ CRIME SCENE

NAVAL CRIMINAL INVESTIGATIVE SERVICE

>> NCIS HEADQUARTERS
>> CAMP LEJEUNE, NORTH CAROLINA
>> 0814 HOURS

"Do you see this scar?"

Will peered over Estrella's shoulder at one of the pictures of Jeff Swanson from when he'd been taken into custody on Wednesday. The scar was old and faded.

"What about it?" Frustration chafed at Will. It was Friday morning, and Maggie still hadn't gotten a judge to sign off on the exhumation.

"I talked to Laura." Estrella nodded to Laura, who sat beside her. "She confirmed that the scar is an old one. When she married Swanson, Jeff was only four. He had the scar then."

"Do you have a point?"

"Yes, sir."

Will knew he was being testy, but he couldn't help it. Last night he'd finally gotten some sleep, but he hadn't rested well. The media pressure on the investigation was snowballing. Chloe Ivers's murder had captured national attention because of the lies and hidden truths and the fact that a well-known congressman was at the eye of the storm.

"At ease, Estrella," Will said. "I'm working on my own issues here. It's not you."

"I know." Estrella pulled up pictures of the car Deanna Swanson had been murdered in. "Since we know now from the bullet Nita recovered from Bryce Ketchum that he was there the day Deanna Swanson was shot and killed, I decided to have the lab try to match his DNA with the two samples the Raleigh police acquired from the car."

"And?"

"Neither of them matched."

"I thought we'd established that."

"We did. I was reminding you. Working on a hunch, I had the lab compare the two blood samples. We're able to do more with it than they could back then. Here's what they found."

Estrella brought up pages of lab results.

"What am I looking at?" Will squinted at the screen.

"The mitochondrial DNA from the two samples matched," Estrella said. "The investigators couldn't test for that back then. The blood came from a mother and a child."

What Estrella was saying slammed into Will. "Jeff Swanson was in the car that day. He saw his mother killed."

"And he was nearly killed himself," Estrella said. "No wonder he's had problems all his life."

"If he was in the car, how did he get back home? The congressman claims his son was with him at the time his wife was killed."

"There's only one way that baby got home. Either Swanson was there when his wife was killed—"

"No, he was at home. There are witnesses."

"—or the killers brought his son back to him."

And that, Will felt certain, must have been what happened. "But why would they bring the baby back if they were just there to take the car?"

"They wouldn't."

Will nodded. "They went there to murder her." He straightened up and looked at Laura Ivers as the full implications of Swanson's deception hit him. "And Swanson lied about his son being there and tried to cover up his relationship with Haskins and Ketchum because he was in on it. It's the only explanation. He must have hired Haskins and Ketchum to kill his first wife." Suddenly it all made sense. Swanson's involvement explained everything. But they still had no tangible proof. Nothing that would stand up in court or be strong enough to bring down a congressman.

"Will?"

Glancing up, Will saw Maggie approaching.

"I found a judge," Maggie said. "He signed off on the exhumation order. We can go."

"All right," Will said. "Get Remy and Shel."

"They're already out front waiting."

Turning to Estrella, Will asked, "Have you been calling Nita?"

"Every half hour. She's still not answering."

A chill ran through Will. If Nita wasn't picking up, there must be a problem. "Keep trying."

"I will."

Laura stood and grabbed her jacket and purse. "I'm going too."

Will looked at her. "This isn't going to be easy."

"None of it has been so far."

Knowing he'd have a fight on his hands if he refused her, Will nodded and headed for the front entrance.

>> ROOM 110
>> MIDDLE TENNESSEE MEDICAL CENTER
>> MURFREESBORO, TENNESSEE
>> 0839 HOURS

Nita came out of the bathroom still feeling nauseous. The toothpaste hadn't really cut the taste of vomit.

"Are you okay?" her mother asked.

"Yes." Nita picked through the clothes she'd bought at the local Wal-Mart Thursday evening. It was the first time in almost fourteen years she'd bought anything that hadn't come from a fashion store.

"You threw up yesterday morning too," her mother said.

"I know, Mom." Nita picked out a pair of jeans and a red blouse.

"You're sure you're not sick."

"I'm sure. I'm a doctor, remember? I'd know if I was sick."

Nita went into the bathroom, showered, and changed into the new clothes. Back in her mother's room, she pulled on a pair of hiking boots and laced them up.

"That blouse really looks good on you," her mother said.

"Thanks."

"It brings out your hair. You've got your grandmother's hair."

"I didn't know that," Nita said.

Her mother looked sad. "I know. Do you feel like eating?"

"Not yet." Nita's stomach still hadn't settled.

"How long have you been getting sick mornings?"

Nita shrugged. "About a week or so."

Her mother was quiet for a moment, picking at the coffee cake that had come with her breakfast. "You know, I was sick every morning for a few weeks when I was pregnant with you."

Nita didn't say anything.

"Did you have morning sickness when you were pregnant with your daughter?"

"Yes," Nita said.

Her mother nodded. "You may have more problems than you thought."

>> OAKWOOD CEMETERY
>> RALEIGH, NORTH CAROLINA
>> 1327 HOURS

What had been—and would again be—Chloe Ivers's final resting place was beautiful. Shaded by trees in the quiet serenity of the Watauga Street side, the grave site seemed peaceful and promising, like there was a better place to go to after leaving this world.

Will hated disrupting the girl's rest and hated bringing the sound of machinery into the cemetery. What he hated most, though, was bringing the media there.

It hadn't taken long for the local news teams to find out the NCIS team was on-site at Oakwood Cemetery. Will had been forced to call reinforcements from the Raleigh PD and the sheriff's office, which hadn't exactly engendered goodwill on the part of either agency. The media and a crowd of spectators stood behind the yellow *NCIS Crime Scene* tape.

The diesel-powered backhoe clanked and snorted as the blade scraped away the earth over Chloe Ivers's casket.

Laura Ivers stood silently by. She looked emotionally drained.

A few minutes later, the backhoe driver pulled away. Shel and Remy climbed into the hole and started digging with shovels. When they were close enough, they got down on their knees and brushed off the remaining dirt by hand.

I'm sorry, Will thought. *But you've got to help us one last time, Chloe. Then we'll put you to rest properly.*

>> ROOM 110
>> MIDDLE TENNESSEE MEDICAL CENTER
>> MURFREESBORO, TENNESSEE
>> 1348 HOURS

Holding on to the sides of the bathroom sink, Nita felt like she was going to throw up again.

This can't be happening.

But she looked at the early pregnancy test again. The plus sign was still there. It didn't fade. It didn't go away.

Nita cried as silently as she could, not knowing what she was going to do.

Her mother called from the room. "Nita."

Wiping her face, Nita tried to get control of herself. She didn't know what she was going to do. She and Joe hadn't been trying to have more children, but they hadn't always used precautions either.

Now—

Now she was pregnant.

She was trapped again. Only this time she didn't have Joe and Celia.

"Nita?"

She threw the test in the trash and walked out of the bathroom.

Her mother looked at her, silently asking the question that neither of them wanted to say out loud. Without a word, she held her good arm out to Nita.

For a moment Nita held her ground. Then she went to her mother and let her mother hold her. Nita's tears came hot and heavy.

"Shhhhh," her mother whispered into her ear. "Everything's gonna be all right. You'll see. You'll figure this out."

Nita let herself be held, feeling lost and overwhelmed. She hadn't expected this. She hadn't seen this coming. She wasn't supposed to be pregnant. She didn't know what she was going to do.

>> OAKWOOD CEMETERY
>> RALEIGH, NORTH CAROLINA
>> 1359 HOURS

"How are you holding up?" Maggie looked at Laura Ivers, standing beside her. Her heart went out to the woman as Shel and Remy finished uncovering the casket and attached chains to extract it from the grave.

"I'm going to be fine," Laura said.

Maggie thought the declaration sounded more like a mission statement than a condition.

Tears leaked from beneath the rims of Laura's sunglasses. "The thing

I keep remembering," she said in a hoarse voice, "is how much time I lost with her. It was a two-and-a-half-hour commute every day to Camp Lejeune. I still had quarters on base because I sometimes had to stay over. Occasionally Chloe stayed with me. Jeff never did because he couldn't bear to be out of his bedroom at night."

"Don't think about the times you weren't there for her," Maggie said. "Think about the times you *were* there."

"It's hard to do that."

"I know." Maggie took a deep breath. "When I was just a girl, my mother was institutionalized. She dealt with clinical depression all her life." She chose not to reveal how Harrison Talbot Foley III had contributed to that with his endless stream of mistresses. "One day, my mother couldn't handle it anymore. She tried to commit suicide. Only she didn't take enough pills. The doctors worked with her and got her better. A few months later, she tried to commit suicide again. This time she used a razor. After her third attempt, my father had her put away. She's still there, and she still thinks that someday she's going to get to come home."

"That's terrible."

"I know," Maggie said. "I could have chosen to believe my mother died. It would be much easier simply to forget her, to never see her. But that's just not who I am. So I go every chance I can, but she's back in Boston and I can't go often." She took a deep breath, feeling the tightness in her throat. "I could remember how I found her after her second suicide attempt, how she acted when she was depressed. Instead I remember how she was during the good times, when she could be there with me and go shopping or take me to the park." She looked at Laura. "I choose to remember my mother when she was healthy. I'll bet Chloe didn't think about the times you were gone. She looked forward to the times you were there."

"I hope so," Laura said.

Maggie took the woman's hand and held it as Remy and Shel climbed from Chloe Ivers's grave.

57

SCENE  NCIS   CRIME SCEN

NAVAL CRIMINAL INVESTIGATIVE SERVICE

>> ROOM 110
>> MIDDLE TENNESSEE MEDICAL CENTER
>> MURFREESBORO, TENNESSEE
>> 1402 HOURS

"Were you and your husband planning to have another baby?"

Emotionally drained, Nita sat by her mother's bed. "We never really talked about it."

"A man always wants a son."

Nita shook her head. "Joe's never said that. I know he wants more children, though. He's always liked the idea of a big family."

"Well, I guess that's all right if he's not the one staying there taking care of them."

Guilt shot through Nita again. "I'm the one who's not there, remember? And even if I were, Joe's not like that. He's the kindest, most wonderful man you could ever hope to meet. He's understanding and considerate. Every spare moment he has he spends with Celia."

"Celia? That's your daughter's name?"

"Yes."

"It's a pretty name."

"She's a pretty girl."

Her mother hesitated. "Do you have any pictures?"

Knowing she was about to cross a line she couldn't uncross later, Nita reached for her purse and took out a picture of Joe and Celia.

"She's pretty." Her mother smiled. "She looks like you."

"She looks like Joe. It's almost like I had nothing at all to do with her."

"You're just not looking at her right, baby girl. Celia—I do love that name; I couldn't think of a better name for a grandbaby—has her daddy's hair and eyes, but she's got your nose and your chin. I can see you in her even if you can't." Her mother looked at her. "Why aren't you in this picture?"

"I was supposed to be. Joe had a family portrait set up. I had to do an autopsy on a Marine who'd died of carbon monoxide poisoning. I couldn't make the sitting. I've . . . missed a lot of things, Mom. A lot of things."

"It must be hard. Doing your job and trying to be a wife and mother too."

"It's impossible," Nita said. "There aren't enough hours in the day, and I just don't have the energy for it. I've never been a good wife and mother."

"Did Joe tell you that?"

"No, but he's been disappointed when I've missed things."

"Well, you can understand that."

"I can, but there's nothing I can do about it. My job doesn't come with regular hours. Not always. It's very demanding."

"You could do something else."

"But I don't want to. I love what I do. When I'm working, trying to figure out what killed someone, trying to give Will and the others a direction to investigate, that's when I feel alive. I'm . . ."

"Worth something," her mother suggested. "For the first time in your life, you feel like you're worth something."

Nita looked at her mother. "Yes."

"I can only imagine what that must be like," her mother said softly.

"But I'm constantly torn over what I should do."

Her mother was quiet for a moment. "That's how real life is, Nita. You show up, and if you're lucky, you have a plan. After that, no matter what you thought you'd be doing, you wing it."

"Winging it isn't good enough."

"Let me ask you something."

Nita hesitated, then nodded. "All right."

"Did your husband—did Joe—ask you to leave?"

"No."

"Then maybe you should ask him what he thinks. Before you start thinking for both of you." Her mother took a deep breath. "In the meantime, there's something I think you ought to see." She lifted the remote control. "While you were in the bathroom, there was a story about the NCIS that started breaking on the FOX News network. Didn't you say you worked with a man named Coburn?"

"Yes."

"Well, he's on this." Her mother turned on the television set.

Not knowing what to expect, Nita looked at the television and watched as a casket was hoisted from the grave. The announcer and the banner at the bottom of the screen gave the information about who was inside. Nita recognized the name at once and knew that Will had probably been calling for her. If he was exhuming a body, there was little doubt that he would need her there.

Rummaging inside her purse, Nita found her cell phone. Then she discovered the battery was dead.

>> OAKWOOD CEMETERY
>> RALEIGH, NORTH CAROLINA
>> 1409 HOURS

"Commander Coburn."

Will watched as Chloe Ivers's casket was gently lowered to the ground. Then he turned to find Detective Mark Broward standing beside him.

The Raleigh police detective looked as rumpled as ever. Will hadn't spoken with him since the tip about George Haskins potentially working with Swanson.

"Detective," Will greeted.

"I reckon you're about to ruffle some congressional feathers." Broward came to a stop beside Will.

"Probably," Will admitted.

"I also heard you had trouble finding a judge to sign off on the exhumation papers. I expect Swanson had a hand in that."

"I haven't asked."

"Well, his attorney—Bledsoe—has been in touch with my captain on an hourly basis."

"Why?"

"Bledsoe wants to know why we don't have Laura Ivers in custody after everything Congressman Swanson gave us."

"You found the pistol?" Will asked.

Broward nodded. "Laura Ivers's prints were all over it. Including the rounds. She loaded the pistol."

Will wasn't surprised that friction ridges, fingerprints, had been found. They lasted up to forty years and sometimes longer on paper and other porous substances. Even on nonporous substances, such as plastic and metal, the oils from the friction ridges could last for many years if kept dry and not subjected to the elements.

"I've got a theory about that pistol," Will said.

"I'm all ears, Commander."

"It's the same kind of sidearm as the one Commander Ivers regularly carried, right? I'm betting it was identical. And I'm betting Swanson knew where she kept it."

"So it would be easy for him to swap it out, let her carry the one we found, then switch again, and suddenly the commander's prints are on the murder weapon." Broward smiled. "You and I have devious minds."

"I'm afraid it comes with the job."

"And we both like Swanson for this more than that poor girl's mother."

"I'm glad we see eye to eye on that. Did you get the GRCs from the round we recovered from Haskins?" He'd had Estrella e-mail the general rifling characteristics of the bullet fragments Nita had found in Haskins's skull.

Broward nodded. "We tested the pistol. It's the one that killed Haskins."

"What was the pistol loaded with?"

Grinning, Broward said, "Two-hundred-thirty-grain full metal jacket rounds. Standard military issue."

"The bullet that killed Haskins was probably two hundred grain."

"I saw that. You didn't mention that in your notes."

"I wanted to see if you would arrive at the same conclusion we had."

"That whoever killed Haskins did so with hand-loaded subsonic rounds. I don't think Laura Ivers would have done that. She would have used what she had at hand. But that doesn't explain how the gun got into the safe-deposit box."

"I think Swanson hired someone to stand in for his wife," Will said. "She bought the carpet. She bought the gun. She took out the safe-deposit box. All it had to be was someone who looked vaguely like Laura. The carpet salesman and the gun shop owner stated they'd never seen Laura Ivers before or after. Except for in the newspapers and on television."

"It would be nice if we could find that woman."

"She hasn't come forward," Will pointed out. "Either she's protecting herself—"

"Or she's in a shallow grave somewhere too."

Will nodded. It was all too easy to add on to the conspiracy they were following.

"Commander Ivers didn't know about the safe-deposit box?"

"No. As part of the divorce decree, Swanson set up a banking account for the division of assets they had. Laura never closed the account out. Some of the assets were stocks and bonds purchased through the bank."

"The imposter Swanson probably hired could have rented the safe-deposit box if the bank people had never met Commander Ivers. But *she* didn't know she was renting a safe-deposit box?"

"Commander Ivers let the people there manage the accounts and transfer money to her as she needed it. Most of it is still there. She didn't want to touch it. Her brother has children and is struggling to make ends meet. Commander Ivers earmarked the funds for their college tuition."

"Generous woman."

Will nodded. "She's the real deal."

"Shame about her daughter."

"I know. I want to make that right."

Remy, Shel, and four police officers hefted the casket and slid it into the back of a hearse.

"If there's anything I can do," Broward offered.

Will grinned at him. "Not worried about congressional repercussions?"

Broward shook his head. "If things go bad, I pull the pin and go into the private sector. There's more money in security work if you know what you're doing. I do. My problem is I just like putting the bad guys away more."

"Me too," Will said.

>> MIDDLE TENNESSEE MEDICAL CENTER
>> MURFREESBORO, TENNESSEE
>> 1428 HOURS

Nita used the pay phone near the waiting area just down the hall from her mother's room. After dialing Will's cell-phone number, she waited, not knowing if she was doing the right thing.

"Coburn," Will answered.

"It's Nita." Nita looked out the window at the brightness of the day. Everything looked so promising, but she was scared.

"I've been worried about you."

"I appreciate that. I just . . . I just had to get some things worked out."

"Is there anything I can do?"

"No," Nita said. "This is my mess to clean up. I've got to figure out what I'm going to do." She hesitated. That wasn't the truth. She knew what she wanted to do. She just didn't know how she was going to get it done. "I called because I thought maybe I could help you. I was watching the news. You exhumed Chloe Ivers's body."

"Yes."

"What are you hoping to find?"

"Something that the original medical examiner missed."

"He wasn't a medical examiner, Will. He was a coroner."

"And there's a lot of difference between those. I remember you telling me that."

"Worlds of difference," Nita assured him. The coroner's office was political, and the person elected to it didn't have to be knowledgeable about pathology, just a licensed physician. Nita had seen coroners who were obstetricians or even—occasionally in rural areas—veterinarians. A medical examiner, on the other hand, was a medical doctor trained in pathology and forensics. "How is the mother doing with this?"

Will hesitated. "She's okay, I think. We know more now than they did then. But we need proof. I'm hoping you can help us with that."

"I can't perform miracles."

"I know, but I'll take what you can do over what anyone else at the camp can do."

Despite every bad thing facing her, Nita smiled at her ghostly reflection in the glass. "As soon as I can find a plane headed to Raleigh, I'll be there."

"All right. I'll have Remy stay here and pick you up at the airport."

"Thanks."

"Hey, Nita?"

"Yeah?"

"You sound good. I hope you found what you were looking for."

Not yet, she thought. But she said, "Thanks, Will."

>> 1441 HOURS

Geraldine was sitting with Carol when Nita returned to the room. Both women looked up at her expectantly. Nita wondered how much her mother had told the old woman.

“Did you get hold of your friends?” Nita’s mother asked.

“Yes.” Nita wanted to tell her she was leaving, but she didn’t know how.

“Well, did they tell you they needed you?”

“Yes.”

Her mother smiled, but Nita knew the effort was forced. “Then you should go, Nita. This kind of thing, this is what you love.”

“I’ve got to go, Mom,” Nita said, her voice thick. “But I’ll be back.”

“I hope so.” Tears leaked from her mother’s eyes. “I’ve missed you. Fourteen years is too long.”

Nita went to her mother and hugged her. “I promise I’ll be back. I’ll call.”

“Do that, baby girl. I want to see my granddaughter.”

“You will, Mom.” Steeling herself, Nita broke the embrace and walked to Geraldine. “Take care of her for me. Till I get back.”

“I will. And you take care of yourself.”

Nita hugged the old woman, then gathered her belongings. She headed for the door, trying not to look back, trying not to cry.

“Nita,” her mother called.

Nita stopped at the door.

“You’d be a fool if you let that man get away,” her mother said.

“I know.” *But it may be too late.* Nita started moving, feeling pushed by the need to get everything in order. She just didn’t know how she was going to achieve that.

S  CRIME SCENE  NCIS  C 

NAVAL CRIMINAL INVESTIGATIVE SERVICE

58

SCENE  **NCIS**  CRIME SCEN

NAVAL CRIMINAL INVESTIGATIVE SERVICE

\>> NCIS MEDICAL LAB
\>> CAMP LEJEUNE, NORTH CAROLINA
\>> 2348 HOURS

Nita took a breath as she looked at the body bag lying on the gurney in the medical lab.

"Are you doing okay?" Will entered the room and stood to one side. He looked tired and haggard.

"I'm fine," Nita said.

"You don't look fine."

"I'm jet-lagged." Nita knew she sounded irritable. She'd left Murfreesboro, driven to Nashville, caught a plane, and flown to Raleigh-Durham. Remy had met her at the airport; then there'd been the two-and-a-half-hour drive to Camp Lejeune. She could have slept in the car, but she'd reviewed Chloe Ivers's X-rays from the coroner's report instead.

Will handed her one of the tall coffees he'd brought back with him. "You look like you need this."

Nita took the cup. "Thanks. While I was gone, Will, I wasn't drinking. I'm not worn out from drinking."

"I didn't ask."

"I know you didn't, but it's important to me that you know." Nita sipped the coffee and put it to one side. "I respect you, Will, and it's important to me that you respect me."

"I do, Nita. If I didn't, I wouldn't have waited on you to do this autopsy."

Nita hesitated. "Not just the work. But me. As a person. I'm trying to get some things worked out, and it's not easy."

Will nodded. "I'm still working on things from my divorce. When you're dealing with family, it's never easy."

"Thanks." Nita pulled on latex gloves. "It's been a long time since I had to post someone this young."

"I can stay," Will offered.

"This isn't what you do. This is what I do. Get out of here and let me do it. When I find something, I'll let you know."

For a moment, Will stood there.

Nita turned on the recording equipment and unzipped the body bag. Despite seventeen years in the grave and some desiccation, Chloe Ivers looked like she was asleep. She wore a long dress and had her hair down around her shoulders. Bruises showed on her face and neck. If she'd had an open casket, it had to have been hard on the family.

A hurt look entered Will's eyes.

"Go," Nita told him.

"If you need me, I'll be in my office." Will left.

Nita looked down at the dead girl and tried not to think that the world was cruel enough to treat Celia in the same fashion if someone wasn't there to take care of her.

"This is the body of a sixteen-year-old girl," Nita began. "Five feet two inches tall. Ninety-five pounds at the time of death. . . ."

>> NCIS HEADQUARTERS
>> 0726 HOURS

A knock woke Will. He swung his feet down from his desk and sat up.

Nita walked through the door and sat in the chair. She looked like she was running on fumes.

"You took a long time," he said. "That's just an observation."

Nita nodded. "I wanted to be sure. And I took the time to put Chloe back together. I don't want her mother to see her like that."

"I wouldn't let her."

"Besides, it made me feel better that it was all done, and you got a few extra hours of sleep. I don't know if what I've found out is going to help."

"I'll take what I can get."

"Chloe Ivers was murdered, but not the way the coroner's report indicated." Nita pulled his computer's USB add-on hub over to her, then inserted a flash drive. She clicked on several pictures, blowing them up as she talked. "The bruising on her neck indicates that she was strangled." She cycled to the next picture. "This is from the coroner's evidence log. Notice the petechiae?"

"Yes."

"It also occurs when a victim is *almost* strangled to death."

"Almost?"

"Yes. Chloe was strangled, but that's not how she died." Nita clicked to another picture. "This one is also from the file that night. If you look closely, you can see the scratches around her neck."

"Made by the person who tried to strangle her."

"Right. But what discrepancy about the scratches do you see that tells you the strangulation didn't kill her?"

Will looked but didn't see anything.

"The scratches had scabbed over," Nita said.

That jarred Will's mind into wakefulness. "It takes six hours for scabs to form. Healing begins immediately after a wound happens. Red blood cells help form the scab, but white blood cells collect there."

"That's right. Polymorphonuclear cells. They're formed only by a living organism. Once you're dead, there's no healing."

"She was alive after she was strangled."

"The bumps and bruises she suffered, the broken bones—those all fit the scenario of a fall down the steps. But she had river mud in her nasal passages. There was still enough for the lab to identify. They can probably narrow down the composition and tell you where it came from. I can't do that."

"I'll check."

"I think someone thought she was dead, Will. I think whoever did it got scared and got rid of her body."

"That would fit with the stepfather. But six hours into Chloe's disappearance, he was telling police officers she'd been kidnapped. The search was getting under way. He couldn't have killed her."

"Doesn't mean he didn't try."

"What killed her?"

"Someone snapped her neck." Nita stood up and came around to Will. She placed one hand behind his head and cupped his jaw with the other. "Like this." She pulled lightly to demonstrate, then sat back down.

Will took that in, watching as Nita took him through the X-rays she'd taken and the photographs of the dead girl's spine.

"I've seen injuries like that before," Nita said. "I'll bet Shel and Remy know how to do that."

"Her killer was a special-forces guy. Or a martial artist." Will sipped his coffee. "Congressman Swanson is neither of those."

"But he did frame his ex-wife for her daughter's murder. He's guilty of something. My money's on the strangulation."

"Haskins and Ketchum weren't in special forces or martial arts either," Will said.

"Then you're looking for someone else you haven't found yet," Nita said. "Because whoever did this knew what he was doing."

>> 1008 HOURS

"So we're at another dead end," Larkin said. They sat in his office, watching the television coverage of the exhumation again with the sound off.

"We've redefined our search," Will said. "We'll just broaden our scope. We know Swanson is lying, and we know whoever he had dispose of his stepdaughter's body was in special forces or knew martial arts. We've gotten specific enough to move faster."

Larkin sighed. "Not fast enough, Will."

Will didn't have anything to say to that. Investigations proceeded at their own pace. Larkin had taught him that.

"Director, Commander." Estrella was at the door. "I've got something."

Larkin waved her in.

"I've been monitoring all the paperwork connected to this investigation. I found this." Estrella placed a printout on Larkin's desk.

"Someone filed on Haskins's death benefits?" Larkin passed the paper to Will.

"His widow," Estrella said.

"Why didn't she do this before?" Larkin asked.

"She did. Seven years after Haskins went missing. The Marine Corps chose to adopt the position that Gunnery Sergeant Haskins had gone AWOL to avoid impending criminal charges. She didn't get to collect them."

"But he's legally dead now," Larkin said. "Where is she?"

"Hopkinsville, Kentucky."

Larkin leaned back in his chair. "It seems like that's where a lot of this started." He glanced at Will. "Why don't you go have a talk with—" he looked at the request form— "Cindy LaPlatte and see what she knows about Haskins and Ketchum or any other of Swanson's associates."

Will nodded and excused himself. He had a plane to catch.

>> HOPKINSVILLE-CHRISTIAN COUNTY AIRPORT
>> HOPKINSVILLE, KENTUCKY
>> 2137 HOURS

Will flew into Hopkinsville, Kentucky, and landed at Hopkinsville-Christian County Airport, where he was met by Police Chief Lyle Duncan.

Duncan was in his midsixties, a no-nonsense kind of guy who dressed in a shirt and tie, not the cowboy hat Will had expected. Duncan had a soft way of speaking but a professional edge.

The police chief had agreed to provide transportation.

"You neglected to say exactly what you wanted to speak to Mrs. LaPlatte about," Duncan said when Will dropped into his passenger seat.

"Mrs. LaPlatte filed for military death benefits on her husband," Will said.

"Roger LaPlatte isn't dead," Duncan said. "And he's never been in the military. He runs a car dealership here in town."

"Her first husband. George Haskins."

Duncan nodded. "I'd forgotten about him. I went to school with his old man and his uncle. None of them were worth the powder it would have taken to blow them up. Cindy married better this time around."

"Good for her," Will said. "I wasn't too taken with her ex either."

Duncan looked at him. "I recognize your name from the news stories. And I know you didn't come up all this way just to talk to a military widow about death benefits on a Saturday night."

"No," Will replied. "We've tied Haskins in with a murder and I want to talk to Mrs. LaPlatte about that."

"The Ivers girl?"

"Yes." Will wanted to keep George Haskins's probable complicity in Deanna Swanson's death quiet for now. What he'd given Duncan was enough.

"That's a sad bit of business."

"It sure is," Will agreed.

The police chief started his cruiser, and they got under way.

>> SANDERSON DRIVE
>> 2209 HOURS

The LaPlattes had a large house on Sanderson Drive. They were also still up when the police vehicle arrived.

"Since you were getting here so late," Duncan said, "I took the liberty of telling them that we'd be dropping by."

"All right." Will let the police chief lead the way to the door.

Cindy LaPlatte was a quiet woman with short gray hair and an air of timidity about her. Her soft features relayed her wariness about her visitors, but she sat them in the big kitchen and brought out coffee and pecan pie.

"I don't mean to be an imposition, Mrs. LaPlatte," Will said.

"It's no imposition, Commander Coburn." Cindy LaPlatte poured coffee with a confidence that told Will she'd probably spent time as a server somewhere. "I'm just confused is all."

"What confuses you?" Will asked.

She looked embarrassed. "All of this, I suppose. Roger told me all I had to do was fill out the death-benefits form. He said we'd probably have to talk to somebody before it was all over." She paused. "I just didn't expect it to be someone I've seen on the news."

Roger LaPlatte was a quiet man with watchful eyes. "She wouldn't even have filed those papers except that I told her she needed to. After all those years of putting up with George Haskins and raising his two sons, she deserved something."

Putting the coffeepot back under the large dispenser, Cindy LaPlatte sat by her husband. "I filed for those death benefits because our sons—my sons by George—could use the money for college. Both of them are in college now, but it's expensive. I thought if there was something there, something that George could give them in death that he would never have given them in life, they deserved it."

"You'll get it, Mrs. LaPlatte," Will said. Larkin had already said he'd make it happen.

"Then I'm afraid I don't understand what you're doing here."

"I think George Haskins had something to do with Chloe Ivers's death."

"That girl in the news? Ben's stepdaughter?"

Will seized on the casual usage of Swanson's given name. "You know Ben Swanson?"

"Of course I know him. He grew up here before George and Bryce Ketchum had to move down to North Carolina. All of them were thick as thieves."

"When did you move back here?" Will asked.

"After George went missing. The military wouldn't say officially that he was dead, but I knew he was. There was nothing left for me in North Carolina, so I came home." She shared a look with her husband. "This is where I met Roger."

"You mentioned that Ben Swanson moved to North Carolina with Mason," Will said. "Who's that?"

"Mason Craddock. He went into the military too. The Navy, I think. He was a SEAL or something. Some kind of special-forces soldier. But he's doing something else now. He owns a club, I think. In Washington, D.C. Mason was the wild one of the bunch. His father owned one of the martial arts dojos in town. I forget which one. I think it was Mason that got Ben to move to North Carolina. He wanted greener pastures."

Will's heart rate sped up. He worked on remaining calm. "Did you know that Deanna Swanson, Ben's first wife, was murdered?"

Cindy LaPlatte's right eye ticked. She hesitated. "I'd heard that. It was a carjacking."

"That's right, but I know now that Bryce Ketchum was one of the carjackers."

The woman put her hand over her mouth and gasped as if in pain.

"When we did the autopsy on Ketchum," Will went on, "we dug a bullet out of his abdomen that matched those that were found in Deanna Swanson. Her son, Jeff, was in the car too. They killed that boy's mother right there in front of him."

Tears leaked down Cindy's face.

"Since Ketchum and George were together so much during those years," Will said, "I wondered if you knew anything about that."

Cindy LaPlatte cried silently.

"Maybe you should go," Roger said. He put an arm around his wife and shifted his attention to the police chief. "We don't have to talk to him if we don't want to, do we?"

"Mrs. LaPlatte, please," Will said softly. "Laura Ivers has waited seventeen years to find out who killed her daughter. Don't you think she's waited long enough?"

"Lyle," Roger said, addressing the police chief again, "I think we've been as understanding about this as—"

"George told me he was going to kill Deanna," Cindy said in a quiet, halting voice. "He told me that Ben was going to pay him and Bryce Ketchum to do it." She took a breath. "I didn't believe it. George was drunk at the time. He was usually drunk."

"Didn't you think it was suspicious when Deanna Swanson was murdered?" Will asked.

"I knew it couldn't have been George," Cindy said. "He was with me when she was killed. I gave birth to Timothy that morning. Our second boy. George was with me." She shook her head. "I told myself that it was just a coincidence, that Ben and his wife must have gotten into an argument and he'd gone off and gotten drunk with George. That was when Ben was getting his political career going. Deanna didn't want him to go into politics. They had Jeff, and she wanted him to stay home more. But Ben—he's always been one to be in the limelight. He wasn't going to stop until he got what he wanted."

"Why would he want his wife killed?"

"For the money." Cindy LaPlatte shook her head. "I swear I didn't think it was Ben who had her murdered. Once I knew George hadn't had anything to do with it, I just thought it was bad luck."

>> 2241 HOURS

Once more back in the police chief's cruiser, Will called Larkin and ran down the information they'd gotten.

"How soon can you be in Washington, D.C.?" Larkin asked.

"Six or seven hours," Will answered. "About the same time it took to get here."

"Then stay there tonight. Get a good night's rest. Let me see what I can do to get warrants together for Mason Craddock's home and business. I'm also going to see what we can do about getting a federal warrant for Swanson's arrest. He won't be able to claim congressional immunity next time we come for him."

"If word gets out, they could both run."

"If they do," Larkin growled, "we'll hunt them down. They're going to pay for this."

59

SCENE  NCIS  CRIME SCENE
NAVAL CRIMINAL INVESTIGATIVE SERVICE

`>> GOD'S LITTLE HOUSE CHURCH`
`>> JACKSONVILLE, NORTH CAROLINA`
`>> 1118 HOURS`

On Sunday morning, Nita sat in a rented Taurus in front of Joe's church and waited till the singing was nearly over and the sermon was about to start. Her Mustang was still at the Nashville, Tennessee, airport and she didn't know when she would be able to go back to get it, but she knew she had to do this first.

She'd dressed in a midnight blue dress that she'd bought yesterday after finishing the autopsy on Chloe Ivers. She usually wore slacks to church, or jeans, because the congregation often went casual, but today she just wanted to be a woman.

Fear thudded through her heart as she thought about what she knew she had to do. She'd thrown up that morning in the hotel room she'd rented for the night, but at least she'd gotten a good night's sleep. She hadn't called Joe. He didn't know she was back in town, but he probably hadn't known she'd left either.

Easing out of the car, she smoothed her dress and walked toward the church. Only a few stragglers saw her. A couple of the women recognized her and quickly looked away. They might as well have pointed accusing fingers at her.

Don't give in to that, Nita told herself. *This isn't just about you. It's about what you and Joe started together. This is about what you want.*

Quietly, she stepped through the front doors, through the foyer, and into the church.

Mr. Dickerson, one of the church elders, held the door open for her. "Good morning, Mrs. Tomlinson. It's nice to see you here."

"Thank you," Nita said. She stood at the back of the church and waited till the singing was finished and Pastor Wilkins asked for a blessing to be on the church.

Most of the congregation, it seemed, had turned out for service this morning. Over four hundred people were crowded into the little church.

Nita's heart was in her throat as she started forward. *Please, God, please don't let me throw up. And let me have the words I need to say.*

As she walked, heads turned in her direction. Pastor Wilkins stared at her. Joe and Celia sat in their normal pew toward the front. Her daughter looked so beautiful in her dress that Nita thought she was going to cry. Celia acted as if she was going to come to her but held back. Joe just looked at her, his eyes restive and uncertain. She could never, *ever* remember seeing him that way.

On trembling legs, during the quietest moment in the church that she could ever remember, Nita reached the front of the church.

"Pastor Wilkins," she said. Her voice cracked and barely got through her lips.

"Yes, Mrs. Tomlinson." The pastor acted like he didn't know what to do.

"If I may, I'd like to address my husband. And the congregation."

"I don't know if that would be a good—"

"Daniel," Mrs. Wilkins hissed from the piano.

The pastor looked at his wife.

Mrs. Wilkins waved him off the stage.

"Well," the pastor said uncertainly, "there you go. Folks, this is Mrs. Tomlinson."

For a moment Nita couldn't move. Her legs stopped working, and she couldn't figure out what it was she was supposed to do to get them to function. Finally she took another breath, then stepped onto the stage. She wished there were a podium. At least she could have leaned on it or partially hidden behind it.

She took a deep breath and tried to speak. But she couldn't. Joe and Celia and over four hundred other people were staring at her.

God, please help me.

"My name is Nita Tomlinson," she said in a weak voice. "Dr. Nita Tomlinson." She wanted to say she was Joe's wife, but she didn't know if that was fair to say anymore. "I came here today to offer an apology and to ask forgiveness."

The congregation kept shifting its attention from her to Joe and back again. Joe just looked at her. Celia took his hand.

"I have not been a good Christian for a long time. Maybe I never have." Nita sipped a breath. "More than that, I haven't been a good person. I was born Nita Purdue. I was raised by my mother, Carol Purdue, who was sixteen years old when she had me."

Every eye was riveted on her.

"I never knew my father," Nita went on. "I was born out of wedlock. My mother tried to grow up while raising me. It didn't work out very well for either of us. We lived hard and we moved often, staying one step ahead of people my mother owed money to or mean-spirited boyfriends or jealous wives."

When she paused, the church remained utterly silent.

"I don't tell you that to excuse myself or my behavior," Nita said, "but to let you know how little I knew about the world. I left home as soon as I finished high school, went to college, and never went back. This week I saw my mother again for the first time in fourteen years."

Joe's eyes widened.

"I've always told people that my parents were dead. Even Joe. It was . . . it was just easier that way. I thought I could re-create myself. Just be who I wanted to be." Nita took a breath. "So I went to college, and I earned a degree in a little under three years. I'd taken some college courses when I was in high school. After I got my degree, I went into medicine and became a doctor. Then I went back for more schooling and became a pathologist. I work as a medical examiner at Camp Lejeune."

A few people whispered. None of them had known that about her.

"I'm a good medical examiner," Nita said. "I take pride in what I do. For the first time ever in my life . . . I'm important. People depend on me and look up to me. Coming from where I did, from how little I valued myself, that means a lot to me."

Nita's voice quavered. *God, if you're truly there the way that Joe believes you are, please be with me as I try to finish this.*

"Almost seven years ago, when I was in my first year with NCIS, I met a man who was unlike any man I'd ever met before." Nita looked at Joe, and she felt like her heart was going to break. "He has the kindest, gentlest soul of any person I've ever met."

Several people in the audience nodded.

"I wasn't looking for what he wanted, though," Nita went on, regretting her choice of words when she saw pain flash through Joe's eyes. "I was looking for a good time, and he was looking for someone to share his life with. I wanted to walk away, but I couldn't get him out of my head.

What he talked about—forever and commitment and true love—I'd never seen in my whole life." Tears drifted down her cheeks. "I have never been more desirous of something that scared me so badly."

Nita took a deep breath. "I married him because I thought I was in love and because he was so different, so *good,* that I didn't even consider that I might be making a mistake."

More pain showed in Joe's eyes, but he didn't look away from her. Nita was afraid that he was just trying to remember everything she said so he could hate her more. She couldn't blame him.

"Less than a year later, we had a beautiful girl."

Celia smiled happily.

"But inside, I knew I couldn't be what Joe or Celia needed," Nita said. "I wasn't trained to be a wife or a mother. I went to school to become a medical examiner. I'm a good medical examiner. But I'm a terrible wife and mother."

Whispering started around the church.

"I got called in, held late, and got caught up in my work," Nita said. "I loved my work. The problem was, I loved my family too." Her voice broke. "I didn't know how to work it out. I felt like I was going to have to make a choice whether to be a wife and mother or to be a medical examiner. I tell you honestly that I'm a much better medical examiner."

Nita's legs trembled so violently that she knew she was going to fall. But somehow she found the strength to keep going. "I kept trying to do everything myself. I kept expecting so much of myself that I couldn't do it. But I wouldn't let myself fail. I couldn't stand failing. That would mean that I had never made it out of my mother's house, had never become the person that I wanted to be. So I felt I had to make a choice."

The church fell silent again.

"Over a year ago, I started taking steps to end my marriage. I stayed gone more. I went out. I got myself into situations that I shouldn't have been in. I kept hoping that Joe would get sick of it and ask me to leave. Then it wouldn't be my fault; it could be his."

Joe closed his eyes.

"Last week, I left," Nita went on. "I told Joe I wasn't coming home anymore."

Celia began to cry, and Joe wrapped an arm around her.

"I was lost," Nita said. "More lost than I'd ever been in my life. I found my mother this week, and I talked to her. And for the first time, I realized that a sixteen-year-old girl who didn't know much and didn't have anything to work with had done the best by me that she could have. Maybe someone else could have done better, but my mother did what she could."

She let out a breath. "I'm standing up here, scared almost senseless, because I don't know if I've ruined the only decent thing I've had in my whole life. I just . . . I just wasn't prepared to find it. I didn't believe it existed.

"What I've come to realize this week, Joe, is that I love you." Nita swallowed and could barely get around the lump in her throat. "I love the way you are with our daughter, how kind and considerate you are. How loving. I love watching you work in your shop when you don't know that I'm watching. I love watching you put those boats together."

Joe looked at her, and there were tears on his face.

"I love listening to your voice when you talk to me. I love your patience and understanding and insight. I love the way you've never put yourself ahead of me and have always supported the things that I've done in my career." Nita took a breath. "I love your faith. Hearing you pray and seeing the way you live your life makes me want to know more about God. More than anything, Joe, I want you to know that I love you and I'm truly sorry for everything I've put you through this last year. I have no excuse for my behavior. I wouldn't want to give you one if I did. I just want you to know the truth about how I feel."

Nita swallowed. "If you never want to see me again, I'll understand. But I wanted you to know how I felt, and that it wasn't your fault. And if you'll have me, Joe, I want to come home. I want to be your wife again."

Unable to stand there any longer, Nita turned to go, heading for the exit she knew was behind the stage. She had to get out of there before she completely lost it. She had to move while she could still—

"Nita."

Joe's voice froze her in her tracks. She tried to turn around and couldn't.

Then his hand was on her shoulder, pulling her around. She looked up into his eyes.

"I'm sorry, Joe," she whispered.

"I know," he said. "I love you too."

"I do love my work, and it's demanding. I can't promise everything will change."

Joe smiled at her gently. "I never asked you to change. I've always wanted you to be happy."

"I know. And I want you to be happy too."

"Mommy." Celia was pulling at her dress.

Nita looked down at her daughter. "What, baby girl?"

"Are you gonna come home now?"

Nita looked at Joe.

He nodded, tears in his eyes.

"Yes," Nita said. "I'm coming home."

NCIS
NAVAL CRIMINAL INVESTIGATIVE SERVICE

60

SCENE  NCIS  CRIME SCEN

NAVAL CRIMINAL INVESTIGATIVE SERVICE

>> CLUB INFERNO
>> WASHINGTON, D.C.
>> 1317 HOURS

Ben Swanson stood at the one-way mirror above the club floor and looked down. Club Inferno wasn't due to open till four, but he knew Craddock would be there.

He returned to the bar and poured himself a double. He had half of it down when Craddock stepped into the office.

"I was told you were up here," Craddock said as he took his seat at the desk.

"The NCIS found Cindy Haskins. She's Cindy LaPlatte these days."

"So?"

"I think they're putting this thing together." Swanson couldn't believe how calm Craddock was being about everything. "Friday they exhumed my daughter's body."

Craddock sighed. "I watch the news."

"I'm getting a bad feeling about this."

"You gave them your ex-wife," Craddock said. "It was a good frame. It'll stick. Just give it a few more days. The media's already made her out to be some kind of avenging angel."

Swanson knew that was true. Several of the news programs had championed Laura's decision to murder her daughter's killer.

"We wouldn't have had to get cute with everything if you hadn't killed George Haskins that night in my den," Swanson said.

"We started needing to get cute the moment you flew off the handle and started to strangle your daughter," Craddock replied.

Swanson wanted to say something to refute that, but he couldn't.

Craddock frowned. "George had a big mouth. He was blackmailing you, threatening to take you down when he got popped by the NCIS."

"As I recall, he was threatening to take *you* down too."

"All the more reason to kill him." Craddock leaned back in his chair. "George was a loose end. And your stepdaughter was too."

Swanson felt suddenly sick. "I never meant to hurt her," he said.

"I know, and believe me, I feel as bad about what happened to her as you do. It wasn't your fault she was listening to your conversation from the top of the stairs. And it wasn't your fault your son had an epileptic fit or something and pushed her down the stairs. You did what you had to do. Making your son believe he killed her and then blaming it all on your ex were both the right moves. Now all we have to do is ride this out," Craddock said. "We're going to be fine. It's been seventeen years. They're not going to find anything."

"It hasn't been seventeen years since we killed Ketchum."

"Ketchum was a loose end too. When he got caught holding all those girls and the drugs, he signed his own death warrant. Don't worry. There's nothing to tie either of us to that," Craddock said confidently. "The gun I did the job with is scrap metal lying on the bottom of the Potomac now. It's over, Ben. We won."

Swanson started to grin. Then he saw Craddock's right hand come up from behind the desk with a silenced pistol.

"And now," Craddock said, "I'm afraid you've become a loose end too."

Panicked, Swanson tried to run and managed only two steps before a thunderclap hit him in the middle of his back.

>> 1328 HOURS

Clad in full assault armor, Kevlar vest, elbow and knee pads, helmet, and radio, Will debarked from the black Suburban and took the M4 assault rifle Shel handed him.

"Radio check," Will said.

Shel started it off, followed by Maggie, Remy, Estrella, Director

Larkin, and the team of a dozen NCIS special agents the director had brought up from Camp Lejeune.

"Surround the building," Will said. "Then we'll kick the door in. Shel, Maggie—you're with me. Remy, Estrella—you've got the rear. Let's move out."

They moved down the street and closed on Club Inferno. Larkin had come through with all the necessary warrants. The site was theirs. They'd already checked at the large downtown apartment Mason Craddock maintained, and the man hadn't been home. The doorman had reported that Craddock was usually at the club at this time of day.

Less than a minute later, Will stood in front of the club. Shel held the heavy siege sledge they were going to use to break the door down.

Will tried the door to make sure it was locked. It was. "Steadfast Six, this is Steadfast Leader. Do you copy?"

"Roger that, Leader," came Remy's reply from the rear of the club. "Six reads you five by five."

"Are you locked?"

"That's affirmative, Leader. We're tight."

"Okay," Will said, "let's open the ball." He nodded at Shel.

The big Marine drew the sledge back and hammered the door. Wood shattered, but the door didn't give way immediately. Shel had to hit it twice more before the door shuddered inward.

Will spun around the corner and dropped the assault rifle into position. Staying with the wall, he went down the short entranceway. Maggie was at his heels, carrying an assault rifle as well.

At the back of the building, Remy confirmed that they'd gained access.

A man stepped in front of Will in the hall. He froze and his eyes widened when he saw the NCIS special agents. Lifting a walkie-talkie to his lips, he said, "Five-O. Five-O!"

"Drop the walkie-talkie," Will ordered. "Up against the wall."

The man did as he was told, quickly placing his hands on top of his head in a manner that suggested he was intimately familiar with the procedure. He turned his face to the wall.

Handing her rifle off to the man behind her, Maggie went forward—carefully staying out of Will's field of fire—and used one of the disposable cuffs she carried to bind the man's hands behind his back. She used another to bind his ankles. Then she forced him to the ground. They left him lying where he was.

Entering the main dance floor, Will discovered that they weren't as alone as he'd thought. There had been no way to investigate the premises further with the equipment they'd had on hand.

Over a dozen men were inside the club. As it turned out, all of them were armed.

A hail of gunfire drove the NCIS agents back into the hallway immediately.

"I guess," Larkin said at Will's shoulder, "we came at a bad time."

"Yes, sir," Will said. He whirled around the corner and pulled the rifle to his shoulder. "Naval Criminal Investigative Services! Put down your weapons and you won't be harmed!"

More bullets cut the air around Will. He fired at the center mass of one of the men racing across the floor and firing. The M4's 5.56 mm rounds chopped the man down, sending him sprawling across the dance floor.

In seconds, the large open area became a killing zone.

Larkin stood at Will's back and fired, hammering another man over one of the bars.

Will moved into the open area, staying low. Bullets smashed into the wall by his head. Splinters ricocheted from his protective eyewear. He knew what to expect in the club's interior from the blueprints Estrella had dug up on the computer.

From the corner of his eye, Will saw Shel stand tall and shoot two other men. The Marine looked grim, like a force of nature in the battle gear.

"Leader is going up," Will said.

"Roger that, Leader," Maggie said. "I've got your six."

"We'll secure everything down here," Shel called out.

Will went up the stairs, taking them two and three at a time, following the assault rifle. Behind him, it seemed like a full-scale war had opened up. He didn't know why all the high-powered resistance was there, but they'd come prepared for it. Most of the men inside the club looked like gangbangers. Will wondered what the odds were that the men who had been hunting Jeff Swanson had been employed by Mason Craddock. Pretty good, he'd bet.

At the top of the stairs, Will tried the door. It was locked, but it wasn't as substantial as the one that led to the street.

Will lifted his foot and rammed it into the door, shattering the lock and driving the door into the room. He paused, waiting for gunfire.

There was none.

Glancing at Maggie, Will nodded. She nodded back. Steeling himself, Will whirled and went in low, dropping to one knee as he brought the rifle to his shoulder. The M4 was easy to handle in enclosed areas. The shorter stock and barrel were designed for urban warfare.

Two men were in the room. Congressman Ben Swanson lay on the ground. He wasn't moving. Above him, Mason Craddock was. The ex–special forces soldier brought his pistol up and fired at Will from twenty feet away.

Will managed to squeeze the assault rifle's trigger once before it felt as if a baseball bat hit him in the chest. He went back and down, twisting so he would slide behind the protective cover offered by the doorway.

He couldn't breathe. Even though he'd been shot before, panic set in. It wasn't something a person got used to. He tried again to suck in air and couldn't.

Maggie's face appeared over him. Concern tightened her features under the ballistic helmet and behind the eye protection. "You're all right," she said. "The bullet hit the vest."

Finally the paralysis over Will's chest went away and he pulled in air. It hurt to breathe, but at least he could. Glancing down, he saw that the bullet had taken him directly over the sternum. The round was expanded and spent, trapped in the layers of Kevlar armor. He'd been lucky. Sometimes getting hit like that could stop the heart between beats.

He pushed himself to his feet and realized he hadn't lost his grip on the M4. Peering into the room, he saw that Craddock had hauled Swanson to his feet and was backing away, holding Swanson in front of him as a shield. Craddock had his pistol muzzle shoved tight against Swanson's neck.

Crouching, profiling himself to make a smaller target, Will peered around the corner of the doorway and took aim at Craddock's head. "Give it up, Craddock," he ordered.

The sound of gunfire in the dance floor below was coming to a halt.

"No," Craddock said. "I want a helicopter to meet me on the roof of this building and a plane waiting at the airport that will take me to Havana."

Estrella's background research had indicated that Craddock had offshore accounts in Cuba.

"You're not getting out of here," Will promised.

Craddock grinned mirthlessly. "Then I'm going to kill the congressman."

Will noted the blood dripping on the floor. Evidently the congressman had already been shot. Will also saw that his own shot had found flesh. Craddock's left shoulder was stained with blood. There was blood spattered on Craddock's face from the wound.

"If you kill the congressman," Will said, "I guarantee you're not getting out of here alive."

"I need help," Swanson gasped. "He's shot me."

"Yes, sir," Will said. "But Craddock doesn't look like he's going to release you."

"I'm going to bleed to death," Swanson said.

"If you do," Will promised, "I'll kill him for you."

"I want that helicopter," Craddock yelled. "You've got twenty minutes."

"Judging from the blood flow, I don't think Swanson's got that long," Will said. "The human body holds six quarts of blood. If a man loses over two quarts, he's going to die." He nodded toward the pool of blood on the floor, knowing that blood always ran and looked like more had been spilled than actually was. "How much do you think you've lost so far, Congressman? A pint? A quart? You don't have much more to lose."

"Get him the helicopter," Swanson gasped. "For God's sake."

"There's not enough time," Will repeated. "Even if I had a helicopter sent in, Craddock isn't going to let you go. He needs to hang on to you till you reach the airport. He's not interested in getting medical attention for you." He tried to make himself sound cold and unemotional. "Here's the game plan: We're going to sit here and talk until you die, Congressman. Then I'm going to shoot Craddock. Unless he chooses to give himself up after you die."

"Why would he do that?"

"Because he may think he can beat the charges the DA brings against him. Right now, all I've got him for is shooting you. I know he did that because the two of you are in this room." Will spoke quickly and concisely. "See, guilt is all about the proof I can put together. If I can't prove that gun he's holding is his, he can say you brought it and tried to use it on him. That you fought and it went off. That it was self-defense. A good attorney might even get him off."

Swanson struggled weakly, but he was thinking now, and that was where Will wanted him.

"I've got evidence that Bryce Ketchum killed your first wife, Deanna," Will said. "We recovered a bullet from his dead body. I figure Craddock probably killed Ketchum, but I can't prove that. Not yet. Maybe not ever. He's getting better at covering his tracks."

The blood pool on the floor grew bigger.

"I know you were going to hire George Haskins to kill your first wife. I've got his ex-wife's testimony on that. And I know Ketchum was involved, because I found a bullet in him from the incident. Unfortunately, Haskins was in the hospital that day while his wife was having a baby. So someone else shot Deanna and Ketchum. I'm guessing that was Craddock, but—again—I can't find any physical evidence. He walks on that, but you don't. I've got you for the murder of your first wife."

Swanson looked pale.

"Shut up," Craddock roared.

Will ignored the man and kept going. No matter how this worked out, he couldn't let Craddock go free. "We've taken apart the frame you put on Laura. The round George Haskins was killed with was different from the ones loaded in the pistol. I can build a case against you for that, too, but it's more circumstantial. And your explanation doesn't cover why Haskins had Chloe's charm on him. If I can take the frame apart, that means you were lying. I'll bet a jury will think you were lying about who murdered Haskins and that you did it yourself." He shrugged, but the rifle sights never wavered.

"I want that helicopter," Craddock repeated. He tightened his grip under Swanson's jaw, causing the congressman to choke.

"Did you know that you weren't the one who killed Chloe that night?" Will asked.

Disbelief showed on Swanson's face. "What are you talking about?"

"I think you tried," Will said. "I think you're the one who strangled her. Maybe you thought she was dead. But she didn't die till at least six hours later. Probably while Haskins was supposed to be disposing of her body. That's how he had the charm in his pants cuff. But she wasn't killed till later. You were at home when she actually died."

Swanson began to see a way out.

"I can make a case for attempted murder against you," Will said. "But you didn't kill her."

"Who?" Swanson asked. "Who killed her?"

"It wasn't George Haskins," Will said. "He didn't have the training. What killed Chloe was a special-forces move. Someone grabbed her head and snapped her neck. Just the way they train SEALs to do." He paused. "There's only one SEAL in the room that I know of."

Swanson struggled again but couldn't make any headway against Craddock's grip.

"My question is this: are you willing to stand there till you die to protect Craddock?"

"You?" Swanson whispered in disbelief. "*You* killed Chloe?"

"Shut up, Ben," Craddock threatened. "He's playing you."

"You shot me," Swanson said. "I came here to warn you, and you shot me."

Will knew that Swanson was fading. His blood pressure would get low enough soon that he would pass out.

Swanson looked at Will. "If he shoots me again, in front of you, that's murder, isn't it?"

"It is," Will agreed.

"And if I tell you something and I don't make it, that testimony counts in a court of law, right?"

"Yes, it does."

"Shut up," Craddock said, tightening his grip.

"I'm not going to let you walk out on this," Swanson replied. "You're not going to get away with shooting me."

"I swear, Ben, I'll kill you if you don't shut up."

Swanson looked at Will. "I got mad that night. When Chloe came tumbling down the stairs, I knew she'd been listening," he said. "Haskins was there, talking to me about Ketchum. He'd been arrested and was in prison. We were both afraid Ketchum was going to talk and tell what he knew about Deanna's murder. When I realized Chloe had been spying on us, I lost it. I went after her. Before I knew it, she was dead. At least, I thought she was dead."

"Shut up, Ben," Craddock roared. "Shut up!"

"Haskins called Craddock," Swanson went on, looking even more faint. "They took Chloe's body away that night. I thought I'd killed her. Later the next day, after Chloe's body had been found and everybody was talking about Isaac Allen Lamont killing her, Haskins tried to blackmail me for more money. Craddock was there. He shot Haskins and—"

Without warning, Craddock pulled the trigger. The bullet tore Swanson's neck out in a bloody rush, then shattered the big glass overlooking the carnage littering the dance floor.

Shocked, Will was a step behind as Craddock lifted his pistol and aimed it at him. Sights still settled on Craddock's head, aware of bullets thudding into the wall beside his face, Will put a round between Craddock's eyes.

Craddock's head snapped back. Incredibly, he stood for a moment longer; then he released Swanson's body and tumbled backward. Both men were dead when they hit the floor.

Cautiously, Will went forward and kicked the pistol from Craddock's nerveless hand. The dead man stared up at the ceiling.

Maggie checked Swanson and shook her head.

"Steadfast Leader," Larkin called over the headset, "are you all right?"

"Roger that," Will said tiredly, feeling all the pressure and fatigue of the past couple weeks eat into him. "It's over. We're secure here."

Larkin entered the room and gazed down at the dead men. "I can't say that I'm sad to see it end this way."

"Neither can I," Will said.

"It's going to be easier like this. Laura Ivers will have more closure. This way there won't be a long, drawn-out court case."

"I know," Will said.

"Did you get Swanson's confession?"

Will reached into his BDU pocket and took out the microcassette recorder. He rewound the tape for a moment, then played it.

"Haskins called Craddock," the player broadcast. "They took Chloe's body—"

Will shut it off and put it back in his pocket. He knew it wasn't going to replace the daughter Laura Ivers had lost. That reunion was waiting for Laura in a better place. For the moment, though, she could make peace with her life in a way that she hadn't been able to in seventeen years.

EPILOGUE

>> NEW RIVER, NORTH CAROLINA
>> 0758 HOURS

Will waved Steven back, guiding his son into the boat launch. Together, warmed by the sun on Saturday morning six days after Congressman Ben Swanson had been been discovered to be a murderer and killed, they pushed the Laser into the water.

Washington, D.C., was still reeling from the blow of one of their own being guilty of such a heinous crime, but Will was jaded enough to know that the city wouldn't reel long. They'd find a new tragedy to mourn soon enough. That was the way of the world.

But that didn't have to be the way of his world.

Steven had surprised him Friday night, calling to say he'd made arrangements with Barbara for her to bring Wren and him to Camp Lejeune. Last week had been Will's visitation weekend, and usually when he missed one because of work, he didn't get to make it up with anyone but Wren. But Steven had called and asked if the weekend get-together was possible.

They'd gotten up early this morning to go sailing.

A few minutes later they were in the boat, and Wren was handing out the muffins she'd picked out at the grocery store.

The wind was fair and the sky was blue. Will didn't think he could hope for a better day.

Nita and Joe were off on an impromptu second honeymoon, with Celia in tow. They'd taken Joe's big sailboat and set out for Miami. Nita had never been there. There had also been some mention of Walt Disney World and Orlando. Any time before, Will wouldn't have believed Nita and the Magic Kingdom would ever be mentioned in the same breath. Will was glad for them though.

He wished he'd been there to see the look on Joe's face when Nita told him she was pregnant with their second child. That was going to make things more difficult for Nita in some ways, Will knew. But he was sure she and Joe would make it. They were good people. Whatever the problems had been, Will hoped they were gone for good.

Steven guided the Laser onto the river with a sure hand.

Will sat back in the boat and thanked Wren for the muffin and carton of chocolate milk she insisted was breakfast.

"You worked on that case involving the congressman who was killed, didn't you?" Steven asked.

That surprised Will. Steven never asked about his work.

"I did," Will said.

"I followed the investigation on the news. They mentioned your name a lot."

Will didn't know what to say about that.

"Some of the reporters said if it hadn't been for you, that woman, the girl's mother—"

"Laura Ivers," Will said automatically. Commander Ivers had returned home after she'd buried her daughter again. Will had attended the service in full military dress, as had the rest of the team. Laura had seemed emotional but more at peace now that she knew the truth.

Laura had taken her stepson, Jeff Swanson, home with her. Will had personally processed the paperwork to get Jeff released from custody. His father's taped confession had cleared him as a suspect in Chloe Ivers's murder. He was a troubled young man, and the death of his father wouldn't help. But Will hoped that with counseling and some positive influences in his life, Jeff would turn out okay. He was happy that Jeff and Laura had each other to lean on in the meantime.

Steven looked at his father. "I never really understood what it is you do, Dad. I mean, I just thought of everything you do as keeping you away from us."

"Sometimes," Will replied, "it does do that."

"I just wanted you to know that I think what you do is pretty cool," Steven said. "I thought about that woman, not knowing what happened to her daughter, and it was sad. People need answers, you know?"

"I'm glad you feel that way," Will said, smiling and wondering at his son, marveling at how much Steven was growing up. *And sometimes you get them when you least expect it.*

"Just so you know, I probably won't always be happy about being away from you, but I'll try to be more understanding."

"That's all I can ask for, Steven."

Steven looked embarrassed. "I didn't mean to talk so much about it. I know you probably didn't need to talk about it anymore. Because it was so sad. But I just wanted you to know."

"I'm glad you told me."

Looking uncertain for a moment, Steven said, "We've got a good wind. Can I let her run?"

Will laughed, remembering what it was like to be fifteen and on a fast boat. *God, thank you for my son, and thank you for touching his heart.*

"Can we finish breakfast first?" Wren asked. "I don't want milk up my nose."

"Breakfast first," Will said, feeling more complete than he had in a long time. "Then we'll make this boat dance."

POLITICAL UNREST BLANKETS THE WORLD

Will Coburn and his team must fight against a countdown to global decimation as they race to uncover the face of true evil.

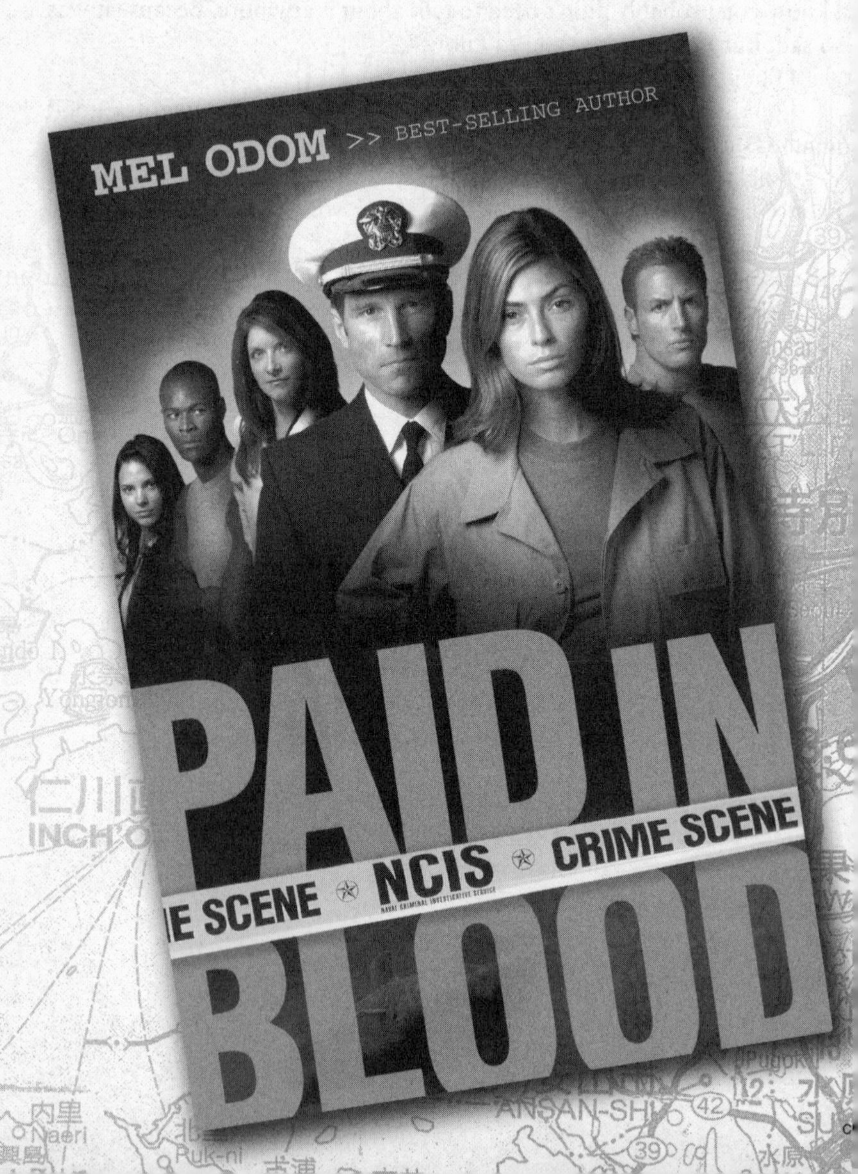